In **Loren D. Estleman**'s "The Pilgrim," a journalist is sent out West to collect stories of frontier adventure, but he may end up writing his own epitaph . . .

A gambler takes a chance working for the Bad Dog Saloon, and his intuition pays off more than he could imagine in "Wherever I Meet with a Deck of Cards," by **Bill Crider** . . .

Bill Pronzini's "Doc Christmas, Painless Dentist" rides into the town of Bear Paw to ply his trade, but a roughneck blacksmith becomes a dissatisfied customer . . .

. . . and 16 more extraordinary tales of the American West in . . .

The Best of the American West II

Don't miss . . .

BEST STORIES OF THE AMERICAN WEST
edited by Ed Gorman and Martin H. Greenberg

THE BEST OF THE AMERICAN WEST II

*Frontier Adventure by
Louis L'Amour, John Jakes,
Loren D. Estleman, Elmer Kelton,
and many others*

**EDITED BY
Ed Gorman and
Martin H. Greenberg**

BERKLEY BOOKS, NEW YORK

THE BEST OF THE AMERICAN WEST II

This is a work of fiction. Names, characters, places, and incidents are either the product of the author's imagination or are used fictitiously, and any resemblance to actual persons, living or dead, business establishments, events, or locales is entirely coincidental.

A Berkley Book / published by arrangement with
Tekno Books and Ed Gorman

PRINTING HISTORY
Berkley edition / October 1999

The Penguin Putnam Inc. World Wide Web site address is
http://www.penguinputnam.com

ISBN: 0-425-17145-0

BERKLEY®
Berkley Books are published by The Berkley Publishing Group, a division of Penguin Putnam Inc., 375 Hudson Street, New York, New York 10014.
BERKLEY and the "B" logo are trademarks belonging to
Penguin Putnam Inc.

PRINTED IN THE UNITED STATES OF AMERICA

10 9 8 7 6 5 4 3 2 1

CONTENTS

v

AUTHOR NOTES

—

Louis L'Amour was the bestselling Western writer of all time. For a number of reasons, it's unlikely that his sales records will ever be equaled by anybody. He wrote a lot of material—far more than most people realize—and from the very start he seemed to understand the mass market better than any other writer of his generation. For all his reliance on careful research, he wrote of the mythic West, of good and evil, in an exciting way that appealed to millions and millions of readers.

John Jakes started out as a writer of genre science fiction, fantasy, suspense, and Western novels. In the seventies, he became one of America's all-time bestselling writers with his historical novels about the origins of America. Since then, Jakes's books have continued to sell in the millions, and many of his older books have been brought back for new generations.

John M. Cunningham's most famous story is "The Tin Star," which moviegoers around the globe know better as the legendary Western film *High Noon*. Cunningham has always given us real people and carefully drawn backdrops for his stories. He has a reporter's eye for the one right detail that brings a setting to vivid life.

Dorothy M. Johnson is frequently referred to as "The First Lady of Western Fiction," a title she richly deserves. Although her work is well known to hundreds of thousands of Western readers, the films based on her stories "The Man Who Shot Liberty Valance," "The Hanging Tree," and "A Man Called Horse" have been viewed by millions of moviegoers.

Dale L. Walker has distinguished himself as an historian, critic, and a creator of serious and innovative Western fiction. When the dust settles on our particular era of Western stories, the reviews and criticism of Dale Walker will be among the work passed on to succeeding generations. He is the author of seventeen books, including *Legends and Lies*, *The Boys of '99*, and *Bear Flag Rising*. His fiction will likely accompany his reviews because he applies his rigid critical standards to his own stories as well, as his story here demonstrates.

Robert J. Conley's Cherokee heritage plays a prominent role in his Western fiction, detailing the struggles of the Native Americans and Europeans to live together without conflict in novels like *Quitting Time*, *Go-Ahead Rider*, and *Killing Time*. Formerly an assistant programs director for the Cherokee Nation of Oklahoma, he is still deeply involved in Cherokee issues in the Southwest. His short fiction also details the intersection of the white man's world with the Cherokee's, and how that meeting can change both sides.

As a reviewer noted, "**Hamlin Garland** wrote about the Midwestern states with the ear of a journalist and the heart of a preacher. He was always listening for the false statement in human discourse, apparently believing that by finding the false he could also identify the truth." Though he was probably a minor artist, Garland wrote beautiful and powerful stories about the heartland, showing us the people and customs of early America.

Gary Lovisi is involved in fiction in a number of ways. He's publisher of the excellent *Paperback Parade*. His Gryphon Press books are among the best example of small-press art.

Over the past few years he's also found time to begin his own writing career, with a number of sales to mystery anthologies and magazines, including more than one Western story.

Judy Alter is the author of several novels, including *Libbie*, based on the life of Mrs. George Armstrong Custer, *Luke and the Van Zandt County War*, which won the 1984 prize for juvenile literature from the Texas Institute of Letters, and *Mattie*, which was named Best Western Novel of the Year by the Western Writers of America. A single parent of four now-grown children, she lists cooking and reading among her hobbies, and likes to travel throughout the American West.

Tom Piccirilli is primarily known as a dark fantasy and horror writer, elements of which are infused in his story in this volume. The author of *Dark Father, Hexes, Shards*, and *The Dead Past*, he is the assistant editor of *Pirate Writings* magazine, and reviews books for the trade magazines *Mystery Scene* and *Mystery News*. His story in this book proves he can cross boundaries while turning out a thought-provoking story.

L. J. Washburn has managed to work in both the Western and the detective genres simultaneously. Her novels about Hallam are set in the Los Angeles of the silent-movie era and involve the stuntman in fair-clue mysteries with a distinctly Western air about them. The Hallam books should be on the shelves of anybody with an interest in Hollywood, private-eye fiction, and realistic Western fiction.

A writer of quality Western fiction and nonfiction for more than forty years, **Bill Gulick** has twice won the Best Short Story Spur Award from the Western Writers of America—in 1958 for "Thief in Camp" and in 1960 for "The Shaming of Broken Horn." His novels include *Bend of the Snake, A Thousand for the Cariboo*, and *Hallelujah Trail*, and his short fiction can be found in the collections *White Men, Red Men,* *and Mountain Men*, and *The Shaming of Broken Horn and Other Stories*.

Michael Stotter has worked at various jobs in publishing, one of which was helping George Gilman (whose violent books about the mythic West became bestsellers in the 1970s) produce a fanzine that kept his readers abreast of the author's forthcoming new books. Stotter is now involved in the British Crime scene, in particular with the fine magazine *Shots*, and has turned to writing his own Westerns.

Loren D. Estleman is the most accomplished Western writer of his generation. He has won the Spur, and been nominated many times more, for fiction that re-creates American history with a vividness and relish found only in the very best Western fiction. His work is, by turns, dramatic, cynical, poetic, humorous, and spellbinding. And all these adjectives can be applied to his crime writing as well. Loren is the best Chandleresque private-eye writer of the past few decades. His Amos Walker mystery novels will endure right along with his Westerns.

Bill Crider is one of the best-kept secrets in American publishing. He has written exemplary novels in so many categories—mystery, suspense, horror, and Western—that his publishers don't quite know what to do with him. But with a recent Anthony nomination, and a ''breakout'' book definitely on the horizon, Bill Crider is bound to become a major star very soon now.

In a full-time writing career that has spanned a couple of decades, **James Reasoner** has written well in virtually every category of commercial fiction. His novel *Texas Wind* is a true cult classic and his gritty crime stories about contemporary Texas are in the first rank of today's suspense fiction. Fortunately for the Western reader, James's Westerns are just as good as his crime work.

Bill Pronzini has worked in virtually every genre of popular fiction. Though he's best known as the creator of the Nameless mystery novels, he has written several first-rate Westerns, as well as a half-dozen remarkable novels of dark suspense. In addition to his novels, Pronzini is an especially gifted short story writer, several of his pieces winning prestigious awards, including the Shamus.

Brian Garfield published his first Western novel, *Range Justice*, when he was just twenty-one years old. Among the more than forty that have followed it are such first-rate titles as *The Vanquished, Sliphammer, Tripwire*, and—his most ambitious work in the field—*Wild Times*. He has also been a prolific and critically acclaimed writer of suspense fiction.

To names such as Owen Wister, Jack Shaefer, and Elmore Leonard, one must add the name **Elmer Kelton**. Like those other men, he took the raw material of the Western novel and shaped it into a means of expression that was wholly his own. Some of his titles alone tell you how different and special his books are: *The Day the Cowboys Quit, After the Bugles*, and *The Time It Never Rained*. Born in Texas in 1926, Kelton brought realism and naturalism to the Western novel. Like other serious writers of his generation, including John Steinbeck, Kelton wanted to show the world what the real old West had been like . . . and, in some of his later novels, what the real West is like today.

INTRODUCTION

This is being written a few months after the death of Roy Rogers. While most of the commentary on his life and death was laudatory, every once in a while a commentator would note that Rogers's movies didn't depict "the real West."

Back in the forties, when your editors were growing up, The Lone Ranger, Gene Autry, Monte Hale, Sergeant Preston and Yukon King, and a whole bunch of other real unlikely heroes represented (to us) "the real West." "Childish," harrumphed the harrumphers.

In the fifties, John Ford's *The Searchers*, Henry King's *The Gunfighters*, and Fred Zinnemann's *High Noon* defined "the real West." Too Freudian, scoffed the scoffers.

In the sixties, the Italian Westerns as embodied by Clint Eastwood and Charles Bronson came into vogue. Several of the writer-directors were left-wing and passionately interested in smearing the United States by examining the old West as they saw it. "Too political," sneered the sneerers.

From its simpleminded origins in the dime novels and on the silent screen, the American Western has taken on hundreds of different shapes, sizes, and meanings. A lot of it is in the eye of the beholder. To some, *Shane* is a masterpiece. To others, *Shane* is a simplistic B movie elevated to A-movie status simply because of the A-level stars and the production budget.

The same holds true with Western novels. "Authentic" Westerns thrill some readers; others want the old-style, the romance of the purple sage (and purple prose).

The Western Writers of America, about as nice a group of people as you'll ever meet, has always made sure that there is plenty of room for every type of Western writer in the organization. And that's what we've tried to do with this book—give readers of every taste something memorable and entertaining to read.

We hope you'll have as good a time reading these tales as we did collecting them. There are few tasks as pleasant as setting yourself down to read through a stack of good Western stories.

—The Editors

THE STRONG SHALL LIVE

Louis L'Amour

The land was fire beneath and the sky was brass above, but throughout the day's long riding the bound man sat erect in the saddle and cursed them for thieves and cowards. Their blows did not silence him, although the blood from his swollen and cracked lips had dried on his face and neck.

Only John Sutton knew where they rode and only he knew what he planned for Cavagan, and John Sutton sat thin and dry and tall on his long-limbed horse, leading the way.

Nine men in all, tempered to the hard ways of an unforgiving land, men strong in the strengths needed to survive in a land that held no place for the weak or indecisive. Eight men and a prisoner taken after a bitter chase from the pleasant coastal lands to the blazing desert along the Colorado River.

Cavagan had fought on when the others quit. They destroyed his crops, tore down his fences, and burned his home. They killed his hired hand and tried to kill him. When they burned his home he rebuilt it, and when they shot at him he shot back.

When they ambushed him and left him for dead, he crawled into the rocks like a wounded grizzly, treated his own

1

wounds, and then caught a horse and rode down to Sutton's Ranch and shot out their lights during the victory celebration.

Two of Sutton's men quit in protest, for they admired a game man, and Cavagan was winning sympathy around the country.

Cavagan was a black Irishman from County Sligo. His mother died on the Atlantic crossing and his father was killed by Indians in Tennessee. At sixteen Cavagan fought in the Texas war for independence, trapped in the Rockies for two years, and in the war with Mexico he served with the Texas Rangers and learned the value of a Walker Colt.

At thirty he was a man honed by desert fires and edged by combat with fist, skull, and pistol. Back in County Sligo the name had been O'Cavagan and the family had a reputation won in battle.

Sutton's men surrounded his house a second time thinking to catch him asleep. They fired at the house and waited for him to come out. Cavagan had slept on the steep hillside behind the house and from there he opened fire, shooting a man from his saddle and cutting the lobe from Sutton's ear with a bullet intended to kill.

Now they had him, but he sat straight in the saddle and cursed them. Sutton he cursed but he saved a bit for Beef Hannon, the Sutton foreman.

"You're a big man, Beef," he taunted, "but untie my hands and I'll pound that thick skull of yours until the yellow runs out of your ears."

Their eyes squinted against the white glare and the blistering heat from off the dunes, and they tried to ignore him. Among the sand dunes there was no breeze, only the stifling heaviness of hot, motionless air. Wearily their horses plodded along the edge of a dune where the sand fell steeply off into a deep pit among the dunes. John Sutton drew rein. "Untie his feet," he said.

Juan Velasquez swung down and removed the rawhide thongs from Cavagan's feet, and then stood back, for he knew the manner of man that was Cavagan.

"Get down," Sutton told Cavagan.

Cavagan stared his contempt from the slits where his eyes peered through swollen, blackened flesh, then he swung his leg across the saddle, kicked his boot free of the stirrup, and dropped to the ground.

Sutton regarded him for several minutes, savoring his triumph, then he put the flat of his boot against Cavagan's back and pushed. Cavagan staggered, fought for balance, but the sand crumbled beneath him and he fell, tumbling to the bottom of the hollow among the dunes.

With his hands tied and his body stiff from the beatings he had taken he needed several minutes to get to his feet. When he stood erect he stared up at Sutton. "It is what I would have expected from you," he said.

Sutton's features stiffened, and he grew white around the mouth. "You're said to be a tough man, Cavagan. I've heard it until I'm sick of it, so I've brought you here to see how much is tough and how much is shanty Irish bluff. I am curious to see how tough you will be without food or water. We're leaving you here."

Hannon started to protest. He had himself tried to kill Cavagan, but to leave a man to die in the blazing heat of the desert without food or water and with his hands bound . . . a glance at Sutton's face and the words died on his lips.

"It's sixty miles to water," he managed, at last.

John Sutton turned in his saddle and measured Hannon with a glance, then deliberately he faced front and started away. Reluctantly, the others followed.

Juan Velasquez looked down into the pit at Cavagan. He carried a raw wound in his side from a Cavagan bullet, but that pit was seventy feet deep. Slowly, thinking as he did it, Juan unfastened his canteen and was about to toss it to Cavagan when he caught Sutton's eyes on him.

"Throw it," Sutton suggested, "but if you do you will follow it."

Juan balanced the canteen on his palm, tempted beyond measure. Sixty miles? With the temperature at one hundred and twenty degrees? Reluctantly, he retied the canteen to his saddle horn. Sutton watched him, smiling his thin smile.

"I'll remember that, Juan," Cavagan said. "It was a good thought."

John Sutton turned his square thin shoulders and rode away, the others following. Hannon's shoulders were hunched as if expecting a blow.

When the last of them had disappeared from sight, Cavagan stood alone at the bottom of the sand pit.

This was 1850 and even the Indians avoided the sand hills. There was no law west of Santa Fe or east of the coast mountains. Cavagan had settled on land that Sutton considered his, although he had no legal claim to it. Other would-be settlers had been driven off, but Cavagan would not be driven. To make matters worse he courted the girl Sutton had marked for himself.

Cavagan stood in the bottom of the sand pit, his eyes closed against the glare of the sun on the white sand. He told himself, slowly, harshly, that he would not, he must not die. Aloud he said, *"I shall live! I shall see him die!"*

There was a burning fury within him but a caution born of experience. Shade would come first to the west side of the pit, so with his boot he scraped a small pit in the sand. There, several inches below the surface, it was a little cooler. He sat down, his back to the sun, and waited.

More than seven hours of sunlight remained. To attempt climbing from the pit or even to fight the thongs on his wrists would cause him to perspire profusely and lessen his chances of ultimate survival. From this moment he must be patient, he must think.

Sweat dripped from his chin, his throat was parched, and the sun on his back and shoulders was like the heat from a furnace. An hour passed, and then another. When at last he looked up there was an inch of shadow under the western lip of the pit.

He studied the way his wrists were bound. His hands had been tied to the pommel, so they were in front of him. He lifted his wrists to his teeth and began ever so gently to work at the rawhide knots. It took nearly an hour, but by the time his wrists were free the shade had reached the bottom of the pit. He coiled the rawhide and slipped it into his pocket.

The east slope was somewhat less steep, with each step he slid back, but with each he gained a little. Finally he climbed out and stood in the full glare of the setting sun.

He knew where the nearest water hole lay but knew Sutton would have it guarded. His problem was simple. He had to find water, get out of the desert, then find a horse and weapons. He intended to destroy Sutton as he would destroy a rabid wolf.

Shadows stretched out from the mountains. To the north the myriad pinnacles of the Chocolate Mountains crowned themselves with gold from the setting sun. He started to walk.

It was not sixty miles to the nearest water, for Cavagan knew the desert better than Sutton. West of him, but in a direction he dare not chance, lay Sunset Spring. Brackish water, and off the line for him.

Twenty-five miles to the northwest among the pinnacles of the Chocolates were rock tanks that might contain water. A Cahuilla Indian had told him of the natural reservoir, and upon this feeble chance he rested his life.

He walked northwest, his chances a thousand to one. He must walk only in the early hours of the morning and after sundown. During the day he must lie in the shade, if he found any, and wait. To walk in the sun without water was to die.

The sand was heavy and at each step he sank to his ankles. Choosing a distant peak in the Chocolates he pointed himself toward it. When the stars came out he would choose a star above it for a guide. At night landmarks have a way of losing themselves and what was familiar by day becomes strange and unfamiliar in the darkness.

To reach the vicinity of the rock tanks was one thing, to find them quite another. Near such tanks in the Tinajas Altas men had died of thirst within a few feet of water, unaware of its presence. Such tanks were natural receptacles catching the runoff from infrequent rains, and so shaded, that evaporation was slow. As there was no seepage there was no vegetation to indicate the presence of water.

The shadows grew long and only a faint afterglow remained in the sky. On his right and before him lay the valley dividing the dunes from the Chocolate Mountains. Now the air was cool and here and there a star appeared. Desert air is thin and does not retain the heat, hence it soon becomes cool, and in the middle of the night, actually cold. These were the hours Cavagan must use.

If he could not find the tanks, or if there was no water in them, he would die. Cavagan was a man without illusion. His great strength had been sapped by brutal treatment, and he must conserve what strength remained. Locating his peak and a star above it, he walked on. A long time later, descending from the last of the dunes, he took a diagonal course across the valley. Twice he paused to rest, soaking up the coolness. He put a small pebble in his mouth to start the saliva flowing. For a time it helped.

Walking in heavy sand he had made but two miles an hour, but on the valley floor he moved faster. If he reached the *tinajas* and they held water he would have achieved one goal. However, he had no way of carrying water and the next water hole was far. Not that one can place reliance on any desert water hole. Often they were used up or had gone dry.

His battered face throbbed with every step and his head ached. The pinnacles of the Chocolates loomed nearer, but he was not deceived. They were miles away.

An hour before dawn he entered a wash that came down from the Chocolates. He was dead tired, and his feet moved awkwardly. In eleven hours he had probably traveled no more than twenty-three or -four miles and should be near the tanks. He found a ledge that offered shade and stretched out. He was soon asleep.

The heat awakened him. His mouth was dry as parchment and he had difficulty in moving his tongue, which seemed awkward and swollen. A glance at the sun told him it was noon or nearly so. According to the Cahuilla he should be within a few yards of water, certainly within a mile or so. In that maze of cliffs, boulders, rock slabs, and arroyos, cluttered with canelike clumps of ocotillo, he would be fortunate to find anything.

Animals would come to water but many desert creatures lived without it, getting what moisture they needed from succulent plants or cacti. Some insects sought water, and he had noticed bees flying past taking the straight line that usually led to hive or water.

His throat was raw and his mind wandered. Far off, over the desert he had recently crossed, lay a lovely blue lake, shimmering among the heat waves . . . a mirage.

Lying down again he waited for dusk. He was sweating no longer and movement was an effort. He had been almost thirty hours without water and in intense heat.

It was almost dark when he awakened again. Staggering to his feet he started to climb. The coolness refreshed him and gave him new strength. He pushed on, climbing higher. His vision was uncertain and his skull throbbed painfully, but at times he felt an almost delirious gaiety, and then he would scramble up rocks with zest and abandon. Suddenly he sat down. With a shock of piercing clarity he realized he could die.

He rarely thought of dying, although he knew it was expected of him as of all men, yet it was always somebody else who was dying. Suddenly he realized he had no special dispensation against death and he could die now, within the hour.

It was faintly gray in the east when he started again. Amazingly, he found the tanks.

A sheep track directed him. It was a half-sheltered rock tank, but it was dry. Only a faint dusting of sand lay in the bottom.

A few minutes later, and a little higher up, he found a second tank. It was bone dry.

Soon the sun would rise and the heat would return. Cavagan stared at the empty tanks and tried to swallow, but could not. His throat was raw, and where it was not raw it felt like old rubber. His legs started to tremble, but he refused to sit down. He knew if he sat now he might never get up. There was a queerness in him, a strange lightness as if he no longer possessed weight. Through the semidelirium induced by heat, thirst, and exhaustion there remained a hard core of resolution, the firmness of a course resolved upon and incomplete. If he quit now John Sutton would have won. If he quit now the desert would have defeated him, and the desert was a friendly place to those who knew how to live with it.

Cunning came to him. To those who knew how to live *with* it, not against it. No man could fight the desert and live. A man must move with it, give with it, live by its rules. He had done that, so what remained?

His eyes peered into the growing light, refusing to focus properly, his thoughts prowling the foggy lowlands of his mind, seeking some forgotten thing.

Think back . . . the rock tanks of the Chocolates. The Chocolates. The Chocolates were a range running parallel to the dunes which the Mexicans called the *algodones*. Bit by bit his thoughts tried to sort out something he knew, but something was missing. Something else the Cahuilla had said. It came to him then like the Indian's voice in his ears. *"If there is no water in the tanks, there is a seep in the canyon."*

Almost due west was the canyon through which ran the old Indian trail . . . maybe five miles.

It was too far. And then he got up without decision and walked away. He walked with his head up, his mind gone off somewhere, walking with a quick, lively step. When he had walked for some distance he fell flat on his face.

A lizard on a rock stared at him, throat throbbing. Something stirred Cavagan's muscles, and he got his hands under him and pushed himself to his knees. Then he got up, weaving a little. It was daylight.

A bee flew past.

He swayed a little, brow puckered, a bee flying straight . . .

hive or water or a hive near water? He took a few hesitant steps in the direction the bee had flown, then stopped. After a bit another droned past and he followed, taking a sight on a clump of ocotillo some distance off. He stumbled and fell, scarcely conscious of it until he arose and stared at his palms, lacerated by the sharp gravel.

When he fell again he lay still for what must have been a considerable time, finally becoming aware of a whistling sound. He pushed himself up, listening. The sound reminded him of a cricket, yet was not a cricket. He listened, puzzled yet alerted for some reason he did not understand.

He moved then, and under a clump of greasewood something stirred. He froze, thinking first of a rattler, although the heat was too great for one to be out unless in a well-shaded position. And then his eye caught a movement, and he knew why the sound had alerted him. It was a tiny red-spotted toad.

Long ago he had learned that the red-spotted toad always lived within the vicinity of water and never got far from it.

Awkwardly he got to his feet and looked carefully around. His eyes could not seem to focus properly, yet down the canyon he glimpsed some galleta grass and walked toward it, coming upon the seep quite suddenly.

Dropping to his knees he scooped water in his palm and drank it. A cold trickle down his throat was painful on the raw flesh. With gentle fingers he put water on his lips, bathed his cheeks and face with it, then drank a little more.

Something inside was crying out that he was safe, but he knew he was not. He drank a little more, then crawled into the shade of a rock and lay on his back and slept.

When he awakened he crawled out and drank more and more, his water-starved body soaking up the moisture. He had found water but had no means of carrying it with him, and the canyon of the seep might well become his tomb, his open tomb.

Cavagan got out the rawhide with which his wrists had been bound and rigged a snare for small game. In placing the snare he found some seeds, which he ate. He drank again, then sat down to think his way forward.

From where he now sat there were two possible routes. Northeast toward the Colorado was Red Butte Spring, but it was at least twenty-five miles away and in the wrong direction.

The twelve miles to Chuckawalla Spring began to loom very large, and leaving the water he had found worried him. The Chuckawalla Mountains were a thin blue line on the northern horizon, and even if he reached them the next spring beyond was Corn Springs, just as far away. Yet the longer he waited the more his strength would be drained by lack of food. He had never known such exhaustion, yet he dare not wait.

On the second morning his snare caught a kangaroo rat, which he broiled over a small fire. When he had eaten he got up abruptly, drank some more, glanced at the notch in the Chuckawallas, and started walking.

At the end of an hour he rested, then went on at a slower pace. The heat was increasing. In midafternoon he fell on his face and did not get up.

More than an hour must have passed before he became aware of the intense heat and began to crawl like a blind mole, seeking shade. The plants about him were less than a foot high, and he found nothing, finally losing consciousness.

He awakened, shaking with chill. The moon cast a ghostly radiance over the desert, the clustered canes of the ocotillo looking like the headdresses of gigantic Indians. He got to his feet, aware of a stirring in the night. He waited, listening. A faint click of a hoof on stone and then he saw a desert bighorn sheep walk into the wash and then he heard a faint splash. Rising, he walked down to the wash and heard a scurry of movement as the sheep fled. He almost walked into the spring before he saw it. He drank, then drank again.

Late the next afternoon he killed a chuckawalla with a well-thrown stone. He cooked the big lizard and found the meat tender and appetizing. At dusk he started again, crossing a small saddle to the north side of the mountains. It was twelve miles this time, and it was daybreak before he reached Corn Springs. He recognized it by the clump of palms and mesquite in the wash before reaching the spring, some clumps of *baccharis,* clusters of small twigs rising two to three feet. And then he found the spring itself. After drinking he crawled into the shade and was asleep almost at once.

He opened his eyes, aware of wood-smoke. Rolling over quickly, he sat up.

An old man squatted near a kettle at a fire near the spring, and on the slope a couple of burros browsed.

"Looks to me like you've had a time of it," the old man commented. "You et anything?"

"Chuckawalla ... had a kangaroo rat a couple of days ago."

The old man nodded. "Et chuck a time or two ... ain't as bad as some folks might figger."

Cavagan accepted a bowl of stew and ate slowly, savoring every bite. Finally, placing the half-empty bowl on the ground he sat back. "Don't suppose a man with a pipe would have a cigarette paper?"

"You started that Mex way of smokin'? Ain't for it, m'self. Give me a pipe ever' time." The old man handed him his tobacco pouch and dug into his duffle for a rolled up newspaper. "Don't tear the readin' if you can he'p. A body don't find much readin' in the desert and sometimes I read through a newspaper five or six times."

Cavagan wiped his fingers on his pants and rolled a smoke with trembling fingers. Then he put the cigarette down and ate a few more bites before lighting up.

"Come far?"

"Fifty-five, sixty miles."

"An' no canteen? You had yourself a time." The old man said his name was Pearson. He volunteered no more than that. Nor did he ask questions. There were not four white men between the San Jacintos and the Colorado River.

"I've got to get to that hot spring this side of the pass, up there by the San Jacintos," Cavagan said. "I can get a horse from the Cahuillas."

The old man stirred his fire and moved the coffeepot closer. "You listen to me you won't go back."

"You know who I am?"

"Got no idea. Figgered you didn't get where you was by chance. Six years I been prospectin' hereabouts an' I ain't seen nobody but a Chemehuevi or a Cahuilla in this here country. A man would have himself an outfit, gun, knife, canteen. Strikes me somebody left you out here apurpose."

"If you could let me have a canteen or a water sack. Maybe a knife."

"How d' you figger to get out of here?"

"West to the Hayfields, then Shaver's Well and the Yuma stage road."

Pearson studied him out of shrewd old eyes. "You ain't no pilgrim. You made it this far on nerve an' savvy, so may-hap you'll go all the way."

He tamped his pipe. "Tell you something. You fight shy of them Hayfields. Seen a couple of gents settin' on that water with rifles. A body could figger they was waitin' for some-body."

The old man helped Cavagan to more stew. He rarely looked directly at Cavagan.

"Are they on the Hayfields or back up the draw?"

Pearson chuckled. "You do know this country. They're on the Hayfields, an' could be they don't know the source of that water. Could be you're figurin' a man might slip around them, get water, and nobody the wiser."

"If a man had a water sack he might get as far as Hidden Spring."

The old man looked up sharply. "Hidden Spring? Never heard of it."

"Southwest of Shaver's . . . maybe three miles. Better wa-ter than Shaver's."

"You must be Cavagan."

Cavagan did not reply. He finished the stew, rinsed the bowl, then filled his coffee cup.

"Nobody knows this country like Cavagan. That's what they say. Nobody can ride as far or shoot as straight as Cavagan. They say that, too. They also say Cavagan is dead, left in the *algodones* with his hands tied. Lots of folks set store by Cavagan. Them Californios, they like him."

Cavagan slept the day away, and the night following. Pearson made no move to leave, but loafed about. Several times he cooked, and he watched Cavagan eat.

Cavagan found him studying some Indian writing. "Can't make head nor tail of it," Pearson complained. "If them Cahuillas can, they won't say."

"This was done by the Old Ones," Cavagan said, "the People Who Went Before. I've followed their trails in the mountains and across the desert."

"They left trails?"

"A man can go from here to the Cahuilla village at Martinez. The trail follows the canyon back of the village and goes back of Sheep Mountain. There's a branch comes down back of Indian Wells and another goes to the Indian village at the hot spring at the entrance to San Gorgonio Pass. There's a way over the mountains to the coast, too."

Back beside the fire Cavagan added coffee to what was in the pot, then more water before putting it on the fire. Pearson watched him. "Met a damn fool once who throwed out the grounds . . . throwed away the mother. Never seen the like. Can't make proper coffee until she's two, three days old."

He lit his pipe. "A man like you, he might know a lot about water holes. Worth a lot to a man, knowin' things like that."

"The rock tanks in the Chocolates are dry this year," Cavagan said, "but there's a seep in Salvation Pass." He poked twigs under the coffeepot. "Twenty, twenty-two miles east of Chuckawalla there's a red finger of butte. Maybe a quarter of a mile east of that butte there's a little canyon with a seep of water comin' out of the rock. Good water."

"Place like that could save a man's life," Pearson commented. "Good to know things like that."

"The Cahuillas used the old trails. They know the springs."

Wind was rustling the dry palm leaves when Cavagan crawled out in the early dawn and stirred the coals to life to make coffee.

Pearson shook out his boots, then put on his hat. When he had his boots on he went to the limb where his pants were hung and shook them out. A scorpion about four inches long dropped from a trouser leg and scampered away.

"Last time it was a sidewinder in my boot. A body better shake out his clothes before he puts 'em on."

Pearson slipped suspenders over his shoulders. "Figger you'll hit the trail today. If you rustle through that stuff of mine you'll find you a water sack. Crossin' that ol' sea bottom out there, you'll need it." He hitched his shoulders to settle his suspenders. "Still find shells along that ol' beach."

"Cahuillas say a ship came in here once, a long time ago."

"If they say it," Pearson said, "it did."

Cavagan filled the bag after rinsing it, then dipped it in water from the spring. Evaporation would keep it cool.

Pearson took a long knife from his gear. "Never catered to that one m'self, but a body never knows when he'll need an extry."

Cavagan shouldered the sack and thrust the knife into his belt. "Look me up some time," he said. "Just ask for Cavagan."

Pearson's back was turned, packing gear, when Cavagan spoke. He let him take a dozen steps, and then said, "You get to Los Angeles, you go to the Calle de los Negros. Ask for Jake. He owes me money an' I expect he might have a pistol. Get whatever you need."

John Sutton sat at dinner at one end of a long table in his ranch house at Calabasas. The dinner had been enhanced by a turkey killed the day before at a *cienaga* a few miles away.

He was restless, but there was no reason for it. Almost a month had gone by. His men had returned to the *algodones* but found no trace of Cavagan. Nor had they expected to. He would have died out on the desert somewhere.

Juan Velasquez saw the rider come up the canyon as he loafed near the gate, standing guard. At the gate the rider dismounted and their eyes met in the gathering dusk. "Buenos noches, Senor," Juan said. "I had expected you."

"So?"

"I have an uncle in Sonora, Senor. He grows old, and he asks for me."

"Adios, Juan."

"Adios, Senor."

Cavagan walked up the steps and into the house where John Sutton sat at dinner.

DEATH RIDES HERE!

John Jakes

Chapter 1

When the wagon blew, Jeff Croydon had no time for thinking.
His dozen high-sided wagons were pulling up, one after another, to the boxcars on the siding in the town of Sooner.
Number four wagon had just pulled away, the skinner bawling lusty obscenities at the mules, and number five was
swinging in toward the car. Jeff Croydon stood near the wagons, the hot dust clouding around him, sweat dripping down
his plain, serious face. Several of the handlers, stripped to the
waist and shining with perspiration, stood in the open door
of the freight car in which the barrels of crude were trans-
ported east, adequately if not safely.

The skinner pulled number five wagon up beside the door.
Someone in the crowd of town loungers standing by the
freight train whistled shrilly. Croydon's head whipped around
as he heard the nervous bray of the mules and the curses of
the skinner trying to frighten them into line once more.

Croydon saw no one in the crowd whom he recognized.
At the moment the thing had the quality of an idle prank, but
Croydon knew and respected the hellish power lying dormant
in the gummy crude. As he turned back to the wagon, something bright flickered in a downward arc across his line of
vision. A short stick, with a flaming rag attached to the end.
With a curse he turned instinctively back to the crowd. They
were brawling now, slugging senselessly at each other, their

16

voices a roaring babel. He still couldn't spot a familiar face, nor a guilty one. Right then his thinking processes stopped.

From down the line he heard the wild shout of Dunc Limerty, the oldster who helped run his freight line. *"Holy God, get that stick outa..."* The wagon exploded. The skinner howled and jumped to the ground. The sweating workers backed into the car, shouting like everyone else. Croydon saw flames licking at the flimsy boxcar walls. Then heat fanned his cheeks like the air from hell's own ovens. The deadly fire so frightening to men here in the oil fields danced out like whirling human figures, extending sudden gouting arms into the car door. Another minute and the whole train might blow. . . .

Croydon had no thought of heroism. He thought only of the flames as a danger. He shoved the frightened skinner out of the way, yelling at the spooked mules as he vaulted onto the wagon seat. In the seconds following the explosion, the mules had begun to move, so the flaming wagon was actually rolling when Croydon hit the seat and gathered up the reins. Banners of flame streaming behind him, he swung the wagon over rows of tracks, cut down a side street and headed past a few last shacks into open country. The rush of wind kept the flames away from him, but the great heat flayed his back. Croydon held his balance, standing wide-legged. He spotted a patch of arid ground ahead. He used all his strength to halt the frantic mules, swing them to the left and brake the wagon.

The mules brayed and threw themselves back and forth in the traces. Croydon dropped to the ground, jerked the pin and let them break free. Then he backed off and watched the wagon burn itself out. He stood there, empty-eyed, counting the loss. Each barrel of crude delivered to eastern oil companies was paid for with monies transferred directly to the well owner, who then paid Croydon a percentage based similarly on barrels delivered to the railroad.

Croydon stared bleakly at the forest of derricks thrusting up all across the face of the land. He freighted crude for none of the big outfits, like that of the wealthy midwesterner, Sen-

ator Lucas Bryant. He handled only the shoestring outfits, and
barely kept his nose out of debt. This calamity, the first in
his three years of management of the small outfit, had come
at a time when success had seemed forthcoming at last. Now,
he didn't know.

A wagon rattled toward him, and he came back to reality.
He squinted against the sun and saw Dunc Limerty driving.
Dunc's weary eyes took in the charred ruin of the wagon as
he braked. He scratched his beard and shook his head.
"T'warn't no accident, Jeff."

"I know," Croydon said, climbing up beside him. "Let's
get back to Sooner."

Limerty swung the mules, and they jogged along back toward the boomtown. The older man reported that the rest of
the shipment had been safely loaded on the train. Croydon
said, "That still doesn't cancel the loss. Dunc, somebody
tossed that burning stick from the crowd. It wasn't just some
fool's idea of a prank. Somebody's out to get us."

Limerty grunted agreement. The clapboards of Sooner rose
ahead of them. The freight train was chugging slowly away
from the yards. "Think it's Hunter?" Limerty asked.

"If it is, I sure as hell don't see why," Croydon answered.
Tom Hunter ran the big freighting outfit in Sooner, handling
shipments for the larger wells including Senator Bryant's
holdings, largest of all in this field. Hunter was the established
business man, Croydon the johnny-come-lately trying to com-
pete. Croydon pointed out that Hunter was making as much
money as any man would want.

"And besides, Hunter's not that stupid. He's got all he
needs. I don't think he'd risk putting us out of business when
we don't even make a dent in his contracts."

"Well," Limerty declared, "you o' course may be right.
But I saw an hombre named Flinch in the crowd. Flinch did
the whistlin' that spooked the mules, and though I didn't see
him toss the stick, he sure as hell got out of there right after
the fire started."

"I don't know this Flinch," Croydon told his partner. "Skinner?"

Limerty spat contemptuously over the wagon side. "Naw. Six-gun artist. Dirty work boy. But he works for Tom Hunter."

"Still," Croydon said, "I can't figure Hunter to make a play like that. It just isn't like him."

No more was said of the matter until they had unhitched the wagons in the freight yard and Croydon lay on his belly on the cot in the cubby-hole office while Limerty slapped liniment onto his back. Driving the flaming wagon had scorched his shirt. "Things can change fast in the oil fields, Jeff," Limerty observed. "I'd sure ask around and see if you can figure out what's going on. You can't get the law to investigate when it looks like Hunter had no reason for jinxing us, even if I did see Flinch. Somebody else would swear he was in the Sooner House having a beer."

Croydon nodded. He pulled on his rough shirt, feeling it prickle against his singed hide. He strapped on his six-gun, more for appearances than anything else, since he was a business man and not inclined to settle matters with lead.

He started on a tour of saloons. He drank beer with drillers, listened to their woes, their laments, their sudden dreams of glory waiting under a new patch of earth, bubbling and black and worth a fortune in the country of quick gains and quicker losses. Slowly he pieced a story together, a story that had come out in the two days he had been out in the field getting this shipment together. When he joined Limerty for dinner at the Sooner House, his mind seethed with anger.

"Wal," Limerty drawled, brushing away foam flecks from his beard, "what did you do, carouse all afternoon? I thought you'd never show."

Croydon ordered a steak and beer. "Hunter's got a damned good reason for wanting us out of the way, Dunc. Senator Lucas Bryant died over a month ago, and nobody knew it until yesterday."

"I can't understand why," Limerty said dryly. "Men forget they's got a Christian name when they smell oil. Nobody in town's interested in anything that can't be put in barrels and sold.'' He frowned. ''But what's the connection?''

''Senator Bryant's widow is arriving here tonight on the train. They say she's a hell of an independent woman. Smart. She's going to look over Bryant's holdings, and the word is she's tossing the freighting contract up for grabs.''

''Hell's bells,'' Limerty exclaimed. He set down his schooner. ''That means we can underbid Hunter and cut ourselves in on the Bryant holdings.''

Croydon nodded. ''Tom Hunter had that contract when I started up here. Now he could stand to lose it. That's reason enough.''

Limerty indicated Croydon's six-gun. ''You better practice up with that thing, and get real good. You may need it.''

He and Dunc Limerty went down to the depot to watch the evening train come in. Croydon felt like a ragged urchin in his grimy clothes. He spotted Tom Hunter sitting in his buggy, heavy-faced, confident, a cheroot tilted in the corner of his mouth. Hunter's clothes were Eastern, expensively tailored.

The funnel-stacked locomotive chuffed its way through the twilight, sparks flying up like red insects. In the smoky glow of the passenger coach lanterns, Croydon saw a woman standing on the platform, obviously impatient to get off. She wore a brown traveling dress, a feathered hat tilted gaily on her head. Her eyes were dark like her hair, and . . . my Lord . . . she was *young*.

Briskly the woman ordered two older women following her to bring her bags. She stepped quickly down the steps when the train halted, and Tom Hunter moved forward, sweeping his hat off and taking her hand. The woman smiled.

''They ain't strangers,'' Limerty muttered sourly. ''He's probably been slickin' his way in by mail. . . .''

Croydon watched Hunter help the woman into the carriage. The maids followed with the baggage, and, amid the awed stares of the depot loungers, the carriage clattered away through the dusk toward the Sooner House. Croydon felt an angry wrath building again. He caught the woman's name. Elizabeth Bryant.

"Come on," he said somberly. "Let's get a drink."

He drank a good deal that evening. Next day he turned up before Mrs. Bryant had awakened, dressed in his best clothes. The maid ushered him into the parlor of the suite at the Sooner House and left the room. He fidgeted, taking in the expensive lamps, the thick, rich carpet, the Eastern furniture. He rolled himself a smoke to calm his nerves.

The bedroom door opened and Elizabeth Bryant swept into the room, skirts belling behind her. She was a damned pretty woman, Croydon reflected. And the way she held her head indicated a strong will and perhaps a temper.

"Well, Mr. Croydon," she said briskly, seating herself, "what can I do for you? I take it this isn't a social call."

"No, it isn't. I run a freighting line, Mrs. Bryant." He hesitated, then decided to show her his hand all at once. "I can haul your crude from the wells to the railroad here in town for one dollar per barrel less than Tom Hunter charges. I came because I heard the contract was open for bid."

"You heard correctly." She gazed at him. Her eyes *were* dark, almost black. "Do you have a cigarette, Mr. Croydon?"

Astounded, he rolled one for her. Here was a woman of a kind he'd never known before; a frank, bold woman from the East. He handed her the cigarette. She smiled her thanks. She inhaled slowly. The smoke drifted through the bars of sunlight streaming in the windows.

"Mr. Croydon, Tom Hunter has the contract for two more weeks. At that time I'll decide whether to keep him on, or hire another company."

"Hunter and I are the only freighters in the territory."

"I know that." Her coolness amazed him. "I base my decision upon a tally that's to be made for me. Men from my wells will check the total number of barrels of crude delivered here in Sooner during the next two weeks. The man who delivers the most oil gets the contract.''

Croydon felt a surge of triumph. He could cancel off yesterday's loss now; he felt sure he could beat Hunter.

He'd hire more skinners, rent wagons . . . it would be two weeks of hellishly hard work, but he could do it.

''I feel I must tell you one thing,'' Elizabeth Bryant added. ''Safety factors also enter into my consideration. Any accidents such as that which occurred yesterday will influence my choice.''

Croydon's eyes blazed. ''Who told you about that? Tom Hunter?''

''Mr. Hunter . . .'' she began.

''One of Mr. Hunter's men caused the explosion.''

''That's a rather strong accusation.''

''I can back it up if I have to.''

Elizabeth Bryant came to her feet. Anger shone in her eyes too. ''Mr. Croydon, I have no personal quarrel with you. You have no reason to shout at me, and I won't stand for it. You've heard my terms. Now please leave.''

Croydon stood there dumbfounded. On one hand the Senator's widow was a lovely, desirable woman. On the other, she was willful and he decided to press the matter no further. He would fight for the contract by delivering the most oil to Sooner.

He put on his hat and said a curt, ''Good day, Mrs. Bryant.'' He slammed the door loudly behind him.

Going down the stairs he met Tom Hunter. The big man started to brush by him, but Croydon caught his sleeve. Hunter whirled, his gray eyes narrowed. ''If you're going to see Mrs. Bryant,'' Croydon said, ''you can tell her how your boy Flinch caused the explosion yesterday. One of my men saw him.''

Hunter laughed, but it was mirthless. ''Croydon, you're a liar. What's more, you're annoying. Stay out of my way.''

''You're going to lose that contract,'' Croydon said.

Hunter dropped his gaze to Croydon's hand on his arm. "Let go of my arm, Croydon."

Croydon hesitated. Hunter wore a gun, and knew how to use it. What's more, winning the contract was the most important thing in the world at this moment. He let go.

Hunter grinned. "My boy Flinch, as you call him, will blow a hole in your stomach if you keep on telling stories about him. Remember that, Croydon."

Hunter disappeared up the stairs.

Dunc Limerty was shouting hoarse orders when Croydon returned to the yard. "Hey, Dunc," he called, "what's the matter?"

Limerty scowled. "Guess you didn't notice when you left." Limerty pointed. "Some polecat got in here last night and sawed through every axle on every wagon we got."

Croydon took in the damage with a bitter gaze. Already the skinners were at work dismantling the wheels. "That's just fine," Croydon said. He described his interview with Elizabeth Bryant.

"She sounds like a real fire-eater," Limerty said when he had finished. "But that don't help the fact that we're due out at noon for the next trip, and we'll never make it. If we don't get our licks in first, we'll fall so far behind we never will catch up with Hunter."

"You don't need to tell me that," Croydon said. "Let's get to work." He tore off his shirt and tossed it on the office steps.

The sun boiled down as the morning wore on, sending salty sweat coursing down his back to make his scorched skin sting even more hellishly. He and Limerty and the others worked tirelessly, repairing axles and cutting and mounting new ones.

Toward the middle of the morning, Elizabeth Bryant appeared. She was driving Hunter's carriage, but she was alone. Croydon put down a hammer and walked out toward her. She kept moving, slowly. He grabbed the horse's headstall. The woman glared at him.

She was dressed differently, he noticed. Rough shirt and

denim trousers. A damned desirable female. But on her hip rested a holstered pistol.

"What do you want, Mr. Croydon?"

"I just thought you might like to know somebody sawed through the axles on our wagons last night. I thought you might have a fair idea of who did it." He couldn't resist a note of bitterness.

"Release the horse," Elizabeth Bryant said.

He stood his ground, staring her down.

Suddenly she had the pistol in her hand, aimed between his eyes. "Move out of the way, Mr. Croydon."

Still he did not move. Her lower lip trembled. She shifted the pistol to her left hand with a lightning movement and pulled the long buggy whip from its socket. She lashed the whip across Croydon's face. The horses reared, throwing him to the ground. The carriage rattled away up the street.

Croydon got up, wiping blood off his cheek. No one looked at him when he came back into the yard. *Looks like she's setting her mind against me*, he thought. *The only way to do it is to beat Hunter's record, with no accidents. She won't be able to refuse the contract then.*

Work went on. Limerty cursed the men endlessly, spurring them on. Croydon dressed after his noon meal and went to the bank. When he returned, he had rented a dozen more wagons and hired additional skinners. They rolled out of Sooner at dusk, toward the oil fields, half a day late. Hunter's outfit had left that morning. Every cent Jeff Croydon had had in the bank was gone now, sunk desperately into the extra gear.

Chapter 2
The Stolen Tally

The days of the following week blended imperceptibly into one another. Croydon's outfit worked day and night. In a haze of weariness, Croydon drove himself and his men, grabbing a wink of sleep when he could, a cup of coffee or a plate of beans. In their first two days they covered the Big Blow Wells, numbers one through five, and the Oh, Nellie! rig, one through four. They wheeled the mules back toward Sooner, rolling through the darkness, and Croydon imagined that his world would forever be one of darkness and eerie fire on the horizon, thundering wheels and braying mules, rattling barrels and loud curses.

They rolled into Sooner at dawn of the third day. Hunter's outfit had gone out again the night before. But Croydon consulted the begrimed tally sheet in the hands of Matheson, a Bryant man, and noticed with pleasure that they were fifteen barrels ahead of Hunter's freighters. The men had one hour off in which to grab breakfast, a shave, or a few jolts of whiskey, and then Croydon had them moving again, popping the buckskin over the heads of the animals as they clattered out of town under a lowering sky.

They covered the Oklahoma Enterprise wells that day, the Golden Garter wells the day after that, and finished with the Illinois Settlement wells at the end of the fifth day. The twenty-three wagons were jammed with tied-down barrels, tier upon tier, until the wagon beds fairly sagged. Limerty begged for a rest, for the other skinners as much as for himself. Croydon listened to the ominous rumbling, his eyes on the black sky beyond the forest of derricks.

"Storm's been brewing for two days now, Dunc," he said. "This load has got to go back to Sooner tonight. We've got enough men, and they've been taking turns sleeping and driving all this week. They can keep it up one more night."

Limerty sighed. "But they won't keep it up much longer. We ain't paying them enough . . ." But despite much grumbling, the freight wagons rolled within the hour.

The storm broke about midnight, filling the world with a black roar of rain. The wheels bogged down, the mules spooked easily, and one of the wagon straps broke, toppling a tier of barrels into the mud.

Lanterns made eerie splotches of light in the gloom as Croydon labored, getting the barrels reloaded. The men grum-

bled louder now. He yelled at them, every angry word an
outward sign of his own inward fear that they'd lose the race.

The storm abated before morning, and dawn found them
again in Sooner. This time, the tally showed them twenty-five
barrels behind Hunter. Croydon was not pleased. On top of
that, the extra skinners and even a couple of the regulars
confronted him and said that they didn't like his kind of hard
work. Too hard, too little pay.

When Croydon returned from the bank this time, a heavy
mortgage lay on his outfit. He doled out salaries, plus a bonus
to each man, and promised them a double bonus if they lasted
until the end of the two weeks. All of them said they'd stay.

Once more they rolled out, splitting up now, working the
smaller outfits, two and three wagons at a time. They returned
to Sooner on the evening of the seventh day, around meal
time. As they swung past Hunter's yard, Croydon saw that
the wagons stood idle. When they had unloaded he told the
men that they had the night off. A few feeble cheers greeted
his words. Croydon smiled grimly at the tally Matheson had
made. Two barrels ahead of Tom Hunter. . . .

He and Limerty decided to eat in the Sooner House dining
room. As soon as they entered, Croydon regretted it. For there
at a secluded table, Elizabeth Bryant sat with Tom Hunter.
The big man wouldn't trouble himself to go into the field. He
had enough skinners to do the work. He stayed in town and
kept Mrs. Bryant busy.

"Ain't that something," Limerty muttered, jabbing his fork
into his fried potatoes. Croydon paid no attention. He watched
the woman, the high tilt of her chin, the lush sweep of her
breast under the severe gown. Her cheeks were slightly
flushed, perhaps from the bottle of wine Tom Hunter had
furnished. She laughed a great deal.

Slowly the dining room cleared, until Croydon, Limerty,
Mrs. Bryant and Hunter were the only ones left, separated by
half a dozen tables. Hunter was leaning forward speaking to
Mrs. Bryant when suddenly his head snapped around and he

fixed Croydon with his gaze. Elizabeth Bryant turned, too, smiling frostily.

Croydon nodded in a pleasant way, blowing smoke from his cigar and noting Hunter's obvious displeasure in being watched. It was only a matter of moments then before Hunter piloted Mrs. Bryant out the door, hand on her arm, brow knotted in a frown of irritation.

Croydon laughed. "Hunter's getting rattled. But I swear that Bryant woman is beyond me."

Despite the fact that he didn't understand her, he still felt an attraction. It was almost with surprise that he found himself knocking on her hotel room door at half past nine that same evening.

The maid ushered him in with protests that Mrs. Bryant had retired. But Mrs. Bryant greeted him, a quilted robe wrapped around her and her dark hair falling across her shoulders, lustrous in the glow of the lamps. Croydon realized that she was truly beautiful.

The maid bustled around for a few minutes, straightening things uselessly, until Elizabeth Bryant dismissed her.

"Well, Mr. Croydon. What is it this time?" Her tone was faintly defensive. She stood close to him, and he caught the fresh-scrubbed smell of her skin, mingling with the scent of her hair. Her features seemed softer in the lamplight.

He juggled his hat in his hands. "I just wanted to inquire if you'd paid heed to the tally. We're keeping up with Hunter."

She laughed. "That's a very lame excuse for calling on me at this hour."

"I know." Their eyes met, held. Croydon's hat dropped from his hands. He seized her shoulders, kissed her hard. She responded for a long moment. And then pulled backwards hastily, anger rekindled in her eyes.

"Damn you," she breathed. "Damn you, Croydon, get out and don't come back."

And then he understood. Senator Lucas Bryant had been a much older man. How she'd married such a man, God alone knew. Family pressure, perhaps. Stranger things happened. But here was no woman born for a cold, passionless marriage. Here was a woman warm and alive and filled with a wild kind of desire. She saw that he knew her secret. Hence the anger.

"You didn't come out here just because of the Senator's wells, did you?" He said it without malice, but she didn't take it that way. Her hand swung up, smacking loudly on his flesh. He wanted to be angry, but he couldn't find it in him.

Croydon turned to go. He didn't look at her. And as he made his way back to the cot in the office, he realized that he might have ruined any chance of ever winning her over. Her pride would have been severely wounded. *You're a fool,* he told himself. He fell into a troubled sleep that night, rolling restlessly on the cot, but knowing he would double his efforts to win the contract now. He had a second stake. The chance it would bring him to be near Elizabeth Bryant.

They headed out early next morning. Before the sun had crawled up the sky to high noon, the raiders struck.

They came pounding down a rise, a dozen of them, dust rolling in gritty clouds behind them, their guns making strangely small flat popping noises in the vast land. Croydon, handling the first wagon, reined the mules, and seized the rifle on the seat beside him. He flung it to his shoulder and fired, jacking it a moment later for another, equally ineffective shot. Croydon had never been a marksman.

The raiders pulled half way between a low hill and the wagons. They all wore stained bandannas across their faces. Croydon leaped down and started forward in a crouch. All along the line of wagons, the skinners were doing the same thing. Dunc Limerty bawled orders. Croydon's stomach tightened as he flattened himself in the dirt, pumping a shot. If another wagon blew, they'd fall far, far behind. Perhaps they'd never catch up at all.

But fortunately the raiding party was a weak one. Croydon had nearly thirty men, and they were stretched out along the wagon line so that their fire could cut into the owlhoots from

many points. Croydon let go a shot and saw one of the raiders
spin out of his saddle and collide with the rider next to him.
The attackers stayed less than two minutes. One of them, a
man in a loud purple shirt, raised his arm and yelled something Croydon couldn't hear. They turned and spurred back
up the rise. Limerty came racing toward Croydon.

"Shall we go after them, Jeff?"

Croydon shook his head. "But let's take a look at that dead
one."

He and Limerty went over and knelt beside the fallen owl-
hoot. They pulled down his soiled bandanna. Croydon didn't
recognize him, and neither did Limerty. But the breed was
familiar enough. He had the vulturish look of a professional
killer, even in death.

Croydon stood up slowly. "Dunc," he said, his voice
barely a whisper, "this is getting pretty tight. These men
couldn't have come from anybody but Tom Hunter."

"Hell, I recognized Flinch, in the purple shirt," Limerty
exclaimed.

"Then if it's killing he wants, it's killing he'll get. Tell
every one of the men to stay ready. Hunter's getting scared."

The men were nervous and obviously displeased about
having to fight as a part of their job. Most of them had no
personal acquaintance with Croydon, no loyalty other than the
fact that he paid them. And none of them had a particular
inclination to get a bellyful of lead in his behalf.

The next two days brought a number of serious foulups.
Men reacted slowly to orders, surly glints in their eyes. One
of the skinners scared his mules so badly that they snapped
the traces and ran off. Another time, a man let a barrel tip
out of his wagon out of pure carelessness. Croydon watched
the crude bubble thickly into the earth. He spoke sharply to
the man, who faced him with dull enraged eyes. Croydon saw
that it would not take much to provoke a fight, so he let him
off with a tongue lashing. It was a bad situation, and Croydon
knew it couldn't last much longer. He was fighting uphill,
and slipping down two inches for every one he gained. Each

day reduced the efficiency of the outfit. The breaking point came on the tenth day.

They arrived in Sooner at noon, with full wagons, and proceeded to unload on the waiting boxcars. The tally showed they were thirty-six barrels behind Hunter.

Reluctantly Croydon gave the men the afternoon off. If he didn't, they would quit, and he would lose out then and there.

He was in the office in the middle of the afternoon when Tom Hunter stormed in, followed by portly Sheriff Hink Peters. Hink knew Croydon, and the freighter liked the law's representative in Sooner. But Peters was scowling. Croydon knew Peters wasn't linked up with Hunter, so this was something bad.

"Afternoon, Hink," he said affably ignoring Hunter. "Have a seat."

"No time to sit down, Jeff. Miz Bryant's man Matheson just turned up in an alley with his skull bashed in. The tally sheet is gone. Plumb disappeared."

"Why would anyone grab the tally?" Croydon asked.

"Maybe you can answer that one, Croydon," Hunter said.

"Now wait a minute . . ."

"Hold off, Jeff." Peters put up one hand, palm outward. "I got to check up on everything. Somebody might want to alter them tallies so's to swing the contract. It's no secret you're fighting for Miz Bryant's business."

"Hunter here is fighting just as hard."

But he saw his own position. In the minds of the citizens of Sooner, he was the johnny-come-lately. He, and not Hunter, would be the obvious and likely one to make such a back-to-the-wall play.

"Just where were you about an hour ago, Jeff?" Peters asked.

"I was sitting right here. I've got a mortgage on the outfit, sheriff, and I was just sitting here stewing about how I could pay it off."

Hunter laughed. "Sheriff, there's one more motive for you.

Croydon's whipped, and he'll pull any kind of stupid trick to save himself.''

''Just try to slap me in jail on the strength of that, Hunter. It can't be done.''

''I know it can't,'' Peters parried. He headed for the door, sad disappointment in his eyes. ''Guess I'll have to do some checking anyways, Jeff. I'll get in touch with you.'' Hunter followed him out and slammed the door loudly.

Croydon stared silently after the two departing men. Any fool could see it was Hunter's trick. Any fool, that is, who didn't have the town's perspective. Everybody would automatically swing over, comparatively speaking, to Tom Hunter's point of view because he had seniority in the matter of reputation. Hunter was tightening the noose around Croydon's neck. And there was not a great deal he could do about it.

The freight yard lay deserted. A hot wind stirred powdery dust. The sun slanting in prickled Croydon's back and he couldn't concentrate. The gun on his hip weighed against his flesh. His palms tingled. He wanted to kill Tom Hunter. But that would only nail the coffin shut completely.

Dune Limerty returned around five, in high spirits, heavily fortified with alcohol. Croydon explained the situation over dinner, and the older man's eyes darkened.

''Lord,'' Limerty said sourly, ''they was even dumb enough to do it in an alley. Nothin' smart about that Hunter. I'm beginning to think he must be going off his head.''

''He's in the position all of Sooner thinks I'm in,'' Croydon said. ''But I can't prove that Hunter's the kind of man who'd pull such a stunt, while I sit by under my halo, ready to go down in honest but pure defeat.'' Deep cynicism edged his words.

''Look out, my friend.'' Limerty's voice became a hoarse whisper. ''Peters just came in, along with Hunter and that Flinch.''

Croydon turned toward the three men. Flinch, bringing up the rear, was a short toad-like man with sunken eyes and sagging cheeks. A witless smile hung on his pendulous lips.

Peters put his arm on Croydon's shoulder. "Jeff, I got some bad news for you." Croydon's eyes flashed to Hunter.

The big man's hard gaze was self-satisfied. "Rip Flinch here went nosing around your office a few minutes ago and found these." Peters extended a sheaf of papers. The tally, smudged with ink and grime.

Croydon rocketed to his feet. "Did you happen to ask Hunter whether he had Flinch plant those things in my office? My God, sheriff, don't be a fool . . ."

Peters shook his head. "I know there's always that possibility. Thing is, I've got to lock you up until I can do some more investigating. Right now you're guilty. Later on . . ." It was hellishly clear. In the delay, Hunter would be assured of the Bryant contract. Whether they ever really found him guilty or not didn't matter.

Croydon didn't wait. He rammed a fist into the sheriff's gut, then shoved Flinch out of the way. Flinch grunted and a bright flash of metal crossed Croydon's line of vision. He tried to dodge out of the way, but Hunter's pistol barrel slammed into his temple. Then Hunter struck him again. He went down and out with frightening suddenness. Next thing he knew, he was lying on his back, staring up at a clay ceiling. He rolled his aching head to the right. Cell bars. Beyond them a deputy lounged, playing solitaire in the glow of a lamp.

Croydon's mind whirled. He was beaten for sure. But something within him wouldn't let him stay beaten. This thing had been business, but now it had taken on a new aspect. Personal between him and Tom Hunter. Elizabeth Bryant's face danced in his mind. Then he forgot about her as the jail door opened. Dunc Limerty made his way past the deputy to the cell. Croydon got up to meet him.

"What's wrong?" Croydon asked.

"Hell, Jeff . . ." He scratched his beard. "It looks like we're through for sure. You know our skinners got pretty stirred up over working so hard these past few days. After

Hink Peters locked you up here, well . . .'' The oldster shook his grizzled head, unwilling to go on.

"Let's have it, Dunc," Croydon said softly.

Limerty's gaze settled on the floor. "Hunter moved fast. He sent Flinch around with a promise of triple the bonus we paid. I tried to stop them, but they wouldn't listen. Most of 'em said they wanted on the winning side.''

"They quit?"

"That's about it, Jeff. We've got three men left, and God knows why they stayed. We've got all them wagons, and nobody to drive them. It wouldn't do us no good even if you was to get out of jail. I hate to say it, but it looks like we're licked in this game.''

Croydon stared through the bars, gripping them, white-knuckled.

Chapter 3
The Thirteenth Day

Croydon languished in jail on the eleventh and twelfth days. In his mind he saw Tom Hunter, slowed down in his pace now, yet still hauling enough crude into Sooner to give him an unbeatable margin, and the contract.

Almost from the moment that Croydon had heard Limerty's announcement of their defeat, he had made up his mind as to the course he had to follow. Escape, that was the only way. And since he could no longer win the contest on the basis of barrels delivered, he had to do it another way. Expose Hunter, thereby putting him out of the running and leaving Elizabeth's only choice his own outfit, which he could rebuild quickly on the strength of her contract.

But for two maddening days no opportunity for escape presented itself. The only escape route was the cell door. That was opened three times a day when the two deputies brought him a tray of food. One deputy held a six-gun on Croydon while the other ducked and set the tray inside. They always

made Croydon retreat to the far wall and stand. Hink Peters
was a thoughtful, methodical man who allowed no carelessness.

When noon of the thirteenth day arrived, Croydon decided
he had to make a desperate try. So far as he knew, Peters had
unearthed no evidence either to clear him or to point conclu-
sively to his guilt. He *had* to get out . . . do something to fight
the sense of defeat rising within him . . .

Instead of waiting until the deputies decided to come into
the cell, he placed himself in position beforehand. He stood
on the cell bunk, which was fastened to the rear wall. He
leaned his elbows on the sill and stared out the small barred
window into the dusty alley. He was standing that way when
the jail door opened and the second deputy arrived with the
food, brought from the Sooner House.

The key rattled in the lock, and Croydon turned around,
desperately trying to conceal his breathlessness. The first deputy pushed the door open, and Croydon noted that he still
held his gun level. The other man put down his tray.

"Well," Croydon said, "guess I'll eat long as you brought
it. The view isn't the prettiest I've seen." He waved over his
shoulder to the window. The second deputy allowed himself
a grin. Croydon shifted his weight as if to step down off the
bunk. His height gave him a slight advantage as he leaped.

The deputies let out hoarse yells as he bowled into them,
knocking them backwards through the cell door. The three
men fell in a heap of thrashing limbs, but Croydon kept his
head, seizing both their guns and leaping to his feet, each fist
full of a heavy weapon.

"All right, boys. Get inside the cell."

They obeyed him without hesitation. He relocked the door
and tossed the keys in the corner, far away from them. Thrusting one gun into his belt and holding the other at ready, he
slipped out the side door into an alley that opened to the main
street.

He slid along in the shadows of the wall, thinking rapidly.
He knew where Sheriff Peters lived. That was his destination.

The house lay on a quiet back street, shaded by big trees. He walked up the lawn and in through the front door without knocking.

He went into the parlor. Mrs. Peters, a ruddy buxom woman with graying hair, saw him first. Then she saw the gun. "Why, Jeff, what are you . . ."

Peters, seated with his back to Croydon, spluttered loudy. He leaped to his feet, his hand dropping toward his holster.

"Easy, Hink," Croydon said. "I don't want trouble."

"What in hell is this?" Peters thundered. "I'll throw the book at you for breaking out of jail."

"I've got to have a chance to prove I didn't take those tallies. You open to a bargain?"

"I sure as blazes am not," Peters shot back.

Croydon had to smile. "Here it is anyway. You know where this Rip Flinch lives?" Peters nodded. "Well, let's stroll over there. If you walk in on him, holding your gun and ask him point-blank whether or not he stole the tallies and planted them in my office, I think you'll have what you really want to know."

"Got this Flinch all figgered, eh?" Peters said. His eyes narrowed thoughtfully. His wife had long since relaxed. She knew Croydon well enough to know that no harm would come to her husband. "I think if you act like you already know he did it, say you got some evidence—he'll spook. He's that kind."

Croydon softened his tone. "But if he doesn't scare, then I'm willing to hand over my gun to you and go back to jail peaceably."

He watched the lawman for reactions. "Hink, I'm betting everything I've got on the hunch that you can scare him into admitting the truth."

Peters hesitated only a moment longer. Then he extended his hand. "All right, Jeff. Hand over your iron right now, and I'll go along with the game. I never did like that Flinch's looks much."

Croydon handed his gun over, followed it with the one at

his belt. Peters led him out through the kitchen, picked up his hat, and the two men moved across the back lawn. From the door Mrs. Peters wished Jeff good luck.

Peters had Croydon ride slightly ahead of him, on one of Peters's own mounts. "So folks don't think I let you run around loose," Peters explained.

Rip Flinch lived in a seedy rooming house near the yards. The landlady informed them that Flinch hadn't yet appeared for the morning. She goggled at the sight of the sheriff herding his prisoner upstairs with his gun.

Croydon flattened himself outside the door while Peters knocked loudly.

When Flinch opened the door sleepily, Peters said gruffly, "Flinch, you're in trouble."

"What?" Flinch grunted. "What's that you're saying, Sheriff? I just got outa bed."

"The stolen tallies," Peters said. "The ones you took from Matheson and planted in Croydon's office." *God*, Croydon thought, *he's really taking a chance for me.* "Come on, Flinch. You took those tallies, and now I can prove . . ."

"Damn you!" Flinch yelped. Croydon was filled with a sense of victory. Flinch tried to slam the door shut, but Peters rammed his shoulder against it and heaved. It spanged open, throwing Flinch to the floor. Peters ran into the room, Croydon on his heels.

Flinch seized his gun from a chair and began a wild volley of shots that blasted the woodwork into splinters but missed Croydon and Peters. They retreated quickly into the hall again. Peters tossed Croydon a six-gun. Croydon poked his head around the edge of the door in time to see Flinch, clad only in trousers and undershirt, heave himself feet first through the window. "Jumped out," Croydon shouted, racing toward the stairs. "Let's go after him!"

Flinch evidently moved fast. They spent twenty minutes prowling the neighborhood around the boardinghouse, but he had eluded them. So they mounted up and rode all the way across town to Hunter's office. The yard man informed them that Flinch and Hunter had ridden out perhaps ten minutes ahead of them, looking excited.

"Ah swear," the yard man drawled, "the feends o' hell was after them, Sheriff."

Croydon vaulted up the office steps, looked in quickly.

"They've skipped all right. The safe's cleaned out."

Peters mounted up. "I'll see if I can get some men. Maybe we can still catch them. You go on about your business. There's no need for you to stay in jail any longer."

Exultantly Croydon headed for the Sooner House. He slammed into Elizabeth Bryant's suite despite the protests of the maid, demanding to see the widow. Elizabeth Bryant appeared in the sitting room abruptly, surprise showing in her dark eyes.

"What's the meaning of all this, Croydon? I thought you were in jail."

"I was. But Flinch spilled his mouth to the sheriff. He stole the tallies, on Hunter's orders. Both of them have cleared out. Hunter's out of business, and I'm the only freighting company owner left in Sooner. So how about the contract?"

"Not on your life. Unless you're ahead in the tally. I'll hire someone to run Hunter's rig. You have till dawn tomorrow to beat his score."

It was stupid, prideful . . . but then Croydon remembered what he had done to her; how he had carelessly exposed her secret. This was her way of retaliating. He jammed his hat on his head and stalked out.

Croydon raced back to the freight yard. There, Limerty greeted him with an expression of amazement. "Jeff! What happened to you? Come on inside, boy, before somebody sees you. If you broke out they'll be after you . . ."

"I did break out," Croydon told him. "But things are all straightened around now." Rapidly he summarized the events of the previous hours.

"Then we got Miz Bryant's contract after all," Limerty said, pleased.

"No we don't. She's a stubborn woman. We've still got

to beat Hunter's tally. Which won't be easy, seeing as we only have till dawn. Now, have we still got those three men?''

Limerty nodded.

"Then with you and me, that will have to do it. I hope to God it does. I'll go down to the yards and check the tally. Just say a long prayer that Hunter's slacked off since I landed in jail.'' He left Limerty wide-eyed as he leaped up into the saddle and went galloping out of the yard.

Matheson, head swathed in bandages, greeted him with apologies. He'd already heard of Hunter's treachery from Sheriff Hink Peters. "But the sheriff and his posse come back about half an hour ago,'' Matheson concluded. "No sign of Hunter and Rip Flinch anywhere.''

Croydon looked eagerly at the tallies. "How far ahead is Hunter?''

Matheson consulted the grimy sheets. "Well, he ain't been pushing near as hard since they salted you away. Let's see . . .'' He frowned, figuring laboriously. "A hundred and three barrels. He ain't done much at all.''

Croydon clapped him on the shoulder. "Thanks. He won't be doing anything after tomorrow.''

And before Matheson could shoot another question, Croydon was into the saddle and away up the street.

He reported the total to Dunc Limerty, who let out a yip of pleasure.

"Round up those three men,'' Croydon said. "We'll need five wagons. We're going to do some mighty fast hauling . . .''

Before sundown, the five wagons careened out of Sooner. Croydon had the lead, howling like a fiend at the mules, cracking the buckskin popper over their ears.

Croydon had already formed a plan of action. Each skinner would take one of the Oh, Nellie! wells, the ones closest to Sooner, and load their wagons with crude. The margin would be close, but Croydon felt they could work it. At a fork, he swung his wagon off and went roaring down a rutted road. The others split up in various directions, having their orders to load up and race hell-for-leather back to Sooner.

Croydon pulled up at Oh, Nellie! number three about ten that evening. He started yelling questions to the drill boss, who informed him they had plenty of crude waiting to be freighted. Croydon sweated in the light of the lanterns, heaving the big barrels up to the wagon bed. The sound of the well, *pump, pump, pump,* echoed in his ears, inexorable as the ticking of a clock.

By midnight the wagon was loaded. Croydon hoped the others would be doing as well. He gigged up the mules, turning their heads back toward Sooner. Driving at a breakneck clip, the wheels flying over the tops of the wagon ruts, he reached Sooner by two. Matheson greeted him by lantern light and chalked up the load on the tally. Croydon rolled himself a cigarette and tried to relax. It was no good. As long as the other men weren't back he couldn't rest.

All the others except Limerty arrived by four o'clock. Croydon scanned the sky anxiously. It would be dawn soon, and without that extra wagon load, they would lose.

Horse's hooves clopped in the street. Croydon turned expectantly, then realized it was a single rider. Elizabeth Bryant, in shirt and denims, rode into the circle of lamplight.

She climbed down, nodded to Croydon and leaned over Matheson's shoulder to glance at the tally. Croydon saw pearly streaks in the east. Nowhere in the silent town did he hear the clatter of Limerty's wagon.

Elizabeth Bryant faced him. "You're still under Hunter's total."

"I've got one more wagon due in."

Elizabeth Bryant smiled a chilly smile, openly defensive against any more attacks. "But Mr. Croydon—it's dawn now."

"Then the contract goes to Hunter's outfit, whether he's around or not?"

"I'm afraid it . . ." she began.

Shots racketed in the night and the lantern exploded in a

hail of glass. Instinctively Croydon swept his arm around Elizabeth Bryant and bore her to the ground.

He snaked his gun free, listening. The whole freight yard was dark. Croydon crept forward along the ground, trying to keep from making noise. Hunter had come back. Defeated, whipped and exposed, the man nevertheless had the will to revenge himself. He wanted Croydon's life.

Croydon scooped up a handful of gravel and tossed it to his right. Nothing happened. He picked up a larger rock and threw it in the same direction. A second later, a gun bucketed, aimed toward the right.

Croydon emptied his gun from where he lay. The powder-flame showed him Rip Flinch, jiggling in the door of a box-car, his chest bleeding.

He teetered forward slowly, and Croydon dodged backward as Flinch fell.

Croydon turned around. Hunter was somewhere around. But where? He took a step backward, and a gun exploded. Fire ripped into his shoulder. He reeled from the pain. Somebody struck a match and touched it to a piece of wood and got a glowing torch.

It was Matheson, standing behind Hunter. Hunter stood clearly outlined, his head turned slightly so that his eyes glowed. His gun rose slowly.

Croydon knew his own gun was empty; it had clicked empty after he had downed Rip Flinch. He had no other.

The pain dizzied him. Another instant and Hunter would kill him. He had to move. He had to *fight*. He took a step forward, trying to lunge at Hunter, but he only succeeded in falling on his face. He heard an explosion, and then something jolted down on his back and didn't move.

A moment later, Hunter's lifeless body was lifted away.

Dunc Limerty stood there, pistol in hand.

"*Dunc!*" Croydon lunged to his feet, staggering.

"Hunter was about to finish you. I couldn't do much else."

Croydon blinked, realization sinking in. "You made it back. You got here! The contract . . ."

Limerty shook his head slowly. "I . . . I came in on one of the mules . . ."

"W—what?" Through the numbing pain, Croydon didn't understand.

"One of them repaired axles gave out, about ten miles out of town. I tried to fix it but I couldn't do it by myself. So I rode in on one of the mules. I seen the tally, Jeff. I'm sorry." The oldster averted his gaze.

Croydon swung bleary eyes to Elizabeth Bryant, standing beside a re-lit lantern. Her face had a dazed bleached quality about it. *Damn her,* Croydon thought, *she isn't going to stop us like that. I won't let her.* He started to walk toward the woman. Limerty put out a hand to restrain him but Croydon shoved it away. He kept walking.

He faced Elizabeth Bryant across the circle of lamplight. She averted her eyes suddenly, and he saw that her cheeks had turned a deep scarlet.

"You heard what Limerty said," Croydon told her. "You know that our last wagon load is stuck outside of town. But for that we'd have won the contract. On your terms."

"I'm sorry," she said, weakly this time. "I set up the rules whereby . . . the . . . the . . ."

Silence.

He moved closer to her so that Matheson, Limerty, and the other three men could not hear.

"What's wrong? Are you ashamed of my finding out that you're a woman and not a machine? I don't think it's anything to be ashamed of."

She looked at him then, the flush deepening. He could see the battle being fought within her, wounded pride against womanly desire. Twice she almost spoke . . . twice she closed her lips again. She shook her head, still unable to speak.

Croydon turned away disgusted. "Well, I guess I had you figured wrong, Mrs. Bryant. And I guess you can find someone to take over Hunter's outfit—"

"Wait." Her voice was barely a whisper.

Croydon turned and stared. "I'll . . . I'm moving the time

up. The final tally will be made at eight A.M. this morning.''
She spun away, then, finding her horse, remounting and
plunging into the darkness as if all the fiends of hell were
pursuing her. *No, not fiends,* Croydon thought, *only emotions,
pride against desire.* And desire had won. He'd found a chink
in her armor.

Dunc Limerty raced to him. ''We've got until eight this
morning to bring that wagon in. Get some of the boys and
use one of their wagons. We'll have that contract.''

''You're damned right we will,'' Limerty exclaimed. He
slapped Croydon on the back. The impact was enough to send
the weakened Croydon toppling. He stretched out on the
ground, dimly aware that the astounded Limerty was bending
over him. The darkness closed . . .

Limerty brought the extra wagon in by seven-thirty. On the
spot, Elizabeth Bryant awarded them the contract to freight
crude for the holdings of the late Senator. When Croydon
awoke, he had his arm bandaged. He sat in his office all day,
doing paper work, thinking of just how long it would take to
pay off the mortgage, what kind of new equipment he could
afford and a hundred other similar details. Now and then he
took a little whiskey for the pain.

That evening he dressed in his best suit and called on Elizabeth Bryant in her hotel suite. They sat opposite each other
on the sofa, a polite distance between them.

''What are your plans now?'' Croydon asked.

''I don't know. I could go back East, but there isn't much
to look forward to there, unless . . .''

''Why not stay here and manage the Senator's business?
You could learn in a year's time, and you could probably step
up production and profit if you took the trouble.''

''I'm afraid I made a botch of things, Jeff.'' She used his
first name casually, as if she were accustomed to it. ''This is
no place for me.''

''I think it is,'' he said. He moved close, tilted her chin
with his hand, and kissed her, long and hard.

She flushed again, but she didn't grow angry. Instead, she

smiled. Croydon knew then that with time, they could have something rich and fine together.

"Would you like to go have dinner?" he asked.

Embarrassed, she smiled. "I think we'd better," she said.

YANKEE GOLD

➖

John M. Cunningham

Hull leaned against the bar waiting for Mourret and looked with faint disgust at his drink. He was sick of shots and bottles; he'd tried to fix up a mint julep and there it stood, tall, pale and stinking, no ice, no mint, no nothing. You might as well drink champagne out of a kerosene can as try to make a julep in a Montana gold-boom town.

He began remembering New Orleans, the smooth mahogany bars, the silver, the river, and somebody said beside him, "Mourret's back. I just saw him go in the hotel. We'd better go up and get things settled for tonight."

Hull looked at Wootten's cold, meek face. "Tonight?" Wootten nodded, his lips compressed. He had a way of looking down, of holding his face and eyes controlled, as though half-blind, or with a kind of secretive mock-modesty which concealed his secret thoughts. Wootten's face always looked as though the coroner had just taken the ice off it. In spite of his downcast eyes he saw everything and when he looked up suddenly you saw not timidity, but pure danger.

"The Negro took Bonnetty's running horse down to be shod. Has to be ready by six tonight. And Rogers heard the black boy and Bonnetty talking out at the barn. It's tonight for sure."

"You didn't find out which way he's going to take it?"

Wootten shook his head and bit the corner of his lower lip. "Not yet. We will. I'm going on over. Don't follow me too closely." He turned and left, head down, walking neatly, modestly, feet straight, close together, everything as proper and controlled as a hangman's thoughts.

Hull looked after him, a helpless sneer faint on his face, a sneer that protected him from his own fear. Wootten was too good for him. Everything about him was efficient—his two clean, modest guns boasted no show. They were a workman's tools. Hull thought of how sometimes a man and wife got to look like each other. A man couldn't kill as many men as Wootten had and not be partly dead himself.

"Now what do you call that there thing you fixed up?" the barkeep said, looking with a yellow eye at the julep.

Hull looked at it and swallowed. "That there thing is known as Dr. Emilius Quack's Jiffy-fix. You feed it to them as they die and save the embalming cost. When are you going to get some really good kerosene in this territory?"

The barkeep's eye turned evil and he slunk down the bar like a fox in a cage. Hull looked after him. He was like the whole damned territory—dry as death, yellow and hungry as a dog—for gold.

Outside he could hear the rattle of wagons, the shout of drivers and crack of whips—bootheels tap-tapping up and down the boardwalks—hammers pounding up the flimsy shanties they had to call palaces or golden globes—nothing as natural as the wide, peaceful saloons in New Orleans, like Garigou's.

In two weeks he'd be there with twenty thousand dollars to set him up again. He smiled to himself. Twenty thousand in Yankee gold.

He walked out into the blazing sunshine and stood blinking at a girl. She was standing still in the middle of the walk. A small package lay at the edge of the walk beside her and her foot, invisible beneath her long skirt, seemed to be trying to kick something. Her face was flushed with embarrassment, yet she did not move.

He frowned with perplexity. She wasn't the kind to make a joke of herself. She was no palace girl, not with that delicacy of face. She was completely out of place here among the saloons, being stared at by every lout that knew how to lean against a porch-pole.

"Excuse me, ma'am," he said, taking off his hat and picking up the package. "This is yours, isn't it?"

"Please hold it," she said, her voice very small. He held the package, and became infected with her own embarrassment.

"What is the matter, ma'am?" She was still doing something with her foot. Somebody sniggered. Her eyelids lowered and she looked down. He looked around. They had a gallery of four or five men, all grinning.

"Who laughed?" he said.

The grins dropped. One of them took an easy step away from the saloon-front, his thumbs hooked in his gun-belt. "I did. What of it, mister?" His hands dropped from his belt.

"Don't you know it's not polite to laugh at young ladies?"

"What lady?"

Hull got him before he could move. He slammed back against the wall, slid down and sat holding his face, blood running down his forearms and chin. Hull stepped to him and gave him a stiff boot in the thigh. "Move out fast."

The other got up, took his hands down and made a pass at his gun. He went back to the wall and Hull took the gun and slung it out into the street.

He turned back to the girl, giving the others a look. They drifted away slowly, with a look on their faces as though they had forgotten to put on their pants that morning and were pretending nobody could see them.

"I'm sorry for that," he said to the girl. She ignored him painfully.

"Please, it's my shoe. Would you be kind enough to give

me your arm—just for a moment?'' She laid her hand on his
forearm and wiggled her foot again. He looked down at her
hand, middle-sized and smooth, very white, and a surprising
warm pleasure made him smile.

"Please don't laugh," she said. "My father told me not to
come down here. I shouldn't have. I was curious. But please
don't laugh at me."

"I wasn't laughing at you, ma'am. I'm glad to be of service."

She gave a little hop to one side and stood balancing herself
on one foot.

"There," she said. "You see? Would you please get it for
me?"

He looked down. Her shoe, a small slipper, sat on the walk,
its heel jammed into a knothole. He knelt and worked it loose,
stood up and offered it to her.

She laughed at him. "I don't want to carry it home, thank
you," she said. He put it down again and she wiggled her
foot into it, stamped lightly and smiled. Her face was pale
again, and her eyes, no longer clouded by embarrassment,
looked up at him clear and laughing.

"Thank you so much," she said. All at once the warm
pleasure in him deepened and he was looking not at her eyes,
but into them. He looked away quickly.

"You're very welcome, ma'am," he said. "Let me walk
with you up the street a way. The—the walks are full of
holes."

She hesitated and then suddenly seemed to collect herself,
frowning very faintly. She gave him a quick, shielded, almost
suspicious glance, then down again. "Please, my package?"
she said remotely.

"Oh," he said and held it out. She took it and looked up
at him again. The shield was still there, but she was peeking
over it.

Her head gave a little bow. "Thank you," she said, and
went past him. He turned and watched her moving, head
down, up the walk, her long, grey dress swinging. Her hair

went bright and dark as she passed under the porches from sun into shadow. Then she turned a corner out of sight.

He stood with her scent still in his nostrils—suddenly astonished that she was not there.

Finally he turned and saw Wootten standing in the street, looking at him with a wooden smile, eyes slyly amused. The pleasure in Hull iced and died.

"What do you want?"

Wootten's little smile faded into his customary prim meekness. "Mourret says to hurry up. He's got a job for you right away." Four men were coming up the walk. Wootten pulled a watch from his vest and looked at it. "Ten o'clock, stranger," he said loudly, and then, after they had passed: "We've got six hours left." He turned and walked off, neatly and collectedly, through the passing wagons.

Hull looked down at the knothole in the walk. A moment before she had been there beside him; now her scent, the pressure of her hand on his arm, had gone and there was nothing left but the memory of her face.

He looked around the street, and it had a new aspect. After all, it wasn't so bad—just new and brawly. The sky had a clean, open look, a quality of bigness he had never noticed before. He thought again of her face. He didn't even know her name—but there were ways of meeting people. New Orleans could wait awhile—at least until he had seen her again. And with fifteen or twenty thousand, whatever his cut might be tonight, there was no telling what he might do here— maybe better than in New Orleans.

He untied his horse, rode a few bucks out of it and managed it up the street to the hotel.

Rogers stopped pacing up and down and looked at him as he closed the door behind him, then started pacing again. Wootten sat on the bed, quietly cleaning his guns.

"I tell you, Mourret," Rogers said, "if you play this too cagey we're likely to lose the whole thing. I say just follow him out of town tonight and hold him up in the mountains, wherever he goes. To hell with all this plotting."

Mourret sat by the front window, looking down over the porch roof at the other side of the street. A quart of brandy stood on a small table beside him and he was quietly enjoying one of his good cigars. He glanced at Hull.

"Fine looking man, isn't he?" he said, nodding across the street. Hull looked out. Bonnetty stood in front of his bank talking to three or four other men. His short, spare figure was straight as a string, and as he moved about slightly, he reminded Hull of an Arab horse—the same smallness, fineness, the same air of quiet dignity. His hair was black and grey, and as he talked he smiled with amusement and content. "A fine looking man," Mourret answered himself. "Pity if we have to kill him." He delicately broke the ash from his cigar into a saucer. "Now there's a man who has sense enough to get gold without a pickaxe. They rush in every afternoon, he buys their dust and they all love him for it. He runs it to Helena and comes back for more, and all it costs him is brains, energy and horseflesh. The only trouble is, he's foxy. He never goes to the same town two times running. Sometimes Helena, sometimes Butte, sometimes Boulder. We've got to get him on the trail, but we can't do that unless we find out where he's going."

"Didn't you hear what I said?" Rogers cried out behind them. "I tell you, to hell with finding out where he's going; follow him out of town and get him anyway."

Mourret sighed. "Have a drink and calm down, Rogers."

"I think he's right, Mourret," Wootten said. "The place is full of dust. Why waste so much time?"

Mourret sighed again. "Now, boys. Now, boys. If it's full this week, it'll be full again next week. And that reminds me, Wootten, no shooting tonight if we can possibly help it. I like the old man. And anyway, we don't kill the golden goose, do we?" Wootten said nothing. "We've got to play it right. If we follow him, we'll have to track him around all day so as not to lose him. We'll have to watch his house, watch wherever he goes, and if he doesn't catch on, somebody else will notice us and pin it on us afterward. We can't have suspicions. I've got a good plan for Hull. We'll get at the Negro, Catlin, or whatever his name is. We'll just wait until he comes for Bonnetty in the buggy at noon.''

Rogers sat on the bed beside Wootten, jaw clamped. "I don't give a damn for this waiting. I say let's hit him once and clear out. He's on to me. I've seen old Catlin looking at me down his nose. Every time he's around the barn out there I think he's going to knife me. He comes around like the devil's shadow. He knows I'm up to something and all he has to do is say a word to Bonnetty and I'm through. It's all right for you, Mourret, to sit around drinking in a hotel—I got to sweat in his lousy barn and work. I'm sick of it." He stopped and waited, looking at Mourret. Mourret drew on his cigar calmly, and Hull saw the lids of his eyes come down. It was a beautiful face, creamy white under pure black hair, as clear in feature and fine in modelling as the best New Orleans blood could make it.

Hull saw Rogers make a mistake as Mourret held his peace. Rogers sat up straighter and his face relaxed in boldness. "So I say," he said loudly, "let's just follow him out. The hell with all this pussy-footing around." He sat staring at Mourret.

Mourret carefully laid his cigar on the saucer, his long fingers balancing it gently. He walked over to Rogers with a slow, easy grace and stood smiling down at him.

"Now, Rogers, you're upset, and so naturally you're upsetting things. You've been very good, very helpful with your spying and your information. But don't try to take on too much. Don't try to tell me what to do." He swung. The blow cracked like a shot and left the red print of his open hand on Rogers's face. "Do you understand what I say?"

Rogers sprang up at him. Mourret caught his wrist and twisted him back down on the bed, kept on twisting and crushing. Rogers let out a cry of pain and lay whimpering.

"Do you understand?" Mourret asked again, still grinding Rogers's wristbones in his one hand. There was no tension, no anger, not even much sign of exertion, and the crushing and twisting went on. Rogers lay squealing. Mourret let go and stepped back.

"Don't tamper with me, Rogers. If I wanted to, I could tear the muscles out of your neck with one hand. You're in this, and you do what I say. Understand?"

Rogers nodded dumbly. "All right," he said. "You're the boss."

"Go back out to Bonnetty's house and hang around the barn. The Negro may let something slip."

Rogers pulled himself off the bed and went out, face sullen and remote.

Mourret glanced at Wootten. He was still cleaning his guns, carefully picking oily dust out of a crack. He did not look up. For all he showed of interest in the affair, he might have been in Texas.

Mourret came back to his chair, gave a wink and a private smile to Hull and sat down again. He picked up his cigar and drew on it till an even red circle appeared under the ash.

"Sit down, Hull, and listen to my plans. I think you're the clever one to pull the trick." He turned in his chair, crossing his legs, and gave Hull a smile that lightened his whole face. He regarded Hull for a moment. "I'll never forget your coming into Beauregarde's tent that night and reporting on your reconnaissance. So modest, so humble, and what an exploit! Do you remember that? The beginning of our acquaintance." The smile faded. "Poor Beauregarde. It broke his heart, Appomattox. That swine, Grant—that brutal, plugging, brainless swine."

Hull looked away through the window. He could not look at Mourret honestly. He had forgotten the meaning of defeat, and Mourret never would. He remembered Beauregarde well enough, the meeting in the tattered tent, even the decoration he had received of that stillborn confederation. But, now, it was all in shadow, an old photograph of people he had hardly known. The war was over, the war was dead, and he realized

that the things that had held him to Mourret were dying, one
by one.

"There are three things we can do," Mourret said. "None
very good, but all possible. First, you take some dust in to
Bonnetty and sell it, and while you are there, try to see something that will tell you where he is going. Maybe the bags
are labelled. He has to write a deposit slip or a receipt or
something, and the name of the bank and the town'll be on
that. Try and see."

He uncrossed his legs and leaned forward. "If that doesn't
work, go at it a different way. Ask him for a job. Get him
talking. Talk about the danger of robbery. You've still got
your old mail-guard ticket, haven't you?"

Hull nodded. "He may have heard about me."

Mourret stuck out his lips and slowly shook his head. "I
don't think so. What was it, after all? A mail-guard in Louisiana is accused of conniving with robbers. It isn't as if you
had been convicted. What is it? Case thrown out of court. It's
a long way from here to Baton Rouge, and who cares to
spread such little news? Ask him to hire you on as a rider, a
guard, anything. You have an honest face, a good way with
you."

Hull looked out of the window silently, thinking again of
her face, remembering her eyes, clear and sparkling as stars.
So he had a good way with him, did he? A way to her? He'd
like to try it. Why? The question hung there without reasonable answer. He had seen her once, and he wanted to see her
again. As simple as that.

And suddenly he did see her again, across the street, in a
buggy, pulling up at the dry goods store two doors up from
Bonnetty's bank. He watched her face as she tied the horse.
Serious, a little pensive, but she did it practically, with sure
movements. He caught a smile on his own face and sup-
pressed it. She picked up her skirt, with a little bowing movement and disappeared into the shadow of the porch. He began
imagining plans. Loose the team and catch them; loose a tug

and fix it for her; take a package out of the buggy, follow her home and give it to her, pretending she had dropped it.

"What's the matter with you?" Mourret's low, hissing voice cut through the smile in his mind and he looked at him hurriedly. Black eyes were fixed on him intensely, at once imperious and suspicious.

"Why aren't you listening? What's the meaning of this daydreaming? Don't you want to go through with this thing? Or are you crazy?"

Hull's mind tuned cold. "Take it easy, Mourret. I'm not Rogers."

"Then listen to me as though you weren't."

Hull looked at Mourret's eyes and a strange perception dawned on him. The look in them was new to him, he felt that he was looking at a stranger, a part of Mourret that had been hidden, or had lately grown—not the casual, graceful, charming Mourret, but a dark, imperious and impersonal one. Hull suddenly felt very awkward and self-conscious, and at the same time Mourret's fixed and accusing stare broke down and some of the old amusement filtered back.

"Sorry," Hull said. "I was thinking about something. You said I was to ask for a job. What's the third plan?"

Mourret shook his head ruefully. "You're changing, Hull, my friend. Daydreaming. Are you in love? Stick to plans and you can have any woman in New Orleans. I was saying, when Catlin, or whatever his name, comes to take Bonnetty home for lunch, I'm going to start a fight with him, order him around. You take a stand against me, be a friend to the Negro, protect him, do a little mild fighting with me. I'll retire beaten. You buy Catlin a few drinks to cheer him up. And in one of them, you put something I'll give you. It's a drug they use in Haiti. I used it in the Army on prisoners to make them answer questions. It'll work, it'll give us what we want to know. Butte, Helena or Boulder. All right?"

Hull pulled out his old mail-guard certificate and looked at it, thinking. "I'm not much of a liar, Mourret. I don't know how well I can put anything over on Bonnetty."

"You were good enough to be a spy under Beauregarde," Mourret said sharply.

"That was war, Mourret. There was a reason."

"It's still war as far as I'm concerned, Hull. Why do you think I came up to this country instead of staying in the South?"

"The gold, I supposed."

"Yankee gold. Do you think I'm a natural thief, Hull? Do you think I'd rob my friends?" He paused and slowly ground out the light of his cigar on the saucer. "Maybe Lee quit, but I never will. As far as I'm concerned, there's no such thing as robbing a Yankee. They have no rights. They gutted the South and they're robbing it blind right now. What about you? Weren't you framed out of that job so that damned Yankee could get it for his nephew? What about you?"

Hull thought a moment. Then he stood up and began wandering around the room. "I don't care, Mourret. I don't care anymore."

Mourret was sitting up straight, looking at him sharply. "You don't care that you were beaten?"

Hull looked full at him. "We were beaten. We took on the North in a fight and we were beaten flat. What more is necessary to make an end of it?"

Mourret stood up. "You just quit and run? You get framed out of a job and just take it?"

Hull's voice came heavy and clear. "The Yankees won. The South is shot. They've got the power. What good does it do to fight a machine you can't lick? Let them have the job. And in any case," he added more softly, "it's better to take your licking and get out than nurse a grudge and stab them in the back."

Mourret's eyelids lowered. "You've got a fine lot of talk there. You know what you are? You're a lick-spittle coward."

Hull took three steps, his hands open and then stopped. They looked at each other steadily for a moment. Then Mourret drew the back of his hand slowly across his mouth, bent his head slightly and said to the floor, "I'm sorry."

Hull looked at him distantly and said to him as though he were on the other side of the Grand Canyon, "That's all right. Maybe I am a coward. It remains to be seen."

Mourret looked up. "Would you mind telling me why you came up here with me?"

"You asked me to. You were pretty good to me—the hospital, the lawyer, all that."

"It didn't have anything to do with money?"

"Yes, it did. I was sore. I figured if they believed I was a thief I might as well make the most of it. I'll tell you one thing, Mourret. I'm not going back to New Orleans with you."

Mourret smiled twistedly. "That's all right. We won't miss you."

"You've sure got a sidling tongue. Some day it's going to get mixed up in your teeth."

"Any day. Any day you pick, after we get through tonight." Mourret turned his back, reached for the brandy bottle and stopped. "My God, Catlin's there. Get going." He ran to the bureau. Hull looked out of the window. The girl's buggy was gone and in its place stood another with a big Negro waiting patiently in the seat.

Mourret tossed him a small sack. "Sell that." He pulled out his wallet, picked a small envelope out of it and handed it over. "Just a pinch will do. Too much will knock him out. Even if you think you found out from Bonnetty, we'll check with Catlin."

Mourret smiled in his old way and Hull felt a faint repulsion that he could have said the things he had said and still expect to go back to their old friendship. "I'll tell you what, Mourret," he said, taking the packet. "I owe you a lot. We've been through a lot together. We'll finish this job, but after that I don't know."

"Pure gratitude. A noble motive. Of course the money means nothing to you."

Blood surged to Hull's head. "As long as you put it that

way, Mourret, I'll make it definite. After this, we're through. The more I see of this outfit, the less I like it. Wootten—nothing but a common murderer. Rogers—a bribed fool. And you. What's come over you since the war?''

Mourret ignored him. "You're going to finish this job all right, whether you like it or not. I'll see you and Catlin later."

Hull went down the hall burning with anger. The more he thought of it, the less he liked the job. The whole thing was dirty; a filthy mess he'd tied himself to in a period of bitterness. He'd cut clear of Mourret, the South and the past, and try his luck in new country. Up here nothing mattered—the place was full of men who had new names, changed them every month, and nobody cared. It was a new land, undiscovered, untouched. Wyoming was filling up with cattle, here the mines were opening like flowers and the earth was full of wealth. He remembered New Orleans with sudden disgust. Defeated, bitter, poor, gaudy, holding itself together with a specious pride—like the white marble tombs that had to depend on their rotting stilts to keep them out of the rotten Mississippi mud. A dead city.

He heard the racket of voices coming up the stair-well. Up here it was raw, but it was new and the dirt was on the hide, not in the bone.

And as he started to go down the steps the thing that had been in the back of his mind, urging all these thoughts, came forward: the girl. His anger eased and he smiled slightly. That was the real reason he wanted to be free of Mourret. Because she and Mourret didn't mix. He suddenly hauled up his mind and looked at himself coldly. Here he was, thinking like this, basing his actions on the look of the eyes of a girl he'd seen for five minutes that morning, whose name he didn't even know. And yet a certain shrewd instinct reassured him—he knew her, knew enough of her to be warranted in acting surely.

He went on down the stairs and out of the lobby to his horse. He'd get the information for Mourret and be quit of him for good.

He mounted his half-broken horse and worked it across the street, dodging teams and wagons. As he pushed it toward the hitch-rail beside the buggy, the girl came out of the store and got in beside Catlin. Catlin took up the whip and brought it back—the lash hit Hull's horse in the face and the horse exploded, bucking and kicking. There was a crash. He fought it down and tied it trembling.

"I'm sorry, suh," Catlin said.

"Oh, I'm so sorry," the girl said. "I know he didn't mean it."

He looked from one to the other, then at Bonnetty's sign over the bank door, then back.

"You're not going to be angry with me after I apologized, are you?" she asked.

"Are you by any chance Miss Bonnetty?"

"Why, yes. Is that any reason for looking so upset?"

He glanced up at Mourret's window and back to her. "No, ma'am." He got hold of himself and took off his hat. "In fact I'm glad the horse was hit—although maybe it's odd to be introduced by a horse. My name is Hull, ma'am. John Hull. And you owed me no apology, Miss Bonnetty, seeing as my horse kicked two spokes out of your wheel." He looked at her and put a question in his eyes. "With your permission, I'll drive your buggy to the wheelwright's to-morrow and have it fixed."

"Catlin can do it, thank you, Mr. Hull."

"I'm sure he can. But why deprive me of that pleasure. I have so few, you know."

She looked up and laughed. "I see," she said. "Very well, you may find the buggy out at my father's ranch. Rogers will have to give it to you, since Father and I live in town." She looked at him with not too secret amusement, and as his face fell, she smiled. "And please return it to my house, if you will. I'll be there to inspect it. Catlin, do you want to take me home? You can come back for Father." Catlin gathered up the lines. "Goodbye, Mr. Hull," she said.

He watched them disappear in the traffic.

"Your horse is a little rough yet," somebody said behind him. He turned and saw Bonnetty. "Thanks for offering to fix my buggy, Mr. Hull. Catlin should have looked behind him."

"You know me?"

Bonnetty smiled. "I was eavesdropping in the door. And I know of no reason why you cannot come to the house without having to kick a spoke out of my buggy for an excuse. As a matter of fact, I've known you for some time."

"I don't understand. How do you know me?"

"Come inside and be at ease. In fact, come into the back office. I want to talk to you."

Bonnetty led him along the counter, past the scales, into the shadows of the rear office. A back window let in a dim light. In one corner stood a large safe. Saddlebags lay on the floor, two rifles stood in one corner, and a heap of empty gold-pokes lay in a large roasting pan. A roll-top desk stood open, littered with papers.

Somebody banged a bell out front.

"Sit down, Hull," Bonnetty said. "Early customer." He went out, shutting the door behind him.

Hull got up and walked nervously to the window, loosened his gun, turned and sat down again. Bonnetty, Bonnetty, he thought. His daughter. And what did he know about him? If she was his daughter, he'd have to get out of the robbery some way—play along with Mourret until the chance came. He had three hours to do it.

He looked at the papers on the desk. There were too many to go through, and then he realized that if he was to edge out on Mourret, he'd better know nothing. He couldn't give him the information now.

He got up and went to the window again. The poke of gold sagged in his pocket. Better return it to Mourret. And how would Mourret like it when he told him? It would mean a fight of some kind, argument, fists, guns. He thought of Wootten.

Then he realized that merely backing out of the robbery solved nothing. Even if he got out of it with his skin, they'd go ahead. If they couldn't find out which town Bonnetty was going to, Mourret would give up his plan, make a good haul and take to the hills. The robbery would come off whether he were in it or not. He'd have to tell Bonnetty—and Bonnetty would know of his part in the plan to rob him, and she would find out, and when she knew, what chance had this little beginning to grow under the doubt and suspicion that would be in her mind?

He turned about restively. Was she worth it, anyway? Was any woman worth it? He recalled her face, remembered her laugh. An amused laugh. Suppose he protected Bonnetty, took the awful chances of bucking Mourret and Wootten, and found out that he was nothing but an amusement to her? And then he remembered what was behind the laugh. Amusement, yes, naturally, but behind it, interest, a shy friendliness, and sincerity. He'd have it out with Bonnetty and take his chances.

The door opened and he turned. Bonnetty came in smiling, sat down at the desk and swivelled around. "Sit down, Hull, sit down. You make me nervous as you are." He began rolling himself a cigarette, shot Hull a side glance and said, frowning as he spilled tobacco, "In fact, you look like a man about to make a confession. Let me save you the trouble." He licked the paper and twisted the end.

"You were hired to guard federal mails between Baton Rouge and New Orleans. You were held up, shot in the battle, killed the driver. You were accused of conniving with the bandits. You pleaded not guilty—said the driver was the conniver, not you, that he got the drop on you when the stage was stopped. You fought him anyway, killed him and were shot by one of the gang. You were acquitted on lack of real evidence, in spite of a general prejudice against you, and you left Baton Rouge two months ago."

Hull looked at him quietly. "That's all very true. What about it?"

Bonnetty winked at him and lighted his cigarette. "The rest
of the story is that one of the nephews of the military governor of Baton Rouge got your job immediately. If you had
had a state job, they would simply have fired you. Since it
was a federal job, they had to frame you. Well, Hull, you
worked as guard for six years and during that time defeated
nine attempts at robbery. A very good record. In case you
want to know how I know all this, the banks all have reports
on things pertaining to mail conditions, and I read them carefully. I have to keep an eye open for odd characters around
town, in my business."

Hull stood up. "That's fine. I'll be around."

"Sit down. It's a sin to be so touchy. Did I say you were
an odd character? Did I? Actually?"

Hull grinned and sat down again.

"It's a fact I need a guard. Somebody to ride gold from
here to the banks in Helena and Butte, sometimes Boulder, a
few times to Ft. Missoula. Somebody I can trust. Up to now
I've ridden it myself—I don't believe in asking any man to
risk his life riding my gold for the little I'd pay him. But it's
too damned hard on me, fifty, sixty miles a night. I've got to
get a good man."

His cigarette fell apart in his fingers. "Blast these things.
I won't smoke the cigars they sell out here. Well, Hull, you're
such a man. A fine record and one bad break."

Hull drew a deep breath, stretched his legs out and laughed.
"You mean you're offering me a job?"

"Yes. Not much pay to start. I want to tempt you, and
tempt you good."

"You're putting a lot of faith in me, Mr. Bonnetty. Lack
of evidence doesn't exactly prove innocence, either."

"You came up here without changing your name. Catlin
tells me you've been hanging around in the saloons drinking
a good deal in a gloomy manner. Not changing your name
shows me you feel innocent. And if you were a real thief,
you wouldn't be drinking in bitterness, but out thieving and
having a good time. My daughter Maura told me how you

helped her this morning and beat up some oaf that laughed at her—drat her, she's just out from Philadelphia and doesn't realize anything—and I, myself, saw your courtesy just now. That might be merely her attractiveness, but I'll wager not, since courtesy's a habit you don't get overnight. Anyway, it's an offer. I take chances all the time and you're a pretty good one.''

''When would I start?''

''Tonight. No point in waiting.''

Hull looked at the rifles in the corner and thought of Mourret. If there were only some way of getting free of Mourret, cutting loose from him and Wootten. Maura, he had said. Maura was her name. What was the matter with him? he suddenly thought. He'd get rid of Mourret some way.

''I'll take it,'' he said. Bonnetty shook his hand. ''And glad to have it.''

''That's fine.'' Bonnetty's face was quiet and shrewd. ''I don't mind telling you there's room in this town for a real banking business. This is no boom. The mines are big. When the gold's gone there's copper. Nobody wants that now, but they will later.''

''I had a little mathematics in school.''

''I can always get somebody that can add. I want somebody with some guts, brains and go. We'll see what you can do, Hull. Come out to my house at two o'clock and I'll go over a map with you.''

Hull stood up. He wasn't going to tell Bonnetty anything. This was too good to spoil. He'd settle Mourret privately.

''You want to sell that?'' Bonnetty asked, pointing to his pocket.

Hull put his hand over the bulge. Mourret's damned gold.

''Come on out and we'll weigh it up.''

He followed Bonnetty out and surrendered the bag. Refusing without a good reason would only look suspicious. He looked through the open door and saw Catlin again waiting in the buggy. He glanced past him and saw Mourret waiting on the hotel porch, slapping a quirt lightly against one leg.

Bonnetty took the bag to the scales, began to untie the knot, stopped and looked quizzically at Hull. "Do you work with old Burrel?"

"What? No, why?" Hull asked in surprise.

"This knot—he always ties his pokes this way." He poured the dust into the pan and began weighing it. "It's funny you and he should use a lover's knot. Most of them just use grannies. What's the idea? You saving up to get married?"

Hull forced a laugh. "I ought to meet him some day— seeing we've got something in common." Mourret was coming down the steps to his horse.

"He's up on Salt Creek, sober old man with a big bushy beard, religious as he can be, in his way. Doesn't smoke, drink, swear or gamble. Just greedy. Once in a while he'll come down to sell a poke for food—most of it he's got stacked up in his cabin." Bonnetty began counting out bills, and lifted his head at a sharp command from outside.

"Get out of my way!"

Mourret was sitting his horse beside the buggy. Catlin was looking up at him with an expression of deep reserve and dignity. Bonnetty stood stiffly watching, the bills unnoticed in his hands. Hull began to move slowly toward the door, feeling anger rise. The act was out.

"Suh, I'm sorry. This is Mr. Bonnetty's hitching place, suh. There's room over there."

Hull reached the door, a dull fog of apprehension in his mind. Mourret was half-drunk, his pale, cool face now flushed, his usually firm mouth loose and smiling.

"Don't speak to me, you black_____—move!"

"I regret, suh, this is Mr. Bonnetty's—"

The quirt slashed out, cutting across Catlin's face. Hull stood shocked. This was no act. Mourret's face flamed with rage. Bonnetty was running around the counter. Hull jumped through the door as Mourret's quirt whistled again.

"Cut it out!" he shouted as the lash cracked viciously. Catlin huddled stubbornly in the buggy seat, defending his head with his arms.

"You ape, when I say move, you—"

Hull reached up and grabbed Mourret's arm.

"Cut it out, you fool!" he shouted. Mourret slashed at him with the quirt, he took it on the neck and with sudden fury dragged him out of the saddle. The horse danced away as Mourret fell in the dust and he hauled him to his feet.

"You're going too far," he breathed heavily in Mourret's face. "This was supposed to be an act."

"Let go of me you trash. No Negro's going to sass me to my face."

Hull stood back and forgot in his anger that there had ever been a plan. "And no cheap New Orleans bum is going to beat a black in front of me and get away with it. You understand that? You're drunk. Clear out."

Mourret's teeth bared and he slashed at him. Hull ducked it, lunging in, and drove Mourret's head back with a snap. Mourret fell to his knees and sat back in the dust. He shook his head and got up clumsily. He suddenly feinted at Hull, Hull parried it with his left arm and Mourret, seizing his wrist, twisted him to his knees. He wrenched against Mourret's grip and coming up threw him off. Mourret staggered back and again stood still, panting, his eyes bloodshot.

"You're right," he gasped. "I'm drunk. It's the only reason I didn't kill you. The next time this happens, I'll be sober."

He turned and walked unsteadily back to the hotel.

"That's twice today you've defended my people," Bonnetty said behind him. "I'm grateful." Hull turned, wiping sweat from his face. Bonnetty's face was calm, but his eyes followed Mourret with a cold, flickering anger. "You all right, Catlin?"

"Yessuh," Catlin said, holding his face and trying to make a smile. "Thanks to Mr. Hull, thank you, suh."

"You'd better come out to dinner now, Hull. I want you

to help me repack the gold, anyway. Catlin and I'll wait for you if you want to clean up in the hotel."

Hull stared at Mourret's window. Now was the time to settle with Mourret. He nodded. "I'll be right with you."

He stopped outside Mourret's door and loosened his gun in the holster. He'd break with them now, take empty saddlebags tonight, let Mourret and the others follow him, and fight it out. He could backtrack and waylay them, as they had planned waylaying Bonnetty, and reduce the odds considerably.

He knocked and said his name in a low voice. The key rattled. Wootten opened the door and smiled at him blankly. Mourret was drying his face with a towel.

"I couldn't get Catlin away."

"I saw that from the window."

"I couldn't find out anything. What's more, I didn't try. I'm through."

"Is that all?"

"That's all."

Mourret looked at Wootten and smiled. He shrugged, slung the towel into a corner and strolled to the bed, casually picked up a gun and pointed it at Hull's stomach. Hull's arms made an instinctive jerk for his own guns, then slowly rose. Mourret's casualness had caught him completely off guard.

"It's not quite all, Hull. I had an idea when you left you were sore enough to cross me. Why didn't you tell me Bonnetty hired you to ride the gold tonight? That you're going out to his house to go over the map? I sent Wootten over. He went in when you and Bonnetty went in the back office. He heard every word." He raised the gun muzzle an inch and his eyes froze. "You're not through, Hull. You're going out and find out where you're taking it, you're going to ride out with it and we're going to meet you. And you're going to hand it over."

Hull looked at the gun muzzle. "And suppose I don't. Suppose I round up the local law and drive you out of town?"

Mourret smiled. "You can't. You've got no evidence. You're forgetting they can't do anything until something's happened. Don't try to cross me any more. If you do, I'll kill you. But you won't cross me, you're going to do exactly what I say. Because if you don't, we're going to get Bonnetty's daughter. You see now?"

Hull looked at him with widening eyes.

Mourret laughed. "You think I don't know what's got into you? Wootten told me about this morning. I saw you and her out there, myself. Doves. Charming. And I see it in your face right now. If you want her alive, you'll do exactly what I say. Get out now, Romeo, and do as I tell you—quickly, obediently, like a lamb. Open the door for him, Wootten."

Hull backed out of the door, still dumb, and stood staring at it as it slammed in his face. He had a raging impulse to kick down the door and have it out now; but he realized he could prove nothing—it would be only murder, even if he succeeded. The only thing to do was to tell Bonnetty.

He turned and made his way slowly down the hall.

Catlin took the last of the dishes off the table and Bonnetty rose. He had been grave all through the meal, speaking very little. Maura had watched his face worriedly. Hull had sat in silence, occasionally forcing himself to speak. Twice he had caught Catlin looking at him with a peculiar expression—one of reserved judgment and perplexity. There was none of that morning's friendliness.

"I'll get a few things ready, Hull, and then call you." Bonnetty went out.

Maura looked at Hull. "What's the matter?" she asked. "He isn't at all like himself."

Hull shook his head.

She regarded him a moment and smiled. "You too. What's got into you?"

He pulled himself out of his depression and anxiety and tried to smile. They rose. The only thing to do was to hope for the best and, at least in front of her, pretend that nothing was wrong. They stood at a window, looking down the street.

"Your father's given me a job," he said. "Riding gold. He seemed to suggest there might be a kind of future in it."

She smiled. "That's fine. He likes you. That means you'll be around for some time, doesn't it?"

He nodded and then looked at her suddenly and fully. "I hope so. There's nothing I'd like more."

She looked away. "I know about your trouble in Louisiana. It doesn't make any difference to me."

"Did your father tell you?"

"I asked him. I asked him why a man like you would be staying in saloons in the mornings—so he told me. Not that I object to a man's drinking," she added hurriedly. "Indeed, in school in Philadelphia, once in a while we used to steal a bottle of sherry out of the pantry and drink it up in our room—so you see I am not as innocent as you might think."

He turned her gently toward him and smiled down at her. She looked up at him quite seriously a moment, examining his face and eyes, and then smiled back.

"Hull!" Bonnetty called. He jumped and immediately a wave of fear swept through his stomach as the whole situation came back to him.

"Coming," he answered, and turned back to her. "Listen," he said. "Do you feel this is a kind of beginning?"

She looked up. "I do feel that way. I don't know of any reason why I shouldn't, so I do."

"Hull!"

He gave her a sudden light kiss and left her, feeling as he went the sudden tightening of her fingers on his arm.

He stopped at the door of Bonnetty's library and drew a deep breath. Just how he could tell him about Mourret and his danger, and yet keep his faith, he could not see—but he had to tell him.

On the floor beside Bonnetty's desk rested the black satchel which Catlin and he had dragged in from the buggy. On the desk stood several large full buckskin sacks. On the floor lay two empty saddlebags. Bonnetty was writing on a pad of forms.

"Help me tie them up, will you, Hull?" Bonnetty said without looking up.

Hull glanced over the paper. Helena, First National. He pulled up a chair and picked up a cord, wound it twice around the sack neck and tied it firmly. He went on to the next.

He was suddenly aware of Catlin behind him and looked up into Bonnetty's eyes. They were grave, sad and remote.

"What's the matter?" Hull asked, dropping his string.

"Catlin has a gun on you, Hull. Don't try to get your own. That's all right, Catlin, leave them where they are. I don't think Mr. Hull's likely to use them."

Hull sat up straight. "What's all this, Mr. Bonnetty?"

Bonnetty pointed to the sacks. "The sack you brought in this morning had a lover's knot—Burrel's knot. I assumed you tied it. I asked you to tie these sacks in order to check that. I find you tie a square knot. That means your sack was tied up by Burrel, not you. Yet you said you did not know Burrel. Then how, I wonder, did you come by Burrel's sack?"

"What's all this about? It's quite true I don't know Burrel—also, I lied about tying that knot. But I came by the sack honestly."

"I don't see how. Burrel was robbed and killed in his cabin last night. Catlin heard it this morning."

Bonnetty's face was heavy and old. "I'm sorry. Looking at you now, I can't believe it. I liked you immediately, Hull, liked your record, your actions. I am sorry also to find my judgment of men so defective. It's rarely been so wrong. I can only conclude, comparing this evidence with the honesty of your face, that you are the damnedest, smoothest, cleverest liar I have ever met."

He shoved his chair back a foot. "If you have no interpretation of this evidence other than what I have given, I am forced to take you down and place you under arrest for murder and robbery. Catlin, take his guns."

Hull looked at Bonnetty helplessly. "I'll tell you the whole truth. I was going to anyway, before you sprung this on me."

Bonnetty listened carefully and thought it over for a long time when Hull had finished.

"Assuming your story is true, Hull, which I'd like to believe, can you make Mourret confess that he gave you the sack? Or even admit that he knows you? He would laugh off the accusation of planning to rob me. You haven't got a case, Hull—all you have is a story."

Bonnetty sat back. "All I can reasonably do is take you down and have you arrested. I don't want to, I prefer to believe you, but I can't do otherwise." He rose. "Catlin, hold him till I get my coat. I hate to do this, Hull. But I can't let you go in the face of evidence. My conscience won't let me."

Hull stood up. "There's something you're forgetting, Mr. Bonnetty. Mourret and Wootten are still on the loose. I told you what they threatened to do. They'll do it."

"I'll have to take my chances," Bonnetty said, and went out, shutting the door.

Hull looked at Catlin, sizing him up. He was big, hard, and had a gun. If he could kick the gun out of his hand, he might have a chance of taking a dive through the window.

Catlin smiled. "That's all right, Mr. Hull, suh. You don't have to look at me that way. It's few times I've had a white gentleman stand up for me against another white man, and take a beating for my sake. You go now, suh, and I'll fire a couple of shots after you. Mr. Bonnetty's conscience won't hurt him none if he thinks I tried—and knows I missed. Here's your guns." He grinned and opened the window. "I reckon you'd better get out of town, suh. He'll think he'll have to report you to the sheriff, suh."

"Don't worry, Catlin. I've got a plan I want to try out." He grabbed his guns and the two saddlebags and scrambled out of the window. As he ran for the barn two shots crashed behind him and dirt spouted far to one side. Catlin began shouting. He ducked into the barn and ran for his horse.

Inside the house, Bonnetty calmly went into his library

again. "You can shut up the shouting, Catlin. I heard you."
He sat down at his desk and sighed. "I hope he does what
he said he'd do." He looked up at Catlin. "You can take the
afternoon off. And you can take my shotgun if you think it
will do any good. You'd better load it with buck."

Hull slung the saddlebags into a corner and poured himself a
shot of Mourret's brandy. Mourret and Wootten watched him
suspiciously.

"Better have one, Mourret," Hull said, grinning at him.
"It's all set. It's perfect. I'm to take the bags out to Bonnetty's tonight, load up and hit for Helena by the Judge Fork
pass. You three can meet me along the road and we'll split
and take off. Sorry I was sore at you, Mourret. Let's forget
it."

Mourret's face relaxed and he stood up with a smile. "I
thought you were going crazy this morning, Hull, old boy. I
never saw such a fast change in a man. Wootten, drink up!"
He began pacing up and down, rubbing his hands excitedly.
Hull watched him as though he were a stranger. "It's four
now," Mourret said. "We'll leave at six and meet you about
ten miles out."

Wootten hadn't moved from the bed, but sat stiffly on the
edge, his knees close together, his round, alert eyes watching
Hull's face. "It sounds too good, Mourret. Too easy."

Somebody knocked at the door.

"Who is it?" Mourret said.

"Me. Rogers. Open up." He burst in, his eyes wide and
face excited. "Something's happened," he chattered at Mourret, not bothering to look around. "Hull was out there. Something went wrong. He busted out of the house and Catlin took
two shots at him. I saw him from the stables. Bonnetty must
have found out some—"

He saw Hull and his mouth opened. Mourret's eyes darted
to Hull. Hull saw the sudden flash in them, dropped his glass
and grabbed for his gun. Before he had it halfway out, Woot-

ten had leaped from the bed and was crouched in the middle
of the room, covering him.

"Drop it," Wootten said, his eyes glaring like a cat's.
"Drop it."

Blood pounded in Hull's head, half fear and half anger. He
let go of the gun and raised his hands. Mourret stepped behind
him, snatched his gun out and skidded it under the bed.

"Talk," Mourret said in a hard, stiff voice, pinching the
word off with tight lips. "What's the deal. What's the meaning of this line about you riding the gold—and getting chased
off the place."

"He's crossed us," Wootten said. "What's behind all this?
He's lying to us for some reason."

"Let him have it," Rogers said. "Get rid of him. We can
get the dust out at the house. I saw them lug it in."

"Shut up," Mourret snapped. "We'll get it all right, but
no shooting here. How much does Bonnetty know? You'd
better tell it straight, or I'll take that dame out and—"

Hull whipped around, slamming his fist down at Mourret,
and missed. Wootten's knees hit him in the kidneys and he
crashed down across Mourret's chair, knocking over the table
and the bottle. He heaved up, trying to throw Wootten off
and somebody jumped on the back of his knees. He saw
Mourret's hand and arm, grabbing up the bottle, made a final
struggle to throw off Wootten, and then as the bottle smashed
down, his brain exploded with a thousand lights and he lay
still.

He woke slowly and lay in dusk, trying to blink the haze
out of his aching brain. He heard low voices, and then realized that the sun had gone. He was tied hand and foot and
lay on the floor arched backward, facing the open windows,
his wrists lashed to his ankles.

He became aware of the extent of his sickness and weakness and lay in an immense weariness, remembering what had
happened and hardly caring. The voice behind him went on,
low, sharp and urgent.

"In the back?"

"Yeah, there's a window."

"All right. I'll go in by the front and cover Catlin. Wootten, you go in and cover Bonnetty and the girl. If it isn't in the house we'll damned soon find out where. The old man won't let thirty thousand dollars worry him when we start on his only daughter."

Hull stiffened all over, his head clearing with rage and the pain shrinking to a small, burning point at the top of his skull.

"Rogers, you stay here and keep a guard on that double crossing_____. When we come back we'll decide what's the best way to get rid of him."

"How do I know you're coming back?" Rogers whined.

"Don't be a fool. Do you think we'd ride out on you with him still alive as a witness? Wootten, you all set? It's about time. Let's go and have a couple of drinks downstairs before we start."

The door slammed. Rogers came over to Hull and sat down beside him, gun in hand. "One peep out of you and I'll crack your head open, Hull."

"Listen, Rogers, you know what this'll mean, don't you? You'll be on the run for the rest of your life. Think it over. Be smart. Cut me loose—we'll go down and get the sheriff and stop this thing."

"Shut up!" Rogers said, raising the gun. "This is my chance to get out of this lousy life. Shovelling manure forever. This is my big chance. Shut up."

Hull lay quiet, listening to the usual evening uproar in the street below, the jangle of pianos, hoarse singing from a dozen saloons, an occasional shot as some lush miner celebrated his luck. Another shout wouldn't mean a thing to anybody down there.

Outside the windows a shadow rose in the dark, faintly outlined by the reflection from the lighted street below. The long black barrel of a shotgun snaked into the room.

"Lay down that gun, suh," Catlin said in a low rumble. "Else I shoot off your leg."

Rogers jerked upright in his chair, his face working.

"Don't want to shoot you, Mr. Rogers, but I reckon—"

Rogers threw himself onto the floor, whipping around and firing at the window. The shotgun spurted orange fire and as Hull's hearing slowly came back he heard Rogers groaning on the floor. Catlin came in through the window like a big black bear, moving slowly and lightly, and began cutting Hull free.

"I sneaked up like a porter, suh. I been lying out there two hours waiting for the odds to come down. I reckoned you might need a little help. You want we should go out and wait for those gunmen to come at Mr. Bonnetty?"

Hull stood flexing his wrists and fingers to get the cramp out of them.

"Wait, hell. We don't dare let them get near that house. You ride out and bring Bonnetty and the sheriff to the bar downstairs. I think I know a way to hold them that long."

He crawled under the bed, gritting his teeth against the blinding pain that flooded his head, and retrieved his gun. As he walked down the hall, he had to steady himself with one hand against the wall. He stood at the top of the stairs, listening to the roar of voices and tinkle of glasses downstairs.

He went on down and edged inconspicuously into the crowded bar. Mourret and Wootten stood together halfway down. He beckoned the bartender.

"Two whiskies, quick," he said. He fumbled in his pocket and took out the little envelope Mourret had given him. The barkeep set the glasses down and as he turned away, Hull slid the powder into them.

"My compliments to those two gentlemen down there. Just say they're on the house."

He drew away from the bar and mingled with the crowd. He watched Mourret and Wootten accept the drinks with surprise and toss them off, and then moved up directly behind them.

"Don't move, Mourret," he said in a low voice, looking

between their heads at their faces in the backbar mirror.
"Don't move at all."

Mourret's eyes glittered back at him from the mirror, and
then he smiled. "You can't stop us, Hull. If you start anything
we'll just kill you in self-defense."

"No. If what you said about that drug is true, Mourret, you
won't be able to lie for a while. Because you and Wootten
just drank it. So we're just going to stand here like this till
the sheriff gets here, and then you're going to answer questions."

Wootten's face lost its neat look and slowly went blank.
"What's the idea? What drug?" Mourret stared at his glass,
his face pale.

"We've got to get out of here, Wootten. It makes you talk.
You double-crossing rat, Hull—I'll kill you for this. Get
out."

"It makes you talk," Wootten repeated in a low voice. He
gave a short laugh. "What kind of nonsense is this? I've kept
my mouth shut for fifteen years and no damned drug is going
to make me into a fool. Hell, they had me in Natchez for a
week after the Connelly murder, and you think I cracked?
They never found out it was me, and if they couldn't, do you
think some punk constable—"

"Shut up! You're talking now, you fool."

"Talking? What did I say?"

"Hull, I'm coming at you in just ten seconds. Get away
while you can. Wootten, you just confessed a murder. Let's
get out of here fast."

"I what?" Wootten said, gaping. "What?" His mouth
opened with amazement. His hand went for his gun. Before
he could draw, Hull stepped in and landed a smashing left to
the jaw. Then everything happened at once. Wootten came
up shooting as Hull dodged, pulling his gun. Maura appeared
in the doorway. Dead silence fell on the crowd. A man
writhed on the floor, holding his stomach. Mourret had both
guns out. The crowd shrank away and lined up against the
wall.

"Don't anybody move," Mourret said. "Hull, I said I'd get you."

"Drop it!" a deep voice said in the door. Wootten fired at the star on the man's chest and he fell. Mourret's gun blasted at Hull as Hull pulled his trigger and he and Mourret went down at the same time. Mourret staggered up. Hull lay still, his right chest flaming with pain. He had dropped his gun.

"Come on," Mourret yelled at Wootten. They moved off toward the rear door, covering the crowd. Hull got to his knees and dived for his gun. Mourret's gun crashed as he grabbed it and the bullet seared his thigh. Wootten whirled as he fired, and he fired again into the blast of his gun. Wootten staggered back and fell, the back of his head blown out.

Mourret sagged against the bar, trying to hold himself up. He turned his head and looked heavily at Hull; his head fell, his hands let go of the bar and he slumped to the floor.

The crowd began to move out of its paralysis, some breaking and running for the doors, the rest mulling around Hull and Mourret's body.

Bonnetty pushed through and knelt beside Hull. "I take it back, Hull, whatever I said. I'm damned glad to know I was wrong about you. They killed Burrel and the sheriff'll be mighty grateful to you for getting them."

Catlin came up with a doctor and Hull sat quiet while he went to work.

"Does Maura know about my being mixed up with Mourret?"

"Yes, yes," Bonnetty sighed. "She made me tell her."

Hull's heart sank. "What did she say?"

"I don't know what's the matter with her, son. She's lost all her morals. She says she doesn't care. She's out in the buggy. Made me let her come. When the doctor's fixed you up, do you think you can walk out?"

"Listen," Hull said, grinning, "when the doctor lets me up, I'm making it on the run."

LOST SISTER

—

Dorothy M. Johnson

Our household was full of women, who overwhelmed my uncle Charlie and sometimes confused me with their bustle and chatter. We were the only men on the place. I was nine years old when still another woman came—Aunt Bessie, who had been living with the Indians.

When my mother told me about her, I couldn't believe it. The savages had killed my father, a cavalry lieutenant, two years before. I hated Indians and looked forward to wiping them out when I got older. (But when I was grown, they were no menace any more.)

"What did she live with the hostiles for?" I demanded.

"They captured her when she was a little girl," Ma said. "She was three years younger than you are. Now she's coming home."

High time she came home, I thought. I said so, promising, "If they was ever to get me, I wouldn't stay with 'em long."

Ma put her arms around me. "Don't talk like that. They won't get you. They'll never get you."

I was my mother's only real tie with her husband's family. She was not happy with those masterful women, my aunts Margaret, Hannah, and Sabina, but she would not go back

75

East where she came from. Uncle Charlie managed the store
the aunts owned, but he wasn't really a member of the family—he was just Aunt Margaret's husband. The only man
who had belonged was my father, the aunts' younger brother.
And I belonged, and someday the store would be mine. My
mother stayed to protect my heritage.

None of the three sisters, my aunts, had ever seen Aunt
Bessie. She had been taken by the Indians before they were
born. Aunt Mary had known her—Aunt Mary was two years
older—but she lived a thousand miles away now and was not
well.

There was no picture of the little girl who had become a
legend. When the family had first settled here, there was
enough struggle to feed and clothe the children without
having pictures made of them.

Even after army officers had come to our house several
times and there had been many letters about Aunt Bessie's
delivery from the savages, it was a long time before she came.
Major Harris, who made the final arrangements, warned my
aunts that they would have problems, that Aunt Bessie might
not be able to settle down easily into family life.

This was only a challenge to Aunt Margaret, who wel-
comed challenges. "She's our own flesh and blood," Aunt
Margaret trumpeted. "Of course she must come to us. My
poor, dear sister Bessie, torn from her home forty years ago!"

The major was earnest but not tactful. "She's been with
the savages all those years," he insisted. "And she was only
a little girl when she was taken. I haven't seen her myself,
but it's reasonable to assume that she'll be like an Indian
woman."

My stately aunt Margaret arose to show that the audience
was ended. "Major Harris," she intoned. "I cannot permit
anyone to criticize my own dear sister. She will live in my
home, and if I do not receive official word that she is coming
within a month, I shall take steps."

Aunt Bessie came before the month was up.

The aunts in residence made valiant preparations. They

bustled and swept and mopped and polished. They moved me from my own room to my mother's—as she had been begging them to do because I was troubled with nightmares. They prepared my old room for Aunt Bessie with many small comforts—fresh doilies everywhere, hairpins, a matching pitcher and bowl, the best towels, and two new nightgowns in case hers might be old. (The fact was that she didn't have any.)

"Perhaps we should have some dresses made," Hannah suggested. "We don't know what she'll have with her."

"We don't know what size she'll take, either," Margaret pointed out. "There'll be time enough for her to go to the store after she settles down and rests for a day or two. Then she can shop to her heart's content."

Ladies of the town came to call almost every afternoon while the preparations were going on. Margaret promised them that, as soon as Bessie had recovered sufficiently from her ordeal, they should all meet her at tea.

Margaret warned her anxious sisters, "Now, girls, we mustn't ask her too many questions at first. She must rest for a while. She's been through a terrible experience." Margaret's voice dropped 'way down with those last two words, as if only she could be expected to understand.

Indeed Bessie had been through a terrible experience, but it wasn't what the sisters thought. The experience from which she was suffering, when she arrived, was that she had been wrenched from her people, the Indians, and turned over to strangers. She had not been freed. She had been made a captive.

Aunt Bessie came with Major Harris and an interpreter, a half-blood with greasy black hair hanging down to his shoulders. His costume was half army and half primitive. Aunt Margaret swung the door open wide when she saw them coming. She ran out with her sisters following, while my mother and I watched from a window. Margaret's arms were outstretched, but when she saw the woman closer, her arms dropped and her glad cry died.

She did not cringe, my aunt Bessie who had been an Indian

for forty years, but she stopped walking and stood staring, helpless among her captors.

The sisters had described her often as a little girl. Not that they had ever seen her, but she was a legend, the captive child. Beautiful blond curls, they said she had, and big blue eyes—she was a fairy child, a pale-haired little angel who ran on dancing feet.

The Bessie who came back was an aging woman who plodded in moccasins, whose dark dress did not belong on her bulging body. Her brown hair hung just below her ears. It was growing out; when she was first taken from the Indians, her hair had been cut short to clean out the vermin.

Aunt Margaret recovered herself and, instead of embracing this silent, stolid woman, satisfied herself by patting an arm and crying, "Poor dear Bessie, I am your sister Margaret. And here are our sisters Hannah and Sabina. We do hope you're not all tired out from your journey!"

Aunt Margaret was all graciousness, because she had been assured beyond doubt that this was truly a member of the family. She must have believed—Aunt Margaret could believe anything—that all Bessie needed was to have a nice nap and wash her face. Then she would be as talkative as any of them.

The other aunts were quick-moving and sharp of tongue. But this one moved as if her sorrows were a burden on her bowed shoulders, and when she spoke briefly in answer to the interpreter, you could not understand a word of it.

Aunt Margaret ignored these peculiarities. She took the party into the front parlor—even the interpreter, when she understood there was no avoiding it. She might have gone on battling with the major about him, but she was in a hurry to talk to her lost sister.

"You won't be able to converse with her unless the interpreter is present," Major Harris said. "Not," he explained hastily, "because of any regulation, but because she has forgotten English."

Aunt Margaret gave the half-blood interpreter a look of

frowning doubt and let him enter. She coaxed Bessie. "Come, dear, sit down."

The interpreter mumbled, and my Indian aunt sat cautiously on a needlepoint chair. For most of her life she had been living with the people who sat comfortably on the ground.

The visit in the parlor was brief. Bessie had had her instructions before she came. But Major Harris had a few warnings for the family. "Technically, your sister is still a prisoner," he explained, ignoring Margaret's start of horror. "She will be in your custody. She may walk in your fenced yard, but she must not leave it without official permission.

"Mrs. Raleigh, this may be a heavy burden for you all. But she has been told all this and has expressed willingness to conform to these restrictions. I don't think you will have any trouble keeping her here." Major Harris hesitated, remembered that he was a soldier and a brave man, and added, "If I did, I wouldn't have brought her."

There was the making of a sharp little battle, but Aunt Margaret chose to overlook the challenge. She could not overlook the fact that Bessie was not what she had expected.

Bessie certainly knew that this was her lost white family, but she didn't seem to care. She was infinitely sad, infinitely removed. She asked one question: "Ma-ry?" and Aunt Margaret almost wept with joy.

"Sister Mary lives a long way from here," she explained, "and she isn't well, but she will come as soon as she's able. Dear sister Mary!"

The interpreter translated this, and Bessie had no more to say. That was the only understandable word she ever did say in our house, the remembered name of her older sister.

When the aunts, all chattering, took Bessie to her room, one of them asked, "But where are her things?"

Bessie had no things, no baggage. She had nothing at all but the clothes she stood in. While the sisters scurried to bring a comb and other oddments, she stood like a stooped monument, silent and watchful. This was her prison. Very well, she would endure it.

"Maybe tomorrow we can take her to the store and see what she would like," Aunt Hannah suggested.

"There's no hurry," Aunt Margaret declared thoughtfully. She was getting the idea that this sister was going to be a problem. But I don't think Aunt Margaret ever really stopped hoping that one day Bessie would cease to be different, that she would end her stubborn silence and begin to relate the events of her life among the savages, in the parlor over a cup of tea.

My Indian aunt accustomed herself, finally, to sitting on the chair in her room. She seldom came out, which was a relief to her sisters. She preferred to stand, hour after hour, looking out the window—which was open only about a foot, in spite of all Uncle Charlie's efforts to budge it higher. And she always wore moccasins. She never was able to wear shoes from the store, but seemed to treasure the shoes brought to her.

The aunts did not, of course, take her shopping after all. They made her a couple of dresses; and when they told her, with signs and voluble explanations, to change her dress, she did.

After I found that she was usually at the window, looking across the flat land to the blue mountains, I played in the yard so I could stare at her. She never smiled, as an aunt should, but she looked at me sometimes, thoughtfully, as if measuring my worth. By performing athletic feats, such as walking on my hands, I could get her attention. For some reason, I valued it.

She didn't often change expression, but twice I saw her scowl with disapproval. Once was when one of the aunts slapped me in a causal way. I had earned the slap, but the Indians did not punish children with blows. Aunt Bessie was shocked, I think, to see that white people did. The other time was when I talked back to someone with spoiled, small-boy insolence—and that time the scowl was for me.

The sisters and my mother took turns, as was their Christian duty, in visiting her for half an hour each day. Bessie didn't eat at the table with us—not after the first meal.

The first time my mother took her turn, it was under protest. "I'm afraid I'd start crying in front of her," she argued, but Aunt Margaret insisted.

I was lurking in the hall when Ma went in. Bessie said something, then said it again, peremptorily, until my mother guessed what she wanted. She called me and put her arm around me as I stood beside her chair. Aunt Bessie nodded, and that was all there was to it.

Afterward, my mother said, "She likes you. And so do I." She kissed me.

"I don't like her," I complained. "She's queer."

"She's a sad old lady," my mother explained. "She had a little boy once, you know."

"What happened to him?"

"He grew up and became a warrior. I suppose she was proud of him. Now the Army has him in prison somewhere. He's half Indian. He was a dangerous man."

He was indeed a dangerous man, and a proud man, a chief, a bird of prey whose wings the Army had clipped after bitter years of trying.

However, my mother and my Indian aunt had that one thing in common: they both had sons. The other aunts were childless.

There was a great to-do about having Aunt Bessie's photograph taken. The aunts, who were stubbornly and valiantly trying to make her one of the family, wanted a picture of her for the family album. The government wanted one too, for some reason—perhaps because someone realized that a thing of historic importance had been accomplished by recovering the captive child.

Major Harris sent a young lieutenant with the greasy-haired interpreter to discuss the matter in the parlor. (Margaret, with great foresight, put a clean towel on a chair and saw to it the interpreter sat there.) Bessie spoke very little during that meeting, and of course we understood only what the half-blood *said* she was saying.

No, she did not want her picture made. No.

But your son had his picture made. Do you want to see it? They teased her with that offer, and she nodded.

If we let you see his picture, then will you have yours made?

She nodded doubtfully. Then she demanded more than had been offered: If you let me keep his picture, then you can make mine.

No, you can only look at it. We have to keep his picture. It belongs to us.

My Indian aunt gambled for high stakes. She shrugged and spoke, and the interpreter said, "She not want to look. She will keep or nothing."

My mother shivered, understanding as the aunts could not understand what Bessie was gambling—all or nothing.

Bessie won. Perhaps they had intended that she should. She was allowed to keep the photograph that had been made of her son. It has been in history books many times—the half-white chief, the valiant leader who was not quite great enough to keep his Indian people free.

His photograph was taken after he was captured, but you would never guess it. His head is high, his eyes stare with boldness but not with scorn, his long hair is arranged with care—dark hair braided on one side and with a tendency to curl where the other side hangs loose—and his hands hold the pipe like a royal scepter.

That photograph of the captive but unconquered warrior had its effect on me. Remembering him, I began to control my temper and my tongue, to cultivate reserve as I grew older, to stare with boldness but not scorn at people who annoyed or offended me. I never met him, but I took silent pride in him—Eagle Head, my Indian cousin.

Bessie kept his picture on her dresser when she was not holding it in her hands. And she went like a docile, silent child to the photograph studio, in a carriage with Aunt Margaret early one morning, when there would be few people on the street to stare.

Bessie's photograph is not proud but pitiful. She looks out with no expression. There is no emotion there, no challenge, only the face of an aging woman with short hair, only endurance and patience. The aunts put a copy in the family album.

But they were nearing the end of their tether. The Indian aunt was a solid ghost in the house. She did nothing because there was nothing for her to do. Her gnarled hands must have been skilled at squaws' work, at butchering meat and scraping and tanning hides, at making tepees and beading ceremonial clothes. But her skills were useless and unwanted in a civilized home. She did not even sew when my mother gave her cloth and needles and thread. She kept the sewing things beside her son's picture.

She ate (in her room) and slept (on the floor) and stood looking out the window. That was all, and it could not go on. But it had to go on, at least until my sick aunt Mary was well enough to travel—Aunt Mary, who was her older sister, the only one who had known her when they were children.

The sister's duty visits to Aunt Bessie became less and less visits and more and more duty. They settled into a bearable routine. Margaret had taken upon herself the responsibility of trying to make Bessie talk. Make, I said, not teach. She firmly believed that her stubborn and unfortunate sister needed only encouragement from a strong-willed person. So Margaret talked, as to a child, when she bustled in:

"Now there you stand, just looking, dear. What in the world is there to see out there? The birds—are you watching the birds? Why don't you try sewing? Or you could go for a little walk in the yard. Don't you want to go out for a nice little walk?"

Bessie listened and blinked.

Margaret could have understood an Indian woman's not being able to converse in a civilized tongue, but her own sister was not an Indian. Bessie was white, therefore she should talk the language her sisters did—the language she had not heard since early childhood.

Hannah, the put-upon aunt, talked to Bessie too, but she was delighted not to get any answers and not to be interrupted. She bent over her embroidery when it was her turn to sit with Bessie and told her troubles in an unending flow. Bessie stood looking out the window the whole time.

Sabina, who had just as many troubles, most of them emanating from Margaret and Hannah, went in like a martyr, firmly clutching her Bible, and read aloud from it until her time was up. She took a small clock along so that she would not, because of annoyance, be tempted to cheat.

After several weeks Aunt Mary came, white and trembling and exhausted from her illness and the long, hard journey. The sisters tried to get the interpreter in but were not successful. (Aunt Margaret took that failure pretty hard.) They briefed Aunt Mary, after she had rested, so the shock of seeing Bessie would not be too terrible. I saw them meet, those two.

Margaret went to the Indian woman's door and explained volubly who had come, a useless but brave attempt. Then she stood aside, and Aunt Mary was there, her lined white face aglow, her arms outstretched. "Bessie! Sister Bessie!" she cried.

And after one brief moment's hesitation, Bessie went into her arms and Mary kissed her sun-dark, weathered cheek. Bessie spoke. "Ma-ry," she said. "Ma-ry." She stood with tears running down her face and her mouth working. So much to tell, so much suffering and fear—and joy and triumph, too—and the sister there at last who might legitimately hear it all and understand.

But the only English word that Bessie remembered was "Mary," and she had not cared to learn any others. She turned to the dresser, took her son's picture in her work-hardened hands, reverently, and held it so her sister could see. Her eyes pleaded.

Mary looked on the calm, noble, savage face of her half-blood nephew and said the right thing: "My, isn't he handsome!" She put her head on one side and then the other. "A fine boy, sister," she approved. "You must"—she stopped, but she finished—"be awfully proud of him, dear!"

Bessie understood the tone if not the words. The tone was admiration. Her son was accepted by the sister who mattered. Bessie looked at the picture and nodded, murmuring. Then she put it back on the dresser.

Aunt Mary did not try to make Bessie talk. She sat with her every day for hours, and Bessie did talk—but not in English. They sat holding hands for mutual comfort while the captive child, grown old and a grandmother, told what had happened in forty years. Aunt Mary said that was what Bessie was talking about. But she didn't understand a word of it and didn't need to.

"There is time enough for her to learn English again," Aunt Mary said. "I think she understands more than she lets on. I asked her if she'd like to come and live with me, and she nodded. We'll have the rest of our lives for her to learn English. But what she has been telling me—she can't wait to tell that. About her life, and her son."

"Are you sure, Mary dear, that you should take the responsibility of having her?" Margaret said dutifully, no doubt shaking in her shoes for fear Mary would change her mind now that deliverance was in sight. "I do believe she'd be happier with you, though we've done all we could."

Margaret and the older sisters would certainly be happier with Bessie somewhere else. And so, it developed, would the United States Government.

Major Harris came with the interpreter to discuss details, and they told Bessie she could go, if she wished, to live with Mary a thousand miles away. Bessie was patient and willing, stolidly agreeable. She talked a great deal more to the interpreter than she had ever done before. He answered at length and then explained to the others that she had wanted to know how she and Mary would travel to this far country. It was hard, he said, for her to understand just how far they were going.

Later we knew that the interpreter and Bessie had talked about much more than that.

Next morning, when Sabina took breakfast to Bessie's room, we heard a cry of dismay. Sabina stood holding the tray, repeating, "She's gone out the window! She's gone out the window!"

And so she had. The window that had always stuck so that it would not raise more than a foot was open wider now. And the photograph of Bessie's son was gone from the dresser. Nothing else was missing except Bessie and the decent dark dress she had worn the day before.

My uncle Charlie got no breakfast that morning. With Margaret shrieking orders, he leaped on a horse and rode to the telegraph station.

Before Major Harris got there with half a dozen cavalry-men, civilian scouts were out searching for the missing woman. They were expert trackers. Their lives had depended, at various times, on their ability to read the meaning of a turned stone, a broken twig, a bruised leaf. They found that Bessie had gone south. They tracked her for ten miles. And then they lost the trail, for Bessie was as skilled as they were. Her life had sometimes depended on leaving no stone or twig or leaf marked by her passage. She traveled fast at first. Then, with time to be careful, she evaded the followers she knew would come.

The aunts were stricken with grief—at least Aunt Mary was—and bowed with humiliation about what Bessie had done. The blinds were drawn, and voices were low in the house. We had been pitied because of Bessie's tragic folly in having let the Indians make a savage of her. But now we were traitors because we had let her get away.

Aunt Mary kept saying pitifully, "Oh, why did she go? I thought she would be contented with me!"

The others said that it was, perhaps, all for the best. Aunt Margaret proclaimed, "She has gone back to her own." That was what they honestly believed, and so did Major Harris.

My mother told me why she had gone. "You know that

picture she had of the Indian chief, her son? He's escaped from the jail he was in. The fort got word of it, and they think Bessie may be going to where he's hiding. That's why they're trying so hard to find her. They think,'' my mother explained, ''that she knew of his escape before they did. They think the interpreter told her when he was here. There was no other way she could have found out.''

They scoured the mountains to the south for Eagle Head and Bessie. They never found her, and they did not get him until a year later, far to the north. They could not capture him that time. He died fighting.

After I grew up, I operated the family store, disliking store-keeping a little more every day. When I was free to sell it, I did, and went to raising cattle. And one day, riding in a canyon after strayed steers, I found—I think—Aunt Bessie. A cowboy who worked for me was along, or I would never have let anybody know.

We found weathered bones near a little spring. They had a mystery on them, those nameless human bones suddenly come upon. I could feel old death brushing my back.

''Some prospector,'' suggested my riding partner.

I thought so too until I found, protected by a log, sodden scraps of fabric that might have been a dark, respectable dress. And wrapped in them was a sodden something that might have once been a picture.

The man with me was young, but he had heard the story of the captive child. He had been telling me about it, in fact. In the passing years it had acquired some details that surprised me. Aunt Bessie had become once more a fair-haired beauty, in this legend that he had heard, but utterly sad and silent. Well, sad and silent she really was.

I tried to push the sodden scrap of fabric back under the log, but he was too quick for me. ''That ain't no shirt, that's a dress!'' he announced. ''This here was no prospector—it was a woman!'' He paused and then announced with awe, ''I bet you it was your Indian aunt!''

I scowled and said, ''Nonsense. It could be anybody.''

He got all worked up about it. "If it was *my* aunt," he declared, "I'd bury her in the family plot."

"No," I said, and shook my head.

We left the bones there in the canyon, where they had been for forty-odd years if they were Aunt Bessie's. And I think they were. But I would not make her a captive again. She's in the family album. She doesn't need to be in the family plot.

If my guess about why she left us is wrong, nobody can prove it. She never intended to join her son in hiding. She went in the opposite direction to lure pursuit away.

What happened to her in the canyon doesn't concern me, or anyone. My aunt Bessie accomplished what she set out to do. It was not her life that mattered, but his. She bought him another year.

IN THE MEADOWS

—

Dale L. Walker

The three men rode down together from Fillmore, took a rest, fed and watered their horses at Cedar City, and passed a few stunted scrub oaks and junipers as they entered the Meadows. Alone among the riders, and the youngest of them, Chris Parr knew the place, knew how it would look when the sun rose high enough: a flat wasteland scarred to a brutal corduroy from a million wagon ruts, leached to ruin by floodwaters, covered by a sharp white gravel like bone shards risen to the surface of an ancient burial ground.

Since it would be midmorning before the prisoner came in from Panguitch, Chris, Mason Ewell, and Tobe Tracy unsaddled, gathered wood for a fire, fetched water from the nearby sunken spring, and filled a sooty tin coffeepot. Arbuckle beans were mashed in a cheesecloth bag and the bag knotted and tossed into the pot, which was set to boil on a ring of stones around the fire. The men lounged by it, smoking and chatting in low voices.

Chris sat, his back against his saddle, long legs stretched out, boots crossed, buckskin jacket pulled tight against him, collar up. He watched the shimmering yellow ball on the horizon. To the northeast, somewhere on the road between the

89

Meadows and Panguitch, the little settlement on the bottom fork of the Sevier, a wagon was bringing Lee in. Today would be the first time since '57, everybody said, that Lee would be in the Meadows.

Not so. Chris Parr knew better. *Lee's here now, been here since '57, and he'll be here long after this day is over.*

Chris and Tracy were blowing their cups of steaming coffee when Ewell returned to the camp from a ride up trail toward Cedar City. He was a bowlegged, potbellied, gray-whiskered Confederate veteran, talkative and inquisitive. Chris knew him as a respected senior guard at the prison in Salt Lake City and the two had struck up a friendship on the trail.

"Thought I heard somethin' up there," Ewell said to the men at the fire. "Too early for the prison wagon; prob'ly that magazine slicker."

He hunkered down at the coffeepot. "'Bout time he showed up. He damn near drove me crazy up at Fillmore yesterdy askin' questions I couldn't answer and wouldn't have if I could. He'll be askin' stuff and drawrin' pictures of old John D. the livelong day 'til we get this business over with."

He took a red-tipped stick from the fire and lit a cheroot butt he found in his vest pocket. He edged closer to Chris. "I still don't reckon it, young 'un. Like that magazine fella said, John D.'s bein' brought down here by his ownself. Why ain't none of the others gittin' what he's going to git? This here is your part of the country. Ye know the answer to that?"

Chris sipped the scalding coffee. "They tell me most of the others are dead and those still alive skipped out of Utah a long time ago."

Ewell considered this. "Was me," he said, "I'd have dragged some of them bastards down with me." He sucked at the dead butt-end of his cigar. "That jury up in Beaver . . . I heard they was all Saints. Looks to me like they just got themselfs a lamb for the slaughter. Not that he ain't guilty as hell. 'Son of Dan' my ass. Nothin' but a damn woman and baby killer.''

Tracy, who had heard Ewell's discourse on Lee before, remained silent while he pulled on a leather glove and poured coffee into the old man's tin cup.

Ewell went on, cocking an eye toward Chris.

"Ye only been up to the prison a few months; how'd ye get roped into this transaction?''

"Volunteered,'' Chris offered. "Figured I better take my turn.''

"The hell ye say,'' Ewell said. "Well, I do admire your grit, young Chris Parr. Me and Tobe here been guardin' up there near twelve year, ever since the war was over. Both of us was with Pap Price at Pea Ridge in '62. This makes . . . four, five times for me, and I never volunteered for a one.''

Tracy, on hearing his name, said, "The extry money comes in handy.'' He didn't look up as he spoke but concentrated on rolling a cigarette from his Durham bag.

"Let me ask you one,'' Chris said. "Did you all know Lee at the prison?''

"We seen him a few times is all,'' Ewell said. "He ain't in our block. He got bailed out about four months past. Never will understand why he didn't ride for Mexico like his hair was on fire. I sure as hell would've. But no, that God-fearin' Avengin' Angel sonavabitch hightailed over to Panguitch where he's got a bunch of wives and a cabin full of kids. Then he went on operatin' his ferry on the Little Colorado 'til they come and got him to stand trial in Beaver.''

Chris fell silent.

"Ye gettin' queasy, young 'un?'' Ewell said, tossing the cheroot end in the fire. "Hell, nobody likes this duty. There's Tobe and me, don't forget, so it ain't like you had to do it by your ownself. Just do what Tobe and me do. Thing'll be over soon.''

"Buckboard!'' Ewell shouted. Chris and Tobe Tracy stood and turned toward the Cedar City trail and watched the wagon descend from the rise of the trail in a crunch of gravel and a swirl of white dust. It drew to a halt twenty feet from them and the driver set the brake and climbed down, brushed himself, and blew his nose loudly in a huge filthy handkerchief.

"Nicholas Forbes, artist and reporter representing *Harper's Weekly* magazine of New York City," the man said, approaching the men. Chris, closest to the newcomer, had his hand grabbed first.

"Well now, here's a youngster. What's the name?"

"Chris . . . Parr, sir."

"Ha! Many thanks. Chris . . . Parr, did you say? Yes, Parr." Forbes had produced a pad from his coat pocket and scribbled something on it. He shook Ewell's hand. "Ha! Mr. Ewell. Indeed—Mr. *Mason* Ewell, late *Sergeant* Mason Ewell, Army of the Confederacy, served with General Sterling Price at—was it Pea Ridge in Arkansas? Correct? I try not to forget these things."

Ewell nodded and grinned sheepishly as Forbes continued on to pump Tracy's hand and jot things on his notepad. The reporter was a tall, bony man in a rumpled black suit and frock coat, both grimed with trail dust, a once-white boiled shirt with starched collar, and a black cravat tied in a mare's nest bow. He wore a too-large bowler, which sat on and bent his ears. He had pale blue gooseberry eyes and a wispy, gray blond Imperial, the moustache and goatee roughly the color of the tendrils of lank hair that fell from his bowler over the back of his neck.

Ewell whispered to Chris, "Looks like a damn undertaker, don't he, like he came down here to bury ol' John D. 'stead of drawrin' his picture?"

Chris, hands thrust into the pockets of his buckskin coat, walked to the sunken spring a few yards from the campfire. *About the same distance from the fire as it was from the Fancher camp in '57.* The ground around the spring was spongy—*like it was in '57 when Captain Fancher had worried that his wagons might bog down in it.* Chris knew that distance from the emigrant camp to the spring had been critical. *When Lee and his gang of Saints and Paiutes laid siege to the train, they took pains to guard the spring and keep the captain's people from it. The torture of thirst had a lot to do with their surrender to Lee . . . and the surrender led to the slaughter.*

"Young Mr. Parr, I'm delighted to find you here." Nicholas Forbes, carrying a canvas bucket, came forward. "I must tend to my faithful old animal," he said, kneeling at the spring and scooping the bucket full. He turned to Chris. "This once must have been a lovely spot, don't you think? The descriptions of how it appeared in '57 are veritable word paintings—lush, green, dewy grass, tall enough to hide a horse; black loamy soil, all that. It is ironic that in such a magnificent setting as this was then, such a savage crime could take place."

The artist put his bucket aside and kneeled again to scoop water to his mouth with his cupped hand. Chris remained silent.

Forbes stood. "You have been here before, am I correct?"

"How did you know?"

"No great trick, really. I talked to your friend Sergeant Ewell a few days ago in Fillmore. He's a fine fellow, I'm sure, but most uncommunicative. To one of my questions about this place he said, 'You need to talk to Chris Parr. He's from Beaver. He knows the Meadows.' "

"I've been here a few times," Chris said cautiously.

"Then can I assume you are interested in what occurred here in 1857? I've had the devil's own time in gaining access to certain details of the story. As you perhaps know, my job is to provide my editor with sketches of the massacre as best I can re-create it, and of Mr. Lee when he arrives here this morning, together with a full recounting of the crime for which he was tried and found guilty."

"I know what the papers say and what some people have told me and that's about all," Chris said. He knew from Ewell that the *Harper's* correspondent had been in the territory for both of Lee's trials at Beaver, and full time since September past when the jury had found Lee guilty of complicity in mass murder and sentenced him to death. "You probably know more about the massacre than anybody around here."

Forbes smiled. "My young friend, I'm grateful for your confidence, but I am a stranger here, a scribbler for hire trying to make sense of a complex tragedy. You know this region and its people. You have been to this very place in times past. You could be more help than you might imagine. Perhaps if I told you what I have learned, showed you some of my work—my sketches are in my buggy . . ." He trailed off.

The man was likeable and seemed honest. "I doubt I can help you, but I'd like to see your sketches and hear what you have to say," Chris said.

"Splendid!" Forbes said, grasping his water bucket.

They walked back to the camp together and passed Ewell, sitting against a buckboard wheel. As the artist produced his portfolio, the old man said to Chris in a too-loud whisper, "You watch him, boy; he'll write a big ol' story 'bout you, and before you know it you'll be famous as the man who hunted down that evil Danite chief, John D. hisself!"

"Not really, Sergeant," Forbes said. He had heard Ewell's remark and joined the others carrying a rolled, leather-covered sketchbook. "I am no Ned Buntline, and dime novels are not my forte. I seek the truth, or as close to it as I can come. You will find me most trustworthy."

After helping the artist remove his horse from its harness, water and tie it with the others, the three men sat on the gravelly ground by the buckboard. The pencil sketches were on a thick, white, nubby paper and ranged from detailed drawings of Lee in his prison cell, Lee conferring with his lawyer, Lee intently watching a witness give testimony, Lee with fingers laced and arms resting on the defense table, to small impressions of the man as he appeared during his latest trial—profiles and full-faces. There were several small sketches of Lee's eyes—something that clearly intrigued the artist, who managed, even in penciled lines, to gave a hint of a zealot's madness lurking there.

"This was drawn solely from testimony and research," Forbes said, turning to a large, unfinished drawing. It was the artist's imagined view of the Fancher camp as it appeared during the siege: wagons arranged in a compact circle, tongues toward the center, wheels buried to their hubs in pits to lower them close to the ground. "Also this." Forbes turned a page of the portfolio revealing a scene inside the camp, women tending the wounded, wide-eyed children peering from the wagons, Captain Fancher pointing toward a knoll behind which he had apparently stationed his sharpshooters.

"I have only begun the picture of the emigrants on the trail after their surrender . . . moments before they died," the artist said. "I had to see these Meadows before I could finish it." He wrapped another page behind the big pad and handed it to Ewing, who studied it at length and passed it on.

Chris gripped the edge of the sketchbook. The scene, made with deft pencil strokes to be refined and detailed in ink before publication, chilled him. It was a mournful panoramic view, as if the artist had stood on a low hill above a faint roadway that wound through the Meadows. The back trail was crowded with slumped, trudging men, escorted by armed guards with bandoliers of cartridges slung across their chests. Ahead of this melancholy file, in the right center of the scene, walked the women, sunbonneted and holding their skirts above the dust, and a number of older children, some of them grinning and skylarking. The entire column was watched by a scattering of horsemen on the trail's flank, and ahead, on the upper right of the page where the trail narrowed in perspective, were depicted two wagons with a man walking between them.

With his pencil, Forbes tapped the tiny figure between the wagons. "That, of course, is John D. Lee," he said. "He walked behind the lead wagon, which carried the babies and small children and the emigrants' weapons. The second wagon contained the wounded from the Fancher camp."

"Where were the Paiutes?" Ewell said.

"Here." Forbes indicated with the pencil a point on the

trail a short distance ahead of the leading wagon. "About here lay their ambush site off the Cedar City road, under a mile from this campsite."

Chris had his eyes fixed on the wagons and the figure who walked between them. "How many all told?"

"Indians? About two hundred from most accounts, but nobody is certain, nor is it certain the number of Saints present. Lee claims there were over fifty white men involved."

"How many in the Fancher party?" Ewell struck a match to a fresh cheroot.

"Again, the count varies. Five men had left the train to seek aid. All these were later determined to have been tracked down and killed. A fair estimate of the balance of the Fancher train surrendering to Lee would be about 135. Of course only about half that number had begun the trek from Arkansas. The others attached themselves to the train at various points along the route from Fort Smith to Salt Lake City."

"The Missourians," Chris said.

"Yes," Forbes continued. "Among the latecomers were the ignoble 'Missouri Wildcats,' called 'pukes' by the Saints. Quite possibly it was this group that precipitated the troubles as they marched south from Salt Lake City."

Chris's eyes were fixed on the drawing. "The sketch doesn't show the man who gave the signal."

It was not a question, but Forbes answered. "True. He was just ahead of the leading wagon, about here, hidden from view in the sketch. I intend to render him separately. It appears that this man, stationed ahead of the lead wagon, turned in his saddle and shouted to those escorting the Fancher men and women, 'Do your duty!' What followed, of course, was the carnage."

"The what?" Ewell scooted closer to Chris and bent over the drawing.

"The bloodshed. The guards and horsemen shot the emigrant men at close range; the Indians erupted from the brush and shot and brained with their war clubs the older children and the women. The wounded were shot, stabbed, and clubbed to death in the second wagon. Only the babies and youngest children in the leading wagon survived. They were taken up to a ranch near these Meadows and there eventually distributed among certain church-faithful families.''

"Jesus," Ewell said, clamping his teeth on his cigar. "I heard the story before but . . . Jesus.''

"The man who gave the signal," Chris said, looking up from the sketch, "was Major Lucas Parr."

Ewell spat. "Parr, did ye say?''

"I had intended asking you about that myself," Forbes said. "Not that the name is all that uncommon, but by chance was Major Parr a relative?''

"He was my father," Chris said.

The prison van from Panguitch was due.

Forbes had spent some time by himself, busy with his sketches and notepad, but Chris saw him approach the campfire.

"Mr. Parr, I am duty bound to say that I must include in my story the extraordinary fact that you are the son of Major Lucas Parr of the Iron County Militia, and that Lucas Parr was one of John D. Lee's, ah . . . cohorts . . . in the massacre.''

Chris studied his coffee, saying nothing.

"As I stated earlier," Forbes went on, "I am trustworthy. I consider it insane to believe the sins of the father should be visited on the son. I shall treat this information fairly, but treat it I must. You have to admit it is of . . . interest . . . that you, son of one of Lee's minions, are to be among Lee's . . .''

"I get the drift," Chris said. "You have your job to do. If I were in your shoes, I'd write it up.''

"My boy, you are wiser than your years should warrant," Forbes said. "Might I venture a step further? After the ordeal this morning has ended, will you give me some of your time? I should like to interview you about your father.''

"I know very little about him. He died when I was a little boy.''

"Even so," Forbes said, "there are a few things I'd like to ask. It will ensure that what I write will be precise and correct."

"How about I ride back to Fillmore with you in your buggy," Chris said.

"Splendid!"

"Wagons' comin'!" Ewell shouted, and all eyes turned again to the Cedar City trail where the prison van passed the crest of the rise and began its descent. A faint blue haze shrouded the Meadows, but the sun was now high enough to light the place.

As the wagon drew up, Chris could see two men in blue uniforms and straight-brimmed hats in the seat and hear the *chick-chick* of the driver as he lightly snapped the reins over the two-horse team. The van made a turn at the terminus of the road, creaking and thumping along in a wide circle to approach the camp. Chris stood, hands thrust in the pockets of his buckskin jacket, as the wagon passed. On its sideboard were the words Utah Territorial Prison.

As the wagon drew to a halt near the fire, Tobe Tracy busied with the horses and chatted with the driver and guard. Chris and Mason Ewell stood at the rear of the vehicle. There, in wrist and leg irons and wearing a heavy overcoat, muffler, and grimy, shapeless felt hat, John Doyle Lee sat, leaning against a long pine box. Only the condemned man's unblinking eyes were visible above the folds of his wool scarf.

By ten o'clock, Lee had been removed from the wagon bed and after his shackles were checked and secured, sat on his rough-hewn coffin a few feet to the side of the van. His guard, the man who had, as Ewell put it, "rode shotgun" beside the assistant warden, now stood stiffly beside the prisoner, his carbine butt under his armpit, barrel across his forearm and pointed toward the ground.

Twice Lee had asked for a cup of water. He stared into the

distance. Chris saw him tremble and gather his coat under his chin.

Ewell, meantime, had talked with the assistant warden, signed some papers, and gathered his men on the opposite side of the fire from Lee and the prison van.

Chris, Tracy, and Lee's guard, a man named Luther Smart, presented their weapons to Ewell. The older man inserted in the trapdoor breech of each rifle a copper-cased cartridge, then snapped the trap shut, checked the firing pin, eased the hammer down, and handed the weapon back to its owner.

"Now, boys, stack your pieces military style right here, out of sight. I'll give you the word when the warden is ready, and he will give us the signal. . . ."

At that moment, the assistant warden appeared beside Ewell. "Mace, the prisoner has asked to speak to you and your men, and I have granted his request. Let's get this over with."

The four-man firing squad lined up near the wagon. The warden escorted Lee to them, the prisoner's leg irons clanking as he short-stepped toward them, hands manacled behind him. He stood a few seconds before Luther Smart, saying something softly and briefly before he shuffled sideways to Tracy. Chris stood last in the line, next to Ewell, and as Lee stood before the senior member of the party, Chris heard the whispered words: "I would appreciate a clean shot," Lee said calmly, "and please aim for my heart. My sons will be here later to take me home for burial."

Lee moved to the last man, paused a second, raised his eyes to Chris's, and softly repeated the words: "I would appreciate a clean shot . . ."

The old man paused, his gunmetal eyes auguring in. Chris met the stare. *John Doyle Lee, bodyguard of the Prophet Joseph Smith during the Latter-day Saints's early days at Nauvoo on the Missisippi; veteran of the Sons of Dan, the secret society of Avenging Angels; one-time confidant of Brigham Young—the man whose name struck terror in the hearts of Saint and Gentile alike.*

Lee said at last, "You *are* a young'un. I don't remember you at the prison."

"No, sir," Chris said. "I'm pretty new up there."

"Well, buck up, lad," Lee said, "This won't take long if you and the boys do it right." His eyes narrowed for an instant and he said, "What's your name?"

All the words came to Chris in that instant: the precise words that would give John D. Lee something to take to hell with him. *My name is Christopher Carson Fancher, Mr. Lee, although for the past twenty years I have used the name of the man who raised me, Lucas Parr. You knew him well, sir. Major Lucas Parr? The man who gave the signal in these Meadows in '57? The signal that began the murder of over a hundred people, including my father, Captain Alexander Fancher, my mother Eliza, my oldest brother Hampton . . . ? Lucas Parr died when I was still an ignorant boy, Mr. Lee, but he left a legacy for me: a letter confessing and repenting his part in the bloodletting here, a letter in which he revealed my true identity and everything that happened in these Meadows. I was one of the children in the first wagon, Mr. Lee. I am here today because I volunteered.*

In a split second, these words, long rehearsed, boiled in Chris's mind. But he could not utter them.

He saw the lines that scored Lee's face like the wheel ruts in the Meadows, saw the stubble of white whiskers leaking cold sweat, the slaty eyes watered by the cold and the fear, the bent and shrunken frame, the pathetic husk of a once-powerful man, bereft of all dignity and hope, readying for his descent into hell.

". . . your name?"

"Chris . . . the name is Chris."

"Well, young Chris," the old man said, "all I can say is *do your duty.*"

The buckboard crunched over the bleached gravel of the Cedar City Trail and Nicholas Forbes stretched his legs, pulled at his cravat, and opened his collar.

"I think its going to warm up now," he said, leaning slightly toward the driver. "We've got some miles ahead of us and time to get there. Suppose we just chat as we go along. Now, why don't you tell me something about your father?"

Chris Parr lightly flipped the reins until the buggy passed over a small rise and settled to the long, level stretch ahead.

"Well, he died when I was just a boy . . ."

BEEHUNTER WORKS IT OUT

Robert J. Conley

Beehunter sat on a cane-bottomed chair in front of his small log cabin at the base of Bald Hill in the Tahlequah District of the Cherokee Nation. He appeared to be aimlessly whittling on a small piece of walnut, but a closer look would reveal that he was involved in the intricate process of carving a small bear. The bear was on its hind legs, reaching up the trunk of a tree. Beehunter was not on duty with Sheriff Go-Ahead Rider, for whom he worked occasionally as a special deputy. He had not, in fact, been called on for some time. Things must be quiet in Tahlequah, he thought.

He'd had time to do some hunting, and he had supplied his wife, Nani, with plenty of venison. He had even caught a fine batch of crawdads, but they had eaten them already. As he sat carving, Nani was off to one side of the cabin cooking some fresh catfish he had caught just that very morning. He hadn't worked for Go-Ahead Rider for a while, but they were doing all right. They had not gone hungry.

And Beehunter seldom needed money. The small garden, his hunting and fishing, and a few fruit trees provided them all the food they needed. In fact, they almost always had

102

enough to give some away to others. He grew and cured his own tobacco. He did like coffee though, and he thought it wise to always have a good supply of shells for his old shotgun. They came in handy when he needed some meat for the table.

He sat and he carved, smelling the catfish cooking just around the corner, and it smelled good. Nani was a fine cook, a good woman. He was proud of his wife, and just now, he was anxious to be tasting the catfish she cooked. After he had cleaned the fish for her, she cut the meat in small strips and dropped them in hot grease in a big iron pot over an open fire. Thinking about it and smelling the odors from around the corner made him hungry.

But there was something else, a feeling, something he could not quite put words to, that was annoying him as he sat there. He felt like someone would be coming to see him soon. He couldn't tell who it would be, but he felt as if it had something to do with Go-Ahead Rider. Rider not only called on Beehunter for help now and then, which gave Beehunter almost the only money he ever made, but Rider was a good friend. Beehunter had often said that there was no better man alive than Go-Ahead Rider.

"The fish is cooked," Nani called out. She spoke in Cherokee, her only language. Beehunter could speak both Cherokee and Creek, but he, like his wife, could speak no English. Oh, he could understand when someone said, "Hello," and he recognized his own name and that of Rider when he heard them spoken in English, but that was about all. He sliced a bit of surplus wood off the nose of his bear and set it aside.

"I'm coming," he said. He stood up and folded his pocketknife. Dropping it in a pocket, he looked up to see a rider leading an extra horse coming toward his house. "Someone coming to see us," he said. He walked toward the corner of his cabin, and Nani stepped away from the cooking pot, wiping her hands on her apron. She met him there and looked toward the rider in the distance.

"Who is it?" she asked.

"I don't know yet," he said, but he thought, it's something to do with Rider. Nani turned away from him and walked back to her fire. Beehunter stood staring at the distant figure, slowly growing larger in his vision. She came back and handed him a piece of fish.

"It's hot," she said.

He took it and took a bite. It was hot. He chewed fast and swallowed it down. "Good," he said. *"Wado."* He put the rest of it into his mouth and chewed it. It was almost as hot as had been the first bite, and it was just as good. "It's Earl Bob," he said. He didn't bother saying it, but he could also tell that Earl Bob was leading the little roan from the sheriff's stable that Beehunter liked to ride.

"Yes," said Nani. "I can see him now. Maybe Rider wants you to come to work."

"Maybe," said Beehunter.

Earl Bob was another of Rider's occasional deputies. He got more work than did Beehunter, because he could speak both Cherokee and English, and even though Tahlequah was the capital city of the Cherokee Nation, there were more and more people there who could not speak Cherokee. Rider had tried several times to get Beehunter a full-time job. Beehunter knew that. But the chief or the council or the judge or whoever made the decisions wouldn't let him do it, because Beehunter could not speak any English. Nani brought him another piece of fish, and he ate it. Earl Bob was almost close enough by then to yell at, but Beehunter just ate his fish and waited.

Soon Earl Bob rode up close to the cabin. " *'Siyo,* Beehunter," he said. He touched the brim of his hat. " *'Siyo,* Nani. *Tohiju?"*

"Uh, tohigwu," said Nani. *"Nihina?"*

"I'm all right, too," Earl Bob said. "Thanks."

"Get down," said Beehunter, and Earl Bob swung down out of his saddle, allowing the reins of both animals to trail on the ground. Nani disappeared around the corner of the house. Beehunter indicated an extra chair, and Earl Bob sat down. Beehunter sat in the chair he had been in before.

"You carving?" Earl Bob asked him.

Beehunter picked up his bear and handed it to Earl Bob. "It's not finished," he said. Earl Bob turned the bear around and around, studying all the details.

"It's looking pretty good," he said. "What's he doing? Looking for honey?"

Beehunter chuckled, and just then Nani came around the corner of the house and handed each man a tin cup full of coffee. *"Wado,"* said Earl Bob.

"There's catfish, too," she said, and she disappeared again. Beehunter looked at the little roan. He wondered just what Earl Bob had ridden all the way out there to tell him, but he didn't say anything. Earl Bob would tell him soon enough. Nani came back with two plates, each piled high with pieces of beautifully fried catfish. She handed one to Earl Bob and the other to her husband. Earl Bob thanked her again, and she went back around to her fire. For a few moments, the two men ate in silence.

"Exie came by the sheriff's office this morning," Earl Bob said. "Rider didn't go home last night. He didn't show up at the office this morning either. He went over to Muskogee to take that white man prisoner to Marshal Lovely, you know, and he should have come home the night before last. We thought maybe something happened over there to hold him up for another day, so we weren't worried about him until Exie came by. She said he should be home by now."

"Probably," Beehunter said, "he's just taking a little more time than he thought he would. Maybe he had more business with that white lawman than he thought."

"That's what I told Exie," said Earl Bob, "but she said that he should have been back even yesterday, but he had told her last night at the latest he would be back. She's worried about him."

Nani appeared at the corner of the cabin with a look of deep concern on her face. "Exie doesn't worry like that for nothing," she said.

Beehunter stuffed the last piece of fish from his plate into his mouth and gulped it down. He wiped his fingers on his britches and stood up. "I'll go find him," he said. He picked up his coffee cup and drained it. Then he turned to his wife. "I have to go now, Nani," he said. "Rider might be in some trouble."

"Wait," she said, and she hurried into the house.

"I brought the roan for you," Earl Bob said. "And the guns you like. I hope you don't need them."

Beehunter walked over to the roan and checked the saddle boot for the single-shot Warner carbine. It was there. The Smith & Wesson .44 American revolver was in its holster, the belt buckled and slung over the saddle horn. Beehunter took it and strapped it around his waist. "Me, too," he said, and he swung himself easily up into the saddle.

Nani came out of the house with a bundle in a white cloth. She hurried around the corner to her fire.

Earl Bob finished his catfish and his coffee and stood up. Turning toward Nani, as she reappeared, he said, "Thank you. The catfish was good. The coffee, too."

Beehunter was already turning the roan to ride out when Earl Bob got into his saddle. "I don't know how long this will take," Beehunter said over his shoulder.

"Be careful," Nani said, hurrying over to his side. She opened a flap on his saddlebags and stuffed the bundle down into it. "Some food," she said.

Then the two men rode off together. They were halfway across the field before Beehunter spoke again.

"Who is this white man prisoner?" he asked. "What did he do?"

"He's a whiskey seller," said Earl Bob. "Rider's been after him for some time now. He finally found out who was bringing all that whiskey in from Arkansas, and he caught him, but he's a white man, so Rider had to take him over to Marshal Lovely."

"Was Rider on his big black horse?" Beehunter asked.

"Yes," said Earl Bob.

"This white man," said Beehunter, "Rider's prisoner, what was he called?"

"He called himself Chunk Harlan," said Earl Bob.

Beehunter said the name over and again to himself, trying to set the uncomfortable English sounds in his brain. "Chunk Hollan. Chunk Hollan," he said. Then out loud to Earl Bob, he said, "What does this Chunk Hollan look like?"

"He's a little bit shorter than you," Earl Bob said. (Beehunter was five feet and seven inches tall.) "He's heavy, though. Solid built. He has yellow hair and a yellow stubby beard. His arms are hairy, too. Also yellow. His eyes are very light blue, and his skin is white, but red shows through. It's ugly."

Beehunter nodded and grunted. "Chunk Hollan," he said.

When they reached the road to Muskogee and Earl Bob turned to ride into Tahlequah, Beehunter rode along with him.

"Aren't you going to Muskogee?" Earl Bob asked.

"I'm going somewhere else first," said Beehunter. "Then Muskogee."

Earl Bob didn't ask any more questions. They rode quietly the rest of the way into Tahlequah. When Earl Bob turned to ride back to the jail, Beehunter turned in the opposite direction. He rode on out of town a few miles, then moved onto a trail that wound through the thick woods. Before long he came up to a small cabin in the woods. An old Cherokee man was sitting in front of the cabin smoking a pipe. He smiled as Beehunter stopped his horse.

"Welcome," he said. "Come down."

Beehunter dismounted and walked over to the old man, who then offered him a chair. Beehunter sat and took off his hat.

"White Tobacco," he said. "I've come about Go-Ahead."

"What's the trouble?" White Tobacco asked.

"Go-Ahead went to Muskogee with a white man, his prisoner," Beehunter said. "He was taking the white man to the white lawman over there. He hasn't come home, and his wife is worried about him."

White Tobacco sat for a while in silence looking thoughtful. At last he stood up and walked into his house without saying anything. Beehunter waited patiently. From a branch overhead in a large white oak tree a squirrel chattered angrily and a blue jay screeched. A small green lizard ran up on top of a rock nearby and seemed to be looking at Beehunter. White Tobacco came back out of the house and sat down again.

"I looked in my crystal," he said. "Go-Ahead's in trouble."

"I have to look for him," Beehunter said.

White Tobacco opened up his hand to reveal a wad of string with a small stone tied to one end. He found the loose end of the string and held it up so that the stone dangled, and he sat still and watched it dangle for a time. Then the stone seemed to move and point directly west.

"He's that way," the old man said.

Beehunter thought it strange, for Muskogee was southwest. If he were to ride directly west, he would be going toward Wagoner. Both towns were in the Creek Nation, but that didn't matter to Beehunter. He wasn't acting as a deputy sheriff anyhow. He was a private citizen, looking for his friend who might be in trouble. And he could talk to Creeks. It was only white men who gave him problems. He just wondered what Rider was doing over there. He thanked White Tobacco, handed him a pouch of tobacco he had grown himself, mounted the roan, and left. He headed for Wagoner.

When the sun was low in the western sky and the day was growing dim, Beehunter had not yet reached the Halfway House at Fourteen Mile Creek. That was all right with him though. He didn't have the money to spend a night in the Halfway House nor to eat a meal there. He stopped beside the road and unsaddled the little roan. There was good grass for her to eat, and there was a clear stream nearby. He dug into the saddlebag to see what Nani had given him for the trail, and he was pleased to find that she had wrapped up some of the catfish for him. It was good even cold. He ate some with some bread she had put in there, and then finished his meal with a peach. It would have been nice to have some coffee, but he would just have to do without. He led the roan down to the stream, and they both had a drink. Then he settled down for the night.

He was up early the next morning. He was hungry, so he had some more bread and catfish. Then he saddled the roan and headed for the Halfway House. As he rode up to the establishment, he saw that there were a number of horses tied to the hitching rail. Effie's business is good, he thought. He found room for the roan, dismounted, and lapped the reins around the rail. Then he walked inside.

The main room was crowded with people having their breakfast there. He could smell the coffee and longed for a cup, but he tried to put that out of his mind. He looked the crowd over trying to find a familiar face. He recognized Effie Crittenden, of course. She owned the place. But he knew that she spoke only English, so he couldn't talk to her. He finally found one Cherokee man to talk to, but the man had not seen Go-Ahead Rider and did not know Chunk "Hollan." He found a Creek man he knew only slightly and tried him.

"Chunk Hollan," the Creek said. "The whiskey man?"

"Yes," said Beehunter, speaking in the Muskogee tongue. "You know him?"

"I know him," the man said.

Beehunter grew more anxious then. "Have you seen Chunk Hollan?" he asked.

The man shook his head. "I haven't seen him for some time," he said, "but I heard that Go-Ahead Rider arrested him over in Tahlequah. Hey, can Rider arrest a white man?"

Beehunter rode on toward Wagoner, hoping that he would encounter more people he could talk to and hoping for some sign of Go-Ahead Rider or of Chunk "Hollan." He saw several people along the road, and a few of them he was able to converse with, but no one knew anything of Rider or Harlan. It was late evening when he reached Wagoner. He rode around the town until it was almost dark, looking for any sign of Rider, but he saw none. He talked to a few more people but learned nothing. He rode to a stream just outside of town and made himself a camp for the night.

Early the next morning, Beehunter was walking the streets of Wagoner. At each place of business he poked his head in to see who he could see. He had come to the end of a street where a stable stood, and he was about to cross the street and check the businesses on the other side when he glanced inside the stable door toward the stalls in there, and he saw the head of a big, black stallion looking over a stall gate. He could hardly believe his eyes. He thought that he must be wrong, but he went inside to be sure.

As he walked up close to the stall, he knew that he was looking at the big black horse Go-Ahead Rider had taken on his trip to Muskogee. And here it was in Wagoner. Old White Tobacco had been right. Rider was in Wagoner. At least, his horse was in Wagoner. The stableman approached, and Beehunter tried to speak to him in Creek and in Cherokee, but the man kept replying with gibberish. Beehunter knew that it was English, of course, but it meant nothing to him. Finally, he walked out in disgust.

He was looking up and down the street for an Indian to approach to use as an interpreter when he spotted Marshal Lovely. He hurried toward the marshal. Lovely looked to see who was coming at him so fast and recognized Beehunter.

"Howdy, Beehunter," he said. "What are you doing over here?"

Beehunter, of course, understood nothing beyond the first two words. "Rider," he said.

"Rider?" said Lovely. "Rider was supposed to have showed up in Muskogee three days ago. He never showed up. Is he here?"

Beehunter didn't understand any of that. He pointed at his

own chest, then at his eyes, then moved his fingers away from his eyes and said, "Rider."

Lovely squinted his own eyes, trying to figure out Beehunter's sign language. "You're looking for Rider?" he said.

Beehunter gestured for Lovely to follow him, then led the way to the stable. He took Lovely to the stall that held the black stallion. The stableman was beside them in an instant.

"What's that Indian telling you about that horse?" the man said. "He was in here a few minutes ago looking at it, but he can't talk no English."

"Where'd you get that horse?" Lovely asked.

"Bought him," the man said.

"When?" said Lovely.

"Now hold on," said the man, "just what—"

Lovely pulled aside the lapel of his coat to reveal the badge on his vest. "I'm a U.S. marshal," he said. "When did you buy that horse?"

"Yesterday," the man said. "Just yesterday. Anything wrong?"

"Unless that horse was sold to you by Sheriff Go-Ahead Rider of the Cherokee Nation," Lovely said, "it's stolen."

"Oh, say," the man said, "I don't know nothing about that. A man came in here wanting to sell a horse. That's all I know."

"You get a bill of sale?" asked the marshal.

"Yeah," the man said. "Sure. I'll fetch it. You want me to fetch it?"

"Yeah. Fetch it," Lovely said.

The man ran for his office, and Lovely and Beehunter looked at one another. Lovely crossed his arms over his chest. Beehunter put a hand on the black horse's head. "Rider," he said. Lovely nodded. "I know," he answered. "God damn it, Beehunter, I wish I could talk to you."

The stableman came back from the office with a piece of paper in his hand. He stuck it in front of Lovely's face. Lovely backed off and jerked the paper from the man's hand. He turned it around to read. "Calvin Brown," he read. "That the name of the man who sold you this horse?''

"That's the name he give me," the man said.

"What does this Calvin Brown look like?"

"I don't know," the man said. "He's about as tall as this Indian here. Maybe a little shorter. Light hair and eyes. Kind of heavy fellow, you know."

Lovely handed the paper back to the man, then shook a finger in his face. "You hold onto this horse," he said. "I'll be back, and if this horse is gone, you'll wind up in federal prison."

"He'll be here, Marshal," the man said. "You can count on that."

Lovely motioned for Beehunter to follow him, and he led the way to a nearby café. Inside, he selected a table, and the two men sat down. A waitress came over to the table.

"Can I help you?" she asked.

"Two cups of black coffee," said the marshal. "You know if anyone in here can talk both Cherokee and English?"

"That's a Cherokee man over there in the corner," she said. "He talks English to me, but I think he can talk Cherokee."

Lovely glanced over his shoulder. He saw the Indian man in the corner. He was seated alone at a table sipping coffee. "We'll join him," Lovely said. He got up and motioned for Beehunter to follow. At the table in the corner, Lovely said, "Excuse me, sir. I'm Marshal Lovely. This is Beehunter. Do you mind if we sit with you for a bit?"

The man seemed puzzled, but he said, "No."

Lovely and Beehunter sat down

"I'm Guy Cornshucks," the man said. "What do you want?"

The waitress brought two cups and a coffeepot. She filled a cup for Lovely and one for Beehunter, and she refilled Cornshucks's cup. Beehunter thought the coffee sure did smell good. He picked up the cup and sipped the hot liquid.

"My friend here doesn't speak any English," said Lovely,

"and I can't talk Cherokee. We need a translator. Can you help us?"

"Oh," said Cornshucks. "Yeah. I do what I can."

"Good. Then tell him for me that— No. Wait. Ask him why he came to Wagoner?"

Cornshucks asked the question of Beehunter and waited for Beehunter's answer. Then he said to Lovely, "He say he come looking for Sheriff Go-Ahead Rider. He say Rider didn't come back to Tahlequah when he should. They worried about him over there. His wife worried. He come looking for him."

"But Rider was supposed to have gone to Muskogee," Lovely said. "Why did he come to Wagoner?"

Beehunter's answer to that one was vague. He did not think it wise to tell the white lawman that an old Indian had dangled a stone on the end of a string, and Beehunter had followed the direction the stone sent him. Lovely chose not to pursue the issue. "All right," he said. "Tell him that the man who called himself Calvin Brown sold Rider's horse to the stable-man. The description of Brown that the stableman gave me sounded like Harlan."

Cornshucks repeated that information to Beehunter, and Beehunter said in Cherokee, "Hollan sold Go-Ahead's horse. That means Go-Ahead's in trouble. I've got to find him. Tell this white man that I have to go. I have to fine Hollan and Go-Ahead."

Beehunter was halfway out of his chair, but Lovely put a hand on his arm to hold him. He looked at Cornshucks, and Cornshucks gave a hurried translation of Beehunter's words.

"Tell him to hold on a minute," Lovely said. "We're working together here."

Cornshucks conveyed the message, and Beehunter settled back down.

"What we have to do," Lovely said, "is ask around town after the whereabouts of Harlan. I'll get some help over at the sheriff's office. We'll check the hotels. If he was here, someone had to see him."

Again Cornshucks translated for Beehunter. Beehunter tipped up his cup and drained it of coffee. He put the cup down and stood up. "*Howa,*" he said. "Let's go then."

"He said okay, let's go," Cornshucks told Lovely.

Lovely stood up, a little disgusted that Beehunter seemed to be ordering him around, or maybe that he was allowing himself to be ordered around by Beehunter. "Thanks," he said to Cornshucks. "I'll pay for your coffee."

"You want me to go along with you?" Cornshucks asked.

Lovely hesitated only a second. "Well, yeah. Sure," he said. "If you don't mind."

"If I minded I wouldn't have said so," Cornshucks said, getting up from his chair.

Outside, Lovely looked up and down the busy street. "Why don't we separate," he said, "since you're along to interpret for Beehunter. You two go down that way. I'll go this way. When we get to the end of this street, if we haven't spotted Harlan yet, we'll cross the street and come back this way until we meet."

"What if we spot him?" Cornshucks said.

"If you spot him," said Lovely, "leave Beehunter to watch him, nothing more, make him understand that, just watch him while you come and find me. You got all that?"

"I got it good," said Cornshucks, and he began to repeat it all in Cherokee for Beehunter as Lovely started on his own way down the street. It was half an hour later when Lovely was about to turn into a hotel just ahead. A man came out the front door. He was short and stocky and pale. He had blond hair and watery blue eyes. His shirtsleeves were rolled up, and Lovely could see that his arms were covered in light blond hair. The man wore boots and his pants legs were tucked inside the boots. He wore a vest that seemed almost too small for his frame, and on his head was a low-crowned, wide, flat-brimmed hat. He was puffing a short cigar. He stepped out onto the sidewalk, stopped, hooked his thumbs in his waistband, and looked down into the street, as if he were waiting for someone. Just under his right hand was hanging a Smith & Wesson .45.

Lovely walked a little closer. "Mr. Calvin Brown?" he said. The man's head jerked around, and watery eyes focused on Lovely.

"You talking to me?" the man said.

"You Calvin Brown?" Lovely asked.

"No," said the man.

"Did you sell a black horse to the livery stable here using the name of Calvin Brown?" Lovely asked.

"You got the wrong man, buster," said the stocky man.

"Maybe I should call you Chuck Harlan," Lovely said. "Are you Chuck Harlan?"

"Go bother someone else," the man said. "I've got business."

"Whiskey business?" Lovely asked

"I don't know what you're talking about. Who are you, anyhow?" the man said.

"I'm Deputy United States Marshal Lovely, and I'm asking you to walk down to the stable with me. We'll find out if you sold that black horse. If you're the wrong man, I'll apologize to you and you can be on your way."

"I ain't got time for that, deputy," the man said. "All right. All right. I sold the horse, but I ain't the man you're looking for."

"What's your name, mister?" Lovely said.

Some way down the street, east, Beehunter walked with Guy Cornshucks. They had not come across anyone who fit the description of Chuck "Hollan." Cornshucks had asked a few questions of people they met, and they had talked to a couple of Creeks and one other Cherokee. Beehunter had an uneasy feeling though. Just then, the image of the small stone on the end of the piece of string dangling from the fingers of old White Tobacco came back into his mind. He saw the stone as it seemed to strain to reach out toward the west.

"Come on," he said to Cornshucks in Cherokee. "We're going the wrong direction."

"But the white catcher told us to go this way," Cornshucks said

"I have to go west," said Beehunter, and he turned to walk in the opposite direction, to walk west. Cornshucks hurried along to catch him and walk again by his side. Beehunter set a fast pace. He wasn't looking anymore. He was just hurrying past everyone. It didn't matter to him, for they were only retracing their steps anyway. They reached the place where they parted company with Lovely, on the sidewalk there in front of the place where they'd had coffee, and Beehunter kept going. Cornshucks walked with him.

They hadn't gone much farther when Beehunter saw Lovely standing on the sidewalk ahead. In another instant he saw the other man, and just as he saw the man, just as his mind registered the man's looks and the description of "Hollan," he saw the man reach for a revolver at his side. He felt a moment of panic as he watched Lovely pull out his own revolver and fire. He watched as the man he knew as "Hollan"clutched at his belly and slowly leaned forward. He watched "Hollan" crumple and fall, and he ran toward Lovely.

When Beehunter and Cornshucks reached Lovely, the deputy was kneeling beside the body of the other man. He looked up into the face of Beehunter. "I'm sorry," he said. "He didn't give me any other choice. He's dead."

"I want Rider's horse," Beehunter said, and Cornshucks repeated the words in English. Lovely stood up slowly.

"What for?" he said

After Cornshucks translated for Beehunter, Beehunter said, "Rider will need him."

"Look," said Lovely, "I've got some things to do here yet. I have to make a report on this mess and have this body taken care of. I can't just shoot a man and walk away. When that's all taken care of, I'll talk to the clerk inside and find out if this man was registered here and if so, under what name. I'll ask

questions about him. We'll try to trace his movements and
see if we can find Rider that way."

Cornshucks did his best to relay all that to Beehunter, and
Beehunter nodded his understanding. He had worked with
Go-Ahead Rider enough to know how lawmen went about
their business.

"I want the horse," he said. "I'm going west."

Lovely sighed when he heard the words from Cornshucks.
"All right," he said. "I'll get the horse for you."

Beehunter rode out of town alone. He was leading the big
black horse. He had no knowledge of his destination. He
knew only that he had learned from White Tobacco that Rider
was somewhere west. For a mile or so along the road, there
were too many tracks to make any sense of any of them, but
then the tracks thinned out. The ones that were there were
easier to see, easier to read, and Beehunter knew the tracks
of the black horse well. He studied the ground closely as he
rode along, and then he saw them. Some were headed west,
others back east. He watched them closely, and in a while he
made the determination that the tracks headed east were the
most recent. The black horse had gone west out of town, and
then it had gone back to town.

Beehunter knew that "Hollan" had sold the horse in town,
and so he figured that Rider had not ridden it back to town.
He also knew, because of White Tobacco, that Rider was
somewhere west, so he figured further that Rider had been on
the horse when it made the tracks headed west. He kept riding, kept watching the tracks.

Back in Wagoner, Lovely had just finished giving the local
sheriff a full report on what happened and why it happened.
The body had been taken care of, and Lovely went back to
the hotel where he had encountered Harlan. He went inside
and walked up to the front desk. The clerk behind the desk
looked up. "Can I help you?" he said.

"I'm deputy Marshal Lovely," said the lawman. "You hear the commotion out there while ago?"

"How could I miss it?" the man said.

"Yeah," said Lovely. "That man that got killed, did you see who it was?"

"I seen him," the clerk said.

"Well?" Lovely said. "You know him? Was he registered here?"

"Yes," said the clerk. "To both questions."

"What name was he registered under?" the deputy asked.

"Calvin Brown," said the clerk with a silly grin on his face.

"And do you know if that was his right name?" said Lovely.

"I do," said the clerk.

"Well?"

"It ain't," the clerk said.

"So what the hell was his right name?" said Lovely, his voice beginning to show irritation with the clerk.

"He was Chunk Harlan," the man said.

"Now listen to me," said Lovely, "you ain't on a witness stand, and I ain't no lawyer. You going to start telling me everything you know without me having to drag it out of you one word at a time. You got that? Because if you let a man resister under a false name, and you knew it was a false name, you broke the law. Did you know that? And if you don't give me answers, I'm going to place you under arrest and take you over to jail in Muskogee. Understand?"

The silly expression on the clerk's face had vanished. It was replaced by a serious look, a little frightened. "Yes sir," the clerk said. "What do you want to know?"

A few miles west, the tracks in the road told Beehunter more. The big black horse had gone west in the company of five other horses. It had gone back to Wagoner with only one horse. Beehunter decided that Rider had been with five other men, "Hollan" and four more. They must have captured him somehow. Then they had taken him somewhere west of Wagoner, and "Hollan" had taken the horse back to town to sell. That could only mean one of two things. They had either killed Rider or they meant to kill him. Beehunter's mission took on more urgency.

He tried to recall the exact words of White Tobacco. The old man had said "Go-Ahead's in trouble." Beehunter wondered if that meant Rider was still alive. Would White Tobacco's crystal have told him that Rider was in trouble if Rider had already been dead? Beehunter didn't think so. He thought that the old man's powers would have known and would have told him, but they had told him only that Rider was in trouble, and that he was somewhere west. Beehunter rode on, anxious and worried, but hopeful.

Lovely looked up at Cornshucks as fast as he could and offered to pay him to ride with him out of town. "I'll need you to interpret for me with Beehunter," he said. "There might be trouble out there though. If there's any shooting, you just stay back out of the way. Will you go?"

"I'll go along," said Cornshucks.

As they rode along on the road going west out of town, Lovely filled Cornshucks in on his mission. "That was Chunk Harlan I killed, all right," he said. "Rider was taking Harlan from Tahlequah to Muskogee. From what I found out here, Harlan had some partners—four of them. They must have waylaid Rider to rescue Harlan—somewhere on the road from Tahlequah to Muskogee. Then they cut across this way. They must have skirted town, because I couldn't find anyone who had seen any of them except Harlan. Anyhow, Harlan sold Rider's horse in Wagoner."

"You think they killed Rider?" Cornshucks said.

"I don't know," Lovely said. "I hope not."

"So why are we riding out this way?" Cornshucks asked.

"I don't know that either," Lovely said, his voice sounding almost angry. "We're following Beehunter. That's all the hell I know."

• • •

Beehunter followed the tracks onto a path that led into the woods. The path was just wide enough for one horse. He slowed his pace. He stopped for a while and listened. The only sounds he heard were of squirrels and birds and the leaves rustling in the slight breeze. He moved ahead slowly. Then he stopped again. He could smell the smoke of a fire, probably a fire in a cookstove. He dismounted and took both horses into the woods, lapping their reins around a small tree. He opened one of the saddlebag pouches, reached in, and pulled out a box of shells. He opened the box and took out all the bullets, stuffing them into his pockets. He put the empty box back into the bag, then pulled the Warner carbine out of its sheath. He walked cautiously back out onto the path.

He moved along as quietly as he could, and soon he could detect the odor of meat cooking. It was a cookstove, just as he had figured, and whoever was up there was fixing a meal. That was good. He thought that he should give them time to start eating. He moved in a little closer, now staying on the edge of the path, almost brushing against the foliage that grew thick there. He saw the cabin and the four horses tied to a rail in front. Four men. He moved a little closer, then edged himself into the brush and under the trees. He watched.

Rider's inside there, he thought. *I have to be careful.* He eased himself through the tangled brush, slowly, making as little noise as possible. He found a spot from which he could watch, and shoot if necessary, and he settled in to wait. He didn't know just what he was waiting for, but he knew that he could not realistically rush four men inside a cabin by himself, especially not with Rider in there.

It wasn't long before a man came out of the door to relieve himself. Beehunter was disgusted. The man hadn't gone three steps away from the door. Even before he had finished his business, the man turned his head to shout back toward the open door. "You about got that meat cooked?" he said. "I should have left for Wagoner already. Chunk's going to be pissed off. He's waiting for me."

A voice came back from inside the cabin, "It's done now. Come and get it."

Beehunter watched as the man finished his chore and went back inside. The four men should be busy eating now, and he could move in on them and take them by surprise. On the other hand, in a few minutes, the one man would leave to meet "Hollan" in Wagoner. Then there would be only three to deal with. Beehunter waited. Then he had a thought, and he worked his way carefully back to the place where he had left the horses.

The man rode along the narrow pathway through the woods. He held a piece of meat wrapped in bread in his right hand and was chewing as he rode. All of a sudden a rider on horseback came out of the brush, bumping him broadside, frightening his horse, throwing him off balance. Beehunter swung the butt of the Warner hard against the back of the man's head. It hit with a sickening smack, and the man fell against his horse's neck.

Beehunter then calmed both horses as quickly as he could and moved them back into the brush. He slid the man's limp body down off his horse and tied the man to a tree, then worked his way back through the woods.

He decided to move on in. He made it all the way to the cabin door without calling any attention to himself. He leaned the Warner against the side of the cabin. It would do him no good inside. Then he pulled out the Smith & Wesson and cocked it. He stepped back, took a deep breath, then burst through the door. The three men at the table all started to jump at once, surprised looks on their faces. Beehunter fired, and one man fell, a dark splotch on his chest. The other two stopped still and raised their hands.

"Don't shoot, mister," one of them said.

On a cot against the wall, Go-Ahead Rider slowly raised himself up. Beehunter could see that the side of Rider's head was covered in matted blood. "You all right, Go-Ahead?" he asked in Cherokee.

"I am now," Rider answered. "Just keep those two covered."

Rider got up slowly and made his way with unsteady steps over to the table. He took the guns from the holsters of the two men, then bent down to take one out of the waistband of the dead outlaw. He tossed two of the guns over to the cot and held the third one on the two prisoners. "I got them now," he said to Beehunter in Cherokee. "Tie them up."

As Rider and Beehunter were loading their prisoners onto the horses there at the cabin, Lovely and Cornshucks rode up. "Rider," Lovely said, "Are you all right?"

"I will be," Rider said, "thanks to Beehunter."

"What happened?"

"This bunch jumped me on the road to Muskogee," Rider said. "They took me along with them as hostage just until they could meet with a big customer of theirs to get paid. Then I guess they meant to kill me and get out of the territory. The money man's in Wagoner. I know who he is. We can pick him up there."

"I'm sure relieved to find you in one piece," Lovely said. "Beehunter did a hell of a job. I just wish he could talk English."

Rider looked at Beehunter and grinned. "Aw," he said, "Beehunter don't need no English."

THE RETURN OF A PRIVATE

— ◢◣ —

Hamlin Garland

Chapter 1

The nearer the train drew toward La Crosse, the soberer the little group of "vets" became. On the long way from New Orleans they had beguiled tedium with jokes and friendly chaff; or with planning with elaborate detail what they were going to do now, after the war. A long journey, slowly, irregularly, yet persistently pushing northward. When they entered on Wisconsin territory they gave a cheer, and another when they reached Madison, but after that they sank into a dumb expectancy. Comrades dropped off at one or two points beyond, until there were only four or five left who were bound for La Crosse County.

Three of them were gaunt and brown, the fourth was gaunt and pale, with signs of fever and ague upon him. One had a great scar down his temple, one limped, and they all had unnaturally large, bright eyes, showing emaciation. There were no hands greeting them at the station, no banks of gayly dressed ladies waving handkerchiefs and shouting "Bravo!" as they came in on the caboose of a freight train into the towns that had cheered and blared at them on their way to war. As they looked out or stepped upon the platform for a moment, while the train stood at the station, the loafers looked at them indifferently. Their blue coats, dusty and grimy, were too familiar now to excite notice, much less a friendly word. They were the last of the army to return, and the loafers were surfeited with such sights.

The train jogged forward so slowly that it seemed likely to be midnight before they should reach La Crosse. The little squad grumbled and swore, but it was no use; the train would not hurry, and, as a matter of fact, it was nearly two o'clock when the engine whistled "down brakes."

All of the group were farmers, living in districts several miles out of the town, and all were poor.

"Now, boys," said Private Smith, he of the fever and ague, "we are landed in La Crosse in the night. We've got to stay somewhere till mornin'. Now I ain't got no two dollars to waste on a hotel. I've got a wife and children, so I'm goin' to roost on a bench and take the cost of a bed out of my hide."

"Same here," put in one of the other men. "Hide'll grow on again, dollars'll come hard. It's going to be mighty hot skirmishin' to find a dollar these days."

"Don't think they'll be a deputation of citizens waitin' to 'scort us to a hotel, eh?" said another. His sarcasm was too obvious to require an answer.

Smith went on, "Then at daybreak we'll start for home—at least, I will."

"Well, I'll be dummed if I'll take two dollars out o'*my* hide," one of the younger men said. "I'm goin' to a hotel, ef I don't never lay up a cent."

"That'll do f'r you," said Smith; "but if you had a wife an' three young uns dependin' on yeh—"

"Which I ain't, thank the Lord! and don't intend havin' while the court knows itself."

The station was deserted, chill, and dark, as they came into it at exactly a quarter to two in the morning. Lit by the oil lamps that flared a dull red light over the dingy benches, the waiting room was not an inviting place. The younger man went off to look up a hotel, while the rest remained and pre-pared to camp down on the floor and benches. Smith was attended to tenderly by the other men, who spread their blankets on the bench for him, and, by robbing themselves, made quite a comfortable bed, though the narrowness of the bench made his sleeping precarious.

It was chill, though August, and the two men, sitting with bowed heads, grew stiff with cold and weariness, and were forced to rise now and again and walk about to warm their stiffened limbs. It did not occur to them, probably, to contrast their coming home with their going forth, or with the coming home of the generals, colonels, or even captains—but to Private Smith, at any rate there came a sickness at heart almost deadly as he lay there on his hard bed and went over his situation.

In the deep of the night, lying on a board in the town where he had enlisted three years ago, all elation and enthusiasm gone out of him, he faced the fact that with the joy of homecoming was already mingled the bitter juice of care. He saw himself sick, worn out, taking up the work on his half-cleared farm, the inevitable mortgage standing ready with open jaw to swallow half his earnings. He had given three years of his life for a mere pittance of pay, and now—

Morning dawned at last, slowly, with a pale yellow dome of light rising silently above the bluffs, which stand like some huge storm-devastated castle, just east of the city. Out to the left the great river swept on its massive yet silent way to the south. Blue-jays called across the water from hillside to hillside through the clear, beautiful air, and hawks began to skim the tops of the hills. The older men were astir early, but Private Smith had fallen at last into a sleep, and they went out without waking him. He lay on his knapsack, his gaunt face turned toward the ceiling, his hands clasped on his breast, with a curious pathetic effect of weakness and appeal.

An engine switching near woke him at last, and he slowly sat up and stared about. He looked out of the window and saw that the sun was lightening the hills across the river. He rose and brushed his hair as well as he could, folded his blankets up, and went out to find his companions. They stood gazing silently at the river and at the hills.

"Looks natcher'l, don't it?" they said, as he came out.

"That's what it does," he replied, "An it looks good. D' yeh see that peak?" He pointed at a beautiful symmetrical peak, rising like a slightly truncated cone, so high that it seemed the very highest of them all. It was touched by the morning sun and it glowed like a beacon, and a light scarf of gray morning fog was rolling up its shadowed side.

"My farm's just beyond that. Now, if I can only ketch a ride, we'll be home by dinner-time."

"I'm talkin' about breakfast," said one of the others.

"I guess it's one more meal o'hardtack f'r me," said Smith.

They foraged around, and finally found a restaurant with a sleepy old German behind the counter, and procured some coffee, which they drank to wash down their hardtack.

"Time'll come," said Smith, holding up a piece by the corner, "when this'll be a curiosity."

"I hope to God it will! I bet I've chawed hardtack enough to shingle every house in the coolly. I've chawed it when my lampers was down, and when they wasn't. I've took it dry, soaked, and mashed. I've had it wormy, musty, sour, and blue-mouldy. I've had it in little bits and big bits, 'fore coffee an' after coffee. I'm ready f'r a change. I'd like t' git holt jest about now o'some of the hot biscuits my wife c'n make when she lays herself out f'r company."

"Well, if you set there gabblin', you'll never *see* yer wife."

"Come on," said Private Smith. "Wait a moment, boys; less take suthin'. It's on me." He led them to the rusty tin dipper which hung on a nail beside the wooden water-pail, and they grinned and drank. Then shouldering their blankets and muskets, which they were "takin' home to the boys," they struck out on their last march.

"They called that coffee Jayvy," grumbled one of them, "but it never went by the road where government Jayvy resides. I reckon I know coffee from peas."

They kept together on the road along the turnpike, and up the winding road by the river, which they followed for some miles. The river was very lovely, curving down along its sandy beds, pausing now and then under broad basswood trees, or running in dark, swift, silent currents under tangles of wild grapevines, and drooping alders, and haw trees. At one of these lovely spots the three vets sat down on the thick green sward to rest, "on Smith's account." The leaves of the trees were as fresh and green as in June, the jays called cheery greetings to them, and kingfishers darted to and fro with swooping, noiseless flight.

"I tell yeh, boys, this knocks the swamps of Loueesiana into kingdom come."

"You bet. All they c'n raise down there is snakes, niggers, and p'rticler hell."

"An' fighting men," put in the older man.

"An' fightin' men. If I had a good hook an' line I'd sneak a pick'rel out o' that pond. Say, remember that time I shot that alligator—"

"I guess we'd better be crawlin' along," interrupted Smith, rising and shouldering his knapsack, with considerable effort, which he tried to hide.

"Say, Smith, lemme give you a lift on that."

"I guess I c'n manage," said Smith, grimly.

"Course. But, yo' see, I may not have a chance right off to pay yeh back for the times you've carried my gun and hull caboodle. Say, now, gimme that gun, anyway."

"All right, if yeh feel like it, Jim," Smith replied, and they trudged along doggedly in the sun, which was getting higher and hotter each half-mile.

"Ain't it queer there ain't no teams comin' along," said Smith, after a long silence.

"Well, no, seein's it's Sunday."

"By jinks, that's a fact. It *is* Sunday. I'll git home in time f'r dinner, sure!" he exulted. "She don't hev dinner usually till about *one* on Sundays." And he fell into a muse, in which he smiled.

"Well, I'll git home jest about six o'clock, jest about when the boys are milkin' the cows," said old Jim Cranby. "I'll step into the barn, an' then I'll say: *'Heah!* why ain't this milkin' done before this time o' day?' An' then won't they yell!" he added, slapping his thigh in great glee.

Smith went on. "I'll jest go up the path. Old Rover'll come down the road to meet me. He won't bark; he'll know me, an' he'll come down waggin' his tail an' showin' his teeth. That's his way of laughin'. An' so I'll walk up to the kitchen door, an' I'll say, *'Dinner* f'r a hungry man!' An' then she'll jump up, an'—"

He couldn't go on. His voice choked at the thought of it. Saunders, the third man, hardly uttered a word, but walked silently behind the others. He had lost his wife the first year he was in the army. She died of pneumonia, caught in the autumn rains while working in the fields in his place.

They plodded along till at last they came to a parting of the ways. To the right the road continued up the main valley; to the left it went over the big ridge.

"Well, boys," began Smith, as they grounded their muskets and looked away up the valley, "here's where we shake hands. We've marched together a good many miles, an' now I s'pose we're done."

"Yes, I don't think we'll do any more of it f'r a while. I don't want to, I know."

"I hope I'll see yeh once in a while, boys, to talk over old times."

"Of course," said Saunders, whose voice trembled a little, too. "It ain't *exactly* like dyin'." They all found it hard to look at each other.

"But we'd ought'r go home with you," said Cranby. "You'll never climb that ridge with all them things on yer back."

"Oh, I'm all right! Don't worry about me. Every step takes me nearer home, yeh see. Well, good-by, boys."

They shook hands. "Good-by. Good luck!"

"Same to you. Lemme know how you find things at home."

"Good-by."

"Good-by."

He turned once before they passed out of sight, and waved his cap, and they did the same, and all yelled. Then all marched away with their long, steady, loping, veteran step. The solitary climber in blue walked on for a time, with his mind filled with the kindness of his comrades, and musing upon the many wonderful days they had had together in camp and field.

He thought of his chum, Billy Tripp. Poor Billy! A "minie" ball fell into his breast one day, fell wailing like a cat, and tore a great ragged hole in his heart. He looked forward to a sad scene with Billy's mother and sweetheart. They would want to know all about it. He tried to recall all that Billy had said, and the particulars of it, but there was little to remember, just that wild wailing sound high in the air, a dull slap, a short, quick, expulsive groan, and the boy lay with his face in the dirt in the ploughed field they were marching across.

That was all. But all the scenes he had since been through had not dimmed the horror, the terror of that moment, when his boy comrade fell, with only a breath between a laugh and a death-groan. Poor handsome Billy! Worth millions of dollars was his young life.

These sombre recollections gave way at length to more cheerful feelings as he began to approach his home coolly. The fields and houses grew familiar, and in one or two he was greeted by people seated in the doorways. But he was in no mood to talk, and pushed on steadily, though he stopped and accepted a drink of milk once at the well-side of a neighbor.

The sun was burning hot on that slope, and his step grew slower, in spite of his iron resolution. He sat down several times to rest. Slowly he crawled up the rough, reddish-brown road, which wound along the hillside, under great trees, through dense groves of jack oaks, with tree-tops far below him on his left hand, and the hills far above him on his right. He crawled along like some minute, wingless variety of fly.

He ate some hardtack, sauced with wild berries, when he reached the summit of the ridge, and sat there for some time, looking down into his home coolly.

Sombre, pathetic figure! His wide, round, gray eyes gazing down into the beautiful valley, seeing and not seeing, the splendid cloud-shadows sweeping over the western hills and across the green and yellow wheat far below. His head drooped forward on his palm, his shoulders took on a tired stoop, his cheek-bones showed painfully. An observer might have said, "He is looking down upon his own grave."

Chapter 2

Sunday comes in a Western wheat harvest with such sweet and sudden relaxation to man and beast that it would be holy for that reason, if for no other, and Sundays are usually fair in harvest-time. As one goes out into the field in the hot morning sunshine, with no sound abroad save the crickets and the indescribably pleasant silken rustling of the ripened grain, the reaper and the very sheaves in the stubble seem to be resting, dreaming.

Around the house, in the shade of the trees, the men sit, smoking, dozing, or reading the papers, while the women, never resting, move about at the housework. The men eat on Sundays about the same as on other days, and breakfast is no sooner over and out of the way than dinner begins.

But at the Smith farm there were no men dozing or reading. Mrs. Smith was alone with her three children, Mary, nine, Tommy, six, and little Ted, just past four. Her farm, rented to a neighbor, lay at the head of a coolly or narrow gully, made at some far-off post-glacial period by the vast and angry floods of water which gullied these tremendous furrows in the level prairie—furrows so deep that undisturbed portions of the original level rose like hills on either side, rose to quite considerable mountains.

The chickens wakened her as usual that Sabbath morning from dreams of her absent husband, from whom she had not heard for weeks. The shadows drifted over the hills, down the slopes, across the wheat, and up the opposite wall in leisurely way, as if, being Sunday, they could take it easy also. The fowls clustered about the housewife as she went out into the yard. Fuzzy little chickens swarmed out from the coops, where their clucking and perpetually disgruntled mothers tramped about, petulantly thrusting their heads through the spaces between the slats.

A cow called in a deep, musical bass, and a calf answered from a little pen near by, and a pig scurried guiltily out of the cabbages. Seeing all this, seeing the pig in the cabbages, the tangle of grass in the garden, the broken fence which she had mended again and again—the little woman, hardly more than a girl, sat down and cried. The bright Sabbath morning was only a mockery without him!

A few years ago they had bought this farm, paying part, mortgaging the rest in the usual way. Edward Smith was a man of terrible energy. He worked ''nights and Sundays,'' as the saying goes, to clear the farm of its brush and of its insatiate mortgage! In the midst of his Herculean struggle came the call for volunteers, and with the grim and unselfish devotion to his country which made the Eagle Brigade able to ''whip its weight in wild-cats,'' he threw down his scythe and grub-axe, turned his cattle loose, and became a blue-coated cog in a vast machine for killing men, and not thistles. While the millionaire sent his money to England for safe-keeping, this man, with his girl-wife and three babies, left them on a mortgaged farm, and went away to fight for an idea. It was foolish, but it was sublime for all that.

That was three years before, and the young wife, sitting on the well-curb on this bright Sabbath harvest morning, was righteously rebellious. It seemed to her that she had borne her share of the country's sorrow. Two brothers had been killed,

the renter in whose hands her husband had left the farm had
proved a villain; one year the farm had been without crops,
and now the overripe grain was waiting the tardy hand of the
neighbor who had rented it, and who was cutting his own
grain first.

About six weeks before, she had received a letter saying,
"We'll be discharged in a little while." But no other word
had come from him. She had seen by the papers that his army
was being discharged, and from day to day other soldiers
slowly percolated in blue streams back into the State and
country, but still *her* hero did not return.

Each week she had told the children that he was coming,
and she had watched the road so long that it had become
unconscious; and as she stood at the well, or by the kitchen
door, her eyes were fixed unthinkingly on the road that wound
down the coolly.

Nothing wears on the human soul like waiting. If the
stranded mariner, searching the sun-bright seas, could once
give up hope of a ship, that horrible grinding on his brain
would cease. It was this waiting, hoping, on the edge of despair, that gave Emma Smith no rest.

Neighbors said, with kind intentions: "He's sick, maybe,
an' can't start north just yet. He'll come along one o' these
days."

"Why don't he write?" was her question, which silenced
them all. This Sunday morning it seemed to her as if she
could not stand it longer. The house seemed intolerably
lonely. So she dressed the little ones in their best calico
dresses and home-made jackets, and, closing up the house,
set off down the coolly to old Mother Gray's.

"Old Widder Gray" lived at the "mouth of the coolly."
She was a widow woman with a large family of stalwart boys
and laughing girls. She was the visible incarnation of hospi-
tality and optimistic poverty. With Western open-heartedness
she fed every mouth that asked food of her, and worked
herself to death as cheerfully as her girls danced in the neighborhood harvest dances.

She waddled down the path to meet Mrs. Smith with a broad smile on her face.

"Oh, you little dears! Come right to your granny. Gimme me a kiss! Come right in, Mis' Smith. How are yeh, anyway? Nice mornin', ain't it? Come in an' set down. Everything's in a clutter, but that won't scare you any."

She led the way into the best room, a sunny, square room, carpeted with a faded and patched rag carpet, and papered with white-and-green wall-paper, where a few faded effigies of dead members of the family hung in variously sized oval walnut frames. The house resounded with singing, laughter, whistling, tramping of heavy boots, and riotous scufflings. Half-grown boys came to the door and crooked their fingers at the children, who ran out, and were soon heard in the midst of the fun.

"Don't s'pose you've heard from Ed?" Mrs. Smith shook her head. "He'll turn up some day, when you ain't lookin' for 'm." The good old soul had said that so many times that poor Mrs. Smith derived no comfort from it any longer.

"Liz heard from Al the other day. He's comin' some day this week. Anyhow, they expect him."

"Did he say anything of—"

"No, he didn't," Mrs. Gray admitted. "But then it was only a short letter, anyhow. Al ain't much for writin', anyhow.—But come out and see my new cheese. I tell yeh, I don't believe I ever had better luck in my life. If Ed should come, I want you should take him up a piece of this cheese."

It was beyond human nature to resist the influence of that noisy, hearty, loving household, and in the midst of the singing and laughing the wife forgot her anxiety, for the time at least, and laughed and sang with the rest.

About eleven o'clock a wagon-load more drove up to the door, and Bill Gray, the widow's oldest son, and his whole family, from Sand Lake Coolly, piled out amid a good-natured uproar. Every one talked at once, except Bill, who sat in the wagon with his wrists on his knees, a straw in his mouth, and an amused twinkle in his blue eyes.

"Ain't heard nothin' o' Ed, I s'pose?" he asked in a kind of bellow. Mrs. Smith shook her head. Bill, with a delicacy very striking in such a great giant, rolled his quid in his mouth, and said:

"Didn't know but you had. I hear two or three of the Sand Lake boys are comin'. Left New Orleans some time this week. Didn't write nothin' about Ed, but no news is good news in such cases, Mother always says."

"Well, go put out yer team," said Mrs. Gray, "an' go'n bring me in some taters, an', Sim, you go see if you c'n find some corn. Sadie, you put on the water to bile. Come now, hustle yer boots, all o' yeh. If I feed this yer crowd, we've got to have some raw materials. If y' think I'm goin' to feed yeh on pie—you're just mightily mistaken."

The children went off into the field, the girls put dinner on to boil, and then went to change their dresses and fix their hair. "Somebody might come," they said.

"Land sakes, I *hope* not! I don't know where in time I'd set 'em, 'less they'd eat at the second table," Mrs. Gray laughed, in pretended dismay.

The two older boys, who had served their time in the army, lay out on the grass before the house, and whittled and talked desultorily about the war and the crops, and planned buying a threshing-machine. The older girls and Mrs. Smith helped enlarge the table and put on the dishes, talking all the time in that cheery, incoherent, and meaningful way a group of such women have,—a conversation to be taken for its spirit rather than for its letter, though Mrs. Gray at last got the ear of them all and dissertated at length on girls.

"Girls in love ain' no use in the whole blessed week," she said. "Sundays they're a-lookin' down the road, expectin' he'll *come*. Sunday afternoons they can't think o' nothin' else, 'cause he's *here*. Monday mornin's they're sleepy and kind o' dreamy and slimpsy, and good f'r nothin' on Tuesday and Wednesday. Thursday they git absent-minded, an' begin to look off toward Sunday agin, an' mope aroun' and let the dishwater git cold, right under their noses. Friday they break dishes, an' go off in the best room an' snivel, an' look out o' the winder. Saturdays they have queer spurts o' workin' like all p'ssessed, an' spurts o' frizzin' their hair. An' Sunday they begin it all over agin.''

The girls giggled and blushed, all through this tirade from their mother, their broad faces and powerful frames anything but suggestive of lackadaisical sentiment. But Mrs. Smith said:

"Now, Mrs. Gray, I hadn't ought to stay to dinner. You've got—"

"Now you set right down! If any of them girls' beaus comes, they'll have to take what's left, that's all. They ain't s'posed to have much appetite, nohow. No, you're goin' to stay if they starve, an' they ain't no danger o' that.''

At one o'clock the long table was piled with boiled potatoes, cords of boiled corn on the cob, squash and pumpkin pies, hot biscuit, sweet pickles, bread and butter, and honey. Then one of the girls took down a conch-shell from a nail, and going to the door, blew a long, fine, free blast, that showed there was no weakness of lungs in her ample chest.

Then the children came out of the forest of corn, out of the creek, out of the loft of the barn, and out of the garden.

"They come to their feed f'r all the world jest like the pigs when y' holler 'poo-ee!' See 'em scoot!" laughed Mrs. Gray, every wrinkle on her face shining with delight.

The men shut up their jack-knives, and surrounded the horse-trough to souse their faces in the cold, hard water, and in a few moments the table was filled with a merry crowd, and a row of wistful-eyed youngsters circled the kitchen wall, where they stood first on one leg and then on the other, in impatient hunger.

"Now pitch in, Mrs. Smith," said Mrs. Gray, presiding over the table. "You know these men critters. They'll eat every grain of it, if yeh give 'em a chance. I swan, they're made o' India-rubber, their stomachs is, I know it."

"Half to eat to work," said Bill, gnawing a cob with a swift, circular motion that rivalled a corn-sheller in results.

"More like workin' to eat," put in one of the girls, with a giggle. "More eat'n work with you."

"*You* needn't say anything, Net. Any one that'll eat seven ears—"

"I didn't, no such thing. You piled your cobs on my plate."

"That'll do to tell Ed Varney. It won't go down here where we know yeh."

"Good land! Eat all yeh want! They's plenty more in the fiel's, but I can't afford to give you young uns tea. The tea is for us women-folks, and 'specially f'r Mis' Smith an' Bill's wife. We're a-goin' to tell fortunes by it."

One by one the men filled up and shoved back, and one by one the children slipped into their places, and by two o'clock the women alone remained around the débris-covered table, sipping their tea and telling fortunes.

As they got well down to the grounds in the cup, they shook them with a circular motion in the hand, and then turned them bottom-side-up quickly in the saucer, then twirled them three or four times one way, and three or four times the other, during a breathless pause. Then Mrs. Gray lifted the cup, and, gazing into it with profound gravity, pronounced the impending fate.

It must be admitted that, to a critical observer, she had abundant preparation for hitting close to the mark, as when she told the girls that "somebody was comin'." "It's a man," she went on gravely. "He is cross-eyed—"

"Oh, you hush!" cried Nettie.

"He has red hair, and is death on b'iled corn and hot biscuit."

The others shrieked with delight.

"But he's goin' to get the mitten, that red-headed feller is, for I see another feller comin' up behind him."

"Oh, lemme see, lemme see!" cried Nettie.

"Keep off," said the priestess, with a lofty gesture. "His hair is black. He don't eat so much, and he works more."

The girls exploded in a shriek of laughter, and pounded their sister on the back.

At last came Mrs. Smith's turn, and she was trembling with excitement as Mrs. Gray again composed her jolly face to what she considered a proper solemnity of expression.

"Somebody is comin' to *you*," she said, after a long pause. "He's got a musket on his back. He's a soldier. He's almost here. See?"

She pointed at two little tea-stems, which really formed a faint suggestion of a man with a musket on his back. He had climbed nearly to the edge of the cup. Mrs. Smith grew pale with excitement. She trembled so she could hardly hold the cup in her hand as she gazed into it.

"It's Ed," cried the old woman. "He's on the way home. Heavens an' earth! There he is now!" She turned and waved her hand out toward the road. They rushed to the door to look where she pointed.

A man in a blue coat, with a musket on his back, was toiling slowly up the hill on the sun-bright, dusty road, toiling slowly, with bent head half hidden by a heavy knapsack. So tired it seemed that walking was indeed a process of falling. So eager to get home he would not stop, would not look aside, but plodded on, amid the cries of the locusts, the welcome of the crickets, and the rustle of the yellow wheat. Getting back to God's country, and his wife and babies!

Laughing, crying, trying to call him and the children at the same time, the little wife, almost hysterical, snatched her hat and ran out into the yard. But the soldier had disappeared over the hill into the hollow beyond, and, by the time she had found the children, he was too far away for her voice to reach him. And, besides, she was not sure it was her husband, for he had not turned his head at their shouts. This seemed so strange. Why didn't he stop to rest at his old neighbor's house? Tortured by hope and doubt, she hurried up the coolly as fast as she could push the baby wagon, the blue-coated figure just ahead pushing steadily, silently forward up the coolly.

When the excited, panting little group came in sight of the
gate they saw the blue-coated figure standing, leaning upon
the rough rail fence, his chin on his palms, gazing at the
empty house. His knapsack, canteen, blankets, and musket lay
upon the dusty grass at his feet.

He was like a man lost in a dream. His wide, hungry eyes
devoured the scene. The rough lawn, the little unpainted
house, the field of clear yellow wheat behind it, down across
which streamed the sun, now almost ready to touch the high
hill to the west, the crickets crying merrily, a cat on the fence
near by, dreaming, unmindful of the stranger in blue—

How peaceful it all was. O God! How far removed from
all camps, hospitals, battle lines. A little cabin in a Wisconsin
coolly, but it was majestic in its peace. How did he ever leave
it for those years of tramping, thirsting, killing?

Trembling, weak with emotion, her eyes on the silent figure, Mrs. Smith hurried up to the fence. Her feet made no
noise in the dust and grass, and they were close upon him
before he knew of them. The oldest boy ran a little ahead.
He will never forget that figure, that face. It will always remain as something epic, that return of the private. He fixed
his eyes on the pale face covered with a ragged beard.

"Who *are* you, sir?" asked the wife, or, rather, started to
ask, for he turned, stood a moment, and then cried:

"Emma!"

"Edward!"

The children stood in a curious row to see their mother kiss
this bearded, strange man, the elder girl sobbing sympathetically with her mother. Illness had left the soldier partly deaf,
and this added to the strangeness of his manner.

But the youngest child stood away, even after the girl had
recognized her father and kissed him. The man turned then
to the baby, and said in a curiously unpaternal tone:

"Come here, my little man; don't you know me?" But the
baby backed away under the fence and stood peering at him
critically.

"My little man!" What meaning in those words! This baby

seemed like some other woman's child, and not the infant he had left in his wife's arms. The war had come between him and his baby—he was only a strange man to him, with big eyes; a soldier, with mother hanging to his arm, and talking in a loud voice.

"And this is Tom," the private said, drawing the oldest boy to him. *"He'll* come and see me. *He* knows his poor old pap when he comes home from the war."

The mother heard the pain and reproach in his voice and hastened to apologize.

"You've changed so, Ed. He can't know yeh. This is Papa, Teddy; come and kiss him—Tom and Mary do. Come, won't you?" But Teddy still peered through the fence with solemn eyes, well out of reach. He resembled a half-wild kitten that hesitates, studying the tones of one's voice.

"I'll fix him," said the soldier, and sat down to undo his knapsack, out of which he drew three enormous and very red apples. After giving one to each of the older children, he said:

"Now I guess he'll come. Eh, my little man? Now come see your pap."

Teddy crept slowly under the fence, assisted by the over-zealous Tommy, and a moment later was kicking and squalling in his father's arms. Then they entered the house, into the sitting room, poor, bare, art-forsaken little room, too, with its rag carpet, its square clock, and its two or three chromes and pictures from *Harper's Weekly* pinned about.

"Emma, I'm all tired out," said Private Smith, as he flung himself down on the carpet as he used to do, while his wife brought a pillow to put under his head, and the children stood about munching their apples.

"Tommy, you run and get me a pan of chips, and Mary, you get the tea-kettle on, and I'll go and make some biscuit."

And the soldier talked. Question after question he poured forth about the crops, the cattle, the renter, the neighbors. He slipped his heavy government brogan shoes off his poor, tired, blistered feet, and lay out with utter, sweet relaxation. He was a free man again, no longer a soldier under a command. At supper he stopped once, listened and smiled. "That's old Spot. I know her voice. I s'pose that's her calf out there in the pen. I can't milk her to-night, though. I'm too tired. But I tell you, I'd like a drink of her milk. What's become of old Rove?"

"He died last winter. Poisoned, I guess." There was a moment of sadness for them all. It was some time before the husband spoke again, in a voice that trembled a little.

"Poor old feller! He'd 'a' known me half a mile away. I expected him to come down the hill to meet me. It 'ud 'a' been more like comin' home if I could 'a' seen him comin' down the road an' waggin' his tail, an' laughin' that way he has. I tell yeh, it kind o' took hold o' me to see the blinds down an' the house shut up."

"But, yeh see, we—expected you'd write again 'fore you started. And then we thought we'd see you if you *did* come," she hastened to explain.

"Well, I ain't worth a cent on writin'. Besides, it's just as well yeh didn't know when I was comin'. I tell you, it sounds good to hear them chickens out there, an' turkeys, an' the crickets. Do you know they don't have just the same kind o' crickets down South? Who's Sam hired t' help cut yer grain?"

"The Ramsey boys."

"Looks like a good crop; but I'm afraid I won't do much gettin' it cut. This cussed fever an' ague has got me down pretty low. I don't know when I'll get rid of it. I'll bet I've took twenty-five pounds of quinine if I've taken a bit. Gimme another biscuit. I tell yeh, they taste good, Emma. I ain't had anything like it—Say, if you'd 'a' hear'd me braggin' to th' boys about your butter 'n' biscuits I'll bet your ears 'ud' 'a' burnt."

The private's wife colored with pleasure. "Oh, you're always a-braggin' about your things. Everybody makes good butter."

"Yes; old lady Snyder, for instance."

"Oh, well, she ain't to be mentioned. She's Dutch."

"Or old Mis' Snively. One more cup o' tea, Mary. That's my girl! I'm feeling better already. I just b'lieve the matter with me is, I'm *starved*."

This was a delicious hour, one long to be remembered. They were like lovers again. But their tenderness, like that of a typical American family, found utterance in tones, rather than in words. He was praising her when praising her biscuit, and she knew it. They grew soberer when he showed where he had been struck, one ball burning the back of his hand, one cutting away a lock of hair from his temple, and one passing through the calf of his leg. The wife shuddered to think how near she had come to being a soldier's widow. Her waiting no longer seemed hard. This sweet, glorious hour effaced it all.

Then they rose, and all went out into the garden and down to the barn. He stood beside her while she milked old Spot. They began to plan fields and crops for next year.

His farm was weedy and encumbered, a rascally renter had run away with his machinery (departing between two days), his children needed clothing, the years were coming upon him, he was sick and emaciated, but his heroic soul did not quail. With the same courage with which he had faced his Southern march he entered upon a still more hazardous future.

Oh, that mystic hour! The pale man with big eyes standing there by the well, with his young wife by his side. The vast moon swinging above the eastern peaks, the cattle winding down the pasture slopes with jangling bells, the crickets singing, the stars blooming out sweet and far and serene; the katydids rhythmically calling, the little turkeys crying querulously, as they settled to roost in the poplar tree near the open gate. The voices at the well drop lower, the little ones nestle in their father's arms at last, and Teddy falls asleep there.

The common soldier of the American volunteer army had returned. His war with the South was over, and his fight, his daily running fight with nature and against the injustice of his fellowmen, was begun again.

TOMBSTONES ARE FREE TO QUITTERS

An Original Western Story

—

Gary Lovisi

Fast Jake was the latest one to turn up dead. Gunned down by someone even faster, a low-down snake who called himself Tucson Jack. Though I was sure he'd never been to Tucson and his name wasn't Jack neither. Didn't matter though, not in this town. No one questioned any of it, least of all the law.

So there we all were, standing on the rough plank sidewalk watching as Old Man Furley, Painless Dental Extractions, Close Shaves, and Prime Undertaking of all Kinds and for All Occasions, slowly rode down the dusty street in his old black undertaking wagon. He looked like the figure of death himself.

In back of his wagon stood a moderate-size tombstone, roughly cut, certainly not Furley's best work. It was a free job for the newly deceased, being paid for by the town fathers of Four Angels. Four men had founded the town long ago, before the railroad came and brought prosperity: the sheriff, his deputy, the judge, and even Old Furley. These worthies had a fund to pay Furley for the burial and tombstone of people who died as paupers. I guess they all, as God-fearing citizens and some kind of Christians, tried to do the proper thing when the deceased had no money. Or so they said.

I knew different.

You see, Fast Jake Whatever-his-name-was, was plum busted broke upon his death. For Jake, he'd quit this life rather unexpectedly, and not of his own choosing, but at least his tombstone was free and he'd get a boot hill grave to rest in peace underneath it.

I always figured, a man comes into this world naked with nothing, and a town like Four Angels will make sure you go on out the same way. If you die broke, a quitter, at least you get a tombstone, a marker all complimentary and at no charge.

So we all watched as Furley rode by in that creaking, moaning wagon of his. I could see where he'd cut into the limestone marker, "FAST JAKE—Died hear this day 12 June 1881, Kilted by Tucson Jack Reynolds."

We all knew Tucson Jack had paid Furley extra for that last bit. Advertising, no doubt.

"I'll tell you, boy . . ." Archie, Sheriff Lee's deputy and a bigmouth drunk said to me, "here in this town, tombstones is free to quitters. Appears Fast Jake turned out to be just another quitter."

"How can you tell, Archie?"

The deputy glared at me, said, "Why, boy, he dead, ain't he!"

Then he laughed and walked—actually stumbled—away.

I kinda nodded. I didn't need no trouble with Deputy Archie. He'd been drinking heavy, even at that time of the morning, and I could see the meanness was coming upon him already. He was a man who did not need excuses.

Just before this Fast Jake died, I had the opportunity to be near him, me being a saloon swamper, it was just natural for me to be ordered to clean up the mess. But Jake weren't quite dead yet, and he half whispered, half cried in my ear, "I lived tough all my life. Never giving quarter, never asking it. No complaints. I thought when it was my time and the curtain come down upon me, I'd go out like a man, cussing and full of spit, but look at me! Look at me! I'm scared-terrifying of dying. I'm a crying baby! A damn crying baby! I'm not going out like a man, I'm going out like a damn pussy . . . !''

I gently closed his eyes, whispered to him, "It's okay, Jake. You're allowed. When a man dies, seems to me he can go out any damn way he pleases. Everyone does. You ain't the first I seen. Won't be the last. Some of us come into this world crying babies and we leave it crying like a baby, too. Only be pain, in between all that bawling. It ain't like it's a big deal.''

That's what I told Jake at the time, before things turned on me. Then I wasn't so sure. It happened when Deputy Archie had his important talk with Sheriff Jackson Lee.

Yeah, Jackson Lee of the old-time Virginia Lees, or so he always claimed and reminded me, and Judge Fenton Rogers. He was a mean one, both of them was, actually. In fact, all three of them was hard-ass, nasty cusses, and dangerous, the worst men in Four Angels. The four angels themselves. Problem was, they ran the town and everyone in it, and the town had a certain reputation for having a real lot of boot hill burials. I was thinking tombstones were the only thing free in Four Angels.

Sheriff Lee said to me, "Cole?" That's my name, Ed Cole. He said, "I'm gonna haveta arrest you for the murder of . . . now let's see . . .'' He thought a moment, looked over to Archie.

Archie said, "Ah, That'd be for the murder of Tom Jenkins of the Silverado Mine, turned up dead this morning. We all know you be the one that saw him last, and that you did it, Ed.''

Judge Rogers nodded sagely, said, "Take Ed Cole into custody, boys. We'll have a proper court tomorrow, and do right by him, then hang his mangy hide by evening for his dastardly, vile deed.''

I froze up, shocked. I didn't murder Jenkins, but in a town like Four Angels that didn't matter at all. That was the way they always did things in that town. I quickly found myself put in irons and marched to the town jail. Hearing the pounding drumbeat of my oncoming doom with every step my booted feet took in the dust and dirt of the streets of Four Angels.

Later Old Man Furley explained to me in my cell—while he was busy measuring me for a coffin, his cheapest model, no doubt—"You got no kin here, Ed. No one to speak up for you, no one to step up and fight for you, if need be. And you is in need. But you got no kin."

I nodded. Doomed.

"Four Angels, you gotta know, boy," he continued, "is the most kin-conscious town ever was. Everyone here is a son, cousin, or uncle of everyone else. Sheriff Lee, Archie, Judge Rogers, even myself, all related here. You're an outsider, boy. A far away outsider at that!"

I nodded, too stunned to say much, knowing that in this town it would not do the least bit of good to complain. I realized too late Furley was right. Judge Fenton Rogers would slam down that gavel tomorrow with a loud pounding when my case was disposed of, as final as that damn trap would open for me when they'd be stretching my neck for the murder of Tom Jenkins. Which I did not do. And by the by, it did not seem to matter a tinker's damn in Four Angels to anyone but me.

"Course, Ed, you know it was Archie kilted Tom Jenkins, to get control of his silver mine," Furley said with a sly wink, as he carefully calibrated me with a tape measure. I stood like a statue in that cell before him, trying to think on what to do next. And coming up busted.

"Archie?" I muttered. "But, how . . . ?"

"How's not important, boy. You got no kin here. No one to stand up for you with serious backing. That means guns, my boy. Ain't no one going up against the law and the powers that be, here. You're going down because knowing sumpting and getting it out and believed is two very far apart things sometimes. Especially in this here town. Especially for your kind."

I said, "I have no kin and no money either, Furley."

"Don't let that worry you, son. Here in Four Angels, tombstones is free. Even if you ain't a quitter yet."

And that was it, cut and dried. I'd be dead by this time tomorrow night. Except, later that evening, Gambling Frank Walsh came into town.

Now you see, this Walsh was a half-breed gambling man from Indian Territory, since his youthful days a tough hard case who had heard about my situation and taken some interest. After he took Sheriff Lee and Archie for a considerable sum of cash in a poker game at the Lucky Lady, Walsh let it be known that he didn't cotton to what was being done to me. From what I heard, he was truly serious about saying it.

They said later he showed sharp gold teeth, then he let everyone get a good gander at his Colt revolver and the notches thereupon.

That kinda got Sheriff Lee and Archie a bit concerned.

Next morning, Gambling Frank Walsh was found dead, shot in the back, and robbed of his winnings by the way, in a hotel room in the Lucky Lady Saloon.

My hope shattered as Furley came in and told me the news. Then he cheered up considerably as he made to leave, telling me, "Well, gotta go now, young fella; business in this town is just too damn good lately. Keeping me plum busy. Gotta measure Gambling Frank Walsh for his final resting. Just one more quitter, it appears. Appears lots of quitters in this here town."

I sure nodded about that.

Furley laughed, said, "Funny though, Walsh died without a red cent on him, I'm told. And him doing so well in poker and all just the other night before his demise. Oh well, you know what they say . . ."

"I ain't a quitter!" I shouted.

Furley just laughed harder as he walked down the hall from my cell, saying, "You got nothing to say on the matter, boy."

He was right.

However, I heard he wasn't laughing later on that day. It seemed my trial and subsequent hanging had been postponed by Judge Rogers. A very reluctant Judge Rogers, I was told.

You see, a new fella had come into town on the heels of Gambling Frank Walsh. A tracker. He was a mean one, scared Sheriff Lee, and that was no simple matter, and put the fear of death into Archie and Judge Rogers, too. No one wanted to mess with him. Yet.

He claimed to be my kin.

He said he was after Gambling Frank Walsh. He said he had a star but never showed it. No one dared ask, either. But he looked and sounded like a lawman, maybe even a Ranger, or one of them serious, hard-ass town-tamers you read about in dime novels: Hickock, Brady, Wyatt Earp before the O.K. Corral. He said his name was Cole. He never let on whether that was his first or last name. No one asked for clarification.

"I been after Walsh. I'm bringing his no-good body back with me, Sheriff," Cole said. Then he looked square in Lee's face and said, "and I'm here to tell you—I've heard all about your lousy little town. Let my kin out of jail!"

Sheriff Jackson Lee was unsure just how to take all this. He didn't think it too wise to go up direct against a man like Cole, but there were other ways.

Lee was considering these when Cole took the initiative and forced the sheriff and Archie, who by the way was behind the bar with Clarence's double-barrel aimed at Cole's back, which did no good either for Archie at all.

Cole was fast and bold, and he was not backing down. He drew quick, faster than anyone ever saw before, dropped Archie with a bullet in the brain, then pistol-whipped the sheriff, took off his badge, and stomped it underfoot of his silver-spurred boot.

Sheriff Lee was white as a sheet with fear and rage. The Lucky Lady cleared out and Old Judge Rogers looked like he'd damn near stroked himself to death. Old Man Furley did not appreciate the turn of events. He deftly pulled a small derringer, but Cole saw him in the mirror's reflection and dropped the undertaker faster than you could say "dead man."

Sheriff Lee choked out his next words. "What? Why?"

"He's my kin, I want him set free."

"I . . . don't unnerstand. He's not, he can't be no kin of yours. I mean, for christsakes, he's a Nigra boy!"

Cole's white face stayed blank, but his eyes burned with fire that put the fear of death right back into Sheriff Jackson Lee.

"I'm a-saying he's my kin. I always back up my words. You got a problem with that, *Sheriff?*" Cole barked that last word like it was a dirty cuss.

"No," Sheriff Jackson Lee squeaked.

"Good. Now, go get the boy and bring him here to me. Then, if you don't mind, we'll just ride on out of your stinking little town and you never need to see either of us again. But you hurt that boy, and I'm coming to hurt you."

Sheriff Jackson Lee understood completely, gulped nervously, and was off. He opened my cell, pushing me out the door, barking, "Now go! Git! Git out of town, git your damn black ass out of our town! Git youself begone, and don't you ever come back!"

Well, I took my sweetass time walking from the jail, across town, and finally over to the Lucky Lady. Everyone watching me, wondering. Myself foremost among them, if the truth be told.

I saw the man called Cole there waiting for me. He took my measure, I took his. He was a serious fellow. A killer, for sure. Dangerous as all hell, but not to me. I could tell.

I walked over, nodded, "Thanks, but I think you are mistaken for me being any kin to a white man like you, mister."

He didn't smile; he just looked at me and said, "Son, we be kin for sure. No doubt about it. Someday you'll understand blood and color is the *least* of what's important in this here world."

That's when Sheriff Lee made his move. Standing off to the side where he thought no one could see him, he quickly drew his Colt in an attempt to gun down Cole. Shoot him in the back.

I yelled in warning, Cole turned and dropped, missing Lee's bullet by inches, at the same time getting off one of his own in return that cut into the sheriff's heart and kilted him dead.

Cole got up, the Lucky Lady was empty. Silent.

"Sorry I had to do that," Cole said, "but the stupid bastard just wouldn't quit. I guess that type never quits."

"Well, he's a quitter now," I said and smiled. Then I went over and took all the money I could find out of the sheriff's pocket and put it in my own. I did the same with the corpses of Archie, Judge Rogers, and even Old Man Furley.

The man who called himself Cole watched me robbing the dead but said nothing.

I said, "In this town, tombstones are free to quitters. I just want to make sure these quitters get the burial they so righty deserve."

Cole smiled then.

And I knew then, whether black or white, we was kin for sure.

Of course the man who called himself Cole had been right, and he taught me well.

Now it's years later, and it's a funny thing, but I just heard they got this ignorant, white-trash, swamp rat up for murder in some backwater town over in Oregon. I had heard bad things about that town. Kinda like Four Angels used to be. I heard they buried a lot of people there, too.

I never been to Oregon.

And funny thing, I just know that hapless, helpless piece of turd didn't do it, another one with no kith nor kin to stand up for him, to be railroaded because no one took an interest.

Well, I was interested.

I smiled when the thought hit me about how surprised that ignorant, young, peckerwood was gonna be when I showed up in that redneck town of his to help him out . . .

. . . and claimed to be *his* kin!

THAT DAMN COWBOY!

—

Judy Alter

Each day the old man wheeled his chair out to the veranda and sat staring over the distant river and, farther, the purplish, faint mountains. Some days he sat as still as the landscape before him; others, when the wind swept across the plains and struck him forcefully, he would shift restlessly, long bony fingers stroking his white stubble of beard and pulling at his shaggy hair. But always, his eyes, intense and blue, seemed fixed on the river.

He rarely talked, and the family had grown accustomed to his silence. The grandchildren treated him dutifully, their parents a slight bit more tolerantly. Friends and neighbors, visiting the house, nearly ignored him, and everyone generally agreed that his mind was gone. "Addled with age," they called it. Still, he was the first thing newcomers to the small ranching community heard about. After all, he had been an artist—no, not exactly famous, but he had lived next door to Frederic Remington once.

But Rufus Jones wasn't really addled. It was just that in the years of his old age he had found the world less absorbing than his own interior battle. Retreating from everyday concerns, he tried, with a desperation born of old age, to puzzle out some reason for the turn of his life. He had to know why, before death closed the question forever.

Some days when the fire of anger was less strong in him, he would muse on the quirk of fate that led his son, Davey, to settle in Montana, bringing the then aged Rufus back to the land which had captivated him years ago.

I loved this country from that first trip . . . 1883, no '84, that time I came to follow the cavalry and do some field sketches. Remember thinking it was like the Scotch highlands . . . rolling hills covered with sage brush and in the distance, those great snowcapped mountains . . . only this was grander, more immense . . . so much space that the very openness could make a man feel caught. And all that light and shade on the whole thing. My first sketches were failures. But they got better, got to the point I was proud of them, thought I had found my place, the subject that was all mine. I was going to be a famous Western artist. What happened?

Other days he would think about that damn cowboy, and the flames of bitterness would rise again within him. Too often, he recalled that day when he had first felt the heat of jealousy. It was in New York where he and the great Frederic Remington were neighbors and, in those days, pretty much equals in the artistic world. Both interested in the West, they often sat late at night sharing experiences, swapping Arizona stories for Montana. They tried to joke about their failures and bragged about the successes—the sale of a painting, the signing of a contract with *Harper's Weekly*. Rufus had never thought of Remington as greater or better than he, at least never until that day. He remembered that afternoon clearly, even now, some forty years later.

Young Davey came running home to tell me that Mr. Remington had a new pony. "And a silver-studded saddle and bridle." I can still see the child's eyes, overcome with excitement and pure envy. I was working on that portrait of the old man collecting buffalo bones. The surroundings, even the pile of bones, were right but I couldn't bring the bone man himself into focus. I was frustrated and it wouldn't have done me any good to keep trying, so I told Davey I'd go see the pony.

But as we crossed the lawn, Remington called: "Rufus! Come here! I've done something splendid."

I remember thinking something about egotists, but it didn't really bother me . . . I was used to the man, his bluster and roar, it was just part of him. And I went to look—at a mass of clay and a bunch of sculptor's tools, and Remington with that stupid, proud grin on his face. He looked so superior, and all I saw at first was a lump of clay.

"What do you think, Rufus? I think this mess is the beginning of something great. In fact, I'm convinced of it. Don't you agree? I may give up oils and become a sculptor."

That was when I saw it—that mass of clay was a horse and rider, well done, too. That flash of anger that went through me, it came so suddenly, it surprised, even frightened me. I'd never been jealous before, yet this was almost an instinct . . . I remember making the effort, saying all the right things and wanting really to reach out and destroy that lump of clay. But I just stood there and watched, fascinated in spite of myself, as he added a bit of clay here, scooped some away there, and that damn cowboy took shape before my eyes.

Going home, I was almost feverish with anger and hate . . . couldn't work at all. That blasted old bone man got worse instead of better, and I even jumped at Davey when he came in for his afternoon visit. Poor kid. He wanted to talk about the new pony, and I flew in a rage, scared him out of the studio.

Wonder if Davey would remember that day now? No, he'd probably dismiss it as old age if I asked him. He doesn't know how I grew to hate Remington—no one knows, I've kept it buried all these years. Everyone assumed all along that Remington and I were the best of friends . . . probably thought it was nice of the great Remington to be so kind to a second-rate artist. Remington sure got so he acted that way, kind of condescending. Or was I touchy?

Sometimes Rufus Jones would relive his own career, the near-success of it, or was it near-failure? No, success, for he had done some important works, had been known and praised in his day. His mind would begin with that mural in the state capitol . . .

Quite an honor to be asked, and I did them a good job. Was pleased with it. And the one in the Woolworth Building . . . by that time, I was known for historical subjects, the history of this great land. Oh, I was riding high.

And then there was that business about cowboys at play . . . I was so proud of that drawing when it came out . . . "Painting the Town Red," four cowboys literally holding a town at bay with their high jinx. Everyone else was so busy painting the cowboy at work, roping cattle, riding herd and all that, but no one paid any attention to the cowboy at play. I was the first—it was my idea!

But barely two years later, Remington did a sketch with the same title, looked a lot like mine, too. Anyway, the idea was the same. It came out in that book of Roosevelt's about hunting trails or whatever. Why didn't TR ask me to illustrate it anyway? I just had that letter of praise from him saying how much he valued my Western work and hoping we could collaborate, then the next thing TR asked Remington to illustrate the book. I thought that was the final insult—using my sketch and title!

Of course, it wasn't the final insult. The worst came

*later in another one of those bronzes Remington did . . .
they were all so popular after that first damn cowboy.
This one he called "Coming Through the Rye," but the
figures were almost exactly those of my painting. And
who got all the credit for capturing the cowboy as he
really was—who else?*

Sometimes Davey would come to stand silently beside his
father, staring at the scene that so absorbed the old man each
day as though by looking, he, too, could see something. But
one late summer day when the wind off the river promised
cold weather soon, Davey came with something on his mind.

"Dad?" The tall man in jeans and denim jacket bent almost gently over the older one who sat erect in his chair,
fingering the lap robe that covered him. Davey had to speak
twice before Rufus turned and looked at him, still saying
nothing.

"There's someone who wants to come see you tomorrow.
She's an artist, or says she is anyway. The town kind of
wonders about her. But, she stopped me on the street today,
said she'd heard a lot about your work and wanted to meet
you. I couldn't do anything else . . . I told her to come on out
in the morning."

Rufus turned away as though none of what Davey had said
meant a thing to him. Davey kicked at a cigarette butt with
one scuffed boot, stared at the river for help, and finally went
on.

"Sir, did you hear me?"

"Ummm."

The next that he had to say made Davey uncomfortable,
and he fidgeted a minute before plunging in. "Dad, you will
talk to her, won't you? She says she knows your work, wants
to talk to you about it. Try to be polite, won't you?"

Davey walked away abruptly, only half hearing Rufus's
mumbled, "Can't you tell her I'll be at work on a new painting, can't see visitors?"

But Rufus had understood that someone had heard of his

work, and he was secretly pleased. Maybe she knew "Painting the Town Red," or, perhaps, some of the Oklahoma pictures. His mind went back to reliving his achievements, and slowly he saw himself standing in the gallery at his 1899 exhibition. Somehow, though, memories of Remington's earlier, more successful exhibition, in 1893, crept in.

> *He looked so cocksure, so smug . . . when I congratulated him, he was almost too hearty, telling me that someday I'd have a success like this too . . . People kept coming up to shake his hand, ooze their flattery all over him, and he ate it up . . . All I could do was wonder what it would really be like to have that much attention paid to your art, have all those compliments and empty words . . . imagine myself standing there saying, "Thank you, Mrs. Vanderbilt, I'm so glad you like my pictures of the West . . . yes, it's a very exciting land . . . and Mrs. Astor, how nice of you to come . . . You like the sculpture? Well, I'm most humble . . ."*

Rufus had thirsted after fame so long, he almost felt himself savoring that of his rival. Bitterly, he brought his thoughts back to the present, surprised himself at how far from reality he occasionally drifted these days.

It was midmorning the next day when Rufus, seated in his wheelchair and staring at the river, heard steps approach him from behind. Not Davey, nor any of the family. They were womanly, small steps that sounded mincing.

"Mr. Jones, it's so good of you to let me visit. I can't tell you how delighted I am to talk to another artist."

Rufus turned slowly and fixed his stare on her. She wore pink, an outfit so unsuitable it seemed to insult the landscape, and she smiled too much.

"I said, I'm glad to meet you after hearing so much about your work. I've long been an admirer of the great Rufus Jones."

No response for several seconds, then a glance, a barely

uttered, "Eh?" and Rufus turned again to the river.

"Mr. Jones, I came to tell you how very much I appreciate your Western work—I've seen it in museums and I just think it's marvelous, so wonderful! Particularly that mounted horse and rider you did in bronze—your first, wasn't it?"

That damn cowboy again! Rufus stared at the river with an intensity so great it even alarmed the lady artist. Finally, long minutes later, he turned to stare at her. Then a wave seemed to sweep over his entire body. The burning look disappeared from his eyes, his face grew calm, and he actually smiled.

"Thank you very much, my dear. I'm glad you like 'The Bronco Buster'—that's what he really is. And yes, he was my first bronze. But I'm afraid you have my name wrong—I'm Frederic Remington."

TRACKING THE DEATH ANGEL

Tom Piccirilli

They told him the wind would haunt him, and drive him to eating dirt like the other man who'd lived in the shack before him, out on the high ridge when the keening came up from the cliffs like the howls of a hundred baying hounds, but they were wrong.

Sometimes the wind was the only thing that could drown his own tooth-and-claw thoughts, sitting on the cold boulders and smoking, with the dying branches burning white in the moonlight.

The other man had always eaten dirt: first as a child performing tricks, teasing the girls with worms and making the older, meaner boys fear him for his actions. Later, he'd done it when he'd first tried to shake his need for whiskey, thrashing and biting in the graveyard, full of want for his dead wife and daughter, his maimed son, his rage at the trail of life. The preachers would hold him down and say he was possessed, shouting passages from the Bible and soaking him with holy water, trying to purge demons.

Sometimes the preachers would just give up and listen instead, and eventually weep and share the whiskey with him.

One of them, by the name of Deed, went so far as to send him to a whore, hoping that the least of sins, that of the flesh, might distract the dirt eater from what they all knew had to be coming.

Only the sheriff and the whore didn't seem to understand, and they both learned together on the same night, after the sheriff broke down the door and held his hands over her chest, and tried to keep the blood from pumping into his face. His cheap tin badge got so stained he had to throw it away and take his deputy's.

By the time the posse had formed, and the dead whore was taken from the house, and Preacher Deed had been awoken from his haze and had the hell slapped out of him by the deputy without a badge, the dirt eater had crawled out of town and become something more, and no one could find him.

That was his brother's first murder, Evans thought, near as he could tell.

Jesus, the wind.

Even after the ruby haze of dawn broke heavily over the ridge, igniting the red mud and dust, it took a few hours to steel himself enough to go to the orphanage and see Jacob.

Evans enjoyed the soft melodious lilt of the French nuns, their English only passable but their meaning always clear. They made the same mistake this time as they had last week when he'd first visited. He heard a squeal and suddenly they were running at him, habits whirling as if they were at a barnyard dance, suddenly grabbing his thin arms to help him inside the infirmary. He shook them off, not bothering to smile because he knew that only made him look worse, with half his teeth gone and the dark lines of his face falling in on themselves.

He struggled with them for a moment and tried to calm the two teenage French sisters who'd lapsed back into their own language. He listened to the anxious music until the mother superior appeared on the steps behind them. She clapped her hands loudly and barked a few words, including his and Jacob's names. The young ladies turned their gazes on him, full of apology and revulsion, and drifted off.

She led him inside to Jacob's room. Most of the children that came spilling into the orphanage lodged in a huge school dormitory, one of the few that hadn't been sacked and burned to the ground. Jacob, though, had been cordoned off, rooming with eight or nine blind boys. Evans understood why but didn't like it.

Jacob sat on his bed reading. That's all he did when he wasn't writing or holding the books to his chest, sniffing them, turning pages of wonderfully bound French novels. Evans had never seen such beautifully crafted books. He briefly wondered where the nuns had hidden them, along with the paintings and silverware that had such finely wrought European detail to it, when the looters had come.

Jacob's one good eye focused on Evans as he entered the kid's room. The blind boys weren't there because even they got to go out and play with the other children, do chores, feel accepted and useful to some degree. Jacob sucked air through his ruined, lipless mouth, and a piece of scarred tongue flashed through for a moment. The kid grabbed up his chalkboard and began writing immediately. He'd been taught to read and write by the nuns, and so he only knew French. The mother superior had to translate for them to communicate.

She glanced at the board filled with tight, cursive scrawls and gave Jacob an admonishing frown. They did not run Jacob the way they did the others. Evans could see respect blended in with the dismay and pity and fear. She started to tap the board angrily. They'd gone through this the last time, too, and Evans had asked her to just read the comments and not argue or hold the kid accountable.

"He thinks you look better than before," she said, "but still like a dead man."

"True enough."

"He notices that you've put on a little weight. Your limp is not so pronounced. He says the awful shack agrees with you."

He addressed Jacob directly. Eventually, the mother superior would drop the "he says" and "he asks" and it would feel like he was only talking with his nephew, dreadful as it had become. "You're right, I do like it there."

"He asks if you have found his father yet?"

"No."

"He asks when will you start?"

"I'm . . . not certain, Jacob."

"Will you kill him when you do?"

"I told you already, not if I can help it."

"Go back to the wind and listen."

"I hear plenty of screams all the time," Evans said. "I don't need the wind for that."

The kid, deformed now and having been forced to watch his mother and sister die, perhaps had a better reason to rage than his father, or maybe not. In the war, and especially in Andersonville, Evans had learned more about other men, and himself, than he'd ever wanted to know.

Jacob took his time writing, using a rag afterward to clear the board. He tried to speak, the tongue throwing off his whole head when he made the effort, so that he had to tilt his face and work upward, like a fish coming up after bait. The mother superior glanced all around the room as if understanding that there weren't enough crosses on the walls to do any good.

"What's he say?" Evans asked.

"*C'est tres terrible.*"

"Tell me, please."

"He wants you to kill his father and to take a long time in doing it. He describes things, *non,* I shall not repeat. *Mon dieu, Non!* Oh, lord."

Jacob continued scribbling, coming as close to a grin as he was able, even as the mother superior tried to pull the board from him, breaking pieces of chalk, yanking at his hands. The kid was still capable of laughing, the guttural and crazed titter coming from all the way back in his throat where it shouldn't have been.

"Your father loves you," Evans said, and left.

• • •

He found Deed at a quarter past seven that evening, the already drunken preacher hanging half in a trough outside the saloon.

Through the window, he saw a few poker players about to brawl, sneering men kicking back their chairs. A woman sang a bawdy song accompanied by a fat, smiling Negro playing piano, and the foot stomps and guffaws pounded out from the swinging doors. Nothing in Devil's Dance, Texas, seemed touched by the war now. He limped forward and grabbed Deed, hauled him up over his shoulder, and carried him to the hotel, past the thickening shadows that milled in the alleys behind him.

The pock-faced desk clerk looked ready to refuse them but stopped short when Evans tossed a few bills on the mahogany counter.

"Oh, hey now, listen, fella, I ain't . . ." the clerk said.

Some of the bills had dried bloodstains on them. Every so often, that caused trouble, shopkeepers thinking it meant he'd robbed the money, a bandit in a dry gulch, but the blood was Evans's own, and he saw no reason to throw away cash because of that. He waited patiently while Deed began to mumble and snore on his shoulder. The clerk clucked at them once more, then shook the bills by their corners and put them away.

He watched Deed sleep for a couple of hours, studying the preacher, noticing the white but unduly long teeth. The firmness of face already beginning to slip as the man rotted himself inside out with whiskey and regret. His sweat smelled of mash, and there was an agreeable sweetness to it. Evans pulled his chair closer and took in deep breaths, thinking about Missouri before the war, the summer afternoons on the banks of the Mississippi when the world grew wide with promise.

The dirt eater. He'd had a name back then—Michael—and used to give this knowing, amiable grin all the time to everybody. Evans remembered Mother calling them in from the fields as darkness settled, with their father just coming home from building the town, his muscles glistening in the twilight. Father was the only carpenter worth anything for eighty miles, and there he was, hired by the other settlers, actually building a livery and church and an entire town from almost nothing.

Deed's mouth worked while he slept, the same way Michael's would in the deep autumn nights when the banshee owls kept the trees alive until the moon finally sank. Evans would listen to his younger brother, putting an ear close to his mouth, trying to make out the words. Once in a while he'd catch pieces of some oddly shaped dream, a few coughs about pretty schoolgirls or a beating from the other boys.

Nearing midnight, Deed woke with a start, apparently one of those men who, as the liquor burned out of them, could open his eyes and be totally aware and shrewd. The preacher took in the room, and his gaze settled on Evans.

Word had gotten around, of course. Deed knew him instantly and understood why he was here. His voice sounded wet and raw from a day of hard drinking. "I can't help you."

"Try. You were with him when it started."

Deed let out a low and humorless laugh that went on too long. It petered into a self-important huff. "Was I? Was I with him? Or were you?"

Evans knew what he meant. "Fair enough, but I haven't seen him in over four years."

"Then you know nothing. He's not the man you called your brother anymore."

"Tell me what he said to you before he murdered the whore."

Grinning now, Deed showed those animal teeth of his, the way they hung over his lip. "I know what you believe. You think that because I'm a preacher I ordered him to do it, don't you? That I filled his head with brimstone and hellfire and turned him out because I'd rather love God and the bottle than a woman. Well, you're wrong."

Deed didn't love God or the bottle, and he didn't have enough hellfire to light a match, much less ignite a man. "I don't think that at all," Evans said. "I think you were his only friend, so you're the only one who might tell me what's driving him.''

The preacher's eyes filled with self-pity and a sheen of tears. He let out two large sobs that didn't seem to have any sincerity to them, and his features shifted with scorn. ''Who do you think you are? What do you know of pain?''

The sneer on Deed's face brought the past up in Evans. He closed his eyes for a second and felt a pleasing tide suddenly sweep and pull within his chest, finally breaking from him with a moan. He backhanded Deed with such speed and savagery that the preacher wheeled over backward and spun against the far wall, whipping his head hard against the nightstand and knocking the empty basin to the floor.

Evans calmly said, ''I followed Sherman to Kennesaw Mountain, dragging a cannon up trails too steep for horses, and spent four months in Andersonville for it. I saw my company murdered one by one, filthy and sick with scurvy and dysentery, beaten by guards until their spines broke. I loved a boy named Obedon Bodeen like I was his father, and watched him die gut shot and starving while he coughed up his lungs from pneumonia for three weeks. Came home to my family and found them all dead, or wishing they were. Tell me I don't know pain, and I'll kill you.''

Deed got off the floor and wiped the back of his hand across his bloody mouth, those teeth slick and dripping. ''He calls himself Azreal now. That's all you really need to know.''

When he left the hotel, his hands were trembling badly and he wanted a drink, although he could trace a great deal of tragedy in his life back to the bottle. He'd volunteered for the army while drunk, had seen the worst fights between Michael and their father caused by too much whiskey burning in one man or the other.

Twisted shadows loomed up and down the street.

They were waiting for him. Another bawdy song followed after him, sung by a different beautiful woman, and ugly laughter seeped from the whorehouse. Murmurs nearby caught his attention, and he turned but saw only darkness. He knew they'd be coming eventually, that the whispers would swell in their corners and bring the families out to face him in their wrath. He had no gun and wondered if anyone had a bead on him from a high roof, and he instinctively scanned for men ready to pull the trigger, willing to kill him just to ease their minds a bit.

He went to the sheriff's office.

At this hour, he expected to find only a deputy sleeping inside an empty cell, but Sheriff Harper sat at his desk, thumbing through papers. Harper looked as if he hadn't slept in three or four days, deep circles under his eyes. His face was the sallow color that afflicts men fighting chronic pain, skin always slick like a fish belly.

Evans sat in the chair opposite, waiting, the same way he had a week ago when he'd come in to introduce himself. The sheriff took his time before he finally glanced up and said, "A man named Lucas Cole got to swearing a might loudly today outside the saddlery, saying he was coming after you."

Evans remembered seeing that name in the newspaper. A blacksmith, his wife Loretta had been killed. "He lost his wife."

"Lost," Harper said. "Yes, he lost his wife. He's got two sons of about thirteen, fourteen, they might be ready to pick up a gun as well."

"Settle them if you can, or lock them up. I didn't come here to do harm to anyone."

Harper nearly smiled at that but stopped just short. Irony made fools of everyone, but especially those who found humor in it. He slid the top piece of paper across the desk to him. "Here, you might be interested in this."

Evans glanced through it, knowing what the news had to be. He touched the paper and it quivered, and no matter how hard he tried, he couldn't still the shaking. The ink seemed to flow, part of his mind reading but another part trying to see beyond the horror to a time when they'd gone on picnics together beneath the oak and hickory trees. Ruth so beautiful in the sunlight holding the babies, Michael eating fried chicken and talking about leaving Missouri to find his fortune elsewhere. Jacob and Emily crawling after the fat hound dog, Barrabas, who let the children climb on his back and pull his long, wide ears without so much as a whine.

"That makes seventeen we know of," Harper told him. "I've seen outlaws, gunmen, who did a lot more damage than that, especially during the war. Carpetbaggers, really vicious men who liked to use their sabers. Someone like you, been in the mud with Sherman, you've seen a thousand men die in a day. I didn't serve, maybe you hold that against me, but I did my share, been sheriff for nine years, through the very worst of it. But never met a man without reason or cause like this, murdering anyone he comes across. Hell, he doesn't even rape the women. Doesn't steal anything. He don't distinguish none, this brother of yours."

Shifting in his seat, Evans felt the moan inside him rising again but bit it back down, thinking about dead children, and Jacob and Ruth and Emily, and what had been done to them all.

"We've had two new posses after him for over a month, and got nothing." Harper couldn't keep the frustration from his voice any longer, letting it crack as his face took on a healthier glow, the ire rising. "Tell me more about him. Tell me what I need to know to stop him, damn you!"

With his hands shaking so severely now he couldn't hold onto the paper, Evans let it waft to the floor and wondered how much life and death he could put into words and what those words would be. He thought he'd have to not only take the sheriff to go see Jacob and visit the graveyard and show him the shack and let him hear the wind, but also take him against the flood of years and bring him to their father's house, where Michael met Ruth, and where she gave birth to Jacob and Emily. Then watch them again pack and move to Texas to escape from the old man and the farm—maybe even to get away from Evans himself—and settle into a piece of land in the Paradise Creek territory that was too red and dusty to do much with. Where Michael first strapped on a gun.

The color drained from Harper's face and again he appeared weak and useless. Whatever had given him strength there for a moment had already faded. "And you, from Missouri? What do you do now?"

"I'm a farmer," Evans said, which was mostly still true, he hoped.

"No, up in that shack. What do you do? What are you waiting for?"

Evans didn't have an answer, except that he didn't want to murder his own brother.

"Go back home, old man," Harper told him. "Before you get yourself killed. A shame for you to survive the war only to die here."

Evans didn't admit to his age of thirty-two. His grandfather, at eighty, still plowed his own fields and did more chores than any three hands.

He got up to leave, and Sheriff Harper called him back. "The news I got, there was some other information on it. Something you didn't tell me before. Says he was a lawman years ago. That true?"

Evans said, "Yes."

The singer was swaying, sort of dancing alone in the sawdust just a few feet inside the batwing doors. When Evans walked in, she saw the chance to have a little fun, so she slid her hand under his chin and made like she was serenading him. The place erupted with laughter. She floated around him, fingers drifting over his collar, reaching through his thin hair as she eased closer and sang against his throat for a moment.

"Amy Lynn, darlin', don't waste your time on that there old goat!" someone shouted. "You just come on over a'right heyah, my lap's big enough for ya!"

She was perhaps twenty but had the world in her smile, dimples flashing and tiny beads of sweat rising across her caramel-colored freckles. Her brown hair fell in ringlets, two lengthy curls uncoiling down the sides of her face and bouncing as she moved. Her eyes were filled with a lewd humor, and she drew her lips so close to his that she sang directly against his mouth. The room roared again. For the first time since he couldn't remember, maybe since Kennesaw Mountain, maybe long before, Evans felt the urge to smile, but he didn't want to show how deep the dark fissures of his face went.

He kept still and just watched her.

She brushed against him, swinging her hips with a little grind, moving toward him the way that could drive a man into a shotgun wedding. He swallowed, and she nodded at him, as if following the course of his Adam's apple. She was so beautiful he felt a stirring of desire despite everything that had happened. The piano player kept in time with her, keys tinkling when she held the long, syrupy notes that never seemed to end, her wet lips smoothing into an O that she blew against Evans's hot forehead.

"Forget both of them and come on home with me, honey pie!" someone yelled, causing a ripple of chuckles. "I'll put my wife out to pasture for the night!"

Amy Lynn's fiery crimson dress fit her tightly, cross-laced at her bosom so that her breasts pressed up and out against his chest. She wore a short feather boa and a headdress with feathers in it, tangled in her curls. She touched his face and kissed him lightly, then again, and once more between the words of her song. If he dared to lean forward, she would leave him, he knew, and so he stood rigid and let her kiss him once, twice more, before moving off to another table where the men hooted and banged their mugs. Amy stuck her boot up on a chair and slowly drew her skirt up to reveal her calf, her knee, and eventually part of her thigh.

Evans stepped up to the bar and asked for a drink, threw it back quickly, and ordered another. The whiskey burned deeply as it threaded into his belly. The few Algonquian and Siouan he'd known back in Missouri had never been able to hold their liquor, not even beer; it went directly to their heads and drove them mad, and he wondered if the same couldn't be said for himself and his family. Something weak and susceptible in the strain. He looked in the mirror behind the bar and watched as Amy Lynn continued to entertain the men. He felt a curious rising of jealousy and shook his head in surprise, wondering what the hell he was thinking.

Moonlight wove through the window, with the roiling silver clouds promising rain. He had to get out of here and start doing something to find Michael. A new name had been added to the growing list: Jasper Winston. Fifty-nine years old, a dry goods seller in the town of Greaves City, about fifty miles north of Devil's Dance, murdered three days ago and found by his wife, who'd watched the last few seconds of it before running to her eldest son. Except for when he'd killed the whore, Michael always made sure that at least one person saw him grinning over the dead. It was his way of securing affirmation, leaving no doubt in anybody's mind. He'd always been like that, needing attention.

Evans paid for his drinks, took a final long look at Amy Lynn, and headed for the door.

A huge hand, the size of his father's, slapped him hard on the back, and the room came to a halt. The piano player and Amy Lynn both stopped in the same second, the crowd hushing. Evans couldn't understand it, how it could happen like this all at once.

Lucas Cole stood taller than Evans, a solid and burly man with extremely thick wrists from hauling an iron hammer all day and working metal. The blacksmith didn't wear a gun, but he had a work belt heavy with the tools of his trade. "You know who I am?"

"Yes."

Evans would have said that he grieved for the man, if he had any grief to spare, and if the blacksmith would have believed him. The Negro who'd been playing the piano slipped off his stool and out the door, and Evans hoped he was going for Sheriff Harper. Fat as the piano player was though, it'd be over by the time they returned.

"I'm here to help," Evans said.

"Help?" Cole couldn't have looked more surprised, the way his entire face pulled back as if tied and drawn. "You're here to . . . help me?"

"To stop my brother, if I can."

Cole burst out laughing, whooping and slapping his knee, and sobered immediately. The guffaws broke through, even while he gritted his teeth and his lips turned purple. Evans hadn't heard laughter like that since the Confederate lieutenants took their turns flogging him.

Cole said, "A man like that, he's born evil. He breeds evil. He comes from evil."

Evans had considered the possibility. Their father had been a stern man. A man of angles and planes, lacking warmth, but generally fair. He never made snap judgments, preferring to look at all points of view, near and distant perspectives, and once his mind was made, there was no changing it. Their father, who could build a town, had married their mother, a Knickerbocker, somewhere on Manhattan Island, where she taught school, and brought her back to Missouri to the ranch he'd built with his own hands. She filled the three floors with a certain radiant grace, an ease that the man didn't have on his own.

"Are you listening to me?" Cole hissed.

"Yes," Evans said.

"Lousy Yankee bastard, I'm talking to you!"

Mother hadn't driven them hard with formal education, preferring to let them work their father's fields and live the way his family had always lived, spending more time at the river with the fishermen than anywhere else. She allowed them to attend to reading and writing matters at their own pace, which caused less strain. Evans took to it more than Michael, spending his mornings studying. He did it for his mother's sake more than his own, enjoying the time with her at the big table.

Cole's hands twitched as if he wanted to reach for a pistol. "You don't even wear a gun."

"No."

"My wife . . ." the blacksmith began, and stopped, gagging on the hate. "She . . ."

Evans didn't want to know anything more. He already knew too much, and to think of what had been done wouldn't change a thing. He looked around to see what else might be happening in the room. He glanced from face to face. At least one other man in the saloon had cause to mourn and lament, sitting alone in a chair at the back of the room, those same eyes on him. The man sipped his drink, staring, and Evans understood that he'd probably have to face him sometime in the future as well, if he didn't find Michael soon.

When he got to Amy Lynn's face, he nearly gasped. She was so beautiful that his mind swirled for an instant, wanting her to kiss him softly again. He could hear Obedon Bodeen's high-pitched, exuberant voice saying, *"I swear to you, Sergeant, I ain't never seen a lady as pretty a sight as she is. Them feathers, oh my, think she'd rightly tickle you with them?"*

"My wife . . ." The blacksmith's tool belt, like the carpenter belt Evans's father had worn, chimed gently like the crystal bell Mother had rung on her deathbed when she wanted water.

Evans said, "Believe me, Mr. Cole, please."

"No!"

"I want to stop this."

"No, I'm the one putting an end to it!" Cole screamed, pulling out his hammer.

Evans moved as best as he could and barely avoided the wide-swinging arc as the hammer breezed past his nose. Cole grunted, having to check his swing or break his own leg, and tried again. Raising the hammer once more, he reached out for Evans with his other hand, hoping to get a grip on his throat to hold him in place. The blacksmith found a fistful of Evans's shirt and smiled, bringing the hammer down aimed at his face.

Evans took a step forward so that the blow overshot past

his shoulder. The handle, though, struck him on the neck, and the pain reared through his head to mix with Obedon Bodeen's voice. *"Sergeant, I think the lady admires you, I reckon she does, the way she's looking over here. Or is she staring at me?"*

Evans reached down into Cole's tool belt in a blur of motion, checking handles one after the other, until he got to the one he wanted and snaked it free. It was a long file. Cole said, "What're you doing, you Yankee son of . . . !"

At ease now, knowing they were almost done, Evans raked the file hard against Cole's forehead, opening a wide gash that gushed blood into the blacksmith's eyes. Obedon Bodeen cheered wildly in the back of the saloon. Cole squeaked and reeled, falling backward into another man's lap, who quickly tossed the blacksmith into the sawdust.

When Evans looked at his hands, he was faintly surprised to see that the trembling had stopped. He had to put his palm up to his lips before he realized he was smiling, and wondered if this was how it had begun for his brother. A harsh, freezing breeze blew through the center of his chest, and when it reached the back of his skull, he looked around the room again, seeing it with a new clarity.

"I'm setting out in the morning after him, Mr. Cole," Evans said, realizing the time had actually come.

They watched from their windows as he walked up the middle of the street. Near the livery he heard someone sharpening a knife in the shadows and knew if he turned, they'd come after him. The kin of his brother's victims gathered and milled, passing judgment.

Women would be alone tonight with shotguns. Their husbands were out in the posses, checking arroyos and looking for scuffs on stone, remnants of a campfire, anything to point the way. If Michael hadn't been found yet, he never would be. He wouldn't take heed of the men pursuing him, since he'd been on too many manhunts himself not to keep hidden. They'd come within yards of him but never close enough.

He'd been taught by two Texas Rangers and a Navajo tracker who'd once brought Ruth a bracelet made of bone and eagle feathers, a gift that was supposed to protect her from evil.

Evans heard an odd clanging as he walked. He glanced down to see that he was holding Cole's tool belt, but didn't know when he'd grabbed it. The file had been replaced in its pocket, a little red but mostly clean. Even the hammer Cole had tried to kill him with was back in its proper loop. Evans hadn't drunk much whiskey, but maybe he was drunk, or maybe Amy Lynn brushing her lips against his had caused the same effect.

He would've handed the tool belt to one of the townsfolk glaring at him now if he wasn't so sure somebody would shoot him in the back if he strayed from the center of the street. He could leave the tools here in the wagon ruts, but that seemed spiteful, even more of an insult than what the man had gone through tonight, after losing his wife. He could bring them back tomorrow, or after Michael was finally dead, and go up to Cole and tell him it was finished. Evans touched the handle of the hammer and wondered at the resolve it took to build a town from nothing. He strapped the belt on.

His leg began to hitch worse as he climbed the narrow trail up the ridge. When he looked out at the red rock and cactus, there seemed to be no such thing in the world as the Mississippi. The wind drove down on him as lightning smeared against the frenzied black and silver storm clouds. Murmurs of thunder met the howls coming up the cliff face.

Their father would have been disappointed at how little care went into the walls of the shack, how many cracks let the cold seep through. Michael had built the shack himself after his perfect white house in Paradise Creek burned down three years ago on Christmas day. Evans still didn't know what had started the fire.

At the time, he'd been with Rosecrans at Stones River, opening the way for Grant's run up to Vicksburg. Jacob had only told him to kill his father, and wouldn't say anything more. Perhaps he didn't know or maybe he didn't think it mattered. Most likely, Michael had been drunk and toppled the lamp, and the lace curtains Ruth and Emily had sewn themselves went up in the night. Evans could see Jacob awakening in bed with the flames already covering him, trying to put the blaze out as his sister's and mother's nightgowns caught fire, and his father stumbled forward holding his guns as if he could fight off anything if he drew fast enough.

Tomorrow morning Evans needed to buy a gun.

It had been seven months since he'd last held one, when firing at the Reb who was sighting down on Obedon Bodeen. Evans had only grazed the Reb's shoulder, and then watched as the Confederate corporal with his overcoat smoking had shook off the shock and shot Obedon Bodeen in the belly. A half hour later, the remaining Union troops surrendered and were headed for Andersonville. Obedon Bodeen had outlived a lot of them in the three weeks it took him to die.

Evans had been meaning to get a pistol since he started out of Georgia, but knowing what he'd have to do with it, he'd never found the will to actually head for the gunsmith. Until tonight.

More grumbling thunder rattled the thin shutters in their weak frames as the rain scourged the roof. It reminded him of the sound the riverboats made as they chewed their way downstream. After what he'd set out to do was done, if he didn't die, he'd get Jacob out of the orphanage and take him back to Missouri. He'd teach the boy how to write in English and how to fish, and perhaps the Mississippi could ease a little of their grief.

Sitting at the small table, Evans fell asleep with his fist propped under his chin. He awoke in the deep night thinking of Deed's teeth and Jacob's watchful eye. He had dreamed his entire life again. The furious keening outside brought him to his feet, those wails broken up only by the soft snorting of a horse.

He realized now what he should have known from the beginning—that he didn't have to track the death angel, he just had to be ready to die, and the bloodletting would come for him instead.

Darkness draped the ridge. The rain hadn't stopped, but the storm had moved off, and smudges of purple lightning lit patches of desert in the distance. Evans stepped out into the mud and whispered his brother's name. Then again. "Michael."

He didn't expect an answer yet. It took a while for the cloud cover to thin enough for moonlight to surge through. White shafts dappled the boulders and arched across a few gnarled dead trees. There seemed to be snow on the ground. The shack groaned like it knew what was coming. As the darkness withdrew, he waited there calmly, until he heard a choked sobbing that sent icy nails of panic into his scalp.

Michael wouldn't be alone. He always left a witness.

Obedon Bodeen said, *"He's no kin of yours, Sergeant."*

The dying lightning finally petered out. Crevices kept pouring their screams until threads of the night snapped past. Over there, settled back on his roan and silhouetted against a bloated moon, sat the dirt eater who'd once been his brother Michael, now calling himself Azreal, the death angel.

Dressed in black like that, he looked carved from shadow, and even in this wind he kept his hat on completely straight. He'd come a long way from grubbing on all fours in the graveyard, but only because he carried the grave with him. His pants had slicing creases and his boots and pistols shone brighter than even Sherman's had. His coat snapped over the horse's ear, and his vest and shirt were clean and recently ironed. He'd been just as fussy in Sunday school. Michael had not drunk in a long time, probably not since the night he'd murdered the whore.

Wrenching sobs dragged Evans's attention to the trees, where he could make out a rope dangling and something crimson hanging from it.

His brother had strung up Amy Lynn.

The noose hung high over a thick limb, tied off to the pommel of his saddle. Her uncoiled curls bounced across her

shoulders as she kicked and tried to keep from spinning in
the gusts. Her hands were lashed together, but she had her
fingers worked between her neck and the rope. On her tiptoes
she barely kept from dying, bringing up coughs that jolted
her entire body. Michael sat atop his horse without bothering
to glance at Evans. He stared off the cliff, peering into that
darkness and listening to the wind as if it had words.

"Look at me," Evans said.

His brother ignored him. Amy Lynn's fiery dress billowed
like dancing flame, but Michael didn't appear to notice the
irony. Evans's breath clumped in his throat. He took another
step forward. Without turning, Michael drove a spur lightly
into the horse's flank. The movement made the roan trot and
the rope jerked taut as Amy Lynn was yanked a foot into the
air, strangling.

There wasn't any choice. Michael wouldn't ease up if
Evans moved away or fell to his knees or scurried in the mud
pleading. He was going to hang the girl to death. It didn't
matter to him which of them he killed so long as there was
someone left to talk about it.

Evans covered the ground between them as quick as he
could. He still wore the tool belt and dropped his hand down
to make a grab even as Michael reached for his gun. Evans
snatched the hammer and hefted it with all he had, just as his
brother drew and fired.

Knowing he was already dying, possibly even dead, but
still bucking like Obedon Bodeen, Evans felt the bullet slam
him square in the heart, or only thought he did. He watched
a splash of liquid yellow sparks spatter in the air and realized
the slug had ricocheted off the head of the hammer, even as
it continued to hurtle forward and knocked Michael out of
the saddle.

The horse reared, and the noose tugged tighter, yanking
Amy higher into the branches. She let out a grunt that nearly
chopped Evans's knees out from under him. He grabbed the
horse's reins, turning his back and knowing his brother could
easily kill him now if he was still conscious. Hooves lashed

out at his skull, but he managed to get his other hand on the pommel and unloop the rope. The noose slid free, and Amy Lynn dropped from the tree into the red mud like a corpse on fire.

She wheezed and gasped between awful sobs. Her throat hadn't been crushed. She'd still be able to sing.

Michael came up as if he hadn't fallen at all, sliding around in the dark and gliding forward. At least his boots were dirty and he'd lost his hat. His hair tousled into his eyes until he looked like a child, the same as when Ruth had run her fingers through it and they'd laughed together down at the riverbank. He trained his Colts on Evans and slipped closer. That was okay, too, for the most part. Amy Lynn would be left alone to bear witness.

Back when Michael had been a lawman, he'd gotten a taste for the gunfight and never taken a nick. Evans should've gotten a pistol the day he hit Texas; he shouldn't have gone a day without one. He stood as tall as he was able but couldn't really get rid of the way he hunched. That didn't matter, either. "What do you want, Michael?"

Obedon Bodeen said it again, a lot louder this time, almost as loud as when he wept when he died. *"He's not any kin of yours, Sergeant, not no more, he ain't!"*

Michael jammed one of the Colts barrel first into the empty hammer pocket on the tool belt.

"What happened that Christmas? Talk to me."

Here we are at the end, Evans thought. *Now he'll have to answer my questions, confess to his blood, or at least say my name.*

Razors of moonlight slashed up the ridge. The boyish features hadn't changed much. Evans searched his brother's face for a sign of recognition, sorrow, or maybe blame. He found nothing and tried to stare deeper, leaning in and swallowing hard.

All he saw there was the trapped unthinkable emptiness, eyes like sacked graves.

Evans said, "You're not my brother."

He seized the pistol as if he was clutching a hand that might save him, remembering the strength and justice of Michael's fist. Azreal reached and plucked his gun. Evans found the grip and drew, pointed the Colt without really knowing where he was aiming, the rush of Ruth's laughter alive in his ears, as he squeezed the trigger without remembering a single prayer, and shot the death angel in the head.

Azreal pitched backward without a sound, rolling for a time before coming to rest against the rocks.

Evans threw both of the Colts over the cliff, rushed inside, and returned to wrap Amy Lynn up in some blankets. She tried to murmur to him but he said, "No, don't talk."

He tossed Azreal's body on the bed and hoped he was leaving Obedon Bodeen's high-pitched voice here as well. Evans flung lamp oil all around and set fire to the miserable shack. It went up quick and warmed his back as he lifted Amy Lynn onto the roan and swung into the saddle. The pyre lit his way back to town, and the dawn slowly sifted through to meet it. He wondered if the tears would ever come and eventually decided he didn't really care. He was going to get his nephew and go fishing and have himself fitted for dentures. The wind quieted to a hushed lament as he held the woman to him.

For Joe Lansdale, Richard Laymon, and Ed Gorman, one helluva posse

YESTERDAY'S TRAIL

——

L. J. Washburn

"It's not like he's crazy or anything," Adabelle Wright said. "He's just . . . forgetful." She reached out and put her hand on Hallam's arm. "You have to find him before he gets himself hurt, Lucas . . . or . . . hurts somebody else."

Hallam frowned. "How's an old man like that going to hurt anybody?" he asked.

"Well . . . Grandpa took his gun with him when he left."

That made a difference, all right. Sam Wright might've been a pretty good county sheriff in his day, but that was a lot of years in the past. Now he was just an old-timer who, according to his granddaughter Adabelle, sometimes forgot where he was and even who he was.

Adabelle's hand tightened on Hallam's arm. "You will find him, won't you?"

Hallam was a young man, tall, lanky, not yet twenty years old. How was he going to say no to a pretty girl?

"I'll find him," Hallam said. "Shouldn't be too much trouble."

He'd been on his way back to Flat Rock from El Paso, a long ride no matter how you looked at it. After a week of sleeping on the ground and eating his own cooking, Hallam was ready for a bed and some woman-cooked food. So he'd stopped in Big Spring, remembering how his father had told him about working with Sheriff Sam Wright, back in the days when John Hallam was still a Texas Ranger. Sheriff Sam had long since retired, of course, but he still lived in Big Spring with his granddaughter. Hallam figured Sam and Adabelle wouldn't mind putting him up for the night.

Truth be told, he was looking forward to seeing Adabelle again, too. She was a couple of years older than him, and just like Sam had been sort of like an uncle to Hallam, Adabelle had been like his cousin. But when Adabelle was fifteen and Hallam had just turned thirteen, she had suddenly seemed even older and somehow mysterious and undeniably beautiful. Unattainable, of course, but still, Hallam was quite taken with her. He always looked forward to the visits back and forth between the families.

It wasn't long after that that things had gone to hell in a hay wagon. John Hallam had been killed, and his son had gone after the men who killed him, and what with one thing and another, Hallam hadn't seen Adabelle for several years. As he rode into Big Spring, he found himself wondering if she was as pretty as ever.

The answer was yes, but her beauty was tempered by a look of worry. She'd been glad to see Hallam but distracted and upset about something, and it hadn't taken him long to find out what was wrong.

"Grandpa hasn't been . . . right in the head . . . for about a year now," Adabelle explained while she and Hallam sat in the parlor of the neat little house. "Sometimes he thinks he's still sheriff, and he puts his guns on and goes downtown to 'clean out the ruffians,' as he calls it. Sheriff Bennett, he's the real sheriff now, he has to take Grandpa's guns away and bring him home. It finally got so bad I had to hide his guns so he couldn't find them."

"But he got hold of them this time?"

Adabelle nodded. She was a vision in the sunshine that

came streaming in through the gauzy curtains, lighting up her honey blond hair. "Yes. I had them hidden up in the attic. I don't know how he found them."

"You're sure he's not wandering around here in Big Spring?"

"No, Sheriff Bennett already had his deputies search all over town. Besides, Grandpa took his horse, and he told some of the old men he plays dominoes with that he was going to ride over to Sweetwater and clear his name, that he was finally going to bring back the McCain payroll. Lucas, that was thirty years ago."

Hallam remembered. Not the robbery itself; that had been before his time, as well as Adabelle's. But he had heard all the stories about how bandits had held up the Butterfield stage and stolen the McCain Mining payroll. Three people had been killed in the holdup: the jehu, the shotgun guard, and a special guard who'd been riding in the coach. Sheriff Sam Wright had gone after the outlaws, vowing to bring back them and the stolen money. He hadn't done either one, and that failure had always haunted him. Even worse had been the rumors that he'd been paid off somehow to let the thieves get away. Hallam had never believed that, but some people had.

"He hasn't even talked about that payroll robbery for years," Adabelle went on. "I wish I knew what set him off."

"Don't reckon it matters," Hallam said as he pushed himself to his feet. "I'll ride on over to Sweetwater and find him. Ought to be back in a day or two."

"Lucas, I . . . I can't thank you enough."

Hallam thought about stealing a kiss right then and there but decided to wait until he'd brought Sam home. Adabelle would likely be in more of a kissing mood then, since she'd be grateful to him and all.

The road between Big Spring and Sweetwater carried quite a bit of wagon and horse traffic, so Hallam didn't even try to follow any specific tracks. He just rode toward Sweetwater, figuring that if Sam had said that was where he was going, that was where Hallam would find him. On the other hand, Sam might've gone part of the way and then forgotten where he was headed. There was really no telling where he might have wandered off to, Hallam realized, and the more he thought about it, the more he worried that finding Sam might prove to be a bigger chore than he'd thought it would be. But Sweetwater was where he was going to start looking. Maybe he'd be lucky.

Sweetwater was a day's ride east of Big Spring, so Hallam had to spend another night on the trail after all. He reached the settlement about noon of the following day. He planned to pay a visit to the local law first thing. If Sam had come over here and raised a ruckus, he might be locked up in the jail. That would be a truly pathetic sight, Hallam thought, Sheriff Sam Wright behind bars, but it would sure make the job of finding him easier.

Hallam heard the gunshot before he found the sheriff's office.

The blast of a .45 came from inside a saloon in the next block. Hallam spurred his horse ahead. He'd never been one to duck trouble; some said he even went out of his way to stick his nose in other people's business, especially when powder smoke was involved. He drew rein in front of the saloon, which was called Hanratty's. A couple of townies were stealing peeks over the batwings. There hadn't been any more shots. Hallam said, "What's goin' on in there?"

One of the townies glanced back at him. "Some crazy old man wavin' a gun around. He let off a shot just now."

"Where's the sheriff?"

"Ain't in town right now, nor any of his deputies. They're out chasin' some rustlers who hit the Diamond S last night."

Hallam grunted. He didn't know if the old man inside the saloon was Sam Wright or not, but it seemed likely. Hallam wasn't going to scoff at good fortune. He swung down from the saddle and looped the reins over the hitch rail.

"Mister, what the hell you doin'?" the other townie hissed at him as he stepped up onto the boardwalk.

"Goin' to go in there and take that gun away from him," Hallam said.

"Better be careful, kid. He's sayin' that he's goin' to shoot everybody in there if he has to."

Hallam put a hand on the batwings and peered over them. He saw a man standing ten feet away, back to the door. The man wore a dusty black suit and hat. He was standing at just enough of an angle to Hallam so that Hallam could see the long-barreled Remington pistol with the ivory handle that the old man was pointing at about a dozen people gathered on the far side of the room.

"You ain't a-foolin' me, Cahoba," the old man said as he jabbed the barrel of the pistol toward the prisoners. "I know it's you. I got the proof at last."

The barrel of the Remington quivered as the old man spoke. The pistol was cocked, and depending on how sensitive the trigger was, it might take nothing more than the tremble of a finger to fire it again.

Hallam pushed one side of the batwings open and stepped into the saloon. "Sheriff Sam," he said. "It's me, Lucas."

Sam Wright flinched a little, and so did the people he was covering with the Remington. But the gun didn't go off, and Sam half-turned to look at Hallam. Hallam recognized the sharp-featured face and the drooping white mustaches. "Lucas?" Sam said. The barrel of the Remington sagged toward the floor.

All it would have taken was a couple of long strides to reach his side and get a hand on the gun, Hallam thought. Then this would all be over, and Hallam could take Sam back to Big Spring, back to his granddaughter Adabelle. Hallam could get that home-cooked meal . . . and maybe a kiss or two.

So why didn't he do that? Hallam wondered. Why didn't he take the gun away from the old man while he had the chance?

Maybe it was the desperation in Sam Wright's eyes.

Whatever the reason, Hallam hesitated, and Sam straight-

ened, his back as stiff as a ramrod. The tremble went out of
his hand as he lifted the Remington again and pointed it toward the group of nervous people on the other side of the
room. " 'Bout time somebody got here to give me a hand,"
Sam said. "Leave it to me to bring in a bunch of desperadoes
by my ownself."

Hallam looked at the people being menaced by Sam's gun.
They didn't look much like desperadoes to him.

There was a slick-haired bartender wearing a bow tie, a
fancy vest, and sleeve garters. He was standing at the very
end of the bar, his hands resting on the hardwood. On the
other side of the bar, nearby, was a plump, middle-aged gent
with white hair and a florid face, wearing a gray tweed suit.
Three men in range clothes stood next to the bar, half-full
mugs of beer in front of them to show what they had been
doing when Sam interrupted them. One was older, in his thir-
ties, while the other two were little more than kids. Ranch
hands from one of the nearby spreads, Hallam judged. None
of them were armed.

Neither were the two women who wore spangled dresses
and plenty of war paint. One of them, the redhead, even had
a feather in her hair. They were probably in their mid-
twenties, which couldn't be considered young in their line of
work. Hallam figured they had been laughing and joking with
the three cowhands, trying to cajole the men into buying them
glasses of watered-down tea that all concerned could pretend
was whiskey.

That left the four men sitting at a table, cards and poker
chips scattered in front of them. One of them had the well-
fed, respectable look of a prosperous merchant or banker,
while the other three had harder edges and wore pistols on
their hips. They seemed to be the only ones who were armed.

Except for Sam Wright and Hallam.

"Be careful, mister," said the white-haired man at the end
of the bar. "He . . . he's crazy!"

"They keep sayin' that," Sam said, "but I ain't. I ain't
thought so clear in a long time. It's like a fog's done lifted."

He glanced again from the corner of his eye at Hallam. "I know you, don't I? You're John's boy, Lucas."

Well, Sam hadn't completely lost his memory, Hallam thought. He said, "That's right. Adabelle sent me to find you, Sheriff Sam. You remember your granddaughter Adabelle, don't you?"

Sam snorted. "O' course I remember Adabelle. I tell you, boy, I ain't addled in the head the way I used to be. It's all come back to me. That there is Frank Cahoba, the fella who masterminded the McCain payroll robbery." Sam pointed at the well-dressed man sitting at the poker table.

"I told you he's crazy!" yelped the man at the end of the bar. "That's Mr. Matthew Grace. He owns the First State Bank of Sweetwater."

"A damned lie!" Sam said. "I know Frank Cahoba when I see him!"

"Young man." That was Matthew Grace, and he was looking at Hallam. "I take it you know this poor, deluded individual."

"If you mean Sheriff Sam, that's right," Hallam said.

"He actually is a sheriff?"

"Was," Hallam admitted with a shrug, keeping an eye on Sam as he spoke. "He's retired now."

"That don't matter," Sam said. "I'm still sworn to uphold the law."

Matthew Grace said, "Mr. Hanratty has already vouched for me, and so will everyone else in here. They all know me. I never heard of this . . . this Frank Cahoba. Your friend is confused and mistaken."

Hallam nodded and said to Sam, "Why don't you put down the gun, and we'll talk about this. You don't want to hurt anybody."

Sam didn't lower the Remington. "I want the McCain payroll back, damn it! And I want that snake yonder behind bars, where he belongs, until he swings for killin' those three men in that holdup!"

Grace swallowed. He was keeping his composure remarkably well, considering the circumstances, but Hallam could tell that the banker was getting worried. "I swear to you . . . Sheriff, is it?"

Sam drew himself up even straighter, though Hallam wouldn't have thought that was possible. "Sheriff Sam Wright."

"Sheriff Wright, I swear to you I am not the man you believe me to be. I've lived here in Sweetwater for over twenty years. I have a business, a wife, a family."

"Mr. Grace even served two terms as mayor," Hanratty, the saloonkeeper, put in.

"That's true. Please, Sheriff Wright, can't you see that you've simply mistaken me for someone else?"

Sam was staring intently at Grace. He blinked a couple of times, then said, "You're not Cahoba?"

"On my word of honor, sir, no, I am not."

"But . . . I don't understand. I got the letter from Dunston . . ."

"Who's Dunston?" Hallam asked.

"Moses Dunston," Sam said. "Cahoba's partner. But Cahoba double-crossed him and stole Dunston's share of the payroll. Dunston never forgave him for it, so he wrote it all down in a letter to me. He was goin' gunnin' for Cahoba, but he left the letter with a lawyer, told him to send it to me in case he got killed, so Cahoba wouldn't get away with it. I just got it last week."

So that was what had set him off, Hallam thought. But like he'd told Adabelle, that didn't really matter now.

"Wait a minute," said the bartender. "Moses Dunston, you said, mister?"

"That's right," Sam said. "You know him?"

"I knew a drunk we called old Mose. I think I heard him say once his last name was Dunston." The bartender shook his head. "But he wasn't any sort of outlaw. He was just an old boozer who hung around cadging drinks."

"That's right," Hanratty said. "I remember him now. He worked here for a while as the swamper, but he couldn't even handle that job. Too feebleminded.'' Hanratty looked at the bartender. "Whatever happened to him?''

"Died a couple of weeks ago. Somebody found him in the alley out back. Doc said his whole insides were pickled from all the rotgut.''

"But I got the letter. . . .'' Sam said.

Hallam said, "You have it with you, Sheriff?''

The question seemed to take not only Sam but the others in the room by surprise. Hanratty said, "You don't believe any of this old man's ravings, do you, mister?''

"I just asked if he had the letter.'' Hallam was starting to feel curious.

Sam reached inside his dusty black coat with his left hand, while holding the Remington steady with the right. "I got it right here.''

"Can I take a look at it?'' Hallam asked.

"Sure.'' Sam brought out a wrinkled envelope and handed it to Hallam.

Hallam saw that Sam's name had been scrawled on the envelope—*Sheriff Sam Wright*—in ink that had faded with the passage of time. The envelope itself was brown with age, and so was the sheet of paper inside that Hallam carefully took out and unfolded. Writing in the same cramped hand and faded ink filled the page. It told how Moses Dunston and Frank Cahoba had planned the robbery of the Butterfield stage that was carrying the McCain Mining payroll and how Frank Cahoba had gunned down the three men in the course of the holdup. Dunston had explained, as well, how they had split up, with Cahoba taking the money so they could rendezvous later and divvy up the loot. Only Cahoba had never shown up, and it had taken Dunston a year to track him down. Dunston had written this letter before going off to have a showdown with Cahoba, so that in case he didn't survive the confrontation, he could still have his vengeance on the double-crosser from beyond the grave. Look in Sweetwater, Moses Dunston had told Sheriff Sam Wright. Look in Sweetwater for a man named Matthew Grace.

Hallam looked up from the letter. The timing worked out all right. If the old drunk called Mose had really been Moses Dunston, this letter could have been sitting in a lawyer's desk for nearly thirty years, unsent. But then, with Mose's death, his instructions had finally been carried out and the letter delivered, only decades later than Dunston had intended. What had happened when Dunston had his showdown with Frank Cahoba? Assuming, of course, that Grace and Cahoba were the same man.

And that was a mighty big assumption, Hallam realized. From everything he had seen, Matthew Grace was a pillar of the community, one of Sweetwater's leading citizens. He had been for over twenty years.

But before that, he could have been Frank Cahoba, killer and payroll robber.

"Well, what does it say?" Hanratty demanded.

"That Mr. Grace here is really Frank Cahoba, the man responsible for the McCain Mining payroll robbery," Hallam said.

"You see?" Sam said. "I told you! I told all of you I wasn't crazy!"

"But I tell you, it's impossible!" Matthew Grace said. "I never stole a payroll! I never killed anyone! I'm a banker, for God's sake!"

Slowly, Hallam said, "Fella with a big stake wouldn't have any trouble changing his name and starting up a bank."

"Good Lord, you believe him," Grace said. His eyes widened. "You're as insane as he is."

Hallam's gaze fastened on the bartender. "You remember anything else about that old drunk?"

"You mean Mose?" The bartender frowned. "Not really. Except . . . the way he'd get folks to buy him a drink. That was pretty odd."

"How's that?" Hallam asked.

"He'd tell 'em that if they'd buy him a drink, he'd let them put a finger in the hole in his head." The bartender tapped his own head, just above the right ear. "Biggest dent you ever saw in somebody's skull. Somebody who was still alive, that is.''

That was it, Hallam thought. That tied it all up. Dunston had confronted Frank Cahoba, all right, and Cahoba had put a bullet in Dunston's head. Only it hadn't killed Dunston, just turned him into a feebleminded drunk who had eventually died from all the Who-hit-John he'd swilled down. Chances were, Dunston had barely remembered his own name, let alone who Cahoba had turned himself into. But he'd written it all down before that, and time had eventually caught up with Mr. Matthew Grace.

"Mr. Grace," Hallam said softly, "who are those men you're playing poker with?"

That question threw Grace for a loop. "Why, they're . . . they're associates of mine."

The men didn't look like bankers. They looked more like gunmen to Hallam. Old habits died hard, he supposed.

"They'd better stand up slow and move off, careful-like. I think the best thing would be for you and me and Sam here to go over to the sheriff's office and wait for him to get back. We can hash it all out then."

"That's preposterous," Grace blustered. "You don't mean to tell me you actually believe this old fool?"

"I believe this letter's interestin' enough for the sheriff to take a look at it," Hallam said, holding up the piece of paper in his left hand.

"A letter written by another old fool!" Grace was sweating now. He pulled a handkerchief from his coat pocket and mopped his brow with it. "You can't honestly put any stock in anything old Mose might have said. A drunk with a bullet hole in his skull—"

"Bullet hole?" the bartender said in surprise. "He always told me a mule kicked him. That's what he told everybody else, too. I never heard him say anything about getting shot in the head."

Hallam looked hard at Grace and said, "If it really was a

bullet hole, the man who put it there would know that, wouldn't he?''

Grace just stared back at him in silence, and Sam said, "You got somethin' there, Lucas. You surely do."

Grace's eyes flicked toward the other three men at the table, and he said, "Kill them both."

Hallam was ready for that. As the three men uncoiled from their chairs, Hallam's hand dipped to the butt of his Colt. He palmed the gun smoothly from the holster. Two of the gunmen cleared leather the same time he did, and the third one was about to. Hallam was going to have to rely on Sam to take one of them.

The Remington roared beside him as Hallam squeezed off two shots. Both bullets went into the belly of one of the men who had cleared leather. The other one spun off his feet, driven back by the slug from Sam's Remington that caught him in the chest. Hallam turned slightly and fired twice more as the third man, the last one to get his gun out, became the only one of the three to actually get a shot off. The bullet sang past Hallam's ear. The third man staggered under the impact of Hallam's bullet and fired again, but this shot went into the floor as the man's arm dropped. He followed it, toppling forward in a heap.

Matthew Grace had a little pistol of his own in his hand by now, but he dropped it as Sam leveled the Remington at him and said, "Go ahead, Cahoba. Damned if I wouldn't like to kill you here and now."

Cahoba dropped the pistol and put his hands over his face.

The other seven people in the room were standing there staring. Everything had happened too fast for them to even dive for cover. The saloonkeeper, Hanratty, said in astonishment, "You mean . . . Mr. Grace really was an outlaw?"

"Looks that way to me," Hallam said as he checked on the fallen gunmen.

The gut-shot man was the only one still alive. He looked up at Hallam and grated through teeth clenched against the agony in his belly, "You . . . damned kid . . . who . . ."

"Lucas Hallam." The name was starting to mean something in certain circles, whether Hallam wanted it that way or not.

"Oh . . . damn . . ." the gunman hissed, then either died or passed out. Hallam didn't know which and didn't much care, either.

Sam moved closer to Cahoba. "Where's the payroll money?"

Cahoba lowered his hands. "Gone years ago, damn you! Gone to start the bank, just like he said." Cahoba looked at Hallam. "Why did you believe him? Nobody else ever would have."

"Because he's Sam Wright," Hallam said simply.

By the time Hallam got Sam back to Big Spring a couple of days later, things had changed. He could see now what Adabelle had meant. Sam didn't know him anymore. He was off in a world of his own most of the time, talking about people and places that Hallam had no knowledge of and calling him by names that weren't his own, usually a different one every time. That letter from Moses Dunston had brought Sam back to reality for a while, but it hadn't lasted.

Hallam hoped that somebody shot him before he got that bad off. The line of work he was in, it was pretty likely.

"I can't thank you enough," Adabelle said to Hallam after she'd hugged the old man a lot and then taken him into the parlor and got him sat down in a comfortable rocking chair. "He . . . he didn't get into any trouble, did he?"

Hallam smiled a little. "He cleaned out the ruffians."

Adabelle's hand went to her mouth. "Oh, no! He didn't."

Then Hallam told her about it, and he wasn't sure if she ever really believed him or not. But either way, she was still happy that he'd brought her grandfather back, safe and as sound as he was ever going to be again. She invited him to stay for supper, of course, to stay as long as he wanted.

Hallam looked into the parlor and watched Sam rocking back and forth for a few seconds, then said, "I reckon I'd better be ridin' on." He figured that home-cooked meal wouldn't taste quite as good as he'd expected it would when he first rode into Big Spring.

He didn't get a kiss, either, but that was no great loss, he supposed.

THE MARRIAGE OF
MOON WIND

—

Bill Gulick

It was their last night on the trail. Off to the northeast the
jagged, snowcapped peaks of the Wind River Mountains
loomed tall against the darkening sky and the chill, thin air
of the uplands was spiced with the pungent smell of sage and
pine. But Tad Marshall was not interested in sights or smells
at the moment. A rangy, well-put-together young man of
twenty with curly golden hair and sharp blue eyes, he leaned
forward and spoke to the grizzled ex-trapper sitting on the far
side of the fire.

"You'll fix it for me?"

"I'll try," Buck Owens said grudgingly. "But don't hold
me to blame for nothin' that happens. Like I told you before,
Slewfoot Samuels eats greenhorns raw."

"He takes a bite out of me, he'll come down with the worst
case of colic he ever had."

"You're cocky enough, I will say that."

"Don't mean to be. It's just that I come west to be a beaver
trapper, not a mule tender."

"With the knack you got fer handlin' mules, Captain Sublette won't want to lose you. He hears about this scheme you

193

got to partner up with Slewfoot, he'll have a foamin' fit.''

Tad shook his head. He liked Sublette and was real grateful for this chance to come west, but he wanted to see a chunk of the world with no dust-raising pack train clouding his view.

"Sublette can just have his fit. Me, I don't intend to go back to Missouri for a long spell."

"What're you runnin' away from—a mean pa?"

"Why, no. Pa treated me good."

"The law, maybe? You killed somebody back home?"

"Nothin' like that."

"Jest leaves one thing, then. Did you have woman trouble?"

Tad ran embarrassed fingers through his hair. "Guess you could call it that. There was three gals got the notion I was engaged to marry 'em. They all had brothers with itchy trigger fingers."

"Three gals wanted to marry you all to once?" Buck said in open admiration. "How'd that happen?"

"Darned if I know. Women have always pestered me, seems like. Now tell me some more about Slewfoot. You trapped with him for five years, you say?"

"Yeah. That's all I could stand him. Got a right queer sense of humor, Slewfoot has."

"A bit of joshin' never hurt nobody. I'll take the worst he can dish out, grin and come back for more."

"An' if you can't take it," Buck said, a gleam coming into his faded old eyes, "you'll stay with the mules like me'n' the captain wants you to do?"

"Sure."

"Fine! I'll introduce you to Slewfoot tomorrow."

The word got around. During the half day it took the fur brigade to reach rendezvous grounds in the lush, grass-rich valley of the Green River, the men gossiped and grinned amongst themselves, and their attitude riled Tad.

Greenhorn though he was, Tad had learned considerable during the trip out from St. Louis. There were several kinds of trappers, he'd discovered. Some worked for wages and some for commissions, but the elite of the trade were the free trappers—men who roamed where they pleased, sold their furs to the highest bidder and were beholden to nobody.

Usually such men worked in pairs, but Slewfoot, who'd been queer to begin with, and was getting queerer every year, did his trapping with no other company than a Shoshone squaw he'd bought some years back. Campfire talk had it that Indian war parties rode miles out of their way to avoid him; she grizzly bears scared their cubs into behaving by mentioning his name; and beavers, when they heard he was in the neighborhood, simply crawled up on the creek banks and died.

None of which scared Tad. But it did make him look forward with considerable interest to meeting the man whose partner he hoped to be.

Shortly before noon they hit Green River and made camp. Already the valley was full of company men, free trappers and Indians from many tribes, come in from every corner of the West for a two-week carnival of trading, gambling, drinking, horse racing and fighting. Tad took it all in with keen, uncritical eyes. But other eyes in the party looked on with far less tolerance.

Traveling with the brigade that year was a minister named Thomas Rumford, a tall, hollow-cheeked, solemn-visaged man who was returning to a mission he had established some years earlier among the Nez Perce Indians, out Oregon way. Parson Rumford had made no bones of the fact that he disapproved of the language and personal habits of the mule tenders, and he liked even less the behavior of the celebrating trappers. While Tad was helping unload the mules, Parson Rumford came up, a reproachful look on his face.

"My boy, what's this I hear about you becoming a trapper?"

"Well, I was sort of figuring on it."

"Do you know what kind of man Slewfoot Samuels is?"

"Tell me he's some ornery. But I reckon I can put up with him."

Parson Rumford shook his head and stalked away. Feeling a shade uncomfortable, Tad finished unloading the mules. Then he saw Captain Sublette approaching, and the amused twinkle in Sublette's dark eyes made him forget the minister.

"Met your trapping partner yet?"

"No. Buck's takin' me over soon as we get through here."

"Well, the least I can do is wish you luck."

"Thank you kindly, Captain."

"And remind you that your mule-tending job will be waiting, in case things don't work out."

Feeling more and more edgy, Tad joined Buck and they threaded their way toward the Shoshone section of camp.

"Lived with that squaw so long he's more Injun than white," Buck explained. "Even thinks like an Injun."

"I'd as soon you hadn't told everybody in camp what I was figuring to do. They're layin' bets, just like it was a dog fight."

"Well, you got my sympathy. Slewfoot's got a knack fer figgerin' out the one thing best calculated to rile a man. Goes for a fella's weak spot, you might say. What's yourn?"

"Don't know that I got one."

"Mine's rattlesnakes. Slewfoot shore made my life miserable, once he found that out." Buck shivered. "Kind of gives a man a turn wakin' up from a peaceable nap to find a five-foot rattler lyin' on his chest—even if it is dead."

"Slewfoot done that to you?"

"Yeah, an' then near laughed himself to death."

They stopped in front of a tepee where a squat, red-headed trapper in greasy buckskins sat dozing in the shade, and Buck nodded his head. "That he is. Ain't he a specimen?"

Before Tad could make much of a visual appraisal, Slewfoot Samuels opened his eyes. Tad got something of a shock. One eye was green, the other black, and they were as badly crossed as a pair of eyes could be. Slewfoot glared up in Buck's general direction, took a swig out of the jug of whisky sheltered between his crossed legs and spat.

"Howdy, Buck. This is the greenhorn you're figgerin' on palmin' off on me?"

"This is him. Name's Tad Marshall."

"Sit," Slewfoot grunted.

They sat and Buck reached for the jug. Slewfoot extended his right hand to Tad. "Shake."

Tad gave Slewfoot his hand, which Slewfoot promptly tried to crush into jelly. Half expecting such a stunt and having a muscle or two of his own, Tad gave just about as good as he got, and they let go with the first engagement pretty much a draw. Slewfoot took the jug away from Buck.

"Drink, Tad? Or have you been weaned from milk yet?"

Tad raised the jug to his lips, held it there while his Adam's apple bobbed six times, then passed it back. "Been watered some, ain't it?"

"Have to cut it a mite, else it eats the bottom out'n the jug."

Slewfoot's squaw, a clean, sturdy-looking woman, came out and got an armload of firewood from the pile beside the tepee, and Slewfoot grunted something to her in the Shoshone tongue. She stared curiously at Tad for a moment, grunted a reply and disappeared inside.

Several dogs lay dozing in the shade. A half-grown, smooth-haired white pup wandered into the tepee, let out a pained yip and came scooting out with its tail tucked between its legs, followed by the squaw's angry scolding. The pup came over to Slewfoot for sympathy, got it in the form of a friendly pat or two, then trotted to Tad, climbed up into his lap and went to sleep.

Slewfoot grinned. "Seems to like you."

"Yeah. Dogs usually take to me."

"Mighty fine pup. I got plans fer him."

A dark-eyed, attractive Indian girl appeared, started to go into the tepee; then, at a word from Slewfoot, stopped and stared in open-mouthed amazement at Tad. He colored in spite of all he could do. Suddenly she giggled, murmured something in Shoshone, then quickly ducked into the tepee.

"Who's that?" Buck asked.

"My squaw's sister. Name's Moon Wind."

"Tad is quite a man with the ladies," Buck said, gazing innocently off into space. "They was three gals at once after him, back home. Caused him some trouble."

"A woman can pester a man," Slewfoot said, "less'n he knows how to handle her. Have to lodgepole mine ever' once in a while."

"Lodgepole?" Tad said.

"Beat her."

"Can't say I hold with beating women."

Slewfoot grinned. "Well, you may have to beat Moon Wind to make her leave you alone. She sure admired that yaller hair of yours." Slewfoot yawned. "I'm hungry. I'll git the women to stir up some vittles."

The squaw came to the tepee entrance. They talked for a spell, then Slewfoot looked ruefully at Tad. "She says we're plumb out of meat. Kind of hate to do this, but when a man's hungry he's got to eat, I'd be obliged, Tad, if you'd pass me that pup."

"This pup?"

"Shore. It's the fattest one we got."

"I ain't really hungry yet. Ate a big breakfast."

Slewfoot grabbed the pup by the scruff of the neck, handed it to his squaw and waved her inside, then turned to Buck and began a long-winded tale. Tad's mind wasn't on the story, but with Buck sliding a look his way every now and then, there was nothing for him to do but sit there and pretend to be enjoying the company. Would the squaw skin the thing, he wondered, or just toss it into the pot with the hair on? For the first time in his life, he felt a little sick to his stomach.

After a while the squaw brought out three wooden bowls of greasy, rank-smelling stew, and Tad, hoping his face didn't look as green as it felt, accepted his with a weak smile.

"Hungry now?" Slewfoot asked.

Glassy-eyed, Tad stared down at the mess in the bowl. If he didn't eat dog he'd have to eat crow, and, of the two, he reckoned tame meat was the easier to swallow. Grimly he dug in with his spoon.

"Why, yeah. I am. Hungry enough to eat a horse. Shame you didn't have a fat one to spare."

When they headed back to their own part of camp a while later, Buck asked, "How'd you like that stew?"

"Fine, 'cept for its being a shade greasy."

"Bear meat usually is."

"Bear? I thought it was dog."

"Shoshones ain't dog eaters. Slewfoot could of lodgepoled his woman till Doomsday an' she still wouldn't of cooked that pup for us. That was just his idea of a joke."

"Didn't think it was very funny myself."

"You said you could take his worst, grin and come back for more."

"I can."

"Well, I'll hang around and watch the fun."

There were times during the next week or so when it wasn't easy for Tad to grin. The day Slewfoot near drowned him while pretending to teach him how to build a trout trap was one. The night Slewfoot put the physic in the whisky was another. But he came closest to losing his good nature the evening he got scalped by Moon Wind in sight of the whole camp.

Slewfoot arranged the thing, no doubt about that, even though it was rigged to look plumb accidental. The boys had got to finger wrestling around the campfire. Two trappers would pair off, face each other and interlace the fingers of both hands. At the word "go," they'd have at it, each one trying to force the other to his knees or break his back, according to how stubborn the fellow wanted to be.

Slewfoot threw all comers. Looking around for fresh meat, he allowed as how a certain young fellow from Missouri would chew good, so there was nothing for Tad to do but climb to his feet and give it a try.

Captain Sublette was watching. So were Buck Owens, Parson Rumford, the packtrain mule tenders and a whole mess of Indians. The bets flew thick and fast as Tad and Slewfoot squared off. Staring over Slewfoot's shoulder, Tad found himself looking right at Moon Wind, who was sitting on the ground with her deep black eyes glittering in the firelight and her soft red lips parted in excited anticipation. Kind of a purty little thing, Tad was thinking. A sight purtier than the girls back home. If only she wouldn't keep staring at him that way.

"Go!" Captain Sublette said.

Slewfoot grunted, heaved, and the next thing Tad knew, he was lying flat on his back on the ground. Dimly he heard the yelling of the crowd as he got to his feet.

Slewfoot gave him a cockeyed grin. "Want to try it again, partner?"

"Sure."

This time Tad kept his mind on the chore at hand. For some minutes they rocked this way and that, then Tad made his move. Slewfoot's knees buckled and he went down with a thud. The crowd roared even louder than before.

"Hurt you?" Tad asked solicitously.

"Once more," Slewfoot grunted, getting up.

They locked hands. Judging from the look on his face, Slewfoot really meant business this time. So did Tad. But the kind of business Slewfoot had in mind was a shade different from what Tad expected. Because they'd no more than got started good when Slewfoot dropped to his knees, heaved and threw Tad clean over his shoulders.

Tad did a complete somersault in the air, landing with his feet in the crowd and his head on the ground right close to Moon Wind's lap. Foolishly he grinned up at her. She gave him a shy smile. Then she whipped out a scalping knife, grabbed a handful of hair and lopped it off.

The crowd went crazy. So did Tad. He jumped up and made for Moon Wind, but she fled into the crowd. He whirled and went for Slewfoot, who was laughing fit to kill. Sublette, Buck Owens and half a dozen other men grabbed him and held him back.

"Easy, son; easy!" Sublette said between chuckles. "There

aren't many men get scalped and live to brag about it!''

After a moment Tad quit struggling and they let him go. His face burning, he stalked off into the darkness.

Morosely Tad finished his breakfast and accepted the cup of coffee Buck poured for him. *Yellow-Hair-Scalped-by-a-Woman*. That was the name the Indians had given him. Buck eyed him sympathetically.

''I told you he was ornery. But you were so cocky—''

''He caught me off guard. It won't happen again.''

''He's too cunning for you, boy. Why, I'll bet you right now he's windin' himself up to prank you again.''

''He gets wound up tight enough,'' Tad said grimly, ''I'll give him one more twist and bust his mainspring.''

''Better git ready to twist, then. Yonder he comes.''

Uneasy despite his brag, Tad ran absent fingers over his cropped head as Slewfoot came shuffling up, looking as pleased with the world as a fresh-fed bear.

''Mornin', gents. Any coffee left in that pot?''

Buck poured him a cup. Slewfoot hunkered on his heels, his black eye studying Tad while his green one gazed at the mountains off in the distance. ''That was a dirty trick we played on you last night, Tad. It's sort of laid heavy on my conscience. So I've decided to make it up to you.''

''I can hear him tickin','' Buck muttered.

''Just how are you going to make it up to me?''

''I know you don't like yore new Injun name. So I had a talk with a Shoshone chief that happens to be a friend of mine. He says he'll fix it.''

''How?''

''Why, he'll just adopt you into his tribe an' give you a new name. That'll cancel out the old one. It'll cost me a mite, but I figger I owe you somethin'.''

''Adopt me?''

''Yeah. Injuns do that now an' then.''

Buck eyed Slewfoot suspiciously. ''Who is this chief?''

''Seven Bears.''

"Why, ain't he the—"

"Yes, sir, he's top man of the whole tribe. No Injun'll dare laugh at an adopted son of his."

Tad thought it over. If there was a catch to it, he sure couldn't see it. He looked at Buck. "What do you think?"

"I ain't sayin' a word."

"Well," Tad said, "in that case—"

The ceremony in Chief Seven Bears' tepee took a couple of hours. A dozen or so of the most important men in the tribe were there, and one look at their solemn faces told Tad this was serious business with them. Slewfoot must have been dead serious, too, because before the palaver began he gave Seven Bears a couple of horses, half a dozen red blankets, a used musket, several pounds of powder and lead, and a lot of other trinkets in exchange for his services.

When the ceremony was finally over, they left the tepee and Slewfoot walked to the edge of the Shoshone section of camp with him. His grin seemed genuine.

"How does it feel to be an Injun?"

"Fine. What was the new name he gave me?"

"White Mule. It's a good name."

"Reckon I'm obliged to you."

"Don't mention it. Well I'll see you later."

Buck was taking a nap when Tad got back to his tent, but at the sound of his step the old trapper's eyes jerked open. "What'd they do to you?"

"It was all real friendly. Name's White Mule now."

"So he did do it! What'd it cost him?"

"Well, he gave Seven Bears some blankets, a couple of horses—"

"Hosses? Fer two hosses he could of bought you a—" Buck suddenly broke off and stared at something behind Tad. He shook his head. "He did too. Look around, boy."

Tad turned around. Moon Wind was standing there, smiling shyly. Behind her were four horses, two of which he recognized as the ones Slewfoot had given Seven Bears a while ago, and all four were laden down with Indian housekeeping gear. As Tad stared at her with stricken eyes, Moon Wind gestured at him and at herself, then made a circling motion with both hands.

"She wants to know where she'd ought to pitch your tepee."

"My tepee?"

"Yourn and hern."

"She's—she's mine now?"

"Reckon she is. Slewfoot bought her for you."

"But Seven Bears—"

"Is her pa. Also happens to be Slewfoot's squaw's pa."

"Tell her I don't want her! Tell her to go home!"

Buck laid a restraining hand on Tad's forearm. "This may be just a prank where you an' Slewfoot're concerned, but I don't reckon it's one Moon Wind and her pa would laugh at much. She must of liked you. An' Seven Bears must have thought a lot of her, else he wouldn't of outfitted her so fancy an' given you back them two bosses of Slewfoot's as a special weddin' present."

"Well, I sure can't keep her!"

"Easy. They's a way out of this, maybe, but it'll take some tall thinkin'. Let her set up her tepee. You an' me are goin' to have a talk with Captain Sublette."

Captain Sublette was not in the habit of losing his temper, but when they told him what had happened he was fit to be tied. So was Parson Rumford. When Tad declared that what he had a mind to do was grab a club and beat Slewfoot half to death, then make him take Moon Wind back to her father and explain the whole thing, the parson gave the idea his hearty approval. But Sublette shook his head.

"You can't send her back. No matter how much explaining Slewfoot did—assuming we could make him do any—the whole Shoshone tribe would be so angry they'd be down on our necks in a minute. You've got to accept her and pretend to live with her until rendezvous breaks up."

"I won't hear to such a thing!" Parson Rumford exclaimed.

"I said 'pretend,' sir . . . When the brigade goes back to St. Louis, you'll go with it, Tad. I'll tell Moon Wind that you're coming back next summer to stay. That will save her pride and our necks."

"But I won't come back? Is that the idea?"

"Yes."

Tad gazed off at the mountain peaks rimming the valley. "Seems kind of a dirty trick to play on her. Lettin' her wait for a man that won't never be comin' back to her. It's downright deceitful."

"Better a little deceit than a full-scale Indian war. She won't wait for you long, I'll wager. Next year I'll cook up some story about your having died of smallpox or something, and she'll be free to pick herself another man."

Reluctantly Tad nodded, but the deceit of it still weighed on his mind. "She's an innocent little thing and not to blame for this. I'd kind of like to give her something to remember me by—for a while, anyhow. Could I draw some of my wages and buy her a trinket or two?"

Sublette smiled understandingly, "Of course."

Pausing with the clerk in charge of the trade goods to pick out a few items he thought might appeal to her, Tad walked back to the spot where his tent had been pitched. But the tent was gone. In its place stood a roomy, comfortable skin tepee around which a dozen or two Shoshone women bustled, chattering happily as they helped Moon Wind set her household in order.

Seeing Tad, the women smiled, exchanged knowing looks amongst themselves, then quickly wound up their tasks and drifted away. When the last one had gone, he went to Moon Wind, who was on her knees building a fire.

"Moon Wind, I got something for you."

Her eyes lifted. Black eyes, they were, black and soft and deep. He got the sudden notion that she didn't know whether he was going to beat her for what she had done to him last night or caress her because she was now his woman. He took her hand and pulled her to her feet.

"These here trinkets are for you."

He dumped them into her hands. One by one, she examined them. First the glittering silver-backed mirror. Then the long double strand of imitation pearls. Then the small gold ring, which by some accident just managed to fit the third finger of her left hand. For a long moment she stared down at them. Then without a word she whirled away from him and ran toward the Shoshone section of camp.

She was gone so long that Tad, weary of trying to figure out what had got into her, went into the tepee and took himself a nap. Except for an unpleasant dream or two about Slewfoot, he slept fine. Presently he was awakened by angry voices arguing violently in the Shoshone tongue outside the tepee. He got up and went out to see what the ruckus was all about.

There, toe to toe, stood Slewfoot Samuels and his woman, jawing at each other like a pair of magpies. Off to one side and admiring her new trinkets stood Moon Wind.

Suddenly Slewfoot saw Tad and spun around. "What in the name of all unholy tarnation do you think you're doin'?"

"Me?" Tad said. "Why, I was just takin' a nap."

"That ain't what I'm talkin' about!"

"What are you talking about?"

"Them things!" Slewfoot roared, pointing a trembling hand at the ornaments Moon Wind was admiring. "That foo-faraw she's wearin'! You got any idea how much that stuff costs?"

"Sure. I bought it. What business is that of yours?"

"My squaw wants the same fool trinkets!"

"Well, buy 'em for her."

"Waste a big chunk of my year's wages for junk like that?"

"Then don't buy 'em."

"If I don't, she'll pester the life out of me."

"Lodgepole her. That'll make her quit."

Slewfoot shot his woman a sidelong glance and shook his head. "Don't hardly dare to right now. She'd raise such a racket I'd have all her relatives on my neck." Slewfoot sidled closer, a pleading look in his eyes. "Look, boy, the joke's gone far enough. Now you take that foofaraw away from Moon Wind an' cuff her a time or two. Then my woman won't be jealous of her no more."

Tad looked at Slewfoot's squaw, who had gone over to Moon Wind and was gabbling with her over the beads, mirror and ring. Sure was queer how some men would spend any amount for their own pleasure, but wouldn't put out a dime for their women. He grinned and shook his head.

"Why, I don't have to cuff 'em to make 'em behave. Treat 'em kind, I say, if you want the best out of 'em. Buy 'em presents, help 'em with the chores, give 'em the respect they're due and crave—that's the way I treat my women."

Slewfoot stared at him. "You're goin' to keep her?"

"Sure am. Going to marry her, in fact, soon as I can get Parson Rumford to tie the knot. Come to think about it, I'll make a real shindig of it. Invite her pa and ma and all her relatives. Invite the whole camp. After the wedding I'll throw a big feed with food and drinks for all."

"That'll cost you a year's wages!"

"What if it does? Man like me only gets married once."

"But when my woman sees it," Slewfoot said hoarsely, "she'll squawl to high heaven fer the same treatment. First thing you know, I won't dare lay a hand on her. She'll keep me broke buyin' her foofaraw. She'll have me totin' wood an' takin care of the hosses an' wipin' my feet 'fore I come into the tepee—why, she'll have me actin' jest like a regular husband!"

"I wouldn't be at all surprised," Tad said, and strolled off in search of Parson Rumford.

It was quite an affair, that double wedding, and the party afterward was real good fun for all concerned. Except Slewfoot Samuels, who didn't seem to enjoy it much. He'd lost his sense of humor, somehow. Maybe he'd get it back after they'd spent a few months in the mountains trapping beaver. Tad sure hoped so, anyhow. Worst thing you could have as a partner was a man that couldn't take a joke, grin and come back for more.

PORTRAIT OF A CATTLE KING

—

Michael Stotter

I was surprised when the editor called me into the office. I'd been working for the newspaper for two months, and apart from hiring me and issuing orders, he had hardly passed the time of day with me. So when he bellowed across the office for me, I naturally thought the worst.

It couldn't have been further from the truth. Frederick Styles, editor of *The Guthrie Chronicle*, sat behind his untidy desk, cup of coffee in one hand and a sheet of paper in the other. The gray-haired man took his time studying something that must have been fascinating written on that paper before he even took his eyes off it and signaled for me to sit down. I took the cane-backed chair set opposite him.

"Well, Mr. Wheeler."

Mr. Wheeler? At least he knew my name, which was a good start.

"I've been keeping my eye on you," he continued. "And, truth being told, I think I could use your expertise for a series of articles I want to run."

Me? An expert?

"You do, sir?"

He nodded sagely. "What I have in mind, and no doubt you'll have your own opinions on how to approach this, is a series of articles on the real men of the West."

I hmmed and nodded.

"See, the way things are heading, I can sense that, well, to coin the phrase, the Wild West is coming to an end, but before it does I want some hard-hitting articles that my paper can be proud of."

"I see." I began to relax a little, seeing that I wasn't going to be fired. "What was it you had in mind, sir?"

"You see, Wheeler, I've read your reporting, and I like it. I like the verve, the tenacity, and the no-nonsenseness of your style. I believe that we could syndicate these articles to the Eastern market. So where better to start than our own country—Indian Territory."

I could see Styles was excited about the series. He had forgotten about his coffee and stabbed the air with his finger as he made his points. I had to agree with him that the concept was a fine idea. Also the fact that the writing would be syndicated appealed to me. I could feel my heart pounding excitedly at the very thought of seeing my name in the Eastern newspapers. Wouldn't that be something? Just three months out of college and already appearing in the national papers, by Christ, this was the break every journalist dreamed of.

"Mr. Wheeler, I've thought long and hard about who should appear in our pages, and here is a list of prospective candidates."

He ironed out the sheet of paper with his hand across the flat of the desk, then passed it to me.

"You'll see that I have highlighted one particular name. He is to be the first; there is no argument about that. I have already arranged a time to conduct the interview, and your train passage has already been booked for you."

"Yes, sir."

Styles smiled and said, "In my opinion, he epitomizes what the West is about. Character, tenacity, strength, cunning, and

above all, the ability to rise from a lowly station in life and
be able to make something of yourself."

I wanted to add: "The Great American Dream" but
thought better of it. I didn't want to sound condescending to
Styles. When I first applied for the post of junior staff writer
at *The Guthrie Chronicle*, several of my classmates had heard
of Frederick Styles. He had been labeled an ignoramus, a
poorly educated man with neither diplomas nor skills in jour-
nalism. Some of what they said might have been true, but he
wasn't illiterate, and he had inherent skills, which many of
his antagonists would never have in two lifetimes.

His voice was still in my head as I traveled in the comfort
of the Pullman coach heading toward my ultimate goal of
Caddo to the south of the country. I doubt if there were very
many people who didn't know of or about Charlie Morrow,
one of the biggest cattlemen in the nation. I certainly had,
and I had been out of the country for some years completing
my education. Before leaving Guthrie, I asked some of the
older townsfolk about him. And what tales they came out
with.

As an infant, he and his family were forced to leave their
homeland in exile and walk with his people; he was born and
bred among the Choctaws, to the Little River country. The
government gave them nothing apart from the bare provi-
sions, and the family was forced to take whatever the wild
country threw up at them. There were no schools, no stores
or farming implements, nor did the promised rations appear.
The Morrow family, along with others, was forced into a life
of hardship. It was the upbringing that would mold Charlie
Morrow into the man that he was.

It was the type of asperity that abounded in the early days
of the West. White settlers suffered as much as those who
were forced to accept their circumstances through government
intervention. I couldn't see how different the Morrow story
was when compared against the degradations forced upon im-
migrants from Russia, Ireland, China, or France. Granted,
Morrow was a Choctaw by birth, but there was white ancestor

blood coursing through his veins. Now, don't get me wrong,
I'm not saying he was a better man for that, but it went to
make up his character.

As the train chewed up the miles, I began to write my
notes. How should I start the interview? What would the best
opening be? Certainly a mention of his early days, that went
without saying, but what would interest the readers in the
East, those who had been brought up on dime novels, yellow-
backs, and the more outrageous tales of word of mouth? How
could a half-breed become so powerful? Could that be the
hook?

I read through my notes going through the rough questions:
early days, family, wealth, best achievement, regrets, beliefs,
and the future. Trigger words to exact information out of the
interviewee. I only hoped that Charlie Morrow was a talkative
man. I'd only interviewed two other people, well, what I
would call serious interviews not on-the-spot reporting, and
they were so monosyllabic that a cracked rib was more en-
durable.

If the rumours were true, then there was one area I should
steer clear of and that was about his son from his last marriage. His first wife and two children had died during those
early days struggling to live around Little River. Charlie Morrow remarried when his business ventures were on better foot-
ing, and the union produced one son. Charlie Jr. had been
educated in private schools in Missouri and now worked for
his father's empire as ranch foreman. Charlie Jr. had gained
a bit of a reputation of being a spoiled brat. Those who op-
posed him were usually dealt with by violence. Nothing had
been proved, but it was widespread knowledge that Charlie
Jr. was an out-and-out killer. Should I pussyfoot around the
question, or did the event add to his father's mystique?

It was early evening when I stepped down off the train.
Carrying my valise and folder down the platform, I stopped
at the ticket office. There I asked directions to my hotel. The
official pointed down the street to the three-story building.
Thanking him, I made my way to the Drover Hotel.

I learned a little about Caddo from the ticket collector on the train journey. It was just another Southwest town that had sprung up where cattlemen would rendezvous in the early days. From there came the influx of business folk to build their wooden structures on either side of a main street. The cattle trade boomed when the railroad came in 1872, and so Caddo became an important business center and attracted those kind associated with a frontier cattle town.

The territory was a law unto itself. I know that's been said of many a place on the frontier before, and mostly it's true, but nonetheless, the Choctaws ran their national affairs under their own justice. It was based on similar lines to the United States constitution, but it differed in that there was an election every two years and the winner would be elected principal chief and rule as the governor. It was a very powerful position to hold. The election date was approaching, and that was another reason why Styles sent me down here. Plus Charlie Morrow was standing for the appointment.

The Drover Hotel was a splendid example of Southwestern architecture. The front was brick built; balconies ringed all three floors, the wood painted a bright blue, a sharp contrast to the dull red of the brick. The ground floor held the reception area, dining rooms, and drinking parlor that doubled for the gambling room, all decorated with some taste. I was shown to my room and ordered a bath to be made ready. The long train journey had taken its toll on me, and I needed an invigorating soak in a hot tub.

An hour later, feeling much better, I went down to the bar. I ordered up a beer and took it over to a seat by the window. Night had fallen, and the lights from the stores that were still open for trade lit the street. The comforting, familiar sounds of townsfolk going about their business filtered into the bar. I felt at ease with the town and settled in my seat to take a draft of the beer.

My glass was half-empty when a stranger came over to me.

"Hiddy, son."

"And to you."

He indicated to a vacant chair. "Mind if I set awhile?"

"No, help yourself."

Looking at the man, I got the immediate impression of a person of authority. He held his body ramrod straight and his head erect. His mustache was typical to those worn across the West: thick and drooping down the sides of his mouth. His Stetson was set at the perfect angle and wasn't removed when he sat. In sitting, he brushed his jacket to one side to reveal a revolver worn in cross-draw fashion; the walnut handle gleamed in the oil lamplight.

"Name's George Youngfellow. I'm the law here in Caddo."

I shook his proffered hand. "Pleased to meet you."

"I'll cut to the chase, Mr. Wheeler," he drawled. "Don't look so surprised. Your boss telegraphed me some time back. It was me who set the interview up for Fred."

"Fred?"

He gave a wry smile and took a sip of his beer. "Known Fred for some time now. Back when we were in the cattle business after the Civil War for a short time."

"That's something I never knew about Mr. Styles," I commented.

"We put up a herd and entrusted it to a drover to take the herd to Fort Scott in Kansas. It fetched a fair price, but when the hands came back to town, the drover didn't. He'd gone to Texas with all our money. Fred and I were broke. Well, Fred he went north and I stayed here. I'm telling you all of this because I want you to know the truth."

"The truth? Truth about what?"

Youngfellow eased his bulky frame in the seat. "When you get to meet Charlie Morrow, you should know what kind of person he really is."

If the town marshal had a hidden agenda in telling me what he knew about Morrow, then I figured it would be easy enough to find that out. "Okay, Marshal Youngfellow. I don't know what your interest in Morrow is or why you should tell me, but I'm prepared to listen." I paused to finish off my beer and slowly set the glass back on the table. Youngfellow's face was unreadable. His eyes kept locked on mine as he toyed with his beer glass, his ring finger running around the rim.

"Let's start with you and Mr. Styles or Fred if you want," I said.

"Like I said, me and Fred tried our hand in the cattle business and got burned."

"Who was the drover?"

"A man named Jim Roberts, came from Arizona way originally."

"Why did you trust him?"

"He knew cattle and we didn't. As simple as that. Fred put in all his money from his general store business, and I had some cash I had put to one side. It was about five hundred dollars apiece. Fred's store went belly up. That's when he headed north and I got work in the stockyard here in Caddo."

"So how does Charlie Morrow come into all of this?"

Youngfellow paused to light up a Long Nine cigar before continuing. "He bought Fred's store and set himself up in an already well-established business. Over the years, he became a canny businessman with interests in town, especially when the railroad came and the territory started shipping cattle east."

"Morrow sounds like he's got a good head on his shoulders when it comes to money."

"He sure has."

"You said about telling the truth. To me that implies something sinister or underhanded, and I don't hear anything like that."

For the first time I got a reaction from Youngfellow. He sat bolt upright in his chair, his right hand fisted around the near-empty beer glass and his mouth curled like he'd just eaten something sour.

He said, "Sinister? Underhanded? Them sound like writer's words. For all you hear about Charlie Morrow, I wouldn't walk on the same side of the street as him."

"But you haven't given any reasons," I sighed.

"Okay then, I'll give you an example. There's a law under the Choctaw constitution that allows one man to fence in one thousand acres. Morrow owns almost fifteen thousand acres around town and the pasture feeds a herd of around four thousand head."

"That indicates a violation of the law. How did he get away with it?"

"That's Choctaw law—whatever deal he'd made with other businessmen legally stands under the eyes of the nation."

I sat back and thought on that for a moment. My first impression was that either Styles or Youngfellow bore a grudge against Morrow even after all these years. Perhaps they considered that it should be them and not Morrow who should have been in such a powerful position. If they were planning to use me as a pawn to get to Morrow, then I wanted nothing of it.

"What you've said about Morrow so far," I said, "indicates nothing more than a little bending of the rules and a good deal of business acumen. You can't deny the man that."

"Son, you don't know the half of it," Youngfellow said.

I excused myself to get our replacement beers. The marshal seemed to have a personal agenda, one that he wasn't ready to tell me yet, but it was glowing like a burning iron of hate in his eyes. My interview with Charlie Morrow was set for the day after tomorrow. I needed that time to gather some background color to the interview. It hadn't occurred to me that someone like Youngfellow would use the chance to muddy the waters.

For me the puzzle was who was Youngfellow or Styles trying to get at? It certainly couldn't be the Texan drover who had stolen their money all those years ago. And Morrow was in such a powerful position that it would be unthinkable that they could try to bring him down. Or was it?

I put the beers down on the table and sat down. Taking in a deep breath I said, "Marshal, I got a feeling that you have information on Morrow, and you want me to use it, am I right?''

"Fred said that you was quick upstairs." Youngfellow grinned, tapping at his temple with his fingertips.

A compliment from my editor? Miracles do happen.

"If that's the case, what's in it for you? A chance for revenge?"

The marshal leaned back in his chair. "Such a dirty word," he said. "I'd prefer justice will out."

"Dress it up as you want, Marshal Youngfellow, but let's have your cards on the table."

"You're not so lenty, Mr. Wheeler."

"Lenty?"

"Green."

I smiled at the compliment from the older man.

"I'm going to tell you a story. As a journalist, you'll like it, I'm sure. Ranch wars are common happenings across the West and usually they end up with bloodshed. This war was no different. A little closer to home than usual, if you get my drift. Let's say a holding of five thousand acres of pasture can bring trouble in its management, especially when it's in the hands of a younker.

"This ranch employed mainly full-blooded Indians, very few whites, and no Negroes. The grazing area was open range and shared with another big cattleman whose interests were equal to his neighbor's. It seems that the rivals' history went back some way when they were both starting out. Let's call the holder of the five thousand acres Williams and the other Barley for want of better names. The foreman of the Williams ranch was seen in town one day talking to old man Barley. It all seemed friendly enough according to passersby, and then the conversation started to become heated. Barley suggested that wrongly branded calves were in Williams's stock. The foreman pulled his revolver and shot Barley dead.''

"Was there an investigation?"

"No. No one was ever brought to trial."

"But you said there were witnesses."

"No one would come forward. Williams wasn't only a rancher but owned the town's main mercantile store, the gin mill, and the coal mine. Not one of those witnesses was prepared to put his life on the line to testify."

These were normal strong-arm tactics used by the big land barons to clear the way of unwanted competitors.

"No doubt it wasn't an isolated incident?" I asked.

Youngfellow shook his head. "Another cattleman used the same open range as Williams and Barley. He also owned a mercantile store but on a much smaller scale. I'll call him Wheat, just to keep the image going. Old man Wheat met his end one night in his store. Two gunmen walked in and shot him down. He lived long enough to identify the men as Williams's son and the ranch scout. Other business associates were attacked, more men were killed, and Williams had grown into a very powerful figure."

"I suppose it was the same story again?" I interrupted. "No interference from the law."

He sat there and silently stared into his beer glass.

"Would it have made a difference?" I asked.

He shrugged. "Everyone has their own moral code to live by. Who knows?"

We sat in silence while we drank our beers. Youngfellow seemed more relaxed now that the telling of his story was off his chest. The clock in the bar struck nine. I looked around us and saw that the room was filling up with more customers. From somewhere in the building came music from a piano and banjo. Both players needed music lessons.

As I sat there drinking in the atmosphere, it suddenly struck me that this could be the real reason why Styles had sent me down here. His story to syndicate the articles was just a subterfuge, and the real story was, in fact, the mysterious rancher named Williams. If Williams—no, let's call him by his real name, Morrow—had now become such a powerful figure that no one would stand against him, what difference would my article make? And who's to say that if I did expose him as the man behind the killings, I wouldn't be next?

By Youngfellow's reckoning, Morrow displayed all the symptoms of a megalomaniac. His portrayal was a classic example of a land baron whose background forced him to reach greater heights without regard to losses, personal or otherwise, which occurred on the way. A picture of the man was formulating in my head.

It was a portrait of evil.

Charlie Morrow, the man whom many epitomized as the classic Westerner, was nothing more than a bully hiding behind others to further his empire. I had convinced myself that I was going to write the article, but my way.

I turned my attention back to Youngfellow. "The election," I said. "The Choctaw's governor election. When are the results due?"

He was growing tired of the questions and said through a mouthful of beer, "That's more than a month away."

"That's time enough."

To give Styles his due, my piece, "An Interview with Indian Territory's Cattle King, Charlie Morrow," appeared in that week's edition of *The Guthrie Chronicle* uncut. He even went out of his way to congratulate me on the piece. No extra cash, though. I had penned the bulk of the article on the return train journey home. And by burning the midnight oil, I had managed to write the next piece based on what Youngfellow and others had told me during my trip to Caddo.

The latter appeared in the following week's copy and written under a byline as though written in reply to the interview. Styles considered this to be even better and was as happy as a hog in mud. That fortnight was the slowest yet most exhilarating period I've ever experienced in my whole life. For most of that time, my head was in the clouds. Ideas ran through my mind and back again. Could I be bold enough to count myself as an investigative journalist rather than a junior reporter?

Dreams are like bubbles. They are made to be burst. My bubble burst on a winter's night in 1888.

I was in my room on the uppermost floor of Mrs. Cooke's boardinghouse, when TJ, the oldest typesetter in Guthrie, came knocking. His face was flushed and his limbs ached with the effort of climbing the three flights of stairs, so I gave him the only seat in the room. Word had got out, in its various forms, of the situation in Caddo. Regaining his composure, TJ felt I should know the facts.

It was a day or so after *The Guthrie Chronicle* carrying the Morrow interview came out when it happened. Charlie Morrow Jr. was found riddled with bullet holes on the territory side of the Red River. The story goes that since he was adverse to Choctaw beer, and Caddo wasn't an open town, Charlie Jr. and his friends crossed over to Texas to get their beer. There they set about getting drunk. Along with Charlie Jr. were his two cousins, Dick and Paul Sommers, and sometime scout, John Monaghan.

It was a fine night for such a time of the year, and the men quickly became intoxicated. They traveled back on the ferry to the nation's side where they decided to build a large fire to keep out the growing chill. More drink was consumed, and soon Monaghan fell into a drunken slumber. Charlie Jr. was able to hold his drink better, and soon only he and Paul Sommers were left awake.

They drank the rest of the liquor, and one thing led to another; insults were exchanged, and the argument became more heated between the cousins. Then it turned violent. First it was wildly swinging fists; then out came the knives, and they circled each other. Both were incapable of clear thought or vision. Suddenly Sommers pulled his revolver and shot Charlie Jr. The first shot wasn't fatal, but in his panic, Paul Sommers emptied his revolver into his kinfolk's body.

The body was found washed up on a sandbar on the nation side of the Red River the next morning. Town Marshal Youngfellow helped in the investigation, but no one was ever arrested. The Sommers boys were spoken to, as was Monaghan, but there was not enough evidence to convict any one of them. That was the official version.

TJ knew all this because Youngfellow had written to Styles explaining what had happened. The letter also contained the information that within the same week of Morrow Jr.'s death the Choctaws voted against his father. He had considered himself the newly elected governor during our interview and often made comments such as, "when I'm elected" or "during my tenancy" and such like. Now he had seemingly lost everything.

Reflecting upon this, I considered the part that my articles might have played in the outcome. I felt neither abomination nor partiality toward the businessman. He was desperate to be the chief, to be the most powerful cattle king in the nation, and to finish his remaining years as a pillar of the community. I closed my eyes and could picture him as he stood in his parlor, back to the picture window that overlooked some of the vast range he owned, his erect posture betraying none of the hurt he felt inside. His silver gray hair swept back and neatly barbered, his face exhibiting the lines and folds gained by the years and the elements. He would take the news without manifestation of emotion. To the end, he would play the role of the true Westerner.

THE PILGRIM

—

Loren D. Estleman

It has been my great good fortune during my sunset years to have made the acquaintance of former President Theodore Roosevelt, and to consider myself, in spite of our rather savage differences (for no other adjective will suffice) over his attempt to split the Republican Party in 1912, his friend. He it was who suggested I set down the facts attending the brief period I spent with that great frontiersman and forgotten American, Asa North; and should I succumb in my present extremity to the damnable cough which my physicians predicted would claim me thirty years ago before I have had time to prepare a proper dedication, let it be known henceforth that he alone is responsible for the narrative which follows.

Before I proceed, some background is necessary. Having been born in 1846 to a family of scriveners and schoolteachers in Portsmouth, New Hampshire, and graduated from Harvard at a tender age, I was disappointed though not much surprised upon joining the Army of the Potomac in 1865 to find myself a company clerk in Rhode Island. The only action I saw there had to do with a heated correspondence between myself and a quartermaster sergeant at Fort Leavenworth involving a shipment of flannel underwear issued in response to a requisition for twelve cases of new Springfield rifles. Following Lee's surrender, and contrary to the wishes of my parents, who had envisioned for me a career in law, I emigrated to New York City and there applied for and was given a position as reporter on James Gordon Bennett's New York *Herald*. In that assignment I distinguished myself so far as to persuade Bennett's son, James Gordon, Jr., not to give me the sack when he assumed control of the journal following his father's death in 1872.

I toiled for eleven more years without rising above my original station, and had given up all hope of so doing when I received a telegram from Joseph Pulitzer, founder of the fledgling New York *World*, offering me fresh status as city government reporter with editorial responsibilities at a monthly salary fully twice what I was receiving at the *Herald*. Naturally I accepted, and it was as a Pulitzer employee that I embarked upon the adventure which has inspired this volume.

Lest the reader think my life impossibly barren prior to that winter of 1885, I should add that during my residency in Babylon-upon-the-Hudson I had married and become separated from a young widow from Albany who proved to have the morals but not the discretion of the common alley cat, immersed myself deeply in municipal politics, served two terms as city alderman, and been a delegate to the Republican national convention which nominated Garfield for the Presidency in 1880—continuing all the while to discharge my journalistic duties at first one paper and then the other. Along the way I had also contracted a most serious case of emphysema which, threatening to turn into consumption, influenced my decision to seek a healthier climate out West.

The official excuse was a proposed series centered around a number of those colorful characters with which the frontier was said to be filled, but in truth the general interest in things western was not what it had been, and to this day I am convinced that the assignment was little more than a working

exile designed to relieve the newsroom of my constant hack-
ing and the fear of exposure to the miasma which was said
to surround sufferers of my type of malady. I flatter myself
that my ability to transform the Machiavellian concepts of
party politics into the most puerile terms for the benefit of
our readers was what prevented my editors from discharging
me.

I do not know what it was exactly that made me settle upon
Rebellion, other than a determination to avoid such picked-
over territory as Dodge City and Tombstone. I am fairly certain that I had never heard the name before I booked passage
on the Great Northern Pacific bound to the Northwest, along
whose right-of-way lay the last vestiges of the frontier, but
by the time I found myself trading the luxury of a Pullman
for a seat in a rickety day coach on the Oregon Short Line I
had heard enough from those of my fellow passengers who
were returning to be convinced that I had stumbled upon an
untapped vein of pure gold for the journalist.

My first glimpse of the bonanza was not promising. Huddled between the Caribou and the Big Hole mountains on the
twisting thread of water that gives Idaho Territory's Snake
River Valley its name, it was a cluster of dark log buildings
that looked as if they had started out weary and had long
since sunk past despair into tragic resignation. Directly overhead, a sky the color of mildew hung so low it seemed to
cast its shadow over the dull snow upon which the shelters
lay scattered as if cast by a gambler's hand. A terrible dread
settled over me as I stepped off the platform, bags in hand,
into the muddy street—not of death or danger, which would
merely have stimulated the creative impulse that had brought
me, but rather that I should have to spend the rest of my days
amid such cruel boredom.

"Is it always like this?" I asked my traveling companion
of the past four hundred miles, a lean old ranch foreman by
the name of Dale Crippen, whose great grizzled moustaches
appeared by their sheer weight to be dragging his sun-
browned flesh away from the bone beneath. A handful of

bearded men in patched logging jackets were gathered near
the platform but made no move to greet any of the trio of
road-weary passengers, all male, that had alighted with us. I
suspected that this was the highlight of their day.

"Why, hell, no," said the cowhand, around a plug of tobacco the size of a baby's fist (which I had been waiting all
day for him to expectorate, in vain). "It will be like this here
for a couple of days at the most, and then things will settle
down and get downright dismal for a while."

His reply took me aback until I glanced at him, saw a faded
blue eye watching me slyly from the forest of cracks at the
corners of his lids, and realized that I had just been treated
to an example of that famous frontier humor about which I
had heard so much. I countered with the Manhattan equiva-
lent.

"Good. I am in need of rest."

To my surprise, for I had expected the sublety to escape
him, Crippen winked broadly and served me a nudge in the
ribs with a bony elbow that gave me an uncomfortable moment lest I subside into a coughing fit. Thus far in my journey, no one west of Park Row knew of my real reason for
leaving New York, and that was the way I would have it. By
the time I had mastered myself sufficiently to renew our conversation we had reached the hotel.

This was a square, three-story frame building, one of only
two in town, whose sign running the length of the front porch
identified it as the Assiniboin Inn. Though it was of fairly
recent construction, the paint on one of the porch pillars came
off in a grayish dust onto my sleeve when I brushed against
it and the iron sconces in which a lantern rested on either side
of the door were brown with rust. In general the building was
a twin of the structure upon the opposite corner, which
sported no sign but which I was to come to know as "Au-
rora's place," whose filly curtains concealed the sort of ac-
tivity one might except of an establishment popularly referred
to, from the nickname of the hotel that faced it, as "the other
side of Sin." I remember experiencing a recurrence of the

nameless dread as I stepped up onto the booming hotel porch behind Crippen and glimpsed a pair of mannish-looking matrons watching us idly from the balcony of the other building. In the harsh light of day their shimmering dressing gowns and faces splotched with rouge and mascara made me think of corpses shrouded and painted by an inexperienced mortician.

I asked Crippen about the stench that seemed to be coming from the alley which wound behind the Assiniboin. Borne upon the crisp winter air, it was overpowering.

"Skins," he replied. "That's where they talley them before paying out the bounties. This here is the wolfing capital of the Northwest."

The front of the building was something of a town bulletin board, plastered over with posters describing various rustlers and horse thieves and offering inducements to cattlemen to ship stock on the Union Pacific, all but buried beneath scribbled advertisements enumerating various items for sale by local citizens. It was indication enough that the town had no newspaper. One poster in particular caught my eye for the black boldness of the block capitals that made up its top line, reading as follows:

$600 REWARD $600

For the Whole Hide, or other Proof of Death or Capture, of a Black-Mantled Wolf weighing in excess of 100 Pounds, and known as Black Jack, Leader of a Large Pack in the Caribou Foothills whose Depredations among local Herds of Cattle and Wild Game have been the Source of much Concern among the Good Citizens of Rebellion.

$5 BOUNTY $5

For each Wolf Scalp taken in the vicinity of the Snake River Valley, or more than Twice what the Territory of

Idaho is offering for the same Item.
Redeemable from any Member of the Idaho Stockmen's
Association.

(signed) Nelson Meredith,
President.

Meredith's signature was a daring indigo slash above the
printed name.

"Six hundred dollars seems rather a stiff bounty to pay for
a wolf," I commented, indicating the circular.

"Not for this wolf."

Though far from elegant, the lobby of the Assiniboin carried a simple dignity in its sturdy construction and utilitarian
furnishings to which no amount of gilt fixtures or burgundy
carpeting could add. A broad staircase of hand-rubbed oak
led to the upper floors on the other side of a large desk fash-
ioned of the same dark wood, behind which a middle-aged
clerk with a round, florid face and blond hair brushed back
carefully from a scanty widow's peak stood beaming at us as
we entered. He was wearing a black beaver coat in need of
brushing and a high starched collar whose exposed seams
revealed that it had been freshly turned. When Crippen
greeted him I learned that the gentleman's Christian name,
unfortunately, was Thanatopsis.

"Is he in?" asked the foreman, after answering a number
of questions about his trip to Chicago. He jerked his head in
the direction of the stairs.

The clerk nodded. "With the others. He said to send you
right up when you arrived."

Crippen started in that direction, leaving behind the worn
carpetbag that was his only luggage. "Keep an eye on that.
And take good care of my friend here from back East. He
knows a joke when he hears one."

" 'R. G. Fulwider,' " read the clerk in his off-key tenor
when I had signed the register. "Is that your full name, sir?"

I assured him that it was and accepted the key to a room
on the second floor. There being no bellboy, and the man
behind the desk pleading gout, I was carrying my own bags

up the complaining staircase when a number of men passed me on their way down. There were eight of them strung out in a line, middle-aged and older, dressed in suits of varying quality under overcoats which seemed a bit heavy for the rather mild temperature outside. Their headgear ranged from derbies not unlike my own, perched at jaunty angles, to the storied "ten-gallon" Stetson, which had proved rarer among the wide open spaces than I had been led to believe. Their faces were either very dark or very pale, with no gradations in between, and there was not a clean-shaven lip among them. To a man they moved with that air of being late for an important appointment elsewhere which I had so often noted in financiers on their way to and from the stock exchange.

Dale Crippen was on my floor speaking with a man who stood in an open doorway with his back to a room full of chairs upholstered in black leather. The stranger was stocky and solid-looking, with a square face admirably suited for his sidewhiskers and a head of thick, wavy auburn hair going silver at the temples. His complexion was hickory brown, fading out as it climbed the planes and hollows of his face and ending in a creamy swath across his forehead where the broad gray brim of the hat he held in one hand would have prevented the sun from reaching. His suit was cut western style, his high boots tilted forward upon two-inch heels and hand-tooled in the Mexican manner, but I suspected that nothing like them was available in town, or anywhere else west of New Bond Street.

Seeing my approach, the foreman broke off the conversation to introduce us. Nelson Meredith regarded me with eyes the shade of blue one sees at the very edge of a tempered blade after a professional sharpener has finished with it, and which flees almost in the time it takes to put it away. It hurt to look at them.

"I hope you will enjoy your stay in my Idaho," he said, offering his hand. I set down a bag to accept it. His grip was like his speech, controlled strength in a guise of softness. He had an English accent. Had I not been told his name, I think I would still have connected him with that bold signature I had seen on the bounty notice downstairs. I guessed our ages to be about the same.

I responded to his welcome with an inanity which escapes me now, and explained the official reason for my trip. He laughed softly, a low, silken rumble that barely stirred the lines of his face.

"I fear that you will be disappointed," he said. "The sort of creature you are hunting no longer exists out here, if indeed he ever did. There is but one Wild Bill Hickok to a century."

"But I am not searching for a Hickok, necessarily. I am certain that our readers back East would be just as eager to learn about big ranchers such as yourself."

"Perhaps, but I am hardly a typical example. My father came to this territory when it was populated only by red Indians and herds of buffalo to whom his title of Knight of the Realm meant nothing. He carved out an empire larger than some European kingdoms with his bare hands and a little help from Mr. Colt. He would have been worth writing about. I was educated at Cambridge and only came out here ten years ago upon my father's death." He smiled without showing his teeth. "I am something of a carpetbagger, you see."

"And the others?"

"You passed some of them on the stairs just now. What is your impression?"

I told him of the comparison I had made with financiers back home. He nodded.

"An apt analogy. They are speculators, mainly, from Europe and elsewhere, who purchased their holdings from men like my father and expanded them by homesteading the sources of water. Which is an illegal practice, though hardly heroic. If it is stories of adventure you want, Dale Crippen is your man. He has brought more cattle up from Texas than the city of Chicago could consume in a decade, and has fought red Indians and outlaws to do it. Unfortunately, his experiences do not greatly differ from those of hundreds of others whose stories have already been repeated for print. I fear that you could merely be covering old ground."

"You paint a bleak picture," said I.

He shrugged, a minimal movement involving but one shoulder. "I am using what colors are available."

"I should like to visit your ranch sometime."

"Dale and I will be returning in the morning. If you would care to accompany us you will be most welcome."

My lungs were beginning to close up. I replied hastily that I would very much like to accompany them, agreed to meet them in Meredith's suite at dawn, and took my leave. I barely got to my room with my luggage when the awful racking began.

When it was done I sat down weakly on the edge of the bed and inspected my handkerchief closely. There was no blood yet. Unstrapping my portmanteau, I excavated a quart bottle of gin from among my shirts, uncorked it, and without bothering to search for a glass tipped it up to dissolve the phlegm which had accumulated in my throat. It worked admirably well. My problem was that I did not stop once it had accomplished its purpose.

WHEREVER I MEET WITH A DECK OF CARDS

—

Bill Crider

My daddy was a circuit-riding preacher. He had a big, booming voice, and he loved to sing those hymns and preach those hell-hot and heaven-high sermons. The biggest disappointment of his life was that I seemed a lot more likely to wind up hot than high when my own circuit in life was finished with.

It wasn't his fault, exactly, except that he took me with him one time to face down an unrepentant backslider who was holed up in a saloon. Once I heard that tinny good-time piano, the clink of the whiskey glasses, and the flipping of the cards, I knew I was a goner.

Especially when I heard those cards.

It was a few years after that when I finally got to sit down at one of those card tables and try my luck. If you've ever been there, you know the feeling you get is like nothing else in this world, and probably the next one, hot or high. I'm talking about that feeling when you fill an inside straight on an all-or-nothing gamble, or when you're down to your last dollar and you run a bluff on some big talker who's holding

three jacks that he gets disgusted with and throws in so that
you never have to show your pair of fours.

If you've played the game, you know what I mean. And
ever since I unfolded my first hand, I've been playing the
game. I've played here and I've played there. I played all one
night across the table from Dick Clark at the Alhambra in
Tombstone long before the drink and the morphine did him
in, and once up in Deadwood I saw Poker Alice bite right
through her cigar after losing when she was holding four
kings.

I've never been one to stay in one place for long; that is,
until one time in a little boomtown when Red Collins, the
owner of the Bad Dog Saloon, asked me if I'd play for the
house.

It was a time when I was a little down on my luck, and I
was tempted. But I had to tell him a couple of things first.

"I won't stay long," I said. "And I won't cheat for you."

Those were my two rules. Like most I said, I never liked
to be in one place for long stretches of time. Most gamblers
are like that. We seem to wear out our welcomes faster than
most folks. Oh, for a while after we first get to a place, we're
liked and even respected, but when a town starts getting settled and proper, most people who're making their homes there
would just as soon the gamblers take up their trade somewhere else.

Even the honest gamblers weren't much welcome, and I
was one of those. I believe in playing the game on the square,
and I've never used a shiner, dropped a card on the floor, or
pulled one out of my sleeve.

I know some gamblers, even good ones, who think that
being able to deal from the middle or from the bottom or use
a false shuffle are nothing more than hard-won skills, and so
to use them isn't really cheating at all, but I don't share that
opinion.

"I'm not asking you to cheat," Red Collins told me. "I
have to say that I could use some help, however."

Red was a big man who wore fancy clothes he had shipped

in from the East. He had red hair, a red face, and big red hands that didn't look like they could cut a deck, much less deal from it, though I'd heard he was a pretty fair gambler himself.

I knew he could use some help because a couple of the men he had working for him were about the sorriest card players he'd ever seen. In a boomtown, you want to look prosperous, so you need a lot of players. If you're like Red, you hire gamblers to play for the house. You pay them well, and they turn any winnings over their salary to the house. Of course you have to make up their losses, if there are any, so you hope they know what they're doing. But you have to take what you can get. Sometimes you get losers. That's what had happened to Red.

"I've been losing steadily," he told me. "Over two hundred dollars last night."

"That's not good," I said.

I knew he was making a lot of it up from liquor sales and from his share of what the whores were taking in and almost certainly from the faro, dice, and roulette tables, where he had real professionals working. I've never known a house yet to come up short at roulette or dice, and not many at faro. But what Red was losing at the poker tables was still more than he could afford.

"What makes you think I can help?" I asked.

"I've been watching you. You don't drink overmuch. You know what you're doing. And I've heard a few things about you. Some people call you 'the preacher's kid.' Everybody says you deal a square game."

I thought about how my daddy would be sorry to hear that nickname, but he'd passed on to his heavenly reward a few years back, so he'd never know.

"I've been having a run of bad luck lately," I said. "I might be just as bad as those other fellas you have working for you."

"Nobody could be that bad," Red said. "You want the job or not?"

"I'll take it." I said. "I'll work for you for a week."

"I hope you'll stay a little longer than that, but if that's the best you can do, I'll settle."

We shook hands on the deal, and I started that night.

The Bad Dog was the only saloon in town that was housed in a real building. It was brand-new, so new you could smell the green wood, and it was nothing fancy. The bar was just rough planking, and there wasn't a mirror behind it, or even a picture, though Red said he'd ordered one. The town's other two saloons were in big tents, which wasn't anything unusual, and they were probably just as nice as the Bad Dog, take it all in all.

But I liked the Bad Dog. There was a fiddle player who knew more than three songs, the drinks weren't watered more than a little, and Red kept trouble down to a minimum. There probably weren't more than two or three fights a night.

I did all right the first night except for once when I tried to buy a pot with a pair of sixes. I knew better, but I thought maybe the other guy was bluffing. Turned out he wasn't.

For the most part, the games were free and easy, so I had a little time to glance at the other tables. The gamblers Red had hired for them were Big Boy Evans, who of course wouldn't go more than a hundred and twenty pounds if you weighed him with all his clothes on and a Colt's Peacemaker in his pocket, and Charlie Helton, a slick-looking, black-eyed gent who could make the cards fly over the table like pasteboard birds but who obviously took too many chances on hands that weren't worth the risk. They both lost money that night, money that Red had to make up. And he didn't like it one bit.

"I tell you," he said, "I don't know how much longer I can go on thisaway. You boys are gonna cost me everything I got."

We were all in his little office in back of the saloon, where he was giving us a little talk about the way the night had gone.

"I'm not talking to you," he told me. "You more than broke even for the house tonight. It's Big Boy and Charlie that have me worried."

"I don't know what the trouble is," Big Boy said. "I've never had a bad luck streak go on for this long. I'll break out of it tomorrow night, guaranteed."

Red shook his head. "That's what you said last night. I didn't notice any change. How much did you say you lost?"

Big Boy looked sheepish. "Seventy-two dollars."

"What about you, Charlie?" Red said. "Did you do any better than that?"

Charlie had done worse. He'd lost over a hundred dollars.

"But counting in the both of us, that's better than last night," he pointed out. "Things are improving."

Red looked disgusted. "If they keep on improving like this, I'll have to look for honest work. And I'd purely hate that. Well, we'll see what happens tomorrow night. You can go on home now."

It was nearly daylight, and I was looking forward to a little sleep, but Red called me back before I could get out the door.

"Stick around for a minute," he said. "I want to ask you something."

He waited until Charlie and Big Boy were gone, then closed the office door. For a minute he didn't say anything. Then he walked over behind his desk and sat down.

"What do you think of those two?" he asked.

"I don't know much about them. I never played against them before."

"Did you ever even hear of them before?"

"Not that I can remember."

"That's what I figured. They're probably not gamblers at all. They're just passing themselves off as gamblers and trying to make a little money. And they're doing a damned poor job of it."

"Well," I said, "at least those other players are drinking your liquor. And some of them are using their winnings to go upstairs with your girls."

"That's all to the good. But so are the men at your table, and you're not losing."

"Luck of the draw," I said.

"Yeah," he said, but I could tell he didn't really believe it.

The next evening I tried to sneak a glance at Charlie and Big Boy whenever there was a lull in the game. It was easy to see that Big Boy was just as bad as Red thought he was. His fingers were so clumsy that it was almost painful to watch him shuffle the cards. Of course I've seen some who shuffled like that on purpose, to distract you from the fact that you were going to get three kings to keep betting against their four queens, but that wasn't the case with Big Boy at all. And even worse, he'd barely have known what to do with four queens if he'd had them.

Charlie was a different story. His shuffle was something to see, and when it came to playing the cards, he knew a hawk from a handsaw. It was just that every now and then he'd have a little lapse in judgment, maybe throw in a decent hand when he should have made a bet, and that would let someone take a pot that he shouldn't have.

And once that someone looked mighty familiar to me. He had a bushy black beard, and he never took off his hat, so it was hard to see his eyes. But there was something about him that reminded me of somebody. I couldn't say why.

After all the hands were folded that night, I asked Charlie who the man had been.

"What's it to you?" he wanted to know. He didn't ask it friendly, either.

"Just curious," I said. "He looked familiar to me for some reason or other."

"I imagine you've set yourself down with him in a game somewhere."

I didn't think that was right. When I've been across the table from somebody, I remember him very well indeed, just in case I ever run across him in another game on down the line.

"That's not it," I said. "How much did he win from you?"

"What do you care? It's Red that's got to make it up."

"Just asking," I said.

As it turned out, the man had taken Charlie for around a hundred dollars on that hand I'd seen and a couple of others. Then he'd left the Bad Dog without spending a dime of it.

Red wasn't too worried about it, however, because Big Boy had more than made up for it.

"I told you I was going to break out of that bad streak," Big Boy said with a big grin.

I didn't bother to say that I knew what had happened, which was that Big Boy had met up with someone who was an even worse player than he was. You couldn't count on that happening very often. If I were a betting man, which I am, I'd say not more than once in a month of Sundays.

The next night was pretty hectic. A man accused me of cheating, which was of course an outright lie. He was just playing poorly and losing, and then trying to make excuses for himself. But when I told him that, he jumped up, kicked his chair back, and pulled a gun.

I don't carry a pistol, myself. I don't much believe in them. Their only purpose is to hurt somebody, maybe kill him, and I learned enough from my daddy's preaching to know that killing, besides being wrong, often doesn't solve much.

That pistol put an end to a lot conversations, and it got real quiet in the Bad Dog. The dice stopped rattling, the roulette wheel stopped spinning, and the fiddle player stopped fiddling right in the middle of "Turkey in the Straw."

Not having any kind of a weapon to fight with other than the five cards I was holding (two pair, jacks over tens), I made do. I flipped the jack of hearts right at the fella's face. It went hard and fast, and the edge caught him straight on the softest, tenderest part of his nose.

His left hand flew to his nose, and I stepped over and knocked his pistol aside. His fist left his nose and hit me right in the middle of the forehead like a wooden mallet. I dropped like a rock, and all hell broke loose in the Bad Dog. Seems like everybody who'd had a little bad luck, or who had a grudge to settle, or who just liked a good fight got into the action.

I missed most of it, being laid out on the floor, but I did get stepped on three or four times and kicked twice.

Then Red was in the middle of the bar letting loose with a shotgun, and that stopped everything cold. There's nothing to stop a good fight like a man with a shotgun and the nerve to use it.

It didn't take long for Red to bounce the fella who'd pulled the gun, and things began to settle down. Someone was even kind enough to put down a hand to help me up. I was a little dizzy, but damned if the fella helping me didn't look familiar. It wasn't the same fella from the night before. He didn't even have a beard. He had black eyes and a straight nose and a couple of little nicks on his cheek and neck.

"Thanks," I told him. "Guess they got you a time or two in the fracas."

He grinned. "Not so's you could tell it. I try to avoid violence when I can."

I told him I didn't blame him, and asked him if we'd met before.

"I don't reckon so," he said. "This is my first time in the Bad Dog."

I thanked him again, and we got back to our gaming. He sat at Charlie's table and won a nice hand or two or three before he left. I wondered where the hell I'd run into him before.

Both Big Boy and Charlie lost that night, though Big Boy didn't lose much. I'd lost around fifty, which I blamed on getting hit in the head. Charlie had lost another hundred or so.

"If this keeps up, I'll have to let you go," Red told Charlie while the swamper was cleaning out the place that night. There were still a couple of sleeping drunks sprawled across the tables, but it was nearly four o'clock and the gambling was over. "You're the worst card player I ever saw."

Big Boy looked right proud to hear that, as if he'd always thought *he* was about the worst there was. He was tickled to find someone who played even more poorly than he did.

Charlie took Red's criticism with good spirits. He said, "Hell, I can understand the way you feel. I can't say as I blame you. The way my luck's been running, I've been thinking it was time to quit, anyhow."

"I'll give you one more night," Red told him, which just showed how hard up he was.

Two things happened the next day.

The first one was that I cut myself while I was shaving. I was still a little shaky from the fight, and I cussed myself good for being so clumsy.

The second was that while I was looking at myself in the shaving mirror, a cold chill went through me as I realized for the first time that the older I got, the more I looked like my daddy. A few more years and a few more gray hairs, and I could pass for his brother.

That wasn't anything I wanted to think about very much, so I started thinking about other things. I finished getting dressed and went on down to the Bad Dog Saloon to see Red.

It was a little after noon by that time, and Red was back in his office, looking over his books. He glanced up when I walked in and said, "You don't look too pert today."

"I was just thinking the same thing. Do you know where Charlie's staying here in town?"

"Hadn't thought about it. Isn't he at the hotel where you are?"

"Nope. Big Boy is, I think, but not Charlie."

"Maybe he's got somebody here in town he's staying with, then. None of my business."

"I think maybe it is," I said, and then I told him why.

"God damn," he said when I was finished. "You reckon that's it?"

"Could be," I said.

"Then we gotta find him."

He was right about part of that. I was pretty sure Charlie wouldn't be coming back in that night, so Red had better find him fast. But it was the other part of what he said that bothered me.

"We?" I said.

"I might need your help on this. I'll pay you."

"I'll do what I can."

The first thing Red did was talk to his girls. He was hoping one of them might have gotten friendly enough with Charlie to know something about him. Sure enough, one of them did. He'd mentioned that he was staying in Maudie Tooke's boardinghouse just at the edge of town.

"We'd better get out there right now," Red said. "Come on."

I went with him to the livery, where the old man who ran the place got Red's buggy ready. It didn't take us too long to get to the boardinghouse, but Maudie Tooke said that we were too late to catch Charlie.

"He left here right after lunchtime. Didn't say where he was going."

"What about his brothers?" I asked.

"Brothers? Didn't know he had any."

There went one idea. But I had another one. "Cousins, then?"

"Oh, them. Nice fellas," Maudie said. "They all went with him."

"How many of them were there?"

Maudie didn't even have to think about it. "Three."

"Did they all have beards when they came here?"

She smiled. "Ever' single one of 'em. But they shaved 'em off. Right good-looking boys without all that hair on their faces."

So I'd been right. The gamblers looked familiar to me because they looked like Charlie. Not much, but enough to nag at me, make me think I'd seen them before. They came in bearded one night, then came back shaved clean a couple of nights later. They could take in five or six hundred dollars in a week or so, then move on. I wondered how many towns they'd pulled the same stunt in.

Red didn't care. All he wanted was to get his money back.

"Which way did they go?" he asked.

Maudie shrugged. "Out of town, I guess. I don't know any more than that."

Red touched up the horses, and we headed out of town as fast as they could take us. I didn't think we'd catch up with Charlie and his kin, but sure enough we did. They hadn't been in much of a hurry, I guess. Probably didn't think anyone would be on their trail so fast, if ever.

They were so surprised to see us, in fact, that they didn't even pull out their pistols. They knew why we were there, though.

"I didn't think you'd figure it out," Charlie said to Red.

"I didn't," Red told him. He looked at me. "It was him."

"Damn," said one of the cousins to me. "I never should have helped you off that floor."

"I appreciate that you did," I told him. "But you ought not to have cheated Red here. He hired your cousin in good faith."

"Yeah," Charlie said. "But now he wants to go back on the deal. Well, it's not gonna work that way."

His hand started for the big pistol that he was wearing, but before it got there, I brought the shotgun out from under the blanket on the seat where Red had put it. He'd thought we might be needing it. He'd been right.

"Damn," Charlie's cousin said again.

"Thou shalt not steal," I said.

"Bible-thumpin' son of a bitch," one of the other cousins said.

My daddy would have been proud of me.

•   •   •

"You're sure you won't hang around?" Red asked.

It was the end of the week I'd promised him, and I'd told him I was going to be moving along.

"Can't do it," I said. "I have a nice stake now, thanks to that little extra you threw in. I've enjoyed working for you, but it's time to pull up stakes."

Red shook his head. "I can't figure you. You're smart, the way you figured Charlie's scheme out. And you're law-abiding. You'd make some town a good sheriff."

Law had nothing to do with it. We hadn't taken Charlie and his cousins to any jail. Red had settled for getting back most of his money, and they'd gone on down the trail, probably to try their scheme again with new beards and new names.

Smart didn't have anything to do with it, either. It was just that I'd noticed those nicks on the cousin's face, and then I'd cut myself shaving, and then I'd thought about my resemblance to my father. Just luck, I guess you could say.

"Well," Red said, "I won't try to stop you."

We shook hands, and I left the Bad Dog Saloon. I knew I'd wind up in another place pretty much like it, but that was what I wanted out of life: a different place every now and then where I can get my feet under a card table and listen to the soft clink of the ante, a different place to listen to the fiddle and the rattle of dice in the cup. A different place to meet that deck of cards.

CALLIE AND THE ANGEL

James Reasoner

—◆—

On mornings like this, Callie wished she could still wiggle her toes in the cool dry sand at the bottom of the back steps. It was already hot, the sky cloudless with a funny, faint silver sheen to it. She paused on the top step, balancing on her crutches, and squinted up at the sky. *Goin' to be a scorcher,* she thought.

Behind her in the kitchen, Mama said, "Are you sure you feel up to gatherin' the eggs, Callie honey?"

"I'm sure, Mama," she said, trying not to sound aggravated. Mama sometimes seemed to think she wasn't capable of doing anything, had acted that way ever since the fever that had stolen the use of her legs came four years earlier when Callie was eight. Callie could have told her right from the start that she wasn't going to let no damn sickness slow her down too much or keep her from doing the things she wanted to do, only of course Mama would have washed her mouth out with soap for saying "damn." Mama had never believed in cussing, and would sometimes sniff a lot and refuse to talk to Daddy for several hours when he got upset and let a bad word or two slip.

When Daddy forgot around Callie and Mama didn't hear, then they would just grin at each other and keep the secret. Callie wished Daddy didn't have to go all the way into Wichita Falls to work and stay there all week and only come home on the weekends when he could hitch a ride on Mr. Jimmerson's buckboard. She wished he was here now.

But then, she always felt that way, so she just clumped down the steps on her crutches and started across the backyard toward the chicken house.

Daddy had built the chicken house, just like he'd built the house they all lived in, so it wasn't fancy. It was just a shed with a big window in the front that had wire tacked over it. Inside were some low shelves where the chickens built their nests and laid their eggs. The door was usually left open so that the chickens could wander in and out. There were no dogs around except Taffy, the big cocker spaniel, and she thought chickens were completely beneath her notice, so they were safe enough. The birds scurried around Callie's useless legs as she levered herself along on the crutches and went into the little building, being careful not to set the tips of the crutches down in the chicken shit, which is what it was, even though Mama insisted on calling it droppings.

Callie had a basket hung over her left arm so that it bumped against the back of her left hand with every step she took. She balanced on the right crutch and kept enough pressure on the left one with her arm to keep it from falling as she let go with her left hand and let the handle of the basket fall into her fingers. It wasn't that tricky a maneuver, and she had done it plenty of times, but still she almost dropped the basket because she was startled as she noticed the man sitting on the dirt floor in the corner of the chicken house.

Callie blinked a couple of times and her grip on the basket tightened as she wondered if she was seeing things. It had taken her a while to make her way across the backyard, and the morning sun had been hot on the top of her head. Maybe she was having a heat stroke, she thought. People who were crippled like she was were more prone to all sorts of illnesses,

Mama always said, which was why she insisted that Callie always dress warmly in the winter and try never to get her feet wet. But it wasn't winter now, and it sure wasn't cold, and there was a strange man sitting inside the chicken house.

The man lifted his right hand and held the pointer finger to his lips. There was dirt under the long fingernail.

Callie blinked again and said, "Who are you?"

The man smiled and whispered, "I'm your guardian angel."

He didn't look like any angel Callie had ever seen in Bible pictures. He had a narrow face and frizzy, reddish brown hair that stuck out around his head, and he wore a plain gray shirt and trousers instead of shimmering white robes and wings curving up gracefully from his back. He was a little bit dirty, too. One of his knees showed through a hole in the pants leg, and it was caked with grime.

Other than being surprised to find a strange man in the chicken house, Callie wasn't sure how she felt about it. She knew she wasn't scared. Some kids might've turned around and run back into the house screaming for their mama, but since that wasn't an option for Callie anymore, the thought didn't even occur to her until later. If this stranger meant to harm her, she sure couldn't outrun him, either, so there was no point in worrying about that. She was curious, she decided. More than anything else, that was how she felt.

"If you're my guardian angel," she said, "why don't you help me gather these eggs?"

The man nodded eagerly. "I can do that." He got to his feet. He was wearing old brown shoes that had seen better days, but there was nothing unusual about that. Just about everybody in Texas was dirt poor these days, and nobody had good shoes except a few rich men and their families. Callie didn't envy them, because even though her feet and legs were like sticks of wood from the waist down, she remembered what bare feet felt like and how it was to curl your toes in the dirt or wiggle your feet in thick, cool grass. That was better than shoes any day.

The man came closer, and Callie could smell him, not real bad, just a little. But Callie didn't think angels were supposed to smell like that. The man's fingers were short and blunt, but the nails had grown long. He picked up an egg and placed it in the basket Callie held out toward him.

"If you're really my guardian angel," Callie said, not knowing where the words came from and not believing for a second that was who the strange man really was, "you can make me able to walk again."

The man frowned as he put another egg in the basket. "That might take some doing," he said. "Angels can't do everything, you know. The Lord can, but we don't have His power."

"Well, if you can work on it, I'd appreciate it."

The man nodded. "Sure, I'll see what I can do. Say, I got something here to show you." He reached for his shirt and pulled the front of it out of his pants. "Look here."

Callie leaned forward and looked. She saw the smooth, curved, wooden grip of a pistol. It was tucked down inside the man's pants with just the handle sticking up. "That's a gun," Callie said.

The man nodded. "Yep, it sure is."

"My daddy has a gun," Callie told him. "He keeps it to shoot snakes."

"I see any snakes, I'll sure shoot 'em for you."

"There's probably some around," Callie said. "Snakes like chicken eggs. We best get the rest of these gathered up."

The man kept picking up the eggs from the nests and placing them carefully in the basket. Callie had got used to the smell of him by now. She was just about to ask him to come inside and eat breakfast with her and Mama when she heard Mama's voice calling from outside the chicken house.

"Callie! Come out here. Now."

The sharp edge in Mama's voice told Callie something was wrong. She glanced up at the man and saw that his eyes had gone wide with fear. He put his fingers to his lips again, and with his other hand he shooed her toward the door, like she was a chicken herself. Callie understood that he didn't want her to say anything to Mama about him being in here.

"All right," Callie whispered. She still wasn't sure if he was an angel or not, but just on the off chance that he might be, and that he might be able to help her walk again, she decided to do what he wanted.

She looped the basket over her arm again, set her hands on the grips of the crutches, and went out of the chicken house into the yard. She saw Mama standing just outside the back door. Mama motioned to her and said, "Come on, girl." Mama was staring off toward the north, and when Callie looked in that direction, she saw the man on the horse plodding toward the farm.

The man was big, Callie could tell that even at a distance, but he rode sort of hunched over in the saddle. As he came closer, she saw that he didn't have a hat on. He had the reins in his right hand and had his left arm pressed across his middle.

When Callie made it across the yard, Mama touched her shoulder and said, "Get in the house and stay there. Don't you come back out." She was scared. Callie clumped up the steps and went in, but she stopped just inside the door. Her daddy's shotgun was leaning there against the wall, close at hand where all Mama would have to do was reach inside to get it. Callie turned around so she could look back out the door.

The stranger brought his horse to a stop about ten feet away from Mama. Either that or the horse just stopped on its own, Callie couldn't tell. The man raised his head, and Callie saw that he was not only big, he was ugly, too. He had bristly black whiskers and a face that looked like somebody had pounded on it for a while with an ax handle.

There was blood on his shirt where he had his arm pressed to it. Callie saw something else on his shirt, too, something shiny. After a minute she could tell it was a silver star on a silver circle.

"Ma'am," the stranger rasped as he looked at Callie's

mama, "I'd sure be obliged if you could . . . give me a hand . . ."

As soon as he'd said that, he fell off the horse. His eyes rolled up in his head and he fell right off, landing with a big thump in the yard. Mama let out a yelp, like a cow had stepped on her foot. She hesitated, then hurried forward to kneel beside the man.

Callie moved onto the top step and said, "Mama? Is he dead?"

"No, honey, he's not." Mama looked around nervously. "But I have to get him inside and help him. He's been shot, and the men who did it could still be around here."

Callie thought about the man in the chicken house and the gun he had tucked in his pants. "What's that star on his shirt? Is he a deputy?"

Mama had hold of the man under his arms and started straining to drag him toward the steps. "No, he's . . . uh . . . he's a Texas Ranger."

"Name's Cobb," the man said a while later, when he was awake again. "From the Ranger post down at Veal Station, 'tween here and Fort Worth."

"You're a long way from home, Mr. Cobb," Mama said. She leaned forward and spooned more stew into his mouth.

Mr. Cobb chewed, swallowed, and licked his lips. "Been on the trail of some killers for a couple of weeks," he said. "Finally ran 'em down up in the breaks this side of the Red River. But they were layin' for me, and I wound up with this hole in my hide. Which you done a nice job of patchin' up, ma'am."

"You're welcome," Mama said with a little smile. She looked tired, and Callie didn't blame her. It had been a lot of work getting Mr. Cobb into the house and then lifting him into bed. Callie had helped as much as she could, but that wasn't much. She'd thought about going out to the chicken house and getting the man who claimed to be an angel, but she remembered that he didn't want her mama knowing he was there.

"Thing is," Mr. Cobb said, "those owlhoots followed me down here. They been huntin' me just like I hunted them. They don't want me on their back trail again."

"I was afraid of that," Mama said. "How far behind you were they?"

"Couple hours. Maybe."

Callie figured it had been almost two hours since Mr. Cobb had showed up at the farm. It had taken that long for Mama to bring him inside, clean up the bullet wound in his side, and wrap some bandages around him.

"My husband's down in Wichita Falls, working," Mama said. "We haven't been able to make ends meet with just the farm, so I take care of it."

Mr. Cobb nodded. "You don't have any boy children?"

"Callie is my only child."

Mr. Cobb turned his head and grinned at Callie, and when he did that, he wasn't quite as ugly. "And a mighty fine one she is, but I was hopin' there was somebody around who could handle that Henry rifle of mine."

"I can shoot a rifle," Callie said. "You don't need legs that work for that."

Mr. Cobb glanced at her crutches, then looked at her and said, "I reckon you probably can, sweetheart, but the kind of shootin' I'm talkin' about is different than shootin' at a tin can or a rabbit."

"You're talking about shooting those outlaws who're after you."

Both Mama and Mr. Cobb looked at her funny, like she shouldn't even understand what was going on. She couldn't blame Mr. Cobb for feeling like that, but you'd think Mama would know by now that not being able to walk didn't mean she was stupid.

Mr. Cobb turned back to Mama and said, "That stew of yours is mighty good, ma'am, but I got to get up now."

"I'll put your horse in the barn. Maybe they'll ride on past and not even look for you."

"One of those gents is half Comanch'. He reads sign too good for that."

Mama sighed. "How many are there?"

"Four." Mr. Cobb swung his legs out of bed. "Go ahead and put the horse away, just in case. And bring in my rifle when you come back."

Mama stood up from the chair where she had been sitting. "All right. Callie, give Mr. Cobb a hand if he needs it."

She hurried out, and Callie said, "What can I do for you, Mr. Cobb?"

He was on his feet now, shrugging back into the blood-stained shirt. "Reckon you can give me that gun belt?" he asked. He pointed to it, coiled on the dresser that sat against the bedroom wall.

Callie was balanced on her crutches at the foot of the bed. She turned and made her way easily to the dresser. She picked up the gun belt. It was heavier than she thought it would be because of the pistol in the holster.

As she handed the gun belt to Mr. Cobb, he said, "You get around pretty good on those things. How long's it been?"

"I got a bad fever four years ago," Callie said. "Mama says she thought I was fixing to die. But I got over it, only I couldn't walk anymore after that."

Mr. Cobb buckled the gun belt around his hips. "Damned shame," he said. Close up like this, he seemed about as big as a mountain.

Callie shrugged. "I get along all right."

Mr. Cobb smiled and said, "I'll just bet you do, little sis."

He walked stiff-like into the front room. Callie followed him. Mr. Cobb moved the curtain over the front window enough to look out. Nothing was moving out there, as far as Callie could see.

She knew he was watching for the outlaws who were after him. She was a little scared that bad men like that were some-where around, but to tell the truth, she had been relieved when

Mr. Cobb told who'd shot him. Callie had been afraid for a minute that the man in the chicken house had been responsible for the bullet hole in the Texas Ranger's side. She didn't like the idea that an angel might've shot a lawman. It just didn't seem right somehow.

Mama came back in the house carrying Mr. Cobb's Henry rifle. Callie could tell by the way she held it that it was heavy, like the Colt pistol in Mr. Cobb's holster. She said, "We have a shotgun and an old single-shot rifle. That's all. My husband has a pistol, but he keeps it with him."

Mr. Cobb took the rifle from her. "I'm sure sorry about bringing this trouble down on you, ma'am. I should've just kept ridin'. I was too out of my head to know what I was doin'."

"If you'd kept riding, you would have bled to death before much longer," Mama said. "You did the right thing by stopping."

She was trying to be brave about it, Callie knew, but the plain and simple fact of the matter was they were all in danger. Most men wouldn't hurt a woman, not even outlaws, but when the four of them got here, they would want Mr. Cobb. Mama could probably save her life and Callie's by turning him over to them, but Callie didn't think Mama would do that. She hoped not, anyway. Big and ugly he might be, but she liked Mr. Cobb.

Callie thought some more about the man in the chicken house. If he really was an angel, surely he wouldn't mind helping folks in need, and it seemed to Callie that she and Mama and Mr. Cobb were mighty in need right now. And if he wasn't an angel, at least he was another man with a gun. That might be enough to even the odds.

She moved toward the back door while Mama and Mr. Cobb were talking quietly to each other. She would ask the angel to help them. She was going to think of him like that from now on, and maybe that would help it come true. She wanted him to be a real angel, and to watch over them like the Good Book said.

The back door squeaked, and Mama said, "Callie?", but by then Callie was going down the steps. When she got to the bottom, she took off across the yard toward the chicken house. Behind her, Mama shouted, "Callie!"

She heard Mr. Cobb say, "Best let her go, ma'am. She probably wants to hide out there, and maybe that's a good idea."

Callie snorted, offended that Mr. Cobb thought she was scared and was running off to hide like a baby. He'd see soon enough. She pushed through the chicken house door and looked around for the angel.

He was gone.

"Damn it!" Callie hissed between her teeth. Wasn't that just like an angel to show up when you weren't expecting him and then not be there when you really needed him. God works in mysterious ways, she'd heard preachers say, and she supposed that went for angels, too, since they worked for God. But why couldn't this one have still been here?

"Callie?"

The voice came from under the shelf where the chickens made their nests and laid their eggs. It was dark under there. The angel stuck his head out and said again, "Callie? That you?"

"Yes, it is," she said impatiently. "Come on out from under there. We need you."

The angel crawled out, apparently not caring that he'd gotten chicken shit on his clothes. "I saw a man out there," he said. "He scared me."

"That's Mr. Cobb. You don't have to be scared of him. He's a Texas Ranger."

The angel wouldn't look at her. "Come to take me back. Come to take me back. I don't want to go."

"Back to where?" Callie asked. "Heaven?"

"No," the angel said slowly. "Not heaven."

"Well, like I told you, he's a Texas Ranger, so you don't have to worry about him hurting you. But there are some bad men coming, and we need your help."

The angel scratched under his left arm with his right hand. "Bad men?"

"That's right. Outlaws." Callie pointed. "We need your gun."

The angel took a step back and shook his head. "Can't give it to you. It's mine."

"I know that," Callie said, trying not to lose her temper. "But we need you to use it. We need you to shoot one of those bad men when they get here."

"Angels don't shoot folks. We . . ." He stopped and thought for a few seconds. "We smite wrongdoers with the fiery sword of the Lord's vengeance. That's what angels do."

"Well, I don't see any fiery swords around here, but you do have a Colt revolver," Callie said. "And I reckon anybody who'd shoot a Texas Ranger is a wrongdoer who needs smiting."

"I don't know . . ."

"You think about it," Callie told him. She turned toward the door of the chicken house and started to step back out into the yard. That was when she saw Taffy, the cocker spaniel, lying on the ground and looking off toward the north. Taffy whined a couple of times, then got up and started barking.

She hadn't barked at Mr. Cobb when he rode up, Callie recalled. Dogs sometimes knew more about folks than people did. Taffy had known that Mr. Cobb wouldn't hurt them.

That wasn't true of the four men riding toward the house now.

Callie drew back into the doorway where the men couldn't see her. "They're coming!" she hissed at the angel. But when she glanced over her shoulder, she didn't see him for a second. Then she spotted him cowering under the shelf again.

"Won't go back," he said. "Won't go back."

Callie looked at the house. She didn't see her mama or Mr. Cobb, but she knew they were in there. She eased an eye past the edge of the door. The four men on horseback were a lot closer now. They reminded her of Mr. Cobb because they were big and ugly and dressed rough, but she knew now there was a big difference between him and them. She could see it easy enough. These were bad men.

But not even outlaws would hurt a little crippled girl, would they?

With that thought still going through her brain, Callie tightened her grip on her crutches and levered herself out into the yard. She smiled big and called, "Howdy!" to the men who reined up in surprise.

One of the men was older than the other three and had gray streaks in his beard. His cheek was swollen with a chaw of tobacco. He spat into the dirt and then said, "You live here, gal?"

Callie thought that was a pretty stupid question, but she just said, "I sure do."

"Who else is here?"

"Nobody right now," Callie lied. Maybe they would believe her and ride on, and there wouldn't have to be any shooting. After all, she wasn't very big, and she had a bunch of freckles scattered across her face, and she was on crutches. They had to believe her.

"Where's your folks?" the gray-bearded man asked.

"My daddy's down to Wichita Falls, working. My mama's over at a neighbor's house." Callie thought fast, remembering things Mama had done in the past. "There's a woman fixing to have a baby, and Mama's going to help. She left me here to look after the place."

Well, all that sounded like it could be true enough, Callie thought. All they had to do now was believe it and ride on. She hoped Mama and Mr. Cobb weren't too worried, there in the house. She hoped they would stay out of sight until the outlaws were gone.

"You seen anybody else this mornin'? A man on a horse?"

"You mean here? Nope, just me and Taffy and the chickens. Taffy's my dog."

The gray-bearded man looked at another of the men, one who had a dark face and black hair and looked like an Indian.

The one who was half Comanch', according to Mr. Cobb, Callie figured. He shook his head and said, "The Ranger rode in here, Vince." He pointed at the ground. "Them tracks ain't more'n a couple of hours old."

Vince ran his fingers through his beard and then looked at Callie again with a stern frown on his face. "Now, listen here, little girl. You best tell me the truth this time. Where's the fella who rode in here a while ago?"

"I told you, mister—"

"Vengeance is mine, sayeth the Lord!"

That was the angel yelling as he came out of the chicken house. Callie jumped in surprise and started to turn toward him, but she overbalanced and her hands slipped on the crutches. She fell to the side, sprawling in the dust of the yard.

The angel was waving the pistol over his head, and he started to pull the trigger. The gun made a loud noise—one, two, three times. All four of the riders jerked revolvers from their holsters and fired at the angel. They had to have hit him, Callie thought, but he didn't fall down. He just kept yelling and shooting, and clouds of dust and smoke filled the air in the yard.

The back door of the house banged open and Mr. Cobb stepped out, the butt of the Henry rifle braced against his hip. He fired as fast as he could work the rifle's lever, and the shots sounded like thunder. Callie screamed and clapped her hands over her ears. Even like that, she heard the roar of the old shotgun as Mama fired it from the kitchen window.

Mr. Cobb must have emptied the rifle, because he dropped it and pulled the pistol from the holster on his hip. He was standing hunched over, like he was hurting again, but he still moved fast as he started across the yard. "Where'd he go?" he yelled.

Callie wasn't sure who Mr. Cobb was talking about. All four of the outlaws were down, having tumbled off their horses when Mr. Cobb and Mama shot them. The horses were jumping around crazy-like now, spooked by the noise and the smell of blood. Mr. Cobb ran over to Callie's side and bent down to scoop her up with his free arm. He grunted like she was heavy, but Callie figured that was just because he was hurt. There was fresh blood on his shirt. She didn't know if he had been hit during this fracas or if his wound had just started bleeding again.

He carried her over to the steps, and Mama was there to take her from him. Mama was crying and shaking now, but she had sure been steady enough when she fired that shotgun, Callie thought. The buckshot had knocked two of those bad men right out of their saddles.

Callie hung on to Mama and Mama hung on to her while Mr. Cobb hobbled around the yard and checked on the outlaws. He came back over to them and said, "They're all dead. We were mighty lucky that other fella distracted 'em. But where the hell'd he go?"

Mama was so happy that Callie wasn't hurt she didn't even say anything to Mr. Cobb about the cussing. She hugged Callie and said, "Don't you ever do anything like that again! Don't you ever!"

"I won't Mama," Callie promised. The way Mama was crying, it made Callie start to tear up, too. She buried her face against Mama's dress and sobbed a little. She figured that was all right, considering everything that had happened.

Mama patched up Mr. Cobb's wound again and rounded up the outlaws' horses. Mr. Cobb stayed a couple of days to get some of his strength back. By then, Mama and Callie had buried the four outlaws. Hot as it was, they didn't have much choice in the matter. Mr. Cobb left the horses when he was well enough to ride back to Veal Station. He said if anybody deserved to have them, it was Mama and Callie.

They never found hide nor hair of the angel, not even any blood. Callie told them about talking to him in the chicken house and how he said he was an angel and all, and they just looked at each other. Callie still wasn't sure what she believed. The man hadn't acted like any angel she'd ever heard of, and she still couldn't walk, of course, but she had to admit that when it came right down to it, he'd saved their bacon and then disappeared.

That was enough like an angel for her.

When Daddy got back from Wichita Falls the next time, he'd already heard all about the outlaws. Seemed that Mr. Cobb had stopped there in town to tell the sheriff about it, and word had gotten around, the way word of such things always does. Daddy had some news of his own, too.

"One of those crazy men Doc Canfield keeps in his house got out and escaped," he told Mama while they were eating supper. "Stole the doc's gun, too. Folks were mighty worried for a while when the sheriff looked all over for him and couldn't find him. But things have settled down some now. Nobody's seen him around, and it looks like he's left this part of the country."

"A crazy man," Mama said. "Stole a gun."

"Yep." Daddy tore off a hunk of corn bread. "That's one reason I've decided I'm not going back to town. I don't want to leave my two gals out here by themselves again. I reckon it's time we make a go of this place, one way or another."

"You're not going back?" Mama sounded like she couldn't hardly believe it, but happy at the same time.

Daddy shook his head and dipped the corn bread in his glass of buttermilk. "Nope." He grinned at Callie. "I'm home to stay."

It wasn't like being able to run again, but Callie found herself grinning back at her daddy anyway.

An angel could only do so much, she supposed.

DOC CHRISTMAS, PAINLESS DENTIST

——

Bill Pronzini

Nothing much happens in an eastern Montana farm and cow town like Bear Paw, even in the good warm days of early summer. So when this gent Doc Christmas and his assistant come rolling into town in their fancy wagon one fine June evening, unexpected and unannounced, it caused quite a commotion.

I was in the sheriff's office, where I conduct most of my civic business, when the hubbub commenced. I hurried out like everybody else to see what it was all about. First thing I saw was the wagon. It was a big, wide John Deere drawn by two bays and painted bright red with a shiny gold curlicue design. Smack in the middle of the design was the words: Doc Christmas, Painless Dentist. Then I saw that up on the seat was two of the oddest looking gents a body was ever likely to set eyes on. The one holding the reins was four or five inches over six foot, beanpole thin, with a head as big as a melon and chin whiskers all the way down the front of his black broadcloth suit coat. The other one, wearing a mustard-yellow outfit, was half as tall, four times as wide, and bald as an egg, and he was strumming an outlandish big banjo and singing "Buffalo Gals" in a voice loud enough to dislodge rocks from Jawbone Hill.

Well, we'd had our fair share of patent medicine drummers in Bear Paw, and once we'd even had a traveling medicine show that had a juggler and twelve trained dogs and sold an herb compound and catarrh cure that give everybody that took it the trots. But we'd never had a painless dentist before.

Fact was, I'd never heard of this here Doc Christmas. Turned out nobody else had, neither. He was brand-spanking-new on the circuit, and that made him all the more of a curiosity.

He drove that gaudy wagon of his straight down Main Street and across the river bridge, with half the townsfolk trailing after him like them German citizens trailed after the Pied Piper. Not just kids—men and women, too. And I ain't ashamed to admit that one of the men was yours truly, Randolph Tucker, sheriff and mayor of Bear Paw.

Doc Christmas parked his wagon on the willow flat along the river, with its hind end aimed out toward the road. It was getting on toward dusk by then, so him and the bald gent, whose name come out to be Homer, lighted pan torches that was tied to the wheels of the wagon. Then they opened up the back end and fiddled around until they had a kind of little stage with a painted curtain behind it. Then they got up on the stage part together and Homer played more tunes on his banjo while the two of 'em sang the words, all louder than they was melodious. Then Doc Christmas begun setting out a display of dentist's instruments, on a slant-board table so the torchlight gleamed off their polished surfaces, and Homer went around handing out penny candy to the kids and printed leaflets to the adults.

I contrived to lay hands on one of the leaflets. It said that Doc Christmas was Montana Territory's newest and finest painless dentist, thanks be to his recent invention of Doc Christmas's Wonder Painkiller, "the most precious boon to mankind yet discovered."

It said he had dedicated his life to dispensing this fantastic new elixir, and to ridding the mouths of every citizen of Montana of loose and decayed teeth so's the rest of their teeth could remain healthy and harmonious. And at the very last it said what his services was going to cost you. Pint bottle of Doc Christmas's Wonder Painkiller, "a three months' supply with judicious use"—one dollar. A complete and thorough dental examination in his private clinic—four bits for adults, children under the age of ten free. Pulling of a loose or decayed tooth—one dollar for a simple extraction, three dollars for a difficult extraction that required more than five minutes. There was no other fees, and painless results was guaranteed to all.

As soon as the Doc had his instruments all laid out, Homer played a tune on his banjo to quieten everybody down. After which Doc Christmas began his lecture. It was impressive. He said pretty much the same things his leaflet said, only in words so eloquent any politician would've been proud to steal 'em for his own.

Then he said he was willing to demonstrate the fabulous power of his painkiller as a public service without cost to the first suffering citizen who volunteered to have a tooth drawn. Was there any poor soul here who had an aching molar or throbbing bicuspid? If so, Doc Christmas invited him or her to step right up and be relieved.

Well, I figured it might take more than that for the Doc to get himself a customer, even one for free. Folks in Bear Paw is just natural reticent when it comes to strangers and new-fangled painkillers, particular after the traveling medicine show's catarrh cure. But I was wrong. His offer was took up then and there by *two* citizens, not just one.

The first to speak up was Ned Flowers, who owns the feed and grain store. He was standing close in front, and no sooner had the Doc finished his invite than Ned shouted, "I volunteer! I've got a side molar that's been giving me conniption fits for near a month."

"Step up here with me, sir," Doc Christmas said, "right up here with Homer and me."

Ned got one foot on the wagon, but not the second. There was a sudden roar and somebody come barreling through the crowd like a bull on the scent of nine heifers, scattering bodies every which way. I knowed who it was even before I saw him and heard his voice boom out, "No you don't, Flowers! I got me a worse toothache than you or any man in sixteen counties. I'm gettin' my molar yanked first and I'm gettin' it yanked free and I ain't takin' argument from you nor nobody else!"

Elrod Patch. Bear Paw's blacksmith and bully, the meanest gent I ever had the misfortune to know personal. I'd arrested him six times in seven years, on charges from drunk and disorderly to cheating customers to assault and battery to caving in the skull of Abe Coltrane's stud Appaloosa when it kicked him whilst he was trying to shoe it, and I could've arrested him a dozen more times if I'd had enough evidence. He belonged in Deer Lodge Penitentiary, but he'd never been convicted of a felony offense, nor even spent more than a few days in my jail. Offended parties and witnesses had a peculiar way of dropping their complaints and changing their testimony when it come time to face the circuit judge.

Patch charged right up to the Doc's wagon and shoved Ned outen the way and knocked him down, even though Ned wasn't fixing to argue. Then he clumb up on the stage, making the boards creak and groan and sag some. He was big, Patch was, muscle and fat both, with a wild tangle of red hair and a red mustache. He stood with his feet planted wide and looked hard at Doc Christmas. He'd been even meaner than usual lately and now we all knew why.

"All right, sawbones," he said. "Pick up your tools and start yankin'."

"I am not a doctor, sir. I am a painless dentist."

"Same thing to me. Where do I sit?"

The Doc fluffed out his whiskers and said, "The other gentleman volunteered first, Mr.—"

"Patch, Elrod Patch, and I don't care if half of Bear Paw volunteered first. I'm here and I'm the one sufferin' the worst.

Get to it. And it damn well better be painless, too.''

I could've gone up there and stepped in on Ned Flowers's
behalf, but it would've meant trouble, and I wasn't up to any
trouble tonight if it could be avoided. Doc Christmas didn't
want none, either. He said to Patch, "Very well, sir," and
made a signal to his assistant. Homer went behind the painted
curtain, come out again with a chair like a cut-down barber's
chair with a long horizontal rod at the top. He plunked the
chair down next to the table that held the Doc's instruments.
Then he lighted the lantern and hooked it on the end of the
rod.

Patch squeezed his bulk into the chair. The Doc opened up
Patch's mouth with one long-fingered hand, poked and prodded some inside, then went and got a funny-looking tool and
poked and prodded with that. He done it real gentle, too.
Patch squirmed some, but never made a sound the whole time.

Homer come over with a bottle of Doc Christmas's Wonder
Painkiller, and the Doc held it up to show the crowd whilst
he done some more orating on its virtues. After which he
unstoppered it and swabbed some thick brown liquid on
Patch's jaw, and rubbed more of it inside of Patch's mouth.
When he was done Homer handed him a pair of forceps,
which the Doc brandished for the assemblage. That painkiller
of his sure looked to be doing what it was advertised to do,
for Patch was sitting quiet in the chair with a less hostile look
on his ugly face.

He wasn't quiet for long, though. All of a sudden Homer
took up his banjo and commenced to play and sing "Camptown Races" real loud. And with more strength than I'd figured was in that beanpole frame, Doc Christmas grabbed old
Patch around the head with his hand tight over the windpipe,
shoved the forceps into his wide open maw, got him a grip
on the offending molar, and started yanking.

It looked to me like Patch must be yelling something fierce.
Leastways his legs was kicking and his arms was flapping.
But Homer's banjo playing and singing was too loud to hear
anything else. The Doc yanked and Patch struggled for what

must've been about a minute and a half. Then the Doc let go
of his windpipe and with a flourish he held up the forceps, at
the end of which was Patch's bloody tooth.

Patch tried to get up outen the chair. Doc Christmas shoved
him back down, took a big wad of cotton off the table, and
poked that into Patch's maw. Right then Homer quit kicking
and caterwauling. As soon as it was quiet the Doc said to the
crowd, "A simple, painless extraction, ladies and gentlemen,
accomplished in less time than it takes to peel and core an
apple. It was painless, was it not, Mr. Patch?"

Patch was on his feet now. He was wobbly and he seemed
a mite dazed. He tried to say something, but with all that
cotton in his mouth the words come out garbled and thick,
so's you couldn't understand none of 'em. Homer and the
Doc handed him down off the wagon. The townsfolk parted
fast as Patch weaved his way through, giving him plenty of
room. He passed close to me on his way out to the road, and
he looked some stunned, for a fact. Whatever was in Doc
Christmas's Wonder Painkiller sure must be a marvel of med-
ical science.

Well, as soon as folks saw that Patch wasn't going to kick
up a ruckus, they applauded Doc and Homer and pushed in
closer to the wagon. In the next half hour, Doc Christmas
pulled Ned Flowers's bad tooth and give a dozen four-bit
dental examinations, and Homer sold nineteen bottles of the
painkiller. I bought a pint myself. I figured it was the least I
could do in appreciation for the show they'd put on and that
stunned look on Patch's face when he passed me by.

I was in my office early next morning, studying on the city
council's proposal to buy fireworks from an outfit in Helena
for this year's Fourth of July celebration, when Doc Christmas and Homer walked in. Surprised me to see 'em, particular
since Homer looked some vexed. Not the Doc, though. He'd
struck me as the practical and unflappable sort last night and
he struck me the same in the light of day.

"Sheriff," he said, fluffing out his whiskers, "I wish to make a complaint."

"That so? What kind of complaint?"

"One of the citizens of Bear Paw threatened my life not twenty minutes ago. Homer's life, as well."

Uh-oh, I thought. "Wouldn't be Elrod Patch, would it?"

"It would. The man is a philistine."

"Won't get no argument from me on that," I said. "Philistine, troublemaker, and holy terror. What'd he threaten you and Homer for? Body'd think he'd be grateful, after you yanked his bad tooth free of charge."

"He claims it was not the painless extraction I guaranteed."

"Oh, he does."

"Claims to have suffered grievously the whole night long," Doc Christmas said, "and to still be in severe pain this morning. I explained to him that some discomfort is natural after an extraction, and that if he had paid heed to my lecture he would have understood the necessity of purchasing an entire bottle of Doc Christmas's Wonder Painkiller. Had he done so, he would have slept like an innocent babe and be mostly fit as a fiddle today."

"What'd he say to that?"

"He insisted that I should have supplied a bottle of my Wonder Painkiller gratis. I informed him again that only the public extraction was gratis, but he refused to listen."

"Just one of his many faults."

"He demanded a free bottle then and there. Of course I did not knuckle under to such blatant extortion."

"That when he threatened your life?"

"In foul and abusive language."

"Uh-huh. Any witnesses?"

"No, sir. We three were alone at the wagon."

"Well, then, sir," I said, "there just ain't much I can do legally. I don't know what to tell you gents, except that so far as I know, Patch ain't never killed anybody human. So the chances are he won't follow up on his threat."

"But he would go so far as to damage my wagon and equipment, would he not?"

"He might, if he was riled enough. He threaten to do that, too?"

"He did."

"Hell and damn. I'll have to talk with him, Doc, try to settle him down. But he don't like me and I don't like him, so I don't expect it'll do much good. How long you and Homer fixing to stay on in Bear Paw?"

"Business was brisk last evening," the Doc said. "We anticipate it will be likewise today and tomorrow as well, once word spreads of my dental skills and the stupendous properties of Doc Christmas's Wonder Painkiller."

"I don't suppose you'd consider cutting your visit short and moving on elsewheres?"

He drew himself up. "I would not, sir. Doc Christmas flees before the wrath of no man."

"I was afraid of that. Uh, how long you reckon Patch's mouth will hurt without he treats it with more of your Wonder Painkiller?"

"The exact length of time varies from patient to patient. A day, two days, perhaps as long as a week."

I sighed. "I was afraid of that, too."

Patch was banging away at a red-hot horseshoe with his five-pound sledgehammer when I walked into his blacksmith's shop. Doing it with a vengeance, too, as if it was Doc Christmas's head forked there on his anvil. The whole left side of his face was swelled up something wicked.

He glared when he saw me. "What in hell you want, Tucker?"

"A few peaceable words, is all."

"Got nothin' to say to you. Besides, my mouth hurts too damn much to talk." Then, Patch being Patch, he went ahead and jawed to me anyways. "Look at what that travelin' tooth puller done to me last night. Hurts twice as bad with the tooth out than it done with it in."

"Well, you did rush up and volunteer to have it yanked."

"I didn't volunteer for no swole-up face like I got now. Painless dentist, hell!"

"It's my understanding you threatened him and his assistant with bodily harm."

"Run to you, did he?" Patch said. "Well, it'd serve both of 'em right if I blowed their heads off with my twelve-gauge."

"You'd hang, Patch. High and quick."

He tried to scowl, but it hurt his face and he winced instead. He give the horseshoe another lick with his hammer, then dropped it into a bucket of water. He watched it steam and sizzle before he said, "They's other ways to skin a cat."

"Meaning?"

"Like I said. They's other ways to skin a cat."

"Patch, you listen to me. You do anything to Doc Christmas or Homer or that wagon of theirs, anything at all, I'll slap you in jail right sudden and see that you pay dear."

"I ain't afraid of you, Tucker. You and me's gonna tangle one of these days anyhow."

"Better not, if you know what's good for you."

"I know what's good for me right now, and that's some of that bustard's painkiller. It's the genuine article, even if he ain't. And I aim to get me a bottle."

"Now, that's the first sensible thing I heard you say. Whyn't you and me mosey on down to the river together so's you can buy one?"

"Buy? I ain't gonna *buy* somethin' I should of got for nothin'!"

"Oh, Lordy, Patch. Doc Christmas never promised you a free bottle of painkiller. All he promised was to draw your bad tooth, which he done."

"One's free, so's the other," Patch said. "Ain't nobody cheats Elrod Patch outen what's rightfully his and gets away with it. Sure not no flimflammin' long drink of water that claims to be a painless dentist."

Well, it just wasn't no use. I'd have got more satisfaction

trying to talk sense to a cottonwood stump. But I give it one last try before I took myself out of there. I said, "You're warned, mister. Stay away from Doc Christmas and Homer and their wagon or you'll suffer worse 'n you are now by half. And that's a promise."

All I got for an answer was a snort. He was on his way to the forge by then, else I reckon he'd have laughed right in my face.

Long about noonday I had an inspiration.

I walked home to Madge Tolliver's boardinghouse for my noon meal, which I like to do as often as I can on account of Madge being the best cook in town, and afterwards I went upstairs to my room for the bottle of Doc Christmas's Wonder Painkiller I'd bought last night. Outside again, I spied the Ames boy, Tommy, rolling his hoop. I give Tommy a nickel to take the bottle to the blacksmith's shop. I said he should tell Patch it was from Doc Christmas and that it was a peace offering, free of charge. I don't like fibbing or having youngsters fib for me, but in this case I reckoned I was on the side of the angels and it was a pardonable sin. Sometimes the only way you can deal with the devil is by using his own methods.

I waited fifteen minutes for Tommy to come back. When he did he didn't have the bottle of painkiller with him, which I took to be a good sign. But it wasn't.

"He took it all right, Mr. Tucker," Tommy said. "Then he laughed real nasty and said he suspicioned it was from you, not Doc Christmas."

"Blast him for a sly fox!"

"He said now he had *two* bottles of painkiller, and his mouth didn't hurt no more, but it didn't make a lick of difference in how he felt toward that blankety-blank tooth puller."

"Two bottles?"

"Got the other one from Mr. Flowers, he said."

"By coercion, I'll warrant."

"What's coercion?"

"Never you mind about that. Patch didn't say what he was fixing to do about Doc Christmas, did he?"

"No, sir, he sure didn't."

I left Tommy and stumped on down to the river to see the Doc. There was a crowd around his wagon again, not as large today, but still good-sized. Doc had a farmer in the chair and was yanking a tooth while Homer played his banjo and sang "Camptown Races." I waited until they was done and eight more bottles of the Wonder Painkiller had been sold. Then I got the Doc off to one side for a confab.

I told him what Patch had said to me and to Tommy Ames. I thought it might scare him some, but it didn't. He drew himself up the way he liked to do, fluffed his whiskers, and said, "Homer and I refuse to be intimidated by the likes of Elrod Patch."

"He can be mean, Doc, and that's a fact. He's as likely as a visit from the Grim Reaper to make trouble for you."

"Be that as it may."

"Doc, I'd take it as a personal favor if you'd pull up stakes and move on right now. By the time you make your circuit back to Bear Paw, Patch'll have forgot his grudge—"

"I'm sorry, Sheriff Tucker, but that would be the cowardly way and Homer and I are men, not spineless whelps. The law and the Almighty can send us fleeing, but no man can without just cause."

Well, he had a point and I couldn't argue with it. He was on public land and he hadn't broke any laws, including the Almighty's. I wished him well and went back to town.

But I was feeling uneasy in my mind and tight in my bones. There was going to be trouble, sure as God made little green apples, and now I couldn't see no smart nor legal way to stop it.

It happened some past midnight, and depending on how you looked at it, it was plain trouble or trouble with a fitting end and a silver lining. Most if not all of Bear Paw looked at it the second way. And I'd be a hypocrite if I said I wasn't one of the majority.

I was sound asleep when the knocking commenced on the door to my room at the boardinghouse. I lighted my lamp before I opened up. It was Doc Christmas, looking as unflappable as ever.

First thing he done was unbutton his frock coat and hand me a pistol, butt first, that had been tucked into his belt. It was an old Root's Patent Model .31 caliber with a side hammer like a musket hammer, a weapon I hadn't seen in many a year. But it looked to be in fine working order, and the barrel was warm.

"Sheriff," he said then, "I wish to report a shooting."

"Who got shot?"

"Elrod Patch."

"Oh, Lordy. Is he dead?"

"As the proverbial doornail."

"You the one who shot him?"

"I am. In self-defense."

He might've been telling me the time of night—he was that calm and matter-of-fact. Practical to a fault, that was the Doc. What was done was done and there wasn't no sense in getting exercised about it.

I asked him, "Where'd it happen?"

"On the willow flat near where my wagon is parked. Homer is waiting there for us. Shall we proceed?"

I got dressed in a hurry and we hustled on down to the river. Homer was tending to one of the bay horses, both of which seemed unusual skittish. Nearby, between where the horses was picketed and the wagon, Elrod Patch lay sprawled out on his back. In one hand he held a five-pound sledgehammer, of all things, and there was a bullet hole where he'd once had a right eye.

"It was unavoidable, Sheriff," Homer said as I bent to look at Patch. "He rushed at the Doc with that hammer and left him no choice."

"What in tarnation was Patch doing here with a sledgehammer? Not attempting to murder you gents in your beds, was he?"

"No," Doc Christmas said. "He was attempting to murder our horses."

"Your horses?"

"It was their frightened cries that woke Homer and me. Fortunately, we emerged from the wagon before he had time to do more than strike one of the animals a glancing blow."

Well, I knew right then that the Doc and Homer was telling the truth. Patch had caved in the skull of Abe Coltrane's stud Appaloosa with nary a qualm nor regret, and I could see where doing the same to a couple of wagon horses would be just his idea of revenge. Still, I had my duty. I looked close at the sledgehammer to make sure it was Patch's. It was; his initials was cut into the handle. Then I examined the bay that had been struck and found a bloody mark across his neck and withers. That was enough for me.

"Self-defense and death by misadventure," I said, and I give the Doc back his .31 Root's. "Patch had it coming—no mistake about that, neither. Too bad you had to be the one to send him to his reward, Doc."

He said, "Yes," but he looked kind of thoughtful when he said it.

Doc Christmas come to see me one more time, late the following afternoon at my office. At first I thought it was just to tell me him and Homer was leaving soon for Sayersville. Then I thought it was to ask if they'd be welcome back when Bear Paw come up on their circuit again next spring, which I said they would be. But them two things was only preambles to the real purpose of his visit.

"Sheriff Tucker," he said, "it is my understanding that you are also the mayor and city treasurer of Bear Paw. Is this correct?"

"It is," I said. "I'm likewise chairman of the annual Fourth of July celebration and head of the burial commission. Folks figured it was better to pay one man a salary for wearing lots of hats than a bunch of men salaries for wearing one hat apiece.''

"Then you are empowered to pay out public funds for services to the community."

"I am. What're you getting at, Doc?"

"The fact," he said, "that Bear Paw owes me three dollars."

"Bear Paw does what? What in tarnation for?"

"Services rendered."

"Come again?"

"Services rendered," the Doc said. "I am a painless dentist, as you well know—the finest and most dedicated painless dentist in Montana Territory. It is my life's work and my duty and my great joy to rid the mouths of my patients of loose and decayed teeth. A town such as Bear Paw, sir, is in many ways like the mouth of one of my patients. It is healthy and harmonious only so long as its citizens—its individual teeth, if you will—are each and every one healthy and harmonious. One diseased tooth damages the entire mouth. Elrod Patch was such a diseased tooth in the mouth of Bear Paw. I did not extract him willingly from your midst, but the fact remains that I did extract him permanently—and with no harm whatsoever to the surrounding teeth. In effect, sir, painlessly.

"For a simple painless extraction I charge one dollar. You will agree, Sheriff Tucker, that the extraction of Elrod Patch was not simple, but difficult. For difficult extractions I charge three dollars. Therefore, the town of Bear Paw owes me three dollars for services rendered, payable on demand."

Did I say the Doc was practical to a fault? And then some! He was a caution, he was, with more gall than a trainload of campaigning politicians. If I'd been a lawyer, I reckon I could've come up with a good argument against his claim. But I ain't a lawyer, I'm a public servant. Besides which, when a man's right, he's right.

On behalf of the healthy and harmonious teeth of Bear Paw, I paid Doc Christmas his three dollars.

RIVERBOAT FIGHTER

Brian Garfield

Clay Goddard came aboard the *Mohave* at Yuma an hour before she was due to depart. He walked around B Deck to his regular tiny stateroom on the portside and remained there only long enough to stow his carpetbag and comb his hair; the cubicle was stifling hot. Coming out on deck, he tugged his brocade vest down and placed his gray hat squarely across his brows. Clay Goddard was a tall man, thin to the point of gauntness, with the hint of a stoop in his broad shoulders. His lion-gray eyes were hooded and his lips were guarded by the full sweep of a tawny mustache.

He was coming around the afterdeck, passing in front of the wide paddlewheel, when his alert eyes shot toward the gangplank. A solid-square man in a dusty blue suit was coming up the plank; sight of that man arrested Clay Goddard: he stood bolt still, watching, while the stocky man ascended to the rail and paused.

A ball-pointed brass star glittered on the newcomer's blue lapel. The ship's captain, coming toward the gangway, nodded and touched the brim of his cap. "How do today, Marshal?"

Marshal Emmett Reese nodded and said something Goddard didn't catch; then the lawman's deliberate voice lifted: "Believe I'll be going up with you this trip, Jack. How's the current running?"

"Slow and easy," Captain Jack Mellon said. He was a legend on the river: he had steamed the Rio Colorado more than fifteen years. It was said he could talk to the river and hear its reply. He said to the marshal, "Ought to make an easy five miles an hour going up. I figure to make Aubrey's Landing in forty-eight hours."

"That's traveling," Marshal Reese observed. Clay Goddard watched the lawman's profile from his stance under the shadowed overhang of the afterdeck. The captain spoke once more and turned to go up the ladder toward his wheelhouse on the Texas Deck, and Marshal Emmett Reese's glance came around idly. His eyes alighted on Clay Goddard and immediately narrowed; the marshal's whole frame stiffened. Goddard's expression remained bleak, unreadable. Across thirty feet of deck space their glances clashed and held. The revolver butt at Goddard's hip touched the vein of his thin wrist.

Emmett Reese seemed about to advance, about to speak; but then the sound of an approaching buggy clattered toward the wharf, and the marshal ripped his eyes away, swinging heavily around, tramping back down the plank.

Clay Goddard's face revealed no particular relief. He turned with deliberate paces and walked into the ship's saloon. The bartender was its only occupant. Goddard took a cup of coffee, went to a table in the back of the room, and laid out an elaborate game of patience. Brooding over the cards, he sipped the cooling black coffee and ran his glance once around the room.

It was neither so large nor so elegant as the cardrooms on the great Mississippi packets; but then, this was Arizona, and rivers did not run so deep or wide here. It was engineering marvel enough that the *Mohave*, one hundred fifty feet long and thirty-three feet abeam, could carry two hundred passengers and a hundred thousand pounds of cargo and still skim over the Rio Colorado's shallow bottom. The water often ran less than three feet deep; the *Mohave* drew only thirty inches, fully ballasted.

Steamboats had been plying the river for twenty-seven years now, but their interloping presence in the desert country never failed to strike Goddard as an odd phenomenon. The ships of the Colorado Steam Navigation Company regularly made the seemingly impossible run up to Callville, Nevada—six hundred miles above the river's mouth, and desert country all the way, except where the big ships had to winch themselves up over cascades through the knife-cut tall gorges up-river.

The saloon was a plain oblong room, low ceilinged and plainly furnished—not at all like the velvet-lined rooms of the New Orleans sternwheelers. But the *Mohave* was the pride of the line, and in the far Southwest she was queen. The barkeep wiped his plain mahogany counter and behind it, between racks of labeled bottles, hung a lithographed calendar with today's sailing date circled: August 24, 1879. Regarding that, and recalling the grim square-hewn face of Marshal Emmett Reese on deck, Clay Goddard thought what a long time it had been, how the years had flowed silently by; and he felt quietly surprised. He was thirty-seven this month; his birthday had passed, he suddenly realized, without notice.

His lean hands darted over the wooden table, placing card upon card. Green sleeve garters held the shirt back from his wrists. He pulled out his snap-lid pocket watch—eight-thirty in the morning, and already he was soaked with sweat. It would hit a hundred and ten inside the saloon today.

His gambler's training laid a cool endurance over him; over the years he had developed the ability to stand off from himself and look on, as if from some long distance. Without it, his life would not have been bearable.

The boat swayed gently as heavy freight wagons rolled up the plank onto the cargo decking. Faintly through the door came the hoarse shouts of teamsters, the profane calling of stevedores. Passengers, early arriving, began to drift in and out of the saloon. With a hissing chug and a resigned clatter, the boilers fired up and began to build up their head of steam. Smoke rose from the twin tall stacks at the front of the pilothouse.

His shirt drenched, Clay Goddard unbuttoned his elaborate vest—the uniformed sign of his calling—and bent over his solitaire board in concentration. He was like that, frowning over the merciless cards, when a great force rammed the edge of the table into his belly, slamming him in his chair back against the wall.

Tautly grinning, a hawk-faced man stood hunched toward Goddard, a tall, powerful man with a stiff brush of straight red hair standing up brightly on his head. Hatless, the grinning man held the table jammed against Goddard, pinning Goddard to his chair. In a quiet, soft tone, the red-haired man said, "Somebody told me you were working this boat."

Goddard said with deceptive mildness, "Take the table out of my gut, Miles."

Miles Williams took his hands away from the table and laughed unpleasantly. "I ain't got my gun on just now. That's a piece of luck for you, Clay."

"Or for you."

Miles Williams's eyes met Goddard's without guile. "Nobody said you weren't tough, Clay, and nobody said you weren't fast. But I can take you."

"You can try," Goddard answered evenly. He pushed the table away from him and straightened his rumpled vest, but he kept his seat. The cards had flown into disarray when Williams had violently rammed the table. Goddard gathered them unhurriedly into a pack, never releasing Williams from his gaze.

Williams said, "I've got a lot to settle with you for, Clay. Too much to let pass. I'm going up to Aubrey on this boat and I don't figure both of us will get there alive."

"That's up to you, Miles."

"We're still in port. You can get off now. Maybe I won't follow you—I got business upriver."

Goddard tilted his head slightly to one side. "You'd offer

me a chance to skin out, would you? I'm surprised."

"I ain't an unfair man," said Miles Williams. "And I don't like killing. Go on, Clay—get off the boat. Save us both a lot of grief that way."

Goddard considered him over a stretching interval of time; at the end of it he shook his head. "I guess not, Miles."

"Suit yourself." Abruptly, with a snap of his big shoulders, Miles Williams swung away and stalked out of the saloon.

At the bar, a few men with cigars and coffee had watched with careful interest. What Goddard and Williams had said had been pitched too low to reach their ears, but the scene had been too charged with action and hard stares to escape their attention. Sweeping them with his guarded eyes, Goddard maintained his cool expression and proceeded to lay out a fresh, slow game on the table.

Shortly thereafter, however, he got up and walked slowly out of the saloon. A deck hand was coiling in the stern rope. The ship was crowded with army men—two companies of infantry on their way to Ehrenberg, shipping point for the inland Apache-fighting garrisons. Goddard threaded his path among the knots of troopers and entered his little stateroom, where he closed the door in spite of the heat building up. Out of his carpetbag he took ramrod, patches, cloth and oil. After locking the door he dismantled his revolver and gave it a careful, methodical cleaning. Then he put it back together, loaded the cylinder with six .44-40 cartridges and let the hammer down gently between the rims of two shells. Standing up, he slid the weapon into its oiled holster and adjusted the hang carefully. His expression never changed; the mustache drooped over his wide lips. He packed the cleaning equipment away, unlocked the door and stepped out on deck just as the captain shouted from two decks above and the boat slowly churned out into the current.

The wharves and shipyard of Yuma slowly drifted past the starboard beam; there was a last glimpse of Fort Yuma, high on the hill with its precious squares of green lawns, and then the massive rolling paddlewheel drove the ship around the outer curve of the first bend, and the only sight to either side was mosquito-buzzing brushy lowlands and, beyond, the flats and dry-rock hills of the vast Southwestern desert.

Goddard stepped past a lashed-down freight wagon, and halted abruptly.

Coming forward, arms linked, were Marshal Emmett Reese and a slim figure of a woman. Holding the woman's left hand was a girl of six, wide-eyed and with hair the same tawny color as Goddard's own. The woman's mouth opened and, quickly, Emmett Reese stepped out in front of her as though to protect her. Reese said nothing but it was plain by his stance and attitude that he expected Goddard to go on about his business without stopping to speak.

The woman put her hand on Reese's arm. "No, Emmett. We'll be on this boat for two days and nights. It's a small boat. We can't pretend to each other that we don't exist."

Goddard stepped forward with the briefest of cool smiles. "It's been a long time, Margaret." His glance dropped to lie on the little girl. "Six years," he murmured.

The woman had both hands on the little girl's shoulders now. Emmett Reese said, "Come on, Margaret, we can—"

"No," she said. "I want to talk to him, Emmett."

Reese's eyes bored into Goddard, but it was the woman his words addressed: "I wish you wouldn't."

"Take Cathy with you, will you? I'll meet you in the lounge." The woman's voice was firm.

Troubled, the marshal reached down to take the little girl's hand. He said to Goddard, "Miles Williams is on board."

"I know."

"This boat's in my jurisdiction. I don't want trouble."

"I won't be starting any trouble," Goddard said.

The little girl watched with her head tilted on one side, looking up at Goddard and then the marshal, puzzled but silent. Soldiers milled past in pairs and groups. An officer moved through the crowd, creating a stir of saluting and mumbled greetings. The woman, tossing her head impatiently, said, "Go on, Emmett." She bent down. "Go with the marshal, sweetheart. Mummy will be along soon."

The little girl stared at Goddard. "Who's he?" she demanded accusingly.

The woman looked up and away; her eyes turned moist. Emmett Reese said gently, "Come on, Cathy," and led the little girl away by the hand, casting one warning glance back toward Goddard.

Goddard moved toward the rail, pushing a path through for the woman. She came up and stood beside him, not looking at him, but watching the muddy flow of the river. Her eyes were still clouded with tears; there was a catch in her throat when she spoke: "I'm sorry. I knew this moment would come. I meant to be strong—I didn't mean it to be this way. But when she asked *who you were*—"

"She looks a little like me," he said musingly.

"She has your hair, your eyes—every time I look at her I—" The woman's head turned sharply down against her shoulder, hiding her face. Goddard's hand came out toward her, but stayed, and he did not touch her. A solemn mask descended over his face. He murmured, "Well, Meg."

He took a folded handkerchief from his vest and offered it to her. She pressed it to the corners of her eyes. She was a blue-eyed woman, slim and pretty but no longer in the smooth-checked paleness of youth: the veins of her hands and the creases around her eyes revealed that she was near Goddard's own age.

He said, "You're traveling with Emmett?"

"In separate staterooms," she said dryly, and then shook her head. "He wants to marry me—marry us, that is. He loves Cathy."

"Maybe," Goddard said softly, "that's because he's had the chance to love her."

Her eyes lifted dismally to his. Plainly gathering herself, she used both palms to smooth back her brown hair. "I am going to be strong, Clay," she said, measuring out each word for emphasis. "You and I, we had our chance together."

"And I ruined it," he finished for her.

"You," she agreed, "and that." She was looking at the worn-smooth handle of his revolver. "And now Miles Williams is here. He's been looking for you a long time, Emmett said. You killed two of his friends in a card game."

"I caught them cheating together. They drew against me."

"Is that an explanation, Clay?" she asked. "Or just an excuse?" She reached out; her fingertips touched the walnut gun grip. "You love that thing."

"No. I hate it, Meg."

She swung half way, facing the river again, the marshes drifting past. The huge paddlewheel left a pale yellow wake stretching downstream with the current. "I wish I could believe you," she said. "If it's true then you've changed."

"I have," he agreed simply.

She threw her head back. Her voice was stronger: "We were married once. It didn't work. I've no reason to believe it would work again."

He nodded; but his eyes were sad—he was looking forward, toward the lounge where the little girl had gone. He said, "What will you tell her about me? She wants to know who I am."

"I don't know," she said, almost whispering. "I wish I did." She turned from him and walked away, moving briskly. He watched the way she walked, head turned over his shoulder, both hands gripping the rail so tightly his knuckles shone white.

A tall, red-topped figure swayed forward, pushing soldiers aside roughly with hands and elbows. Miles Williams reached Goddard's side and grinned around the cigar in his teeth. "Who's the lady, Clay?"

When Goddard made no reply, Williams said, "I saw you talking to Emmett Reese. With him on board, we're going to have a little problem, you and me. Either one of us starts trouble, he's likely to step in. So I've got a little proposition for you. I gave you your chance to get off the ship. You stayed, so I guess that means you want to play the game I called. All right, we'll lay down some ground rules. We wait, you and me. These soldier boys get off at Ehrenberg in the morning and the boat'll be less crowded tomorrow. Tomorrow night the decks ought to be pretty clear. We wait until everybody's asleep. No witnesses, that way. We have at each other, and no matter who's standing up afterward, ain't nobody can tell Emmett Reese who started the fight. The winner claims self-defense, and Reese can't dispute it, see? No law trouble, no trouble afterward for the one of us that's still alive."

"You're a coldblooded buck," Goddard observed without much emphasis.

"I just like to keep things neat," Miles Williams said, and turned aft. A holstered pistol slapped his thigh as he walked through the crowd.

Showing no sign of his feelings, Clay Goddard went into the saloon, picked a table, and set the pack of cards out, advertising his calling. It was not long before five soldiers were gathered round his table, playing low-stake poker.

The day passed that way for Goddard, bar sandwiches and coffee and poker—a steamy hot day that filled the room with the close stink of sweat weighted with tobacco smoke and the smells of stale beer and whisky. He did not leave the saloon until suppertime, when he went forward into the dining salon. He saw Emmett Reese and Margaret and little Cathy at the captain's table. His eyes lingered on the blond little girl. Margaret's eyes found him once, but turned away quickly; she swung her head around, tossing her hair, to respond to some light remark of Captain Jack Mellon's.

Miles Williams was not in the room. Goddard took his customary place at the first officer's table, between the deck steward and an Army doctor, and ate a silent meal. Afterward he had a cigar on deck, and returned to the saloon for the evening's trade. The crowd was thoroughly penny ante; he made a total of seven dollars for the day's gambling, and went on deck at midnight. He had to pick a path over the heaps of sleeping soldiers.

The heat had dissipated with darkness. He lay down on his

bunk, knowing he needed sleep in order to be alert for the following night's encounter; but sleep evaded him and he lay in the dark cabin with his hands laced under the back of his head, staring sightlessly at the ceiling. The engines throbbed soporifically, but he was still awake at three when the boat scraped bottom on a sandbar and the engines reversed to take her off. She lurched forward once again, going around the bar, and finally Goddard drifted into a semiwakeful drowsiness that descended into fitful sleep.

He was awake and dressed at dawn when the *Mohave* berthed at Ehrenberg. The town was a drab oasis at best. Miles Williams came by and said, "You could still get off right here and wait till the boat comes back down. But then maybe you'd rather not wait another three years for me to come after you again."

"Never mind," Goddard told him.

"All right," Williams drawled. The sun picked up glints in his bush of red hair. He grinned and ambled away. Goddard noticed Emmett Reese standing not far away, watching him inscrutably; it was hard to tell whether Reese had heard what had been said.

The soldiers disembarked with their baggage and wagons, and thus lightened, the boat made faster headway upstream. Its decks were lashed with wagonloads of mining machinery for the camps served by Aubrey's Landing, but pedestrian traffic was light and there was hardly any trade in the saloon all day.

After supper he was on deck, savoring his cigar, when Margaret came out of the dining room and sought him out. If he was surprised, he did not show it. She said, in a voice that showed how tightly throttled were her emotions, "That may be your last cigar. Have you thought of that?"

"Yes."

"How can you keep such a rein on yourself, Clay? Aren't you frightened?"

He made no answer. He squinted against the cigar smoke and Margaret said, "You're scared to death, aren't you?"

"I guess I am."

"Then that's changed, too."

"Maybe I've learned to care," he said. He turned to look at her. "Sometimes it takes a long time to learn a simple thing like that."

His talk appeared to confuse her. She folded her arms under her breasts. "Cathy still wants to know about you."

"Have you decided what to tell her?"

"I'll tell her the truth. But I'm going to wait until tomorrow."

He said quietly, "You think I'll be dead by then, don't you, Meg?"

"One way or the other," she said. "Dead to us, anyway. Whether you're still walking and breathing won't matter." She dropped her arms to her sides; her shoulders fell. "Emmett told me that Miles Williams gave you the chance to get off at Ehrenberg."

"I might have taken it," he said, "except for you and Cathy. I wanted to have another day—this is as close as I've ever been to her. I couldn't give it up."

She said in a muted voice, "If you'd gotten off the boat," and did not finish; Goddard finished it for her:

"You'd have come with me?"

"I don't know. How can I say? Maybe—maybe."

Twilight ran red over the river. The great paddles slapped the water and a lone Indian stood on the western bank, silhouetted against the darkening red sky, watching the boat churn past into gathering night. A shadow filled the dining room doorway, blocky and sturdy—Emmett Reese, who wore the star. Reese stood there, out of earshot, watching but not advancing. Goddard said, "I guess he loves you."

"Yes."

"And you him?"

She didn't answer right away. There was a sudden break in Goddard's expression and he seemed about to reach out and grasp her to him, but he made no motion of any kind and his face resumed its composure. He said slowly, "I have always been in love with you. But I have to meet Miles Williams tonight and my love for you can't stop that.''

''Nor my love for you?'' she cried out.

''I'm sorry,'' he said dismally.

Her voice subsided in resignation. ''I can't give my little girl a father who fights to kill.''

''What about Emmett Reese?'' He was looking at Reese, outlined in the doorway, still as a mountain.

''It's his job. Not his pleasure.'' Her lip curled when she said it.

''It's no pleasure to me either,'' he said. ''God knows there are a lot of things I regret, Meg.''

''But you won't give up your pride.''

''Would I be a man without it?''

She had no answer for him. She turned and walked from him, toward the waiting shadow of the marshal.

The cigar had gone dry and sour. Goddard tossed it overboard and went into the saloon. Lamplight sent rays through the smoky air; the crowd was thin and for an hour no one came to Goddard's table. He sat with the pack of cards before him; he sat still, his head dipped slightly like a tired man half asleep.

Miles Williams came at ten-thirty and sat down opposite him. Williams had a cheroot uptilted between his white teeth. His face was handsome and brash, the eyes half-lidded. ''A friend is a close and valuable thing,'' he said. ''I lost two friends one night.''

''They forced it on me.''

''Then they should have won.'' Williams picked up the deck of cards and shuffled it. ''Blackjack suit you?''

And so they played a macabre game of cards while the hours ran out, while the passengers drifted away one by one and lamps winked out around the ship. The engines thrummed, the paddles hit the water with a steady slap-slap, and when the saloon was empty but for the bartender, Miles Williams said in a suddenly taut voice, ''All ready, Clay?''

''Here?''

"On deck. Loser goes overboard. Neat—neat that way."

"All right," said Clay Goddard.

Williams thrust his chair back with his knees and stood. "After you?"

"Right beside you," Goddard answered, and they left shoulder to shoulder.

The decks were deserted; lamps were off, except two decks higher up on the Texas, where the keen-eyed captain swept the river vigilantly for shifting sandbars. Miles Williams said, "Jack Mellon's got eyes in the back of his head. We'll go on down to the afterdeck—he can't see that from up there."

They tramped along the port B Deck and Goddard felt moisture on his palms; he wiped them on his vest and heard Williams chuckle. "Got you nervous, ain't I? Get a man nervous, you got the edge." Williams was flexing his fingers. Starlight glittered on the river. Not a single lamp glowed in the after section of the ship. The two men reached the platform behind the cabin structure. Here the smash of the paddles against the water was a loud racket in the night; the paddles lifted overhead and swept down, splashing drops of water against the stern and the aft yard or two of deck planking. The iron railing protected passengers from the cruel, deliberate power of the great paddlewheel.

Miles Williams stopped six feet from the rail and wheeled, planting his feet wide apart. "You can step back a way," he said calmly, "or do you want it point-blank?"

"Right here will do," Goddard said. "A man wouldn't want to miss his shot for bad light."

A startled brightness gleamed from Williams's eyes. "You steadied down quick, didn't you?" he observed. Then he laughed with raucous brashness. But the laugh fell away and his face grew long. The brush of his hair stood up against the sky and he suddenly cried, *"Now!"*

Williams's hand spilled for his gun butt. Close in to the man, Goddard did not reach for his own gun; instead he lashed out with his boot. The hard toe caught Williams's wrist just as the gun was rising. The gun fell away, bouncing off

Goddard's instep; and Williams, rocked by the kick, wind-milled back, off balance. His feet slipped on the wet planking; the small of his back rammed the stern rail and Goddard, rushing forward, was not in time to prevent Williams from spilling over backward into the descending paddlewheel.

The paddles caught Williams and dragged him down relentlessly; there was a brief awful cry, and that was all.

Gripping the rail, Goddard looked down into the churning blackness of the descending paddles. His eyes were hollow. Heavy footsteps hurried toward him along the deck and he turned, nerved up to high pitch.

Emmett Reese said, "I couldn't stop it before it started. But I saw it. He wasn't fast at all—you could have outdrawn him with no trouble."

"I knew that."

"You didn't figure on this?"

"No. I expected a good beating might have changed his mind." Goddard smiled bleakly. "I was always pretty good with my fists."

"Better than guns," Reese said quietly, staring at the heavy falling paddles. He added in a murmur that was barely audible over the slapping wheel, "You're a far better man than I gave you credit for, Clay."

Reese's hand reached out and clenched Goddard's arm. Goddard shook his head slowly back and forth, as if to clear it. He pulled away and walked forward along the empty deck.

He was in his cabin, unhooking his gun belt, when light knuckles rapped the door. When he opened it, Margaret stepped inside. The lamp washed her face in warm light.

She said, "Emmett told me what happened. You could have drawn on him. You could have shot him down, but you didn't—you tried to save his life."

"I told you," he said wearily. "A man learns a few things as time goes by, Meg."

She said, "Cathy's asleep now, and I didn't want to wake her. But in the morning when she asks me who you are, I'll be able to tell her. We'll have breakfast together, the three of us."

"What about Reese?" he said.

She moved into the circle of his arms. "He understands," she said. She turned her face up toward him.

THE LAST INDIAN FIGHT IN KERR COUNTY

Elmer Kelton

In later times, Burkett Wayland liked to say he was in the last great Indian battle of Kerr County, Texas. It happened before he was born.

It started one day while his father, Matthew Wayland, then not much past twenty, was breaking a new field for fall wheat planting, just east of a small log cabin on one of the creeks tributary to the Guadalupe River. The quiet of autumn morning was broken by a fluttering of wings as a covey of quail flushed beyond a heavy stand of oak timber past the field. Startled, Matthew jerked on the reins and quickly laid his plow over on its side in the newly broken sod. His bay horse raised its head and pointed its ears toward the sound.

Matthew caught a deep breath and held it. He thought he heard a crackling of brush. He reached back for the rifle slung over his shoulder and quickly unhitched the horse. Standing behind it for protection, he watched and listened another moment or two, then jumped up bareback and beat his heels against the horse's ribs, moving in a long trot for the cabin in the clearing below.

He wanted to believe ragged old Burk Kennemer was coming for a visit from his little place three miles down the creek, but the trapper usually rode in the open where Matthew could see him coming, not through the brush.

Matthew had not been marking the calendar in his almanac, but he had not needed to. The cooling nights, the curing of the grass to a rich brown, had told him all too well that this was September, the month of the Comanche moon. This was the time of year—their ponies strong from the summer grass—that the warrior Comanches could be expected to ride down from the high plains. Before winter they liked to make a final grand raid through the rough limestone hills of old hunting grounds west of San Antonio, then retire with stolen horses and mules—and sometimes captives and scalps—back to sanctuary far to the north. They had done it every year since the first settlers had pushed into the broken hill country. Though the military was beginning to press in upon their hideaways, all the old settlers had been warning Matthew to expect them again as the September moon went full, aiding the Comanches in their nighttime prowling.

Rachal opened the roughhewn cabin door and looked at her young husband in surprise, for normally he would plow until she called him in for dinner at noon. He was trying to finish breaking ground and dry-sow the wheat before fall rains began.

She looked as if she should still be in school somewhere instead of trying to make a home in the wilderness; she was barely eighteen. "What is it, Matthew?"

"I don't know," he said tightly. "Get back inside."

He slid from the horse and turned it sideways to shield him. He held the rifle ready. It was always loaded.

A horseman broke out of the timber and moved toward the cabin. Matthew let go a long-held breath as he recognized Burk Kennemer. Relief turned to anger for the scare. He walked out to meet the trapper, trying to keep the edginess from his voice, but he could not control the flush of color that warmed his face.

He noted that the old man brought no meat with him. It

was Kennemer's habit, when he came visiting, to fetch along a freshly killed deer, or sometimes a wild turkey, or occasionally a ham out of his smokehouse, and stay to eat some of it cooked by Rachal's skillful hands. He ran a lot of hogs in the timber, fattening them on the oak mast. He was much more of a hogman and trapper than a farmer. Plow handles did not fit his hands, Kennemer claimed. He was of the restless breed that moved westward ahead of the farmers, and left when they crowded him.

Kennemer had a tentative half smile. "Glad I wasn't a Comanche. You'd've shot me dead."

"I'd've tried," Matthew said, his heart still thumping. He lifted a shaky hand to show what Kennemer had done to him. "What did you come sneaking in like an Indian for?"

Kennemer's smile was gone. "For good reason. That little girl inside the cabin?"

Matthew nodded. Kennemer said, "You'd better keep her there."

As if she heard the conversation, Rachal Wayland opened the door and stepped outside, shading her eyes with one hand. Kennemer's gray-bearded face lighted at the sight of her. Matthew did not know if Burk had ever had a wife of his own; he had never mentioned one. Rachal shouted, "Come on up, Mr. Kennemer. I'll be fixing us some dinner."

He took off his excuse of a hat and shouted back, for he was still at some distance from the cabin. "Can't right now, girl. Got to be traveling. Next time maybe." He cut his gaze to Matthew's little log shed and corrals. "Where's your other horse?"

"Grazing out yonder someplace. Him and the milk cow both."

"Better fetch him in," Kennemer said grimly. "Better put him and this one in the pen closest to the cabin if you don't want to lose them. And stay close to the cabin yourself, or you may lose more than the horses."

Matthew felt the dread chill him again. "Comanches?"

"Don't know. Could be. Fritz Dieterle come by my place

while ago and told me he found tracks where a bunch of horses crossed the Guadalupe during the night. Could've been cowboys, or a bunch of hunters looking to lay in some winter meat. But it could've been Comanches. The horses wasn't shod.''

Matthew could read the trapper's thoughts. Kennemer was reasonably sure it had not been cowboys or hunters. Kennemer said, ''I come to warn you, and now I'm going west to warn that bunch of German farmers out on the forks. They may want to fort-up at the best house.''

Matthew's thoughts were racing ahead. He had been over to the German settlement twice since he and Rachal had arrived here late last winter, in time to break out their first field for spring planting. Burk Kennemer had told him the Germans—come west from the older settlements around Neu Braunfels and Fredericksburg—had been here long enough to give him sound advice about farming this shallow-soil land. And perhaps they might, if he could have understood them. They had seemed friendly enough, but they spoke no English, and he knew nothing of German. Efforts at communication had led him nowhere but back here, his shoulders slumped in frustration. He had counted Burk Kennemer as his only neighbor—the only one he could talk with.

''Maybe I ought to send Rachal with you,'' Matthew said. ''It would be safer for her there, all those folks around her.''

Kennemer considered that for only a moment. ''Too risky traveling by daylight, one man and one girl. Even if you was to come along, two men and a girl wouldn't be no match if they jumped us.''

''You're even less of a match, traveling by yourself.''

Kennemer patted the shoulder of his long-legged brown horse. ''No offense, boy, but old Deercatcher here can run circles around them two of yours, and anything them Indians is liable to have. He'll take care of me, long as I'm by myself. You've got a good strong cabin there. You and that girl'll be better off inside it than out in the open with me.'' He frowned.

"If it'll make you feel safer, I'll be back before dark. I'll stay here with you, and we can fort-up together."

That helped, but it was not enough. Matthew looked at the cabin, which he and Kennemer and the broken-English-speaking German named Dieterle had put up after he finished planting his spring crops. Until then, he and Rachal had lived in their wagon, or around and beneath it. "I wish she wasn't here, Burk. All of a sudden, I wish I'd never brought her here."

The trapper frowned. "Neither one of you belongs here. You're both just shirttail young'uns, not old enough to take care of yourselves."

Matthew remembered that the old man had told him as much, several times. A pretty little girl like Rachal should not be out here in a place like this, working like a mule, exposed to the dangers of the thinly settled frontier. But Matthew had never heard a word of complaint from her, not since they had started west from the pineywoods country in the biting cold of a wet winter, barely a month married. She always spoke of this as *our* place, *our* home.

He said, "It seemed all right, till now. All of a sudden I realize what I've brought her to. I want to get her out of here, Burk."

The trapper slowly filled an evil black pipe while he pondered and twisted his furrowed face. "Then we'll go tonight. It'll be safer traveling in the dark because I've been here long enough to know this country better than them Indians do. We'll make Fredericksburg by daylight. But one thing you've got to make up your mind to, Matthew. You've got to leave her there, or go back to the old home with her yourself. You've got no business bringing her here again to this kind of danger."

"She's got no home back yonder to go to. This is the only home she's got, or me either."

Kennemer's face went almost angry. "I buried a woman once in a place just about like this. I wouldn't want to help bury that girl of yours. *Adiós,* Matthew. See you before dark.'' He circled Deercatcher around the cabin and disappeared in a motte of live-oak timber.

Rachal stood in the doorway, puzzled. She had not intruded on the conversation. Now she came out onto the foot-packed open ground. "What was the matter with Mr. Kennemer? Why couldn't he stay?"

He wished he could keep it from her. "Horsetracks on the Guadalupe. He thinks it was Indians.''

Matthew watched her closely, seeing the sudden clutch of fear in her eyes before she firmly put it away. "What does he think we ought to do?" she asked, seeming calmer than he thought she should.

"Slip away from here tonight, go to Fredericksburg.''

"For how long, Matthew?''

He did not answer her. She said, "We can't go far. There's the milk cow, for one thing. She's got to be milked.''

The cow had not entered his mind. "Forget her. The main thing is to have you safe.''

"We're going to need that milk cow.''

Impatiently he exploded, "Will you grow up, and forget the damned cow? I'm taking you out of here.''

She shrank back in surprise at his sharpness, a little of hurt in her eyes. They had not once quarreled, not until now. "I'm sorry, Rachal. I didn't go to blow up at you that way.''

She hid her eyes from him. "You're thinking we might just give up this place and never come back . . .'' She wasn't asking him; she was telling him what was in his mind.

"That's what Burk thinks we ought to do.''

"He's an old man, and we're young. And this isn't his home. He hasn't even got a home, just that old rough cabin, and those dogs and hogs . . . He's probably moved twenty times in his life. But we're not like that, Matthew. We're the kind of people who put down roots and grow where we are.''

Matthew looked away. "I'll go fetch the dun horse. You bolt the door.''

Riding away, he kept looking back at the cabin in regret. He knew he loved this place where they had started their lives together. Rachal loved it, too, though he found it difficult to understand why. Life had its shortcomings back in east Texas, but her upbringing there had been easy compared to the privations she endured here. When she needed water she carried it in a heavy oaken bucket from the creek, fully seventy-five yards. He would have built the cabin nearer the water, but Burk had advised that once in a while heavy rains made that creek rise up on its hind legs and roar like an angry bear.

She worked her garden with a heavy-handled hoe, and when Matthew was busy in the field from dawn to dark she chopped her own wood from the pile of dead oak behind the cabin. She cooked over an ill-designed open fireplace that did not draw as well as it should. And, as much as anything, she put up with a deadening loneliness. Offhand, he could not remember that she had seen another woman since late in spring, except for a German girl who stopped by once on her way to the forks. They had been unable to talk to each other. Even so, Rachal had glowed for a couple of days, refreshed by seeing someone besides her husband and the unwashed Burk Kennemer.

The cabin was as yet small, just a single room which was kitchen, sleeping quarters and sitting room combined. It had been in Matthew's mind, when he had nothing else to do this coming winter, to start work on a second section that would become a bedroom. He would build a roof and an open dog run between that part and the original, in keeping with Texas pioneer tradition, with a sleeping area over the dog run for the children who were sure to come with God's own time and blessings. He and Rachal had talked much of their plans, of the additional land he would break out to augment the potential income from their dozen or so beef critters scattered along the creek. He had forcefully put the dangers out of his mind, knowing they were there but choosing not to dwell upon them.

He remembered now the warnings from Rachal's uncle and aunt, who had brought her up after her own father was killed by a falling tree and her mother taken by one of the periodic fever epidemics. They had warned of the many perils a couple would face on the edge of the settled lands, perils which youth and love and enthusiasm had made to appear small, far away in distance and time, until today. Now, his eyes nervously searching the edge of the oak timber for anything amiss, fear rose up in him. It was a primeval, choking fear of a kind he had never known, and a sense of shame for having so thoughtlessly brought Rachal to this sort of jeopardy.

He found the dun horse grazing by the creek, near a few of the speckled beef cows which a farmer at the old home had given him in lieu of wages for two years of backbreaking work. He had bartered for the old wagon and the plow and a few other necessary tools. Whatever else he had, he and Rachal had built with their hands. For Texans, cash money was still in short supply.

He thought about rounding up the cows and corraling them by the cabin, but they were scattered. He saw too much risk in the time it might take him to find them all, as well as the exposure to any Comanches hidden in the timber. From what he had heard, the Indians were much less interested in cattle than in horses. Cows were slow. Once the raiders were ready to start north, they would want speed to carry them to sanctuary. Matthew pitched a rawhide *reata* loop around the dun's neck and led the animal back in a long trot. He had been beyond sight of the cabin for a while, and he prickled with anxiety. He breathed a sigh of relief when he broke into the open. The smoke from his chimney was a welcome sight.

He turned the horses into the pole corral and closed the gate, then poured shelled corn into a crude wooden trough. They eagerly set to crunching the grain with their strong teeth, a sound he had always enjoyed when he could restrain himself from thinking how much that corn would be worth in the settlements. The horses were blissfully unaware of the problems that beset their owners. Matthew wondered how content they would be if they fell into Indian hands and were driven or ridden the many long, hard days north into that mysterious hidden country. It would serve them right!

Still he realized how helpless he and Rachal would be without them. He could not afford to lose the horses.

Rachal slid the heavy oak bar from the door and let him into the cabin. He immediately replaced the bolt while she went back to stirring a pot of stew hanging on an iron rod inside the fireplace. He avoided her eyes, for the tension stretched tightly between them.

"See anything?" she asked, knowing he would have come running.

He shook his head. "Not apt to, until night. If they're here, that's when they'll come for the horses."

"And find us gone?" Her voice almost accused him.

He nodded. "Burk said he'll be back before dark. He'll help us find our way to Fredericksburg."

Firelight touched her face. He saw a reflection of tears. She said, "They'll destroy this place."

"Better this place than *you*. I've known it from the start, I guess, and just wouldn't admit it. I shouldn't have brought you here."

"I came willingly. I've been happy here. So have you."

"We just kept dancing and forgot that the piper had to be paid."

A silence fell between them, heavy and unbridgeable. When the stew was done they sat at the roughhewn table and ate without talking. Matthew got up restlessly from time to time to look out the front and back windows. These had no glass. They were like small doors in the walls. They could be closed and bolted shut. Each had a loophole which he could see out of, or fire through. Those, he remembered, had been cut at Burk Kennemer's insistence. From the first, Matthew realized now, Burk had been trying to sober him, even to scare him away. Matthew had always put him off with a shrug or a laugh. Now he remembered what Burk had said today about having buried a woman in a place like this. He thought he understood the trapper, and the man's fears, in a way he had not before.

The heavy silence went unrelieved. After eating what he

could of the stew, his stomach knotted, he went outside and took a long look around, cradling the rifle. He fetched a shovel and began to throw dirt onto the roof to make it more difficult for the Indians to set afire. It occurred to him how futile this labor was if they were going to abandon the place anyway, but he kept swinging the shovel, trying to work off the tension.

The afternoon dragged. He spent most of it outside, pacing, watching. In particular he kept looking to the west, anticipating Burk Kennemer's return. Now that he had made up his mind to it, he could hardly wait for darkness, to give them a chance to escape this place. The only thing which came from that direction—or any other—was the brindle milk cow, drifting toward the shed at her own slow pace and in her own good time for the evening milking and the grain she knew awaited her. Matthew owned no watch, but he doubted that a watch kept better time than that cow, her udder swinging in rhythm with her slow and measured steps. Like the horses, she had no awareness of anything except her daily routine, of feeding and milking and grazing. Observing her patient pace, Matthew could almost assure himself that this day was like all others, that he had no reason for fear.

He milked the cow, though he intended to leave the milk unused in the cabin, for it was habit with him as well as with the cow. The sun was dropping rapidly when he carried the bucket of milk to Rachal. Her eyes asked him, though she did not speak.

He shook his head. "No sign of anything out there. Not of Burk, either."

Before sundown he saddled the dun horse for Rachal, making ready. He would ride the plow horse bareback. He climbed up onto his pole fence, trying to shade his eyes from the sinking sun while he studied the hills and the open valley to the west. All his earlier fears were with him, and a new one as well.

Where is he? He wouldn't just have left us here. Not old Burk.

Once he thought he heard a sound in the edge of the timber. He turned quickly and saw a flash of movement, nothing more. It was a feeling as much as something actually seen. It could have been anything, a deer, perhaps, or even one of his cows. It *could* have been.

He remained outside until the sun was gone, and until the last golden remnant faded into twilight over timbered hills that stretched into the distance like a succession of blue monuments. The autumn chill set him to shivering, but he held out against going for his coat. When the night was full dark, he knew it was time.

He called softly at the cabin door. Rachal lifted the bar. He said, "The moon'll rise directly. We'd better get started."

"Without Burk? Are you really sure, Matthew?"

"If they're around, they'll be here. Out yonder, in the dark, we've got a chance."

She came out, wrapped for the night chill, carrying his second rifle, handing him his coat. Quietly they walked to the corral, where he opened the gate, untied the horses and gave her a lift up into the saddle. The stirrups were too long for her, and her skirts were in the way, but he knew she could ride. He threw himself up onto the plow horse, and they moved away from the cabin in a walk, keeping to the grass as much as possible to muffle the sound of the hoofs. As quickly as he could, he pulled into the timber, where the darkness was even more complete. For the first miles, at least, he felt that he knew the way better than any Indian who might not come here once in several years.

It was his thought to swing first by Burk's cabin. There was always a chance the old man had changed his mind about things . . .

He had held on to this thought since late afternoon. Maybe Burk had found the tracks were not made by Indians after all, and he had chosen to let the young folks have the benefit of a good, healthy scare.

Deep inside, Matthew knew that was a vain hope. It was

not Burk's way. He might have let Matthew sweat blood, but he would not do this to Rachal.

They both saw the fire at the same time, and heard the distant barking of the dogs. Rachal made a tiny gasp and clutched his arm.

Burk's cabin was burning.

They reined up and huddled together for a minute, both coming dangerously close to giving in to their fears and riding away in a blind run. Matthew gripped the rawhide reins so tightly that they seemed to cut into his hands. "Easy, Rachal," he whispered.

Then he could hear horses moving through the timber, and the crisp night air carried voices to him.

"They're coming at us, Matthew," Rachal said tightly. "They'll catch us out here."

He had no way of knowing if they had been seen, or heard. A night bird called to the left of him. Another answered, somewhere to the right. At least, they sounded like night birds.

"We've got to run for it, Rachal!"

"We can't run all the way to Fredericksburg. Even if we could find it. They'll catch us."

He saw only one answer. "Back to the cabin! If we can get inside, they'll have to come in there to get us."

He had no spurs; a farmer did not need them. He beat his heels against the horse's sides and led the way through the timber in a run. He did not have to look behind him to know Rachal was keeping up with him. Somehow the horses had caught the fever of their fear.

"Keep low, Rachal," he said. "Don't let the low limbs knock you down." He found a trail that he knew and shortly burst into the open. He saw no reason for remaining in the timber now, for the Indians surely knew where they were. The timber would only slow their running. He leaned out over the horse's neck and kept thumping his heels against its ribs. He glanced back to be sure he was not outpacing Rachal.

Off to the right he thought he saw figures moving, vague

shapes against the blackness. The moon was just beginning to rise, and he could not be sure. Ahead, sensed more than seen, was the clearing. Evidently the Indians had not been there yet, or the place would be in flames as Burk's cabin had been.

He could see the shape of the cabin now. "Right up to the door, Rachal!"

He jumped to the ground, letting his eyes sweep the yard and what he could see of the corrals. "Don't get down," he shouted. "Let me look inside first."

The door was closed, as they had left it. He pushed it open and stepped quickly inside, the rifle ready. The dying embers in the fireplace showed him he was alone. "It's all right, Rachal. Get down quick, and into the cabin!"

She slid down and fell, and he helped her to her feet. She pointed and gave a cry. Several figures were moving rapidly toward the shed. Matthew fired the rifle in their direction and gave Rachal a push toward the door. She resisted stubbornly. "The horses," she said. "Let's get the horses into the cabin."

She led her dun through the door, though it did not much want to go into that dark and unaccustomed place.

Matthew would have to admit later—though now he had no time for such thoughts—that she was keeping her head better than he was. He would have let the horses go, and the Indians would surely have taken them. The plow horse was gentler and entered the cabin with less resistance, though it made a nervous sound in its nose at sight of the glowing coals.

Matthew heard something *plunk* into the logs as he pushed the door shut behind him and dropped the bar solidly into place. He heard a horse race up to the cabin and felt the jarring weight of a man's body against the door, trying to break through. Matthew pushed his own strength upon the bar, bracing it. A chill ran through him, and he shuddered at the realization that only the meager thickness of that door lay between him and an intruder who intended to kill him. He heard the grunting of a man in strain, and he imagined he could feel the hot breath. His hair bristled.

Rachal opened the front-window loophole and fired her rifle.

Thunder seemed to rock the cabin. It threw the horses into a panic that made them more dangerous, for the moment, than those Indians outside. One of them slammed against Matthew and pressed him to the wall so hard that he thought all his ribs were crushed. But that was the last time an Indian tried the door. Matthew could hear the man running, getting clear of Rachal's rifle.

A gunshot sounded from out in the night. A bullet struck the wall but did not break through between the logs. Periodically Matthew would hear a shot, first from one direction, then from another. After the first three or four, he was sure.

"They've just got one gun. We've got two."

The horses calmed, after a time. So did Matthew. He threw ashes over the coals to dim their glow, which had made it difficult for him to see out into the night. The moon was up, throwing a silvery light across the yard.

"I'll watch out front," he said. "You watch the back."

All his life he had heard that Indians did not like to fight at night because of a fear that their souls would wander lost if they died in the darkness. He had no idea if the stories held any truth. He knew that Indians were skillful horsethieves, in darkness or light, and that he and Rachal had frustrated these by bringing their mounts into the cabin.

Burk had said the Indians on these September raids were more intent on acquiring horses than on taking scalps, though they had no prejudice against the latter. He had said Indians did not like to take heavy risks in going against a well-fortified position, that they were likely to probe the defenses and, if they found them strong, withdraw in search of an easier target.

But they had a strong incentive for breaking into this cabin. He suggested, "They might leave if we turn the horses out."

"And what do we do afoot?" she demanded. Her voice was not a schoolgirl's. It was strong, defiant. "If they want these horses, let them come through that door and pay for them. These horses are *ours!*"

Her determination surprised him, and shamed him a little. He held silent awhile, listening, watching for movement. "I suppose those Indians feel like they've got a right here. They figure this land belongs to them."

"Not if they just come once a year. We've come here to stay."

"I wish we hadn't. I wish I hadn't brought you."

"Don't say that. I've always been glad that you did. I've loved this place from the time we first got here and lived in the wagon, because it was ours. It *is* ours. When this trouble is over it will *stay* ours. We've earned the right to it."

He fired seldom, and only when he thought he had a good target, for shots inside the cabin set the horses to plunging and threshing.

He heard a cow bawl in fear and agony. Later, far beyond the shed, he could see a fire building. Eventually he caught the aroma of meat, roasting.

"They've killed the milk cow," he declared.

Rachal said, "We'll need another one, then. For the baby."

That was the first she had spoken of it, though he had had reason lately to suspect. "I shouldn't have put you through that ride tonight."

"That didn't hurt me. I'm not so far along yet. That's one reason we've got to keep the horses. We may need to trade the dun for a milk cow."

They watched through the long hours, he at the front window, she at the rear. The Indians had satisfied their hunger, and they were quiet, sleeping perhaps, waiting for dawn to storm the cabin without danger to their immortal souls. Matthew was tired, and his legs were cramped from the long vigil, but he felt no sleepiness. He thought once that Rachal had fallen asleep, and he made no move to awaken her. If trouble came from that side, he thought he would probably hear it.

She was not asleep. She said, "I hear a rooster way off somewhere. Burk's, I suppose. Be daylight soon."

"They'll hit us then. They'll want to overrun us in a hurry."

"It's up to us to fool them. You and me together, Matthew, we've always been able to do whatever we set our minds to."

They came as he expected, charging horseback out of the rising sun, relying on the blazing light to blind the eyes of the defenders. But with Rachal's determined shouts ringing in his ears, he triggered the rifle at darting figures dimly seen through the golden haze. Rachal fired rapidly at those horsemen who ran past the cabin and came into her field of view on the back side. The two horses just trembled and leaned against one another.

One bold, quick charge and the attack was over. The Comanches swept on around, having tested the defense and found it unyielding. They pulled away, regrouping to the east as if considering another try.

"We done it, Rachal!" Matthew shouted. "We held them off."

He could see her now in the growing daylight, her hair stringing down, her face smudged with black, her eyes watering from the sting of the gunpowder. He had never seen her look so good.

She said triumphantly, "I tried to tell you we could do it, Matthew. You and me, we can do anything."

He thought the Indians might try again, but they began pulling away. He could see now that they had a considerable number of horses and mules, taken from other settlers. They drove these before them, splashing across the creek and moving north in a run.

"They're leaving," he said, not quite believing.

"Some more on this side," Rachal warned. "You'd better come over here and look.'

Through the loophole in her window, out of the west, he saw a dozen or more horsemen loping toward the cabin. For a minute he thought he and Rachal would have to fight again.

Strangely, the thought brought him no particular fear.

We can handle it. Together, we can do anything.

Rachal said, "Those are white men."

They threw their arms around each other and cried.

They were outside the cabin, the two of them, when the horsemen circled warily around it, rifles ready for a fight. The men were strangers, except the leader. Matthew remembered him from up at the forks. Excitedly the man spoke in a language Matthew knew was German. Then half the men were talking at once. They looked Rachal and Matthew over carefully, making sure neither was hurt.

The words were strange, but the expressions were universal. They were of relief and joy at finding the young couple alive and on their feet.

The door was open. The bay plow horse stuck its head out experimentally, nervously surveying the crowd, then breaking into a run to get clear of the oppressive cabin. The dun horse followed, pitching in relief to be outdoors. The German rescuers stared in puzzlement for a moment, then laughed as they realized how the Waylands had saved their horses.

One of them made a sweeping motion, as if holding a broom, and Rachal laughed with him. It was going to take a lot of work to clean up that cabin.

The spokesman said something to Matthew, and Matthew caught the name Burk Kennemer. The man made a motion of drawing a bow, and of an arrow striking him in the shoulder.

"Dead?" Matthew asked worriedly.

The man shook his head. *"Nein, nicht tod.* Not dead." By the motions, Matthew perceived that the wounded Burk had made it to the German settlement to give warning, and that the men had ridden through the night to get here.

Rachal came up and put her arm around Matthew, leaning against him. She said, "Matthew, do you think we killed any of those Indians?"

"I don't know that we did."

"I hope we didn't. I'd hate to know all my life that there is blood on this ground."

Some of the men seemed to be thinking about leaving. Matthew said, "You-all pen your horses, and we'll have breakfast directly." He realized they did not understand his words, so he pantomimed and put the idea across. He made a circle, shaking hands with each man individually, telling him *thanks,* knowing each followed his meaning whether the words were understood or not.

"Rachal," he said, "these people are our neighbors. Somehow we've got to learn to understand each other."

She nodded. "At least enough so you can trade one of them out of another milk cow. For the baby."

When the baby came, late the following spring, they named it Burkett Kennemer Wayland, after the man who had brought them warning, and had sent them help.

That was the last time the Comanches ever penetrated so deeply into the hill country, for the military pressure was growing stronger.

And all of his life Burkett Kennemer Wayland was able to say, without taking sinful advantage of the truth, that he had been present at the last great Indian fight in Kerr County.

CREDITS

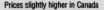